ACCLAIM FOR

THERE BLEEDS THE LIGHT

There Bleeds the Light is a glorious and hopeful story for our generation. With prose that rivals the greats—making you want to read lines over and over for sheer enjoyment—a plot that keeps you spellbound and on the edge of your seat, and characters that feel so true to life you'll walk away thinking they are friends, Renae weaves a tale that not only entertains but also brings life to weary hearts burdened by darkness and called to the light.

—VICTORIA LYNN, The Chronicles of Elira

In *There Bleeds the Light,* Renae dives even deeper into the conflicting hearts and souls of humanity. With haunting and lyrical language that highlights the melancholy and beautiful world, a question keeps rising to the surface: where does darkness truly dwell? In this book, we are reminded why seeking light can come at a cost, but a cost that is worth every dark and dangerous valley we pass through.

—EMILY BARNETT, *Thread of Dreams*

Between the world-building, magical prose, and realistic characters with raw struggles, Andrea Renae weaves a breathtakingly vivid story about light in the darkness. I found my own personal misgivings splayed out on the page, worded and kneaded and breathed in such a way that spoke of healing amidst turmoil. Andrea is a wonderfully talented author, and I wholeheartedly believe *There Bleeds the Light* will bless every reader who turns these pages.

—ANNE J. HILL, *What Darkness Fears*

There Bleeds the Light is a stunning continuation of a truly beautiful story. An expanded world, new revelations, and even more characters to love make this a sequel that will simultaneously bring Renae's readers satisfaction and leave them hungry for the next installment.

—RACHEL LAWRENCE, *Seashells & Other Souvenirs*

We need books that contain truth unapologetically. This one does. *There Bleeds the Light* is for autumn evenings and hope in darkness. It is a book for quiet afternoons, bright winds, and warm days with a hint of chill. Andrea has drawn us into a world that is both harsh and beautiful, grasping and lovely, and I hoped and longed with the characters as they wrestled and fought. This book was a delight, like an iced cup of black tea with a constant thread of sweetness through the middle.

—DANIELLE BULLEN, *Frost Light & Sparrow in the Sun*

Another compassionate depiction of the battle of light against darkness, *There Bleeds the Light* shows readers what's beyond the Vale and within our own hearts with a depth and honesty that cannot be ignored. Drawing portraits of lives we can relate to, yet cast in the stark shades of Shrouded beasts and light enchanting each page, this book refuses to shy away from the idea that just because the light has found you doesn't mean the battle is over.

—EMMA HILL, The Maybe Duology

Renae draws us in with three-dimensional characters who grip our hearts and refuse to leave us even after we shut the book. You'll spend days turning this story over searching for all the profound theological connections and unravelling the magical mysteries within.

—LARA D'ENTREMONT, *The Painted Fairytale*

SONG OF THE SOLAS | BOOK TWO

there *bleeds* the *light*

ANDREA RENAE

there *bleeds* the *light*

ANDREA RENAE

there *bleeds* the *light*

First Edition printed November 2024

Edited by EditElle — editelle.com

Proofread by Anne J. Hill — annejhill.com

Cover Design, Map, Interior Formatting, Graphic Design,
Artwork, and Sheet Music by Andrea Renae — authorarenae.com

ISBN paperback: 978-1-7388647-4-4
ISBN hardcover: 978-1-7388647-5-1
ISBN ebook: 978-1-7388647-6-8

For those who feel so weak
And the promises that sustain us

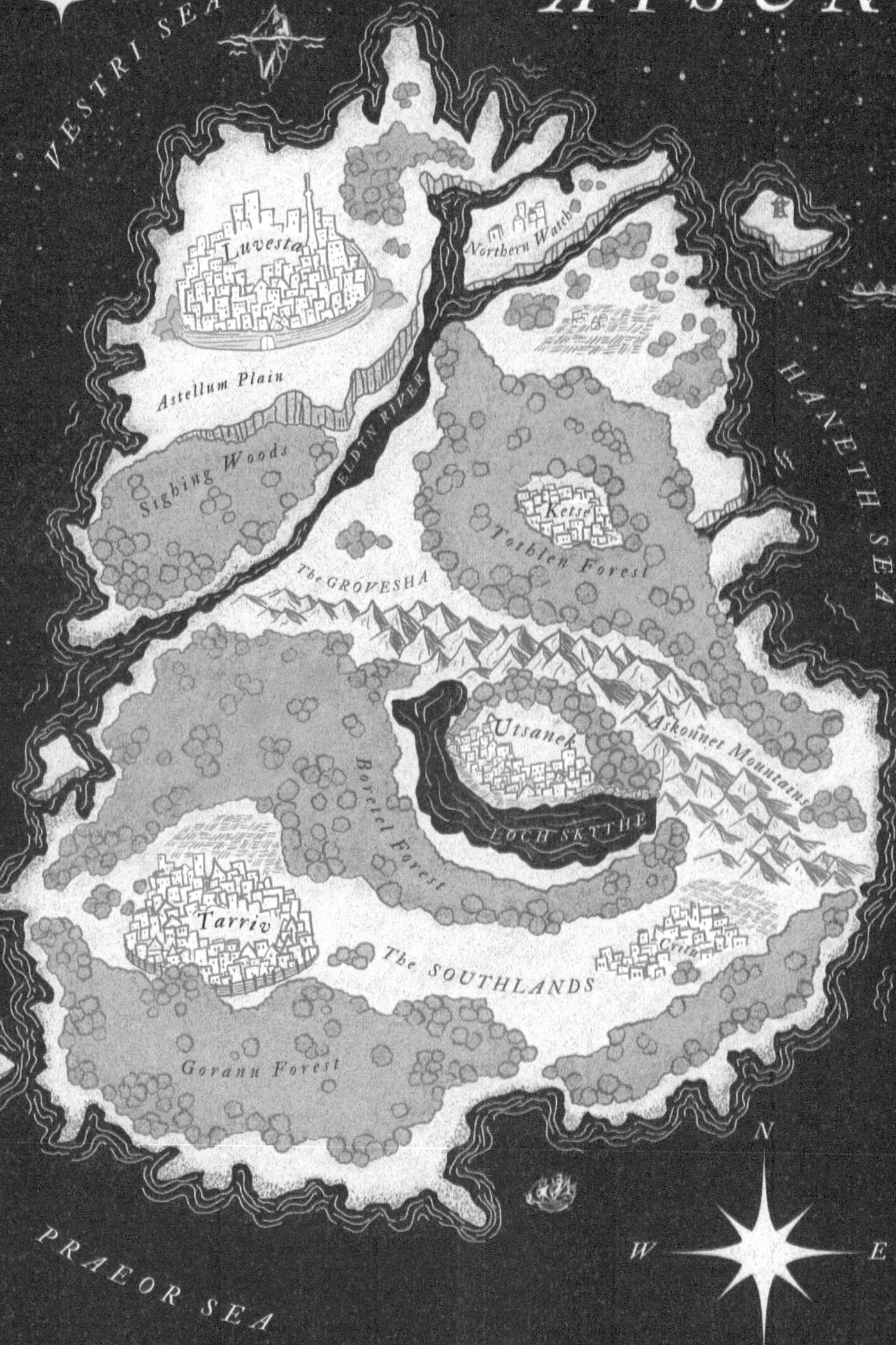

ATSUN
VESTRI SEA
HANETH SEA
PRAEOR SEA
Luvesta
Northern Watch
Astellum Plain
ELDYN RIVER
Sighing Woods
Ketse
Tothlen Forest
The GROVESHA
Utsanek
Askonnet Mountains
Borelel Forest
LOCH SKYTHE
Tarriv
The SOUTHLANDS
Goranu Forest
N
W
E
S

PROLOGUE

You must be more than they expect.

The words have driven me for most of my life, and I cling to them now as my exhausted eyes begin to blur the Vale's cloaking shadows with the clear skies of my Southland home. As my thoughts drift back to my tent and the cot that awaits me.

You are an úramech of Tarriv, not someone with the luxury to spend her days reclining on padded furniture. You chose this life of discipline, not one that would give you a soft backside.

I let out a long, measured breath and roll my shoulders in a slow circle.

Do not give them the satisfaction of seeing you fail.

"The watch is not over yet, Seyla." My partner's voice is like a rasp on raw wood, and I flinch as he sheathes his sword noisily for the thousandth time this night. He chuckles. "Didn't expect you'd have the stamina to make it to sunrise."

Ordin moves off down the shores of the loch, and I throw his stout backside a scathing look. As if I need him breathing down my neck, keeping me accountable. But I grit my teeth and bite back a retort because I must give the Agmen no reason to find fault with me if I have any hope of advancing through the úramech ranks.

Of course, out of all the soldiers in our regiment, Commander Verrek paired me with the one who refuses to see me as anything other than a woman.

"Just keeping my muscles loose, as you should," I say, failing to stifle my irritation. "How can you expect to protect us from the Vale's phantoms with those old joints?"

Ordin merely grunts, refusing to turn and acknowledge my insult. I sigh and scan where the shining waters meet the impenetrable wall of black. The Loch Skythe posting would be much less wearisome if there were something more interesting to look at.

But nothing has crossed these waters in decades.

My eyes snag on a break in the shadows, sending my pulse into a sudden spike. Frowning, I cross the beach until the waters lap at the toes of my boots.

"It must be an illusion," I whisper, knowing how difficult it is to differentiate between water, waves, and darkness at the end of the night watch.

Narrowing my eyes and scanning the silent loch, I find no evidence of anything abnormal, and my heart rate slows. An overwhelming desire to make it out of this shift without incident consumes my thoughts.

But when the irregularity appears again, I know I am not imagining it.

Sensing my distraction from a distance, Ordin runs to my side with heavy, bumbling footsteps.

"What is it? What do you see?"

Saying nothing, I point toward the unnatural horizon.

The big man's face, already cemented with folds and creases, squishes into more fleshy furrows.

"Can't be," he mutters, jaw going slack.

A wind picks up from the north, teasing the waters into jagged peaks uncommon on this side of the loch at this time of year. My úramech cloak snaps behind me.

We stand side by side, at a loss for words. This level ground is a nice change. For once, Ordin can't lord his experience and masculinity over me.

A battered skiff soon comes into full view, carried along with the relentless rise and fall of the waves. When it is close enough to see that it's carrying cargo, I wade a few steps into the water.

Ordin spits on the ground. "Well, tell me what you see, úramech."

At any other moment, I would bristle at being ordered around by him, but my breath is trapped in my chest.

A tattered pile of cloth lies heaped in the bottom of the craft, covered in black stains. A knot of pressure forms in my chest. *Dried blood*. A lot of it.

Ignoring Ordin's impatient growl, I reach out and wait for the prow of the boat to bump into my fingers. When it does and I draw it in, my mouth drops open.

A small creature nestles in the middle of the shredded tatters. Peaceful, as if asleep. It reminds me of a fox, but with a broad, flattened tail, sail-like ears, and dull patterns curling in its short fur. I withdraw my hand, wary, but it does not move or even breathe. Its tired, gray color is like driftwood on the beach, long sapped of life. Though there is no visible sign of decay, I am sure the thing is dead.

"Seyla? Oh, for Vale's sake. I *am* your superior. D'you think you could treat me like one, for once?"

Ordin splashes into the water next to me, his ranking medallions clinking together, and all his bluster drains away. "What in Elyōn's name is that?"

"I-I don't know." I gulp down an unwanted swell of emotion. Decades ago, my younger sister and I used to make up tales of the day when something would finally breach the Vale's borders and cross Loch Skythe's black waters. We imagined ferocious monsters with poison fangs that would devour us while we slept, whispering about them so often that I half believed them to be true.

This image doesn't match our childhood frightfables at all.

"Well, go on. Pull it in."

I steel myself with a breath before doing as he says.

When the boat hits the rocks, the bloodied heap shudders, and my heart responds with a violent convulsion.

"*Sea's fury*," Ordin yelps, scrambling back onto the shore.

His churlish fright snaps me to my senses. I reach in and flip back a fold of fabric to reveal a blood-drained face.

It's a man, older, but not much more than me, with creases spreading from the corners of his eyes like sunbeams. I peel the glove from my hand and hold the backs of my fingers underneath his nostrils. A faint flutter of air hits them.

He's breathing, but barely.

Compassion flickers in my chest like a single ember under a mountain of ash. When did I last feel its warmth?

"If he came from there, then he's one of them valefolk," Ordin says. His sword slides out of his sheath with a cold *shing*.

I shift my hand to my side, fingers finding my khukuri's hilt.

"We have our orders," he says, determination in his voice. "The Imperii is clear about what we are to do in this situation."

With a lightning-quick motion, I spin around and bring the curved dagger's point so it sits right under Ordin's chin, where I can see the flutter of his pulse in his neck.

"What in—"

"Elyōn's name?" I cock an eyebrow and enjoy the flush of scarlet that tinges his features.

"You'll lose your station in the Agmen for this," he says through gritted teeth.

I do not flinch. "For keeping you from murdering a man a breath from death?" Ordin's mouth works with formless arguments. My hand shifts so the sharpened edge presses closer to his throat. "Until he awakens, we know nothing of him. He could be from anywhere. Perhaps you think angering the Imperii is worth whatever thrill you'd get from snuffing out a dying wick?"

The fury does not subside in Ordin's eyes, but he drops his sword to the ground and holds out his hands in submission.

My mouth slants into what I hope is an expression of confidence as I withdraw my khukuri, turning away to hide the way my hands tremble.

"So that's it, then? I let you defy me and bring in this corpse, and we forget this little act of insubordination ever happened?" He spits again, like I am a foul taste he wishes to rid from his mouth.

Unfortunately for him, I am used to his intimidation, and I've been dreaming of challenging him ever since we were assigned to patrol this barren stretch of waterfront a month ago.

"If you breathe a word of this to anyone in the Agmen," I say almost lazily, bending to peel back the wounded man's garments and assess the damage, "if you so much as think of taking out your displeasure on me or doing something to him, I promise I will find you when you are least expecting it, and I will put an end to . . . Well, use your imagination."

"You wouldn't dare," Ordin says, seething.

I straighten and spin to face him, taking two steps forward and fingering the khukuri again. "Oh, wouldn't I? Well, that should help you sleep at night. If you're wrong, though, know you won't see it coming."

He snorts. "You underestimate me, woman."

I raise an eyebrow. "No, that's your specialty."

Throwing me the filthiest look of which he's capable—impressively hideous in that lumpy face—he retrieves his sword and takes up the patrol without another word.

I turn back to the man. He clings to the barest threads of life, and I have no plan on how to get him to my tent, let alone out of this boat. The ember winks out in my chest.

Seyla, for ancestors' sake, what are you doing?

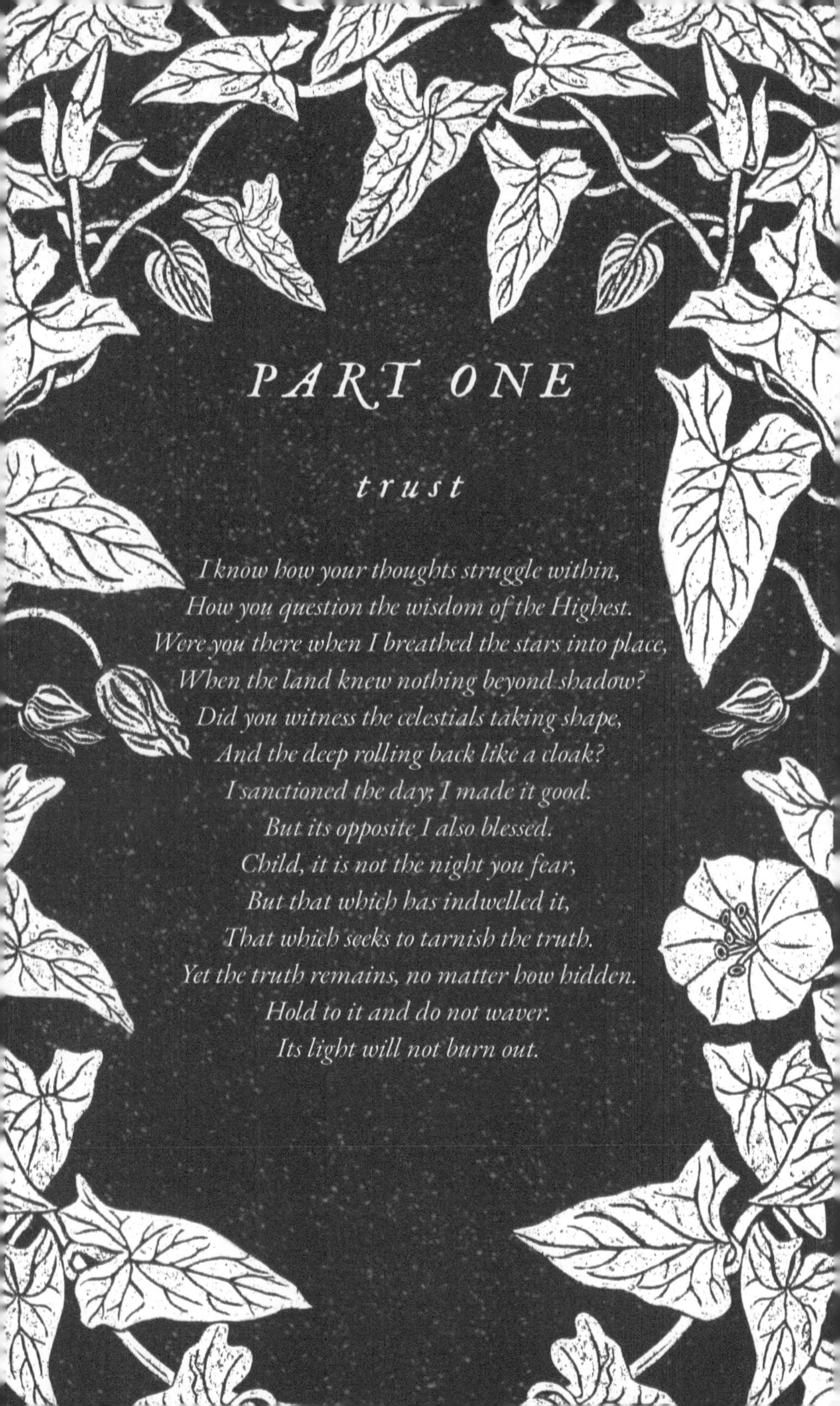

PART ONE

trust

I know how your thoughts struggle within,
How you question the wisdom of the Highest.
Were you there when I breathed the stars into place,
When the land knew nothing beyond shadow?
Did you witness the celestials taking shape,
And the deep rolling back like a cloak?
I sanctioned the day; I made it good.
But its opposite I also blessed.
Child, it is not the night you fear,
But that which has indwelled it,
That which seeks to tarnish the truth.
Yet the truth remains, no matter how hidden.
Hold to it and do not waver.
Its light will not burn out.

I

AMYRAH

I NEVER IMAGINED THE NIGHT would make my soul sing.

In the Vale, darkness searches for a way to choke out every trace of light. Its sinews spread like a poison vine, stalking our days and haunting our dreams. But out of the ténesomni's hungry grasp, where everything I thought I knew has been rewritten, it is something beautiful.

Breath trapped in my lungs, I watch the day part with a lover's embrace, sighing as she turns her face away. The night descends upon her shoulders like a blanket as she lays down her flaming head. The lesser burning stars begin their shy courtship, casting a gentler glow that eases the shadow's passing. They drip wealth and wisdom and aching warmth into my soul. The Highest sings over me his song of love in a language my heart understands.

Standing at the peak of the Askonnet Mountain Pass with my back to the wall of shadow, I drink in this new freedom and pretend that I have always dwelled here, that all the mysteries of who I am will become as clear as the firelights. I look upon the expanse as I would a long-lost friend, begging her to confide all her secrets.

The sound of careful footfalls makes me turn. Belwyn gazes at me curiously, and heat floods my cheeks to be caught in this moment of pure delight.

"Why stare at me when you could be looking at the stars?" I pull my hair over my shoulder and raise an eyebrow accusingly.

His playful smile shines in the moonlight, making me forget my embarrassment. "They aren't going anywhere."

His eyes linger on mine for a breath, then trail down my frightful hair. Something rich and wonderful and new swirls in my core, and I press a hand to my stomach to still it.

"They've waited long enough." The words escape as a whisper, and my eyes flick up to the splendor once more.

Belwyn closes the space between us, stepping around the mountain lupines. My heart quickens, wrestling between the desire to be held and the need to be left alone. He does neither, instead gently tucking a strand of hair behind my ear and offering me his other hand. I bite the inside of my cheek and hold my breath as my fingers slip between his.

He always seems to understand what I need before I can even comprehend what it is. Right now, I realize, it's simply to know he's here.

Silently, we turn to the cabin perched atop the Askonnet Mountain Pass. It's a forlorn place, where a mother's bereft arms crave something beyond her reach and a father's purpose-stripped hands struggle to fix everything he touches. My shoulders tense as we approach the building's, humble silhouette.

I shouldn't dread being in the presence of my friend's parents like this.

The dull sound of ax rending wood cuts unfeelingly through the night's melody. Arlyn, Wehna and Arvo's father, stands in the warm glow cast from the cabin's only window, tossing a split log onto a pile nearly as tall as he is.

"He has enough to fill the Reckoning Grounds pit by now," Belwyn says, and I glance at him. His expression is muddied—the skin between his brows creases with pain, yet the corner of his mouth lifts in odd amusement.

Seeing us, Arlyn embeds the ax in a stump and straightens, stretching his neck. His eyes follow our arms, landing on our entwined fingers.

"Did you two have a pleasant walk?"

The way his rumbling voice hitches on the word 'pleasant' belies how he feels about the notion. Like it doesn't belong in a world where parents cannot be reunited with their children.

I free my hand from Belwyn's grasp, pretending not to notice his questioning look. How can I explain that every time I see Arlyn, I think of my father? And when I think of my father, I wonder how he would take me wandering through the night, hand in hand with a boy—even if that boy was the one who made sure my father's sacrifice wasn't for nothing.

A quiet pain sloshes in the cage of my chest.

"Is Rael inside?" I ask, even though I know his wife wouldn't be any other place this late. Arlyn rubs his hands together and tips his copper-bearded chin in confirmation. Smiling my thanks, I swing open the crooked door. When Belwyn moves to follow, Arlyn holds out a hand.

"Could I have a word with you?"

I glance back, catching Belwyn's apprehensive look.

"Goodnight," I whisper before the door closes out the world. And for the first time in my life, my heart trusts the word.

Nothing more than a bed, a table, and a few other essentials furnish the cabin, a space so small that it would be inhospitable for housing more than two people. It's merely a roof overhead for the watchmen of the Grovesha, who monitor the ténesomni and the kaligorven to ensure everything is contained.

It is uncomfortable to think that there exists a whole world of strangers who view my home as an evil in need of guarding.

Home. Longing, grief, and guilt accumulate in my chest as the word stumbles uninvited through my mind. A shiver like the teasing fingers of death travels down my arms. I rub my hands over them to shake off the chill.

I have no home.

Blinking, I force the warm interior to come back into focus. Wehna's mother and I have been sharing the cabin while the men camp under the night sky. If I'm honest, I envy them. The first evening of the arrangement, Rael questioned me about what I knew of her children. I told her what I could while leaving out that the last time I saw Wehna, she was sprawled in an Utsanek alley, blood covering her face. No matter what other detail I gave, Rael did not seem satisfied, yet she eventually let the matter drop. There has only been uncomfortable silence between us since.

My gaze drifts across the room to where Rael sits in a wooden chair facing the fire. She seems oblivious to my presence, her turbulent thoughts disfiguring her features with invisible claws.

I finger my necklace's eight points through the pocket of my dress.

At first, I didn't understand why it ruined her to see it around my neck when Belwyn and I stepped through the ténesomni, until the name of her daughter spilled from her lips in a broken question. Since then, I have kept it in my pocket, and she has kept her emotions under a carefully monitored layer of ice.

Even without much conversation, I have been able to put together a tattered picture of the events that led them here. Arlyn and Rael had been bringing aid and encouragement to one of the Vale's poorest districts on the outskirts of Utsanek when a Shrouded beast attacked them. Without any means of defending themselves, they fled northward, through the forest and toward the mountains. Rael had sustained a serious injury by the time the kaligorva grew bored of them. They sought refuge at this cabin, a place they knew from their years living outside of the Vale. The man who had been stationed here agreed to let them make use of it while he returned to Ketsé, the forest city north of the mountain range. Where my mother was from.

I don't know why they haven't ventured back into the ténesomni to reunite with their children, though, and I'm too wary of upsetting Rael to ask.

The slightest sound of swishing fabric breaks Rael's trance where voices and the creaking door could not. She turns to me with alarm in her gaze, and it's like I am looking at Wehna's face. Same black spirals of hair and heart-shaped face. Same hazel eyes. Guilt tugs at my conscience like stubborn brambles as I remember my friend.

I should have listened to her. We should have never stayed at the market that day.

What became of Wehna?

Rael's confusion clears with a few quick blinks, and she moves to get up.

"Don't." I hold out a palm and force a smile. "You look so cozy by the fire."

"I've sat too long." Pulling her shawl taut around her shoulders, she stands. My eyes hitch on the rusty stain she's attempted to hide within the folds of fabric. I haven't asked her where she's injured, but the way she favors her right leg tells me enough.

"Were you able to get a clear view tonight?" she asks with fabricated cheerfulness.

"Better than ever." I pull off my cloak and drape it across the foot of the bed. No matter how much I've protested, Rael has insisted that I take the mattress while she sleeps on the floor. She is stubborn in a way that her daughter is not. I turn to face her, sighing. "I don't think I will ever tire of looking at the stars. Of being able to see."

Rael gathers the air-dried dishes and stacks them on a shelf. "Most of the people living outside the Vale take them for granted."

I sink to the bed, a breathy laugh escaping me. "How could they possibly do that?"

"Those with the freedom to look up don't always use it," she answers slowly. "And those who do still have to notice what they see." She tilts her head toward the flames. Delicate beaded earrings, no doubt her daughter's creation, waggle back and forth. "Pain and trials tug a person's eyes downward, no matter where they were raised."

Try as I might, I cannot imagine the thrill of a light-drenched world ever growing old, or of a person becoming blind to its splendor. Maybe that's because I grew up in the Vale, maybe not, but I find comfort in knowing that I won't ever have to face that darkness again.

2

BELWYN

MOONLIGHT SPILLS OVER THE MOUNTAIN as I begrudgingly follow Arlyn away from the cabin. I inhale the mountain air and let the sights distract me, picking out faint rusty hues in the rocks and greens in the trees that I would have never noticed in the woods outside Utsanek. There is color out here, even in the dead of night.

I grew up dreading the times when my father would call me aside to talk. Often it was to inform me of a fresh disappointment or to lay some crushing expectation on my shoulders.

Arlyn, though, is nothing like my father. He serves his wife with humility, which is something I have never seen modeled in my own home. He is quiet and attentive to the needs present around him. Words are slow to leave his lips, as if he knows what weapons they can be if not wielded with care. Perhaps most foreign to me, his sorrow and regrets have not embittered him, made him lash out at those he is supposed to love, or given him an excuse to erect thorny barricades around his heart.

So why did it fill me with dread when he asked to speak with me?

I follow him to the wall of shadows that separates us from the Vale. A wicked presence hangs about the blackness, setting my teeth on edge. Even night out here does not seem dark in comparison to it. Only a few days have passed since we stepped through its barrier, and already I cannot recall what it was like to dwell within its confines.

Where Mother, Shem, and Korvin are still contained.

The cloying tangles of guilt spill into my memories, souring the choice I made on Amyrah's behalf.

"Do you understand what this is?" Arlyn's rich voice severs my line of thought. He faces the wall and crosses his arms, inclining his chin to see where the plumes end.

I stand beside him and follow his gaze. "It's darkness." My answer feels unintelligent and obvious, and I scratch behind my ear awkwardly.

He sighs, shaking his head. "I wish it were that simple, but darkness is passive and easily chased away when exposed. This . . ." His eyes narrow and a measured breath expands and contracts his chest. "No, there is no doubt that this thing is evil. And alive."

He extends a hand toward the ténesomni. A few curious trails of shadow stretch out to meet his fingertips. Giving me a pointed look to ensure I'm watching, Arlyn holds his palm parallel to the wall and walks forward.

Expecting to see the black billow around him until he is no longer within view, I struggle to grasp what's happening when he leans his full weight against the mass as if it is a solid thing.

Cold disbelief prickles my skin. *No. There must be a way back in.*

Arlyn continues to push against it until sweat beads on his brow and the tendons of his arms bulge with exertion. After a while, he slumps, his chest lurching.

No . . .

When he turns to face me, tears shine on his pale cheeks. He sniffs and wipes them away but not in haste, as if he's ashamed of their existence, like my father would be. He had always mocked me and my brothers if our emotions dared to draw out real tears.

My boys will not cry.

Yet another of the hundreds of ways I brought him shame.

But there is no shame in Arlyn.

"Perhaps you would like to give it a try?" He directs a defeated gesture at the barrier, and I approach it prepared for a similar result.

Except it isn't the same for me. The cold chill of the ténesomni is what it should be: a hungry mist, swallowing my hands whole. I recoil from it and look at Arlyn in bewilderment.

"I don't understand. Why would it welcome me, but not you?"

His brows lower. "Interesting. I would assume it is because you are born of the ténesomni and I am not."

Born of the darkness.

Though the phrase makes me shiver, it doesn't make sense. "Didn't your family come to the Vale only a few years ago?" I ask.

Arlyn nods.

"And you had no trouble entering then?"

"No one has ever been prevented from crossing the boundary before." He paces a few steps along the wall, and fingers of ténesomni reach for him as he passes. "I can't explain it. These borders have been monitored by all the people groups inhabiting the Grovesha for generations, since they were established. Without the ability to see into the shadowlands, it was wise to be aware of anything that passed in and out of the Vale. The kaligorven, we knew, would be contained within the boundary. But people? They've always been free to pass through. That is why the Watch is so vital. Those who have wandered too far have been lost to the shadows far too many times." He pauses, studying it again with a pull to his mouth, like he has swallowed a bitter enatuberry. "But something must have shifted after we left."

As worrying as this change is, my mind catches on the fact that the ténesomni has only been kept to the Vale for a few generations. If that is true, then how has the light beyond its borders been so thoroughly wiped from memory?

Arlyn approaches and clamps his hands around my forearms. "Think, Belwyn. Have there been any recent developments in the Vale?"

Everything is new. Weariness overwhelms me, but I force myself to think over the last several weeks.

I sigh and raise an eyebrow. "You must know some of what happened. The Light Creatures returned out of nowhere for the first time since I was a child."

A distant look clouds Arlyn's eyes. "Yes. When my family moved to the Vale three years ago, we learned all about the system Utsanek had adopted to survive. Solas are rare enough outside of the Vale that we were surprised to learn that they would venture there at all. But not for thirteen years, correct?"

I nod. "After the Blood Reckoning Ceremony, the kaligorven grew displeased and forbid us from using the sola bones for light. And those who ignored the warnings suffered . . ." My lungs turn to iron. I fight for breath and drop my gaze to the ground, crunching a pine cone underneath my boot. "Suffered their wrath."

Despite my efforts to prevent it, the image of my brother Rhun's terrified face as I shoved him into the night tumbles to the surface of my thoughts. I was so fixated on obeying the kaligorven that I made him go outside and bury the sola bones he had swiped from the carcass of a Light Creature, regardless of the danger it could put him in.

A curse cracks Arlyn's lips, shaking me from my regret. "Those wicked sola brossa," he spits. "How Rael and I desired to rid the valefolk of their dependence on them for light."

Bile rises in my throat. If it weren't for the sola bones, my brother might still be alive.

Yes, I hate them too.

"I know of the kaligorven attacks that followed during those black days," Arlyn says, making an effort to regain his calm. "It was then that my wife and I were chased into the forest." His voice catches in his throat and he presses his knuckles to his lips. "And it was then that we were separated from our children."

A breeze picks up over the mountain, stirring the trees and washing us in a whispered hush. I look away to give Arlyn time to ride the swell of his grief.

"Can you think of anything else?" he asks after a moment.

I take a slow breath, resigning myself to relive things that dredge up pain I don't know what to do with. "You know most of what I know. Except for . . ."

My veins burn like they have been injected with ignati.

I am such a morvus. How could I forget the reason I felt compelled to accompany Amyrah out of the Vale in the first place?

I clear my throat. "There was a newcomer. A man who claimed to possess an extraordinary amount of knowledge about the kaligorven."

Arlyn, still clutching my upper arms, tightens his grip. "Did this man have a name?"

"Myrzeth," I answer, unable to hide my bitterness.

Surprise flickers in Arlyn's eyes, chased away quickly by anger that appears no less caustic than my own. He stares somewhere past me, and his hands drag away from my arms. "Myrzeth," he repeats, the word jumping from his tongue like a spit husk.

"You know him?"

His brows knock together, animated by uncomfortable thoughts. "I know of him, you could say. It's not easy to forget someone who disowns his people."

His people? Myrzeth betrayed his sister, his brother-in-law, and his niece. Does his treachery reach beyond that, to the Luvesti themselves?

Arlyn folds his arms and drums his fingers on his elbow. "He must be controlling the Shrouded, giving strength to their shadows. Enacting some curse long kept hidden away by the Luvesti."

My ears prick at the offhand mention of Amyrah's race, as if it is common knowledge. I had never heard the word until she spoke it.

She should be here for this.

Arlyn's barely contained emotions get the better of him. I flinch as he roars, kicking a rock the size of my fist into the black curtain. "If I had known I would not be able to make it back to my children, I would have never left them." He chafes his rusty head with his palms and strides away.

My eyes follow the trail of the rock through the billows, where it punches a hole and disappears. Can physical objects pass through like people with darkness running through their veins—people like me?

I stare at the obsidian mass as the hole fills in. I stare at it until I realize . . .

It's drawing closer.

My eyes search for an anchor, for some way to confirm it. I spot a pine tree close to the boundary and jog over to it, laying my hand against its rough trunk.

"What is it?" Arlyn asks, catching up with me.

I jut my chin toward the ténesomni. "Watch."

The lines of bark sink as if into tar. My hand is soon marooned on a narrow strip of trunk. I draw it back before the black can touch me.

Arlyn's face pales in the moonlight. "Elyōn, no."

"What does it mean?" I ask, dread slipping into my stomach like a stone into a slough.

He runs a hand over his beard. "I-I don't know. Perhaps that the kaligorven are growing in number, that they are on the move."

"This isn't a usual occurrence, then?"

"Not since they were contained in the Vale a hundred years ago."

A hundred years. How has everyone outside of the valley justified keeping an entire civilization trapped with those beasts for that long?

I turn back to the wall to hide my disgust.

Arlyn's words travel to me in a muted way, like he doesn't mean to voice them. "The timing of this . . ." He presses his knuckles to his brow, deep in thought. "The Nocilium will need to hear of it." He comes to stand beside me and watches the darkness's subtle, smoke-like advance, grimacing. "I doubt we will be able to linger here. The night isn't safe."

I feel like laughing. To a darkness-born, this doesn't qualify as night, but since I'm standing in an impossible world I never could have imagined existed a week ago, I won't argue.

We stare ahead defeatedly, until a sliver of an idea presses into my mind. I turn to Arlyn. "How were the kaligorven contained?"

Arlyn's lips part as if my question perplexes him. "How? I'm not sure of the specifics."

"Did the Luvesti have something to do with it?"

His forehead lines deepen. "Yes, they are given credit for it."

This may be a gamble, but if it means we won't have to rush out of here unprepared, it's worth a try.

I shout for Amyrah, surprising both Arlyn and myself. I feel bad when she bursts out of the door, worry painting her features. Her wild hair drifts into her face when she stops by my side.

"What is it?" She brushes a strand out of the way with the back of her hand and searches my eyes.

I rush to explain what Arlyn told me about the shadows not behaving like normal and how their territory is advancing as we speak. "He says it was the Luvesti who contained them a century ago."

Her eyes widen at the mention of her race, like I have violated an unspoken secret we seem to have agreed on. But this feels pressing. This feels right.

"Amyrah, you might be able to slow their progress."

"How?" Rael catches up to Amyrah in her limping fashion, hugging her shawl around her shoulders. Arlyn holds out his arm in invitation, and his wife leans into his side. Her irises appear like black chasms in the darkness. Yawning. Desperate.

I open my mouth to answer, but Amyrah gives me a look of warning and I relent. This is her story to tell.

She faces Wehna's parents, her long hair dancing around her in the slight breeze. "I can repel the shadows."

Rael and Arlyn exchange meaningful glances.

"Are you one of the Luvesti?" Arlyn's voice is sterner than seems necessary. His fingers dig into the soft flesh of his wife's arms.

Undaunted, as always, Amyrah nods. "By half. My mother was one of them, but my father is—"

Her explanation falls dead on her tongue.

I move to stand beside her, and she seeks out my hand. "The Vale has always been his home," I finish for her.

Arlyn's lips thin, but he doesn't press the issue. "Well." He clears his throat and jerks his head toward the ténesomni. "If you think you can affect the ténesomni, we won't stop you." He sounds confident, but a wariness lingers about his face.

Nodding faintly, Amyrah turns around, dropping my hand. She watches the wall for a while, as if needing proof that it is coming closer before exerting herself. I move to give her space, but she grabs my sleeve and whispers, "*Please*, Belwyn. Stay with me."

"Always," I say, warmth creeping into my fingertips.

As if it is second nature, as if she has been trained to do so since she could walk, Amyrah holds up her hands and bows her head. The familiar sense of awe that accompanies her gift washes over me.

Where does she take her thoughts when confronting an evil like this?

For a while, nothing happens. Her face is serene, more ethereal than usual in the frozen light of the night sky. Then, her arms begin to shake and sweat beads along her brow. Concern creases my forehead. Is this normal? She has always seemed to dismiss the waves of black with such little effort.

Have I asked too much of her?

With a quick intake of air, she raises her face to behold the heavens. I watch her lips move with words I cannot hear, although the name of Elyōn rushes past my ears like a wild wind.

When it is too intense, when I feel compelled to stop her from giving so much of herself, a bright blast radiates from her extended hands. It hits the cascading darkness and ripples along its surface, burning it up like flames consuming flour. The ténesomni shudders in response. Amyrah stumbles back, and I lunge and catch her in time to spare her from hitting the ground.

"Are you alright?" I breathe into her hair.

"Yes," she says weakly. "Just tired."

I lower her down, sitting behind her so that she can rest against me.

Wehna's parents step forward, their attention trained on the sable force.

"Did that do it?" Amyrah asks in a breathy voice. I resist the urge to press my lips to her temple.

Arlyn crouches and digs a line into the earth with a jagged stone. He stays down for several heartbeats, watching.

"For now, it seems to be held at bay."

Amyrah exhales and the muscles of her back relax.

Brushing his hands on his trousers, Arlyn straightens and turns to look at us. "In the morning, we will set out for Ketsé."

An odd sadness tries to creep in, but I deny it entry. I do not regret leaving the Vale with Amyrah. It—*she*—is a purpose that I threw my whole heart into. What we are, I don't quite know, but *together* is something I do understand. Something I can give myself to without holding back, even if staying underneath the kaligorven's shadow and wondering what is happening on the other side has been difficult.

Still, I can't help wondering how my purpose with Amyrah can be so clear, yet the fact that I have abandoned my family still weighs like lead on my mind.

My exhale flutters Amyrah's loose curls. I draw my arms in around her. We're moving forward now. That's what matters.

Rael limps to Arlyn's side. Her injury might make her seem weak, but I am sure strength rumbles beneath her skin. No one would choose to live in the Vale without it.

"Are you sure, my love?" She rests a trembling hand against Arlyn's cheek and probes his eyes with hers. "You know what waits for us." They share a silent moment heavy with understanding.

Eventually, a resigned sigh escapes Arlyn. He drags his wife's hand down and holds it between his own.

"Yes." His gaze travels up to where the obscuring presence meets the wild expanse of the sky. "But if the ténesomni is changing, then we owe it to them to bring warning."

Rael's face crumples. Arlyn pulls her close and whispers, "Elyōn has watched over our children this far. He won't abandon them now."

3
WEHNA

I STAND ON A PRECIPICE in that space between worlds.

To my left, warmth and light swirl in a dizzying dance. Their fragrance is like a song I can't quite recall, like the promise of spiced tea on a cold day. It tugs at memories and dredges up longings I can't explain. I stretch out my hand to feel the glow on my skin, but the wisps of gold shift out of reach. They don't want me.

Come back, I whisper.

My words are stolen by a wind as black as the abyss. It glances up my right side and I shiver as it throws my hair into chaos, circling around my throat. Where the curls of illumination were demure, resistant to be known, the tongues of ténesomni claim me with brazen cords.

I am entrapped in their seductive grasp, and though I know I should fight against them with every drop of strength in my bones, another part of me listens to their siren call.

Come to me. I'm waiting for you. I am where you belong.

There is a word for this moment, a phrase embedded somewhere in my memory to arm me against temptations like this, but I can't remember it now.

Or maybe I don't want to.

I open my mouth and the last of my resistance drains away like water through sand. The ténesomni pulls me into its dead embrace, and I let it take me.

The light fades as I am dragged back into the Vale, back into the shadowlands.

I am in the darkness and the darkness is in me.

The bonds of shadow continue to press on my chest long after the dream has released me. I blink away the stupor of it and try to make sense of where I am, of what confines me. The room is oppressively dim even though a fire crackles nearby.

The Vale. I am in the Vale. My chest squeezes tighter.

The last thing I remember is my own voice twisted and stretched into an alien scream as I watched men drag Amyrah away. There was an explosion of pain and . . . nothing. Nothing but nightmares.

A rounded shape covered in springy coils of hair bobs under my chin. The faint fragrance of the oil I apply to my own tight curls mingles with the scent of an active little boy.

"*Arvo*," I wheeze, stabs of pain piercing my skull. "Get off."

My brother's face lifts into view, and my relieved exhale at the sight of him is augmented by his sharp elbow in my gut.

I free my arms from under him and make a weak effort to target his ticklish places. He shrieks and dodges, fixing me with a reproachful look that would make me laugh if he weren't camped on my diaphragm. If my voice still remembered how to make the sound.

"Let me sit up," I say.

Arvo's lips pull to the side for a beat before he abandons his dog-pile position. It takes tremendous willpower to rise from the bed. The mere effort to move that small amount sends my head throbbing. I catch my bottom lip between my teeth and fight the urge to cry out. Arvo scuttles onto the mattress and tucks into my side once I'm upright. The room spins, and the pressure behind my eyes grows so intense that my brain stops registering it as pain. It's something in a dreadful category all its own. A cold sweat emerges on my brow and I pull Arvo close, grateful for the extra support. As I focus on the rise and fall of his chest, my pulse begins to steady itself.

"You slept a long time, Wehna," he says, tugging the simple braided bracelet on my left wrist. "Days and days."

"Did I?"

I slot my fingers into my hair and suck in a sharp breath when they brush a hot lump of flesh. The room drops out of focus, tears assaulting my eyes and my scalp catching fire.

Oblivious to my anguish, Arvo nods. "Miss Tress told me not to be scared because Elyōn wouldn't let anything bad happen to you." He turns his eyes on me, and I force my grimace into submission. "But something bad *did* happen to you, didn't it?"

The apprehension written across his face strikes at my heart. I can't lie to him, but how can I tell him the truth?

I let my silence answer for me.

At his widened gaze, I rush to say, "But things are fine now, Vo. I'm feeling better." I tap a finger to his nose, which he scrunches. "Miss Tress was right, wasn't she?" The smile that spreads my lips is a liar. "Elyōn looks after us."

Arvo tilts his chin, tasting the words for truthfulness.

Please, please accept it. I don't have the energy to fight for his faith as well as mine. Because a part of me understands his confusion and demands answers from the deity that my parents devoted their whole lives to. That left us parentless.

Childlike trust wins out, and Arvo nestles his head back into my shoulder. His innocence is a heavy burden, and I am not sure I have the strength to bear it while keeping my own struggles out of his reach. I must, though, because the only way we will make it through this day, and the next after that, is if I leave every doubt undisturbed, like silt on the riverbed.

But Arvo is too earnest a soul to let things go unsaid. "Like he's looking after Mada and Pada right now." His words are as untainted as Morpa's snows, but they release an avalanche in my soul.

An internal fire rises to meet it, one not meant for warmth and illumination but for wrath and consumption. It is alarming how real the flames feel. My arm stiffens around Arvo's little shoulders. I wonder if he can feel the storm he has set ablaze.

"I'm glad you're with me, Wehna."

I close my eyes tightly and release a slow breath. Arvo is like a shining thread in an expanse of black. If I fix my gaze to that hope of dawn, I might have enough strength to endure the night.

What would happen if that light was taken from me? Would I give myself to the shadows, like I did in my dream?

The sound of bustling life interrupts these disturbing thoughts, and peals of girlish laughter fill the house.

Arvo sits up straight and grins from ear to ear. "I forgot to tell you, Wehna."

The door bursts open and five blond-headed girls spill into the room.

"Mister Bryn let us get kittens."

For the next while, the bed is overwhelmed with limbs and skirts and puffs of fur mewling and latching onto everything with tiny, barbed claws. The commotion is enough to set the room spinning again, and injections of pain race around my skull. As Arvo giggles and delights in the simple joy of a purring kitten, I wonder how, in the midst of this trial, Elyōn is still good.

"Girls." Tress enters the room with one hand fixed to a hip, a plate in the other, and a look of reprimand claiming her brow. "I have told you again and again that Wehna is not to be disturbed."

Elodie, the oldest of the daughters, holds a white kitten with eyes the same shade as hers under her chin and turns toward her mother sheepishly. "But, Ma, don't you think kittens make everything better?" Her voice holds a practiced sweetness. She's thirteen, as enchanting as Zomré's blossoms, and I'm sure, a source of constant worries for her father.

Tress raises an eyebrow and points to the door.

When the last girl has scampered out of the room and Tress has issued stern instructions to keep the cats out of the pantry, she turns her attention to Arvo.

"You too," she says, not unkindly. Arvo detaches the last kitten from the comforter, hopping off the bed as Tress bends to his level. "I hope I can count on you to keep an eye on those troublemakers."

I'm not sure if she means the kittens or the girls. She scratches the furball between the ears as Arvo gives a dutiful nod.

"Bye, Wehna." Before he slips out the door, he turns around and holds the kitten up high, waggling it back and forth so its miniature paws sway. It lets out an indignant meow as they both disappear behind the doorpost.

Tress sets down a plate of enatuberries, soft cheese, and kifa crackers on the bed. Her gentle fingers find the weal on my head and probe it. I suck my lips in as I fight the rush of pain.

"Good. The swelling is beginning to go down." She sits back and assesses me with concern in her gaze. "How does your head feel?"

I laugh dryly. "Like it's pinned between two boulders."

She bites her lip and gives a slight nod. "That's to be expected. Bryn found you unconscious in an alley. You suffered a significant blow that will take time to heal, but I'm more concerned about other side effects. Is anything else troubling you?"

"A little dizziness."

I should tell her more, like how light and sound make my stomach churn, but Tress has enough to worry about without me adding to her burdens.

"Because you're starving, no doubt. That's something we can fix." She smiles and covers my hand with hers. "I'd like you to rest in our home for a while longer."

I open my mouth to object, but she squeezes my hand and won't hear it. "You don't have to worry about anything. We're privileged to help you. Arvo fits in well here, and my younger daughters are rather enjoying having a boy to play with."

She means well, but sorrow seeps through me with her words. Is that what we are? Stray cats adopted into a home already full to bursting with its own established rhythms?

I push aside these feelings, faking a smile of gratitude.

Tress moves to leave, but I grab her forearm and search her face. "Please. Do you know . . ." The question doesn't want to leave my tongue. I swallow and try again. "Do you know what happened to Amyrah?"

Tress sits, silent, as if she is struggling with what to say. I grit my teeth to keep the frustration under control.

Tell me.

She sighs. "Myrzeth wanted to make an example of her." Her brows cinch together and her lips purse like she has tasted something sour. "By offering her to the kaligorven."

The room grows blacker around the edges, and my hands ball around the bed's linens.

"It's alright, Wehna. They didn't hurt her. It was her—" She catches the words as a wave of sadness slips across her features. Her hands wring the blanket on my lap and her gaze drops. "Her father sacrificed himself in her place."

Oh. I turn my face to the hearth and wish the white noise of its crackling could consume the pain.

My poor, sweet friend.

I clear my throat, but my eyes do not leave the blaze. "I need to see her."

"That isn't possible."

With the sudden turning of my head, the world lurches around me. Pain screams through my senses and nausea pools in the pit of my stomach.

I rush to disguise my gasp with words. "W-why not?" Tears trail down my cheeks, and they could be mistaken for the product of sadness rather than pain. "She's my friend. I should be there for her."

Tress takes a moment to come into focus. Her face is not stern like I would expect, but apologetic. "Wehna, I'm sorry." She stands, hands disappearing into her dress's pockets. "No one knows where she went."

"But that . . . that doesn't make sense. Has no one looked for her? What if she's been attacked or—"

Or she's lying wounded in some alleyway with the life draining out of her?

I gulp down a sob as the memory of the beggar woman I encountered after my parents' disappearance grips me between clammy hands. I can picture the look on her pallid face as she backed away, repeating over and over again that it wasn't me she'd seen lying in the street.

It was my parents.

"It isn't safe to leave Ellithïm. Right now, it's Utsanek's last haven." Tress kneels on the floor and grabs my hands, lending me her strength and making sure my eyes stay on her. "The Shrouded have been on a rampage for the past week, and Myrzeth's followers are eager to expose everyone who would stand against them. The shadows have been growing thicker than ever. This is a storm that we must weather from inside this community. Do you understand?"

I shake my head, though it hurts. She is wrong, and there is no way I will agree to losing another person I care about.

Tress's grip intensifies. "Wehna, please listen to me. It's dangerous out there right now, and you need to recover your strength. You must consent to the care Elyōn has placed you under and release Amyrah to him."

The conversation and exertion have exhausted my weak body, my troubled mind. I slump into the pillows and let the tears trickle into the hair at my temples. Tress stands and passes her hand over my brow.

"Elyōn will take care of her."

She leaves, and my last cohesive thought before fitful slumber takes me is that this would all be so much easier if I still believed in him.

4
AMYRAH

MY SOUL DOES NOT WANT to leave the mountaintop, and I fight the fear that if another wilderness takes me and blocks out the sky, it will be like entering the Vale's shadows again. The thought is suffocating.

Anxiety drives my heart into a lurching rhythm that my lungs struggle to keep time with as we descend the north face of the mountain range. The warmth from the burning star above is a reminder of what will be taken away from me too soon. I drink it in.

We stop many times to replenish ourselves, to let Rael rest her injured leg. I try to take in all the intricacies of this open landscape before I lose the view for good. Belwyn, too, must be going through his own emotions about traveling the opposite direction of the Vale, because he doesn't try to fill the pauses with words. Maybe he is grieving what he will soon lose. What he's let go.

We pass the night in the foothills, camped beneath the stars and surrounded by whispering grasses. Ahead, the secretive Tothlen Forest cuts into the night like the jagged teeth of a saw blade.

It's only been just over a week outside the ténesomni's realm, but already I have become addicted to the openness of this world. My soul yearns for it the way a bird seeks the open air to fly.

Before the next morning dawns, we enter the gloomy forest, which will define the next few days as we journey to the city of Ketsé. The air is close, and I have to intentionally suppress my fears as we travel deeper into the trees' folds. The sun soon rises, quickly lightening the world and my heart.

Since he had to take such care with his wife on the mountainside, Arlyn had asked Belwyn and me to go ahead of them. Now he leads the journey, coming in and out of sight as the path winds before us. Our pace is still easy to accommodate Rael, who trusts her walking stick on terrain that no longer conspires to throw her headlong down a precipice. The reprieve is welcome. My encounter with the ténesomni drained me more than I let on, and I am grateful for more time to soak in this new world.

"Could you have ever imagined anything as beautiful as this?" Belwyn asks, jaw hanging loose as we pass between the trees.

I almost laugh when I glance at his face, not because his expression is humorous, but because it so completely mirrors my own relieved awe.

It turns out that a forest that isn't indwelled by the ténesomni is the most exhilarating, soul-filling kingdom in all creation.

The shadows beneath the boughs are brighter than day in the Vale, revealing a whole new host of rich hues in the foliage. I marvel at how all the sounds that would have brought me such unease in the ténesomni are sources of delight outside the wall. I take silent notice of a squirrel soaring from branch to branch, a hare disappearing between curling ferns. Birds send the leaves quivering above, and a bee absentmindedly bumbles to blossoms as if browsing market booths.

"I mean . . ." Belwyn bends to cup a vibrant fiddlehead in his hands. "I had no idea what we were missing."

"How could we have known?" My eyes land where dappled sunspots bring out reddish hues in his auburn hair. He catches me staring and grins, and I wonder if the blush to my cheeks is also amplified by this vivid realm.

He straightens and jogs a few paces to catch up with me, his quiver bouncing on his back. "I think most of the valefolk have a longing within them that the darkness can't satisfy, but they don't know it's there unless something, some*one*, shows them."

I bite my lip. He means me, and I don't know why it bothers me so much. It's probably meant to be a compliment, yet it dredges up something else I don't want. "Belwyn, I wasn't the one who showed you that."

He turns, a question in his eyes.

I curl my shaking fingers, remembering what my light cost. "Please stop treating me like some miraculous creature that changed your life." My words snap in a way I don't intend.

He blinks a few times before his bemused smile returns. "But didn't you? I would never have realized what a hopeless path I was on if you hadn't gotten in my way, shown me the meaning of light."

A dry laugh climbs up my throat. "Anyone could have done that for you."

"No," he says, stepping in front of me and waiting until I look him in the eye. "Not just anyone. You."

The earnestness written across his face threatens to soften my guard, but I can't let it. I can't let him gain purchase in my heart just so he will leave a throbbing wound when he's ripped away.

"It wasn't me," I say, practically plead. "If you want to thank anyone, thank Elyōn. He's the one that gave me the gift. My . . . my *heritage* is beyond my control. I didn't ask for this ability, and I didn't try to wake anyone up with it."

I hug my arms around my chest, and it feels as if all the warmth has been leached from the Zomré morning.

What bothers me most is that I had no say in this destiny. No matter what I do, no matter how I strive to make my heart pure or choose to do the next hard thing, all anyone will ever see is the way light favors me.

Belwyn frowns, his expression conflicted. I am not certain what he thinks of Elyōn, or if he believes in him. I wouldn't blame him if he thought it was all a joke.

My own faith is a tremulous thing, newly acknowledged, barely understood. I've always accepted the Highest's existence and taken it for granted that he was the one who created the world, but I don't understand why I believed it so whole-heartedly when I grew up in a place that worshipped the kaligorven. My father didn't speak of Elyōn often, if ever.

Do I owe this understanding to my mother's careful instruction? Is it possible that the work she did to teach me Elyōn's truths so long ago could have laid the foundation for my faith today, struggling though it may be?

How much more would I understand if she hadn't been stolen from me when I was four years old?

I want to learn more about you, Mada, my mind whispers, although I know she can't hear. *If I learn who you were, I hope that will show me who I am supposed to be.*

Belwyn's lips tense, then part. His voice emerges quiet and firm, breaking into the cage of my thoughts. "Maybe you didn't mean to wake me up, but you did anyway. You showed me what I was missing. There's a reason you were supposed to be that for the Vale."

I almost laugh. *Is there really*? I don't see anything remarkable in myself.

He spares me from having to respond and holds out a hand, gesturing toward the sack of supplies Arlyn gave me to carry. I slide it off my back gratefully, and Belwyn shoulders it with ease.

Side by side, we continue walking until the birds' refrains no longer carry so far through the warming air. The sun bears down on us from straight above. I never knew its name, but I used to feel the heat of it in the open places of Utsanek during midday. How strange it seems now to have benefited from its touch but not known it existed. Do the animals see what we cannot? I often wondered how they seemed so unaffected by the ténesomni. Perhaps it does not enslave them like it enslaves people.

I rub the back of my neck. Truth feels as hazy as the shadows. Rael tells me that without the sun, nothing grows. That the fact that life exists in the Vale is a mercy from Elyōn. Ordinary darkness is the absence of light, but the shadow I grew up in seeks to hide the knowledge of light's presence. It distorts the truth into a compelling farce that valefolk have never thought to question.

As we push farther into the heart of this foreign forest, my gloomier thoughts have time to catch up. I begin to avoid the trees, which have ceased to draw my gaze upward. They surround me like an army of witnesses, glaring down as if they can hear the nagging question that pricks my conscience like a pebble in my boot.

If I was supposed to be the one to show the Vale the light, then who will do so now that I have run away?

"Belwyn, Amyrah. Come rest with us."

Arlyn's voice draws me out of the place where my anxieties reside. The path continues ahead, but he and his wife have stopped next to a laughing brook that kisses the roadway, then curves away into the trees.

Rael settles onto a moss-covered bank and leans against a boulder, closing her eyes with a long exhale. A sheen of sweat caps her brow. Arlyn's gaze rests on her for a moment, concern weighing down the corners of his lips.

"How much farther is Ketsé?" Belwyn asks, setting down the gear and stretching out his back.

"Another four days' journey at least." Arlyn grimaces, his eyes not leaving Rael. "Perhaps more."

Thinking about that makes me want to cry. It's been no more than a day and a half of traveling, yet I feel so drained. But I hide how it bothers me and crouch to unlace my boots, then wade into the shallow water. The shock of cold makes me groan as my sore feet find relief. I resist the urge to plunge my whole exhausted body in, but the desire to wash some of the journey's dirt away is too strong to ignore. Glancing back at the bank, I see Arlyn settling down next to his wife and drawing her to rest on his lap. We will be here a little while, at least. Long enough to rinse out my hair.

Belwyn's voice follows me as I move downstream. "You shouldn't wander off."

At his nervous tone, a guilty grimace finds my lips.

He's afraid I'll leave him again.

It was unkind of me to send him on an errand, then run after he had helped me escape to my cottage when my father sacrificed—

No. I can't think about this.

"I won't do that to you again." My voice sounds like a stranger's, too bright and certain. It's foolish to make promises I don't know I can keep. But it isn't exactly a lie; I *want* it to be true. "And I don't think we have anything to fear out here."

Belwyn's face relaxes, and he tucks his hands into the pockets of his trousers as he trails me. "Well, I'm not sure about that. I got the impression Arlyn is as wary of these woods as the ones surrounding the Vale."

"As long as it isn't a kaligorva, I don't care."

I find a flat rock and sit, pulling my hair over a shoulder. Belwyn crosses to the other side of the shallow stream and angles away to give me privacy. I cup the water into my tresses until they are heavy and dripping with twinkling droplets. My fingers work the knots, gently tugging them apart. For a moment, I pretend that this is the stream that flows beside my cottage, that I will turn around and find my father scolding the goats or tripping over chickens. I pretend that I don't feel this nagging drive to prove what all the loss was for.

There are lots of things I wish I could forget.

"I can still see it."

I turn, surprised to find Belwyn standing so close to me, jacket and cloak thrown onto the bank. He still wears his belt with the sword tucked into it. His tunic is a soft gray color, almost blue. I never noticed it before, nor how it pulls across his broad shoulders and clings tightly to his arms. I wonder if the secret of what it feels like to be wrapped within them is mine alone.

My face warms. Water drips onto my lap, but I hardly care. I swallow. *Focus.*

"What can you see?" I ask.

He tilts his head. "Your light. I thought it wouldn't be visible out here, but it is." His eyes narrow, passing over me. "You just have to look really closely."

My cheeks burn hotter, and I glance down and coach myself to breathe. "Well, hopefully no one will have the occasion to look at me *that* hard." I scrunch the excess water out of my hair and stand. "I'm afraid what I can do will be conspicuous, even out here." When I lift my eyes, my heart jumps to my throat for an entirely different reason.

Belwyn opens his mouth to respond but stops when he notes my changed expression. His hand travels to his sword hilt as he spins around.

A tall form emerges from behind the bend, raising a nocked arrow to eye level.

"Hands off that blade, my friend. You'd be wise not to test my skill with a bow."

Belwyn's shoulders heave for a few breaths before he relents, sheathing his sword and raising his hands.

"That's better. Now, if the both of you would kindly walk ahead of me, we'll rejoin the rest of your party."

I follow Belwyn's lead, wishing I could tuck close to his side. I risk a glance back at the stranger, which prompts a jerk of the arrowhead. He wears a close-fitting uniform that resembles Rael and Arlyn's clothes in material and rich color. I catch a glimpse of his face—young, olive-skinned, with deep-set eyes and a chin marked with a small scar—before he jabs me in the back to keep walking.

When we round the bend, another two strangers await us, each bedecked in a similar fashion, but their weapons remain on their backs and in their sheaths. Arlyn paces with his hands on his hips, Rael beyond him pulling her shawl close.

"I know you don't like it, Arlyn, but you know the rules," the broader stranger says, his tone rough. "I'll reap the consequences as it is for not requiring the same of you and your wife."

Rael touches Arlyn on the shoulder. He stills.

"It's alright, my love. We expected this, didn't we?" she asks quietly.

Arlyn's lips press together, but he gives a tight nod and turns to face us. "I'm sorry about this," he says as a hood is yanked over my head.

Now I think I really will suffocate.

5
BELWYN

I HAVE NEVER LIKED TO CONSIDER what a doomed afterlife in Ikktar would feel like, but it's probably something like this.

The hood over my head would be enough to make me miserable, but the day is also sweltering, and my throat is coarser than sand. The men who bound our hands behind our backs deposited Amyrah and me in a rolling cart pulled by sweaty horses. Being spared the walk isn't a blessing, though, because the path through the forest is narrow and laced with thick roots. I tense as the wagon lobs me to the right for the hundredth time. Without the use of my arms, it takes incredible effort not to crush Amyrah, who sits beside me. I fall against her and hear her exasperated exhale as I struggle to right myself.

"Sorry," I mutter after my elbow lodges into her side. She doesn't respond but manages to help us both back into a sitting position. I rest my neck against the rough wood railing and feel a trickle of sweat drip from my nose.

Shades, what I wouldn't do for a breath of fresh air.

The tones of serious conversation find my ears from behind me, where I assume the strangers and Arlyn are leading the procession, but between the fabric over my face, the creak of the cart, and the heavy breath of the horses, I cannot make anything out other than deep voices. A much more colorful expletive slips off my tongue.

"Izra, they've had more than enough of this."

The voice is Rael's, feminine and firm, and it issues from close to my feet. Of course, they wouldn't make her walk any longer with the way her leg is paining her. She had remained so quiet, though, that I didn't realize she was riding in the cart with us.

Commands are issued to the animals, and the cart lumbers to a halt. Footfalls scrape the ground, stopping to my left.

"If they are from the Vale, as you say, then I cannot let them walk into the city unguarded," says the man I assume must be Izra.

"They won't be unguarded." Arlyn's voice rises in support of his wife. "At least remove their hoods, unbind their hands. Let them breathe and see the world around them. They aren't a threat."

"I'm under orders—"

"*Please*." Rael's voice cuts through. "They've been in darkness long enough, and we will have to make camp soon. Better to have their help, don't you think?"

After a lengthy pause, a hand grabs my hood and a fistful of hair with it. The burlap slips off, and oxygen and daylight are returned to me. I drink in both, blinking until my eyes adjust. The scenery looks different now, with shadows slanting lengthwise across the open ground. Amyrah gasps, her face relaxing after her hood is removed. Her hair, which was wet when the sack went over it, is plastered to her head and crowned with a halo of frizz.

"Lean forward, friend."

I bristle at the ironic term. "What makes you think I'm your friend?" I say, turning to glare at the man who apprehended us at the stream. The shadow of his cloak hides any reaction I'd hoped to see. Silent, he bends over the side of the cart and produces a dagger from his hilt. My body jolts forward as he cuts my bonds, then rounds to Amyrah's side of the wagon to do the same for her. She rubs her wrists, her eyes seeking mine.

"Are you feeling well?" I ask, stretching my arms and finding a more comfortable position to sit between the casks and crates.

She tugs her long hair over her shoulder, combing it out with her fingers. "Better now."

The cart resumes rolling, and it's remarkable how much easier it is to handle the bumps when I have my bearings and can hold myself upright. I glance to the end of the cart, where Rael sits, her shadowed eyes fixed on Amyrah. No emotion claims her face, yet the expression isn't unfriendly. Merely reserved.

"I'm sorry you had to endure that. The Watch is particular when it comes to outsiders." Rael leans forward and pulls the shawl off her shoulders, folding it into precise quadrants.

"Would've been nice to have some warning that we were going to be treated like criminals," I mutter.

Rael tilts her head. "And would you have consented to it willingly? Ketsé is the only place we can go. Would you rather have ruined your peace of mind by fretting about what was to come?"

Amyrah's hand slips over my wrist. "It's alright," she says, maybe to me. Maybe to both of us.

"One action I don't like, and those ropes and hoods are going back on. Got it?"

I don't have to turn around to know that the warning issues from Izra. His voice already sets my teeth on edge.

So much for forming good relationships with the Ketsans.

But I'm too irritated to care how juvenile my behavior is. "Don't you have other things to worry about, like how your kingdom of light is shrinking?"

Amyrah elbows me in the ribs.

Nobody responds, and it's probably for the best.

The silence stretches on for what feels like an eternity. Even though they are no longer treating us like prisoners, our hosts are less willing to talk now that they can see our faces. The men walk in conspicuous quiet that rubs on me like new wool, and I can't stand to let the awkwardness persist.

I turn to Rael. "What do we need to know about Ketsé?"

She regards me with a lowering of an eyebrow. "What do you want to know?"

"How about you start with your connection to it."

She inhales sharply and looks past me to the road ahead. "It was our home."

My chin bobs. That much was obvious, but something doesn't add up. "Why did you leave in the first place?"

And why are you so reluctant to return?

Rael's arms tense around her. Her face hardens as though entombed behind a wall of stone. Unreachable.

"We didn't want to leave. Not really. But we were compelled to, nonetheless."

"Compelled by who?" Amyrah asks as she ties off a loose braid with a strip of fabric. She looks different with her hair pulled back. Withheld, somehow. I am so used to her carefree appearance that I'm not sure I like it.

I turn back to Rael. A smile that looks like it's meant to be easy trips across her mouth but stays well away from her eyes. "By Elyōn."

The cart lurches to a halt, the horses pulling it whinnying and stamping the ground. I look over my shoulder to see the man driving them struggling to keep them under control, crooning soft commands and holding the reins tight.

"Steady, girls."

The man to our left tenses, raising his bow with one hand and pulling an arrow from his quiver with the other. When I move to hop over the side of the cart, he throws me a look of warning. I freeze, gripping the cart's rail and looking around at the others. Swords are out, arrows nocked. The fading evening light etches the men's grim faces.

I listen.

A low growl issues from the trees, and before I can decide what kind of animal it came from, a haunting howl follows it, so close it reverberates around my chest cavity.

Cold fingers fix around my arm, and I turn to find Amyrah's wide eyes dominating her face.

"Belwyn, the sola. Do you think—"

I give a subtle shake of the head, but the man closest to us whips around and stares at her.

"What did you say?"

Amyrah bites her lip, but her eyes do not leave mine.

Before he can question her again, the forest erupts in a chorus of howls.

"Holden, we need fire. Quick," Izra says.

The man closest to us turns and curses. As he rummages through a sack at my feet, his hood falls back, revealing his face. He's younger than I thought.

"Here." Holden thrusts a bundle into my hands. "Get busy while we ward them off."

I unwrap the leather and find flint and steel inside. "Stay here," I say, turning to Amyrah. It isn't a question, but her determined expression is an answer.

"No. I'm helping."

I don't have time to argue with her. A shadowed shape darts to the right, and Holden responds before I can blink, piercing the creature with a white-fletched arrow.

"*Blazes*," he hisses after crouching and examining the heap of fur. Another lupine beast launches toward him, and he grabs a dagger secured to his thigh, plunging it into its chest. The huge canine thumps to the earth.

"Belwyn. Make fire. Now."

I jump out of the cart, Amyrah close behind.

"I'll find wood," she says, running into the trees.

Shades!

An arrow whizzes past me and takes out another wolf.

"Go. I'll cover you," says Holden.

I sprint to catch up with Amyrah, and the two of us manage to break an armful of branches off a fallen tree within moments. When we run back to the group, I get a clearer picture of what's happening.

There are at least twenty of the animals, the smaller ones staying near the back of the attack. They are not as big as the wolf-sola Amyrah and I met outside of Utsanek, but still larger than any dog I have ever seen. Arlyn, Izra, and Holden are overwhelmed with keeping them back while the third man attempts to keep the horses under control. The wolves snarl and dart in and out of the shadows, impossible to target with an arrow. I frown. This aggressive behavior toward a group of humans isn't normal.

A soft sound of frustration burns through my confusion. Amyrah is crouched at my feet, flinging spark after useless spark into the pile of wood.

"Give it here."

She stands and watches the battle as I try to get a blaze going.

"It's not going to work," I huff after several attempts. "We need some sort of kindling or we'll never get it going."

Amyrah fingers her cloak. "What about this?"

"No good. Wool is terrible for burning."

Shouts ring out as the circle of wolves presses the men closer. The horses rear and shriek, their handler all but thrown off the wagon as it lurches forward a few feet.

"How's that fire coming?" Holden says over his shoulder, his voice strained.

I grunt and flake the magnesium. The spark hits the branches and winks out.

A curse escapes me right before Amyrah's hand thrusts in front of the deadwood. Her fingers crunch a handful of yellowed papers. I seek out her face and find tears streaming down her cheeks. Her other hand presses an old book to her chest.

"What's this?"

"Take them," she gasps, shaking them under my nose.

The wolves erupt into a chorus of yipping howls. I glance at the papers again. "Are you sure?"

Her chest puffs up and she nods.

I grab them. Within moments, the paper has ignited, and the dry branches soon follow. Holden whoops and grabs a flaming brand. "Izra, *catch*." He lobs it toward the older man.

Amyrah selects her own torch, advancing on the pack, and I do likewise. With fire on our side, the wild canines retreat into the forest, their eerie wails fading into the distance.

A relieved chuckle passes from man to man. Rael presses her hand to her mouth and closes her eyes.

Heart racing, I sag beside Amyrah, taking her branch and throwing it into the fire with mine. "What a rush."

Closing the book, Amyrah holds it to her heart. Her lips pull back in a grimace.

Concern fills me. "Did you get burned?"

She shakes her head.

I reach out to touch her shoulder, but she pulls away, her braid jerking. "Really, Belwyn. It's nothing."

What happened to the closeness we shared, and why can't I seem to get past this shell around her emotions?

"What in all Atsun is that?" someone calls.

"It explains why they were so eager to attack. They were protecting their meal."

"But . . . isn't that also a wolf?"

I get up and join the men fifty paces into the trees. They stand around a huge mound of fur punctuated with shimmering rivers of luminescence.

My jaw drops as recognition dawns, but I can't form the words.

"It's a sola." Amyrah approaches, her soft voice bleeding with emotion.

Izra and the cart driver look at each other, an expression I can't interpret passing between them. The young man, Holden, keeps his eyes trained on Amyrah. Something sharp and corrosive expands in my chest as he watches her.

"How can you be sure?" he asks, more like he is testing her rather than requesting proof.

"Because it saved us from a kaligorva in the Vale," I say before Amyrah can reveal her strange connection with the Light Creatures. I leave out the part about how I stabbed the Shrouded beast in the heart.

Holden glares at me, his eyes narrowing. I glare back.

Amyrah passes between us and kneels before the creature. Holden blinks and watches, and I return my focus to her. She lifts the creature's head and rests it in her lap, stroking its long, lupine snout like a mother with her child.

6

WEHNA

"LISSI, I SAID *I* WAS GOING TO have the blue ones."

"Well, tough. I have them now and there's nothing you can say to make me give them away."

I struggle to keep my hold on the flaxen strands I'm attempting to coerce into a braid as three of the Peren sisters battle it out for hair ribbons. Why did I volunteer to help get them ready for the caeruméni service? I don't know what I'm doing. Elodie's hair is such a different texture than mine—slippery, fine, straight, and needing constant brushing—but I do the best I can. I understand what it's like to be the oldest, although I don't have four younger siblings like she does. Sometimes it's nice having someone look after you for a change.

Elodie stills, allowing me to make progress with the braid. She strokes the puffball of a feline in her lap. "I'll trade you Bear for them," she says, her voice quiet.

"Elodie!" six-year-old Téah shrieks indignantly.

I trap the inside of my cheek with my teeth when a fresh wave of pain assails my head with the noise. She stomps over to us and plants a hand on a hip, her other arm clutching two more kittens to her middle a little too tightly. She and Arvo make quite the combustible pair when they're together. "You said there was nothing in Atsun you loved more than Bear."

The teen withdraws her hands from the kitten and picks at her cuticles. "Bear doesn't bring out my eyes like those ribbons."

I roll my eyes. It's a good thing her father isn't in the room to hear this.

Lissi crouches before Elodie's lap, where the kitten purrs, a perfect picture of contentment. "Are you sure? You aren't going to steal him back?"

The braid slips from my fingers when Elodie shakes her head.

Téah moans. "But that's not fair. I would have traded you my entire bolétis collection for him. It's not like anyone's going to notice the color of your stupid eyes."

But her older sisters have made the transaction before she can complain further, and Elodie hands the satin ribbon over her shoulder for me. Lissi scoops up the poof and whispers, "I'm so sorry she doesn't love you like I do," into its white fur. I have a hard time holding in a chuckle.

I tie off the plait and Elodie swings it over her shoulder. She stands and gives me a hug. "Thank you, Wehna." Before I can object, she yanks two generous sections out of the intricate hairstyle. She giggles at my horrified expression. "What? They frame my face."

"Come, girls. It's time to go," Tress calls from the hallway.

We emerge into Ellithïm's main street, finding it stuffed with people heading toward the fenced-in forest that houses the weekly worship meetings. I like to think of it as "the cathedral." Arvo sees me, drops the crude bow he's been working on, and runs to catch up with Téah.

I freeze. He didn't even stop to say hello.

People move forward, brushing my shoulders. Each jostle is like a lightning bolt of pain, which I have convinced my hosts I no longer feel. It's as if my brain is clamped between two fists as amiable chatter assaults it. I take a step back, then another, and another, until the pressure lessens and the whole community has entered the cathedral without me. Chest squeezing, I escape through Ellithïm's hidden gateway that leads out to the rest of Utsanek.

I'm so tired of this incessant push to be strong.

Because right now, I'm pretty sure all I'm being is stupid. And I really don't care.

It is Satus morning, the word meaning "rest" in Atsunic, and the Vale is taking that definition to heart. It's a good thing, I tell myself, because it means I'm less likely to come across anyone who will give me trouble. That helps soothe my festering conscience. The only people I see are those cracking open their doors to replace the stale offerings to the kaligorven with fresh loaves and fragrant blooms, giving me no more than a cursory glance as I walk by. With every step I take, my ease grows feebler. I don't want to admit that I'm repaying my hosts' kindness and protection poorly by wandering the city alone.

With no real destination in mind, my feet find familiar alleyways, even though the last thing I want is to revisit the places I know. Everything about my life has changed, so why is this hateful city the same as it has always been? I switch directions, choosing all the forlorn passages I come across. Even the fear of the ténesomni has faded to something halfhearted and hazy in the recesses of my mind. Or perhaps the constant presence of pain has forced it aside. Whatever the case, I am oddly freed of my inhibitions, and all I want are the corners of Utsanek that are untouched by light.

Despite my efforts to get lost, I soon find myself standing in a shadowy street before my family's old apartment building. A single, pathetic sola brossa is suspended above me—a tooth, maybe?—illuminating the building's sad façade.

"*Falling firelights*," I whisper into the silence.

My eyes hitch on the first landing, where my former neighbor Gotrel has rearranged her ever-struggling collection of depressing plants. The lingering scent of scallion, cabbage, and lanuum soup drifts from her open window. I want to stop there, to forbid my eyes from wandering to the second story, but with one flutter of my eyelashes, I take in the only home I've ever known in Utsanek.

I am up the stairs before I can stop myself. The front door stands open a sliver, prevented from swinging shut by a pile of broken earthenware spilling out onto the landing. I kick a pot aside, anger igniting as I realize someone's been scrounging through our things. Our life.

The door squeals as I push it open all the way to allow the glow of the street's sola brossa to spill into the small space.

A stench of something rotten meets me, and I press a hand to my mouth as I step inside. Hollow sadness cinches around my lungs.

Nothing is as I remember it. The few remaining pillows that I'd helped my mother sew for our home worship gatherings are scattered, torn open with their stuffing blanketing the floor like snow. The old table is upended, one of its legs missing, and the chairs are nowhere to be seen.

On the other side of the room, the two large beds we all shared remain, piled with soiled linens I dare not touch. My mother's meticulously labeled shelf of dried herbs and grains has been knocked over, and rat droppings are mixed in with the diminutive grain spilled across the wooden planks.

A rustle sounds to the left, and I startle when two beady eyes reflect the sola bone light back at me. I take a hasty step backward, something cracking beneath my shoe.

Fear forgotten, I crouch and discover a small, broken mug on the floor. It's a rough thing, unglazed and forgettable, but I recognize it immediately. Careful of the sharp edges, I pick up the shard of memory and turn it over.

The words 'Wehna loves Mada' are scratched into the side in shaky letters, put there by my own hand when I was not much younger than Arvo. When we were still living in Ketsé and I had no fears to speak of.

The broken pottery falls from my hands as a quick inhale shudders my chest.

What am I doing here?

Trembling, I back out through the door and stumble down the steps.

"This isn't a nice neighborhood, you know."

The voice makes me start. I whip around, press a hand to where my heart lurches in my chest, and glare at Elodie's smirking face.

"What are you doing here?" I force the question through a tight throat, guilt sliding through my conscience, like I've been discovered doing something I shouldn't. I close my eyes for a beat. "You shouldn't have followed me."

"I wanted to see where you were sneaking off to." She crosses her arms, a lantern swaying beneath them, and turns to take in the dilapidated building. “What is this place?”

I clench my jaw and grab Elodie’s small shoulders, spinning her away from the sight, as if it isn’t something fit for innocent eyes. “Never mind. We shouldn’t be here.” I take hold of her wrist and attempt to march her down the street.

Elodie wrenches herself free of my grip. A tinkling laugh dances from her lips. “Wehna, come on. Can’t we have a little fun? The caeruméni won’t be over for a while yet, and it’s so packed, no one will notice we’re gone.”

Tilting my head back, I stare above and exhale. I know I shouldn’t give in to her, but I also don’t want to go back yet. “Your father is going to kill me.”

Warm fingers clasp my arms, and I look down to find Elodie’s blushing face below mine. “I saw a cute boy a couple blocks back.”

My mouth opens in wordless reply as she drags me behind her like a pup on a lead.

We slip around a corner and find a better-lit street, marginally cheerier than the one we left. Elodie gasps and yanks me into the shadows when voices reach us. She opens the door of the lantern and blows out the candle before I can protest.

My temples pound, and I bite my tongue to keep from snapping at her. She doesn’t know the kind of pain I’m in, and I don’t need to give her mother any more reasons to fuss over me.

“Do you see him there? Leaning against the wall?” Elodie whispers.

I squint and make out two shapes lingering a few houses down the street. The smaller one crouches and aims a slingshot at a pyramid of old jars. He gripes when his rock sails past its target.

The taller boy has broad shoulders for his young age, wavy hair, and a carefree demeanor that reminds me of someone.

"He's *adorable*," my companion squeals.

"You shouldn't be pining after boys, Elodie," I say, although I don't have the right to judge. It wasn't that long ago that I was thirteen and keeping a close watch on the baker's son down the street.

Back in Ketsé.

My gut twists and my head throbs.

I tug Elodie's sleeve. "Please. We need to get back."

She opens her mouth to argue, but irascible shouting spills out of the dwelling at the boys' backs, stopping her.

"Korvin, you useless boy. Where are you?"

A large man trips over the threshold and stumbles into the street, and a waft of stale liquor hits me. I shrink farther into the shadows, pulling Elodie back.

"What is it, Father?" The older boy stands straight, unfazed by the outburst.

Reaching to steady himself, the man blinks and seems to gulp down his torrent of words. "Your mother needs you in the kitchen," he mutters.

Korvin motions for the younger boy to follow. They slip into the house, but the man stays there, gripping the doorframe and staring into the black-painted sky. Rings of tattoos stand out around his bicep, illuminated by the shard of sola brossa suspended down the street. A long, dark slash cuts the tattoos through, negating their significance. I squint, recognizing him from city gatherings. My parents often made me stay at home with Arvo whenever those were called. I'm certain, though, that I'm looking at the former Foremost of the Vale.

I look around the street again, realizing that I've been to this area of Utsanek before.

That's Belwyn's father.

My teeth catch the inside of my lip. I wonder where Belwyn is and if

Amyrah's absence has affected him like it has me. I watch his disheveled father until Elodie tugs me away.

Our scuffling feet alert the man to our presence. He bellows after us, but Elodie and I have already escaped down an adjacent street.

Breathless, we lean against an old stone wall underneath another sola bone shard, and Elodie bursts into a fit of giggles. "So, what did you think of him?" She bats her long eyelashes, holding the extinguished lantern under her chin.

I don't remember what it's like to have my head turned by someone, or to feel a bashful warmth claim my cheeks and settle in my abdomen. I'm seventeen, and I've already lived enough life to make me weary of it.

"I think," I pause, summoning my last reserve of levity to fight against the painful gloom settling over my mind, "that although he may have some agreeable traits—"

Elodie's eyebrows arch up hopefully.

"Your parents would rather I tell you to forget about him."

I only catch a glimpse of the girl's crestfallen face before an immense cloud of darkness envelopes the street. Terror like I've never experienced steals the breath from my chest. I can't even scream. Grabbing the girl by her shoulders, I draw her back to my chest and wrap my arms around her. I can't tell if she is the one shaking, or if it's me. We withdraw as far back into an alcove as we can, then remain still, save for our heaving chests.

Black wisps of shadow unroll like a carpet along the street, barely missing the toes of our shoes. I struggle to keep my breaths quiet. Elodie's soft scent tangles with the sharpness of sweat and something putrid. This is different from the odor that permeated my old home, and it fills me with terror. The sable mists intensify and clamber over each other, rising well past our waists, and a living mass of ténesomni steps into full view, held loosely in place by a towering form that is neither human nor beast.

I clap my hand over Elodie's mouth before she can scream and resolve to swallow my own.

The kaligorva halts directly in front of us, and for an awful moment, I fear it can sense our presence. Its horned head rotates atop massive shoulders, and I pinch my eyes closed.

Elyōn, if you are here, be with us now.

Whatever horror I'm expecting doesn't come. All I can hear are the kaligorva's labored breaths, the wet sound of its giant maw opening and closing. Even Elodie remains perfectly silent. My arms begin to ache from holding her so tight. I risk easing my grip around her and peel my hand from her face. When she doesn't utter a sound, I feel brave enough to open my eyes.

The Shrouded has turned away from us and angled its muzzle to peer at the minuscule sola bone dangling above it. Its tongues of liquid night reach and grasp for the light but then pull back as if burned. A hiss pours into the air like acid, making my entire body erupt in gooseflesh.

"Elïatova."

That voice. It makes me feel like water hovering around the freezing point is rushing beneath my skin, crystalizing the blood it touches. I crane my neck as far as I dare, but I cannot see past the walls of the alcove to confirm whom the voice belongs to.

"Elïatova atéro."

The command is firmer this time. Helpless, I watch the beast's shadows advance on the sola bone. The sickly green-gold illumination wavers, then seeps down in weeping rivulets to meet the ténesomni. The two opposing forces connect, and the filthy black spreads into the light, leaching it. Devouring it.

Extinguishing it.

We are left in suffocating blackness.

A moan of twisted pleasure escapes the kaligorva. Although I cannot see anything, I feel its presence grow and the shadows brushing my skin like cobwebs. And I hear it move away, down the street.

As attentive as I was to every noise the beast made, I am more-so to the soft footsteps that fill its void. They slow as they approach our hiding place. My heart thunders as I try to decide what to do. I don't wish to be caught like a cornered rabbit, and I think I've faced this monster before.

Shoving Elodie behind me and warning in an abrasive whisper for her to stay hidden, I step into the street.

Cold laughter greets me, filling the shadows as a rush of fetid wind pushes my hair behind my shoulders. I shiver. The billows of ténesomni part around me, revealing a black-clothed man with white skin and hair without pigment. He holds his book between his hands, the ink slithering across its pages and arms like nightcrawlers.

"Well," he says softly after an assessing glance, his lip curling. "I was wondering if we would meet again."

"Foremost." I refuse to speak his name. He is not worthy of a proper greeting.

"I trust you witnessed my new little trick." He closes the book with a thud, and my heart thuds along with it.

I bite my lip and say nothing, the pain in my skull unbearable.

Undeterred by my reticence, Myrzeth moves closer, clasping his book behind his back with both hands. "What do you think?"

"I—" My sluggish, fear-addled brain cannot form an intelligent reply.

He chuckles. "I know. It's rather overwhelming to see the might of the kaligorven on full display."

A shiver races up my spine. Or perhaps it's a tendril of ténesomni. "You would call this 'might'?"

He gazes at the sky, as if studying the stars his darkness has shrouded.

"What is it you said to me when we first met? Let's see if I can recall it. I daresay I've heard your Ketsan kinfolk repeat the phrase as well. *The darkness may assail the light, but it won't overcome it.* Did I get that right?"

At my stunned expression, he widens his eyes dramatically. "Oh, yes. I know you aren't from here, Wehna Qaith." A grin stretches his lips. "You and I have the advantage over the rest of the Vale in that respect."

"How—how do you know that?"

He raises a shoulder, then lets it drop. "I have my sources. All I needed was the name of your parents to confirm my suspicions." He tilts his head as though paying his respects. "So sorry for your loss, by the way."

For the first time, those words don't make me want to scream. They are true, aren't they? I have lost them. And, if anything, seeing the physical remnants of my old life broken to pieces has made me accept it.

I breathe in through my nose and raise my chin. "You were saying some nonsense about dark and light?"

His eyebrows raise and he bobs his chin. "Yes. Light has this legendary reputation of dispelling shadows wherever it goes, does it not? And yet, in every possible manner, I have shown you that the power I possess is greater than either." Myrzeth holds the book before him again, and his eyes gleam. "Do you need any more proof of my mastery than that?"

When I offer him no reply, he lowers his head and comes to stand within a foot of my face.

"I have invited you once, and I extend that invitation again. Give yourself to the night." He reaches a pale hand forward and fingers a spiral of my hair. "You don't have to live in fear or doubt. You can choose the side of strength. More will see the wisdom of my actions in the days to come." He stares me in the eyes, letting his hand fall away. "Why shouldn't you be the first?"

I had my initial encounter with Myrzeth inside the fanum shortly after he arrived in the Vale. The same frightening pull I felt to his words plagues me now, but I also remember how I stood against him.

The air crackles as if touched by the flames of Ikktar. I lick my dry lips and whisper hoarsely, "You will not succeed in winning many to your side by siphoning their light."

His mouth shifts to the side, bunching his cheek into a tight fold. It's too stiff to be called a smile. He clicks his tongue against his teeth. "Miss Wehna, are you concerned for me?"

My cheeks warm, and I grit my teeth and call on the fire of indignation to burn the embarrassment away. "Not at all. Why would I waste a single thought on someone who tried to have his niece killed?"

I almost said 'my friend,' but my better sense cautions me about revealing my connection to Amyrah.

Myrzeth backs away, his face growing hard. "I can't expect you to understand what was at play during that whole scenario, Wehna. I will admit, that was not my finest moment. However, it turns out the kaligorven were well-satisfied with her substitute." A wicked pleasure claims his features.

Her father sacrificed himself in her place. That's what Tress said.

I feel sick.

"But it will comfort you to hear that I have no intention of repeating those actions, as I also have no intention of winning anybody." The corners of his lips lower, and his irises pool with shadows. He leans in as though sharing a secret. "Make no mistake. I will have the valefolk one way or another."

I draw back, and my knees almost give out beneath me. He laughs again, and it is no less chilling than the kaligorva's hiss.

"Well, you had better run along, little rabbit, and tell your Elyōn-loving friends to prepare themselves."

Turning on his heel, Myrzeth saunters back down the street. He raises a hand into the air, clicks his fingers. The ténesomni piles back in around me, thick enough to make me feel like I'm choking.

"W-Wehna. What was th-that?"

Through great heaving sobs, Elodie calls to me, and I stumble to locate her, kneeling at her side when my boot finds her on the ground.

"Nothing. We'll be fine." I pat around until I find her arms, following them up to her shoulders. "He didn't see you there." Slipping an arm around her waist, I help her up. I begin the terrifying task of feeling along the buildings, hopeful we can find our way out of this pitch-black maze.

"Do you know that man?" Elodie whispers.

"That's Myrzeth, the new Foremost of the Vale. You know that, Elodie."

I feel her torso wiggle as she shakes her head. "No, I mean, it sounded like there was more between you and him."

My groping fingers find the corner of a building, and once we go around it, I can feel a narrow passageway has opened before us. A few steps into it, the unwavering glow of a shard of sola brossa breaks through the ténesomni.

"Trust me, Elodie, there is nothing more."

Except that's a lie, because a strange desire to experience the strength of which Myrzeth boasts has implanted in my mind.

7
AMYRAH

THE LITTLE STAR PENDANT IS WARM to the touch. I roll its pointed shape between my fingertips, trying to recall the feeling of hope it infused within me when I found it dropped in Utsanek's market.

Hope has felt like a phantom as of late.

I sit a fair distance from the fire, farther than I should, and still, I am within the ignati's glow. If we were in the Vale, it would have been choked out long before it reached me. In the Grovesha, it seems as though illumination, no matter how small, can go on forever.

The rest of the group relaxes on the other side of the blaze, their humming conversation low enough that it cannot be heard over the fire's aggressive cracking and popping. A frigid breeze rises to challenge the fire's heat, sending shivers up my spine. I pull my knees up and hug them close to ward off the chill.

"Can I get anything else for you?"

I blink away the spots in my eyes and tilt up my chin. Belwyn curves over me, holding something that issues ribbons of steam and wearing an expression of concern. Maybe I should open up to him, but I am scared what will follow if I give voice to my excruciating thoughts about my father.

My father, whom I had just gotten back. My father, who must have seen some value, some purpose for my life that was worth dying for. My father, who loved me—

No.

Shaking my head to dislodge grief's hold, I fold my legs to the side, accept the carved wooden mug with one hand, and tuck the necklace into a pocket with the other. Eyes closed, I breathe in the steam of the hot liquid and take a sip. It's spiced and nutty, and much too reminiscent of the tea Orlagh brought me up on. Swallowing proves difficult. I open my eyes and make a lame attempt at a smile.

"No, this is perfect."

Belwyn nods a little, like he expected that response and doesn't believe a word of it, and gazes across the flames.

The warmth of the tea reaches to my marrow.

"What do you make of them?" Belwyn asks, looking toward the other side of the blaze.

My eyes trail the figures lit up by the orange glow. I know he is referring to our new acquaintances from Ketsé, but I can't look past Wehna's parents. Arlyn sits with his back against a tree, caught up in a somber discussion with Izra. His wife cozies up under his arm, her beautiful hair cascading in tight spirals across her face as she rests her head on his shoulder. As a couple, they couldn't be more different from each other. He is tall with a fair complexion, thinning red hair, and easy faith shining out from green eyes. Her skin is rich, her hair blacker than ténesomni, and tortured thoughts remain trapped behind her dark irises. Yet one look at them together and I knew that neither would be whole without the other.

Would my father have been different if my mother was never taken from him?

The question announces itself before I have a chance to slam the door, to shut it out. I draw in a sharp breath, feeling the pressure building behind my eyes.

I can't let myself think of him again, or all will be lost.

"They seem alright," I choke out.

A small grunt issues from Belwyn at my weak response. I force another gulp of tea down my tight throat.

"I'm not sure going to Ketsé is the best thing for us."

Resting the cup on my lap, I turn my attention back to Belwyn. "Why is that?"

He scuffs the dirt with a leather-shod foot. "I can't really say. I don't get a good feeling from Izra and Holden. They treat us like we are *different*."

What an unfeeling word. Coming from anyone else, it might be offensive, but I can't deny that he's right. Something is strange about the Ketsans' behavior toward us. Maybe Arlyn and Rael told them I am Luvesti.

I take another gulp of tea, running my thumb over the cup's smooth exterior. It must belong to the Ketsans, because I haven't seen it before. I wonder if countless hands have held it, if its shape has comforted them as it comforts me now. My gaze shifts back to Belwyn. "What else can we do? Arlyn is right. We need to warn the Grovesha of what's coming. I can't let my heritage get in the way of that, and I need to find out more about my mother."

Pity arcs Belwyn's lips, and I quickly look away, focusing on Izra. The older man has perfect posture, even while seated. He has the air of someone well-trained, ready to jump to action at the slightest disturbance. His shoulders are not as broad as some, but he is thick around the chest and arms. He runs a hand across the white stubble coating his chin and gives Belwyn a look that makes my skin go cold.

Belwyn's voice softens, a contrast to Izra's scorn. "I know. I want that for you too." He takes a breath, then lets it out slowly. "But I hope we won't regret it."

One of the horses nickers from deep within the shadows, prompting the man I have yet to meet to excuse himself from the fireside. I observe the last person by the ignati, Holden, and clutch my mug under my chin. He leans against a tree, arms folded, engrossed in the conversation. With his hood down, I can see more of his face and the light-brown hair that reaches to his jaw. His features appear stern, almost brooding, until they break into an infectious smile when the horseman shouts a wisecrack over his shoulder.

"Do you think they mean us harm? There's a lot we don't know about the world outside the Vale." I sip my tea. "Maybe they are only being cautious."

"I guess it's possible." Belwyn settles on the ground beside me. I wish he would have sat closer. "But I'm sure you can feel it. Something is off about this."

"I'm used to being the odd one out, Belwyn." My voice is little more than an exhale, and the words slip from my grasp before I've thought them through. "It might be a new feeling for you, but it's been my life. I've learned to ignore what others think of me, and you should too."

I can feel his gaze, but I don't face him.

"Do you think this is about me, about some petty desire to be liked?" he asks, a soft laugh escaping him as he runs his fingers through his hair. "I don't care if they don't like me, but this is something deeper. I thought you'd be safe when we got out of the Vale. Now, I am no longer sure if that's the case."

I am ashamed for insinuating that his motives are selfish. He's protecting me. Again. *Always.* I let out my trapped breath and turn my eyes upon the stars twinkling through the gaps in the trees.

When I was held in the Vale, longing for light, all I could think about was the way everything would be so much clearer if it weren't for the never-ending ténesomni. How could fear and secrets exist where light has free rein? But as I ponder that question now, the answer is obvious.

Darkness doesn't merely exist around us. It makes its home in our hearts.

"So what should I do? Hide my ability?" I ask. My shoulders shift upward as I struggle to hold in my frustration, if that's the right word for it. "Because if I did, there would be no point to what my father—" I swallow and close my eyes, hiding the stars from view. The snapping fire and my ragged sobs fill the pause.

Belwyn's hand finds my forearm, and his gentle voice slips through the heartache. "I need—I *want* you to be careful."

I catch my lip between my teeth.

"And I'm here for you."

We sit quietly, the night air cool and damp despite the heat of the ignati.

"I need you to be," I whisper after a while.

Across the fire, the conversation shifts, and Holden turns to stare at us. At *me.* I match his gaze for a moment, but when he doesn't look away, heat crawls over my skin. I seek freedom in the surface of my tea as it mirrors a diluted image of the night sky.

The ground crunches underneath approaching footsteps, and Belwyn straightens, shifting closer to my side.

"Tomorrow is going to be quite the day for you both, friends. I hope you're prepared for it."

Holden's voice is gentle, with a slight rasp to it. He slips his hands into his pockets and stands over us. When he calls me "friend," I want to believe he means it, despite Belwyn's apprehensions. I open my mouth to respond, but Belwyn gets there before me.

"What does that mean?"

Holden's mouth slants into his cheek. "Ketsé is not a place accustomed to receiving strangers. I'm afraid that given where you come from and the news you bring with you, the Nocilium won't be eager to welcome you."

Belwyn's hand slips from my arm. "Why? Because we have darkness in our veins?"

Surprised by his sharp tone, I face him. What does he mean?

He leans forward, resting his forearms on his kneecaps and clasping his hands between them, and pins Holden with a look of challenge.

The smile retreats from Holden's face. "Yes, but if we handle this well," he says, parrying Belwyn's expression with a pointed look of his own, "it shouldn't be a problem."

"You mean it won't be a problem if we hide who we are."

Holden raises his hands and angles away from us. "I don't mean to give offense; I only want to encourage caution when we enter Ketsé. It might go better for everyone if you appear as regular travelers, not—"

"Reminders of the nation you'd rather pretend didn't exist?" Belwyn's glare issues a silent dare to deny it.

Tension chokes the air like a swarm of gnats. I set down my mug and rest a hand on Belwyn's arm to assure him I'm on his side before addressing Holden. "What is the Nocilium?"

Holden peels his eyes away from Belwyn. "Ketsé's high council. It's because of the Nocilium that the woodfolk remain safe and prosperous."

Belwyn barely suppresses a snort.

Holden's jaw flexes, and he strips the leaves off a nearby branch, then drops them to the ground one by one. His expression eases. "Peace, friend. Believe me when I say that it will go better for everyone if we keep the implications of who and what you are hidden for now." He turns to retake his spot by the fire, attempting to pat Belwyn on the shoulder as he passes. His eyes crinkle good-naturedly when Belwyn recoils.

The words *who and what you are* circle through my mind until I'm nauseous. When we left the Vale behind, I never would have thought that there could be something more unwelcome to those living in the light than the kaligorven. And that something could be *me*.

"Amyrah?" Belwyn's voice makes my world stop spinning, and I suck in a cool breath of air. His hazel eyes lock with mine. "Do me a favor."

I wipe my cheeks with a fold of my cloak. "Yes?"

"Tomorrow, when we get to Ketsé, make sure you put that necklace on."

At least the little star still symbolizes something encouraging to him, even if it no longer does to me.

The trees grow denser and wilder as we travel, their branches cast overhead like a living net. The midday sun struggles to penetrate the forest floor, where the air is as thick as a simmering stew. Dew beads on the delicate fern leaves, dampening my dress from the knee down, and the strands of hair that have escaped my braid wind into loose coils in the humidity. The path which was once so obvious between the trees becomes more and more difficult to find. Izra leads the way, never appearing to doubt his direction. We spend an absurd amount of time navigating the wagon around fallen trees and dense undergrowth. Soon, the way becomes so crowded and craggy that the wagon cannot go on. Belwyn and I stand aside as the Ketsans unharness the horses and unload the provisions.

I peer ahead into the trees. "Why would they abandon all the supplies here?" I ask him.

Belwyn tilts his chin as he watches the men pile crates and barrels into the mouth of a gargantuan log with a hollowed-out center, then secure what remains to their backs. "This must be some sort of cache."

"That's exactly what it is." Holden approaches Belwyn, holding out his satchel, cloak, and weapons. "We have them all over in areas of the forest that aren't that accessible."

Belwyn raises his eyebrows but takes his possessions without question, returning the sword to its place at his side.

I guess the Ketsans no longer view us as threats. That's an improvement, at least.

"Won't the animals get to it?" Belwyn asks, adjusting the belt around his waist.

Holden shakes his head. "As soon as we reach the gates, they'll send out a crew to retrieve what we couldn't bring."

"That seems like an inefficient system."

"It's how we're accustomed to operating on the south side of the city." Holden turns his attention to me. "I'm sorry you don't get to see Ketsé from the north. The gate is rather impressive."

"That's alright," I answer with a smile, and I can feel Belwyn's eyes on me.

Izra calls Filippos—the man I hadn't met—to assist him, and they approach what looks like an unassuming knoll. Digging their hands into the moss, they carefully pry away a camouflaged door and roll it to the side. A small cave is revealed, big enough to wheel in the wagon. Filippos retrieves two leather saddles and bridles from within before they push the wagon inside and replace the door. With a little adjustment and tucking in of moss around its edges, the hole is concealed from view.

"Clever."

I don't miss the dry tone to Belwyn's voice.

"Onward?" Holden asks, and I turn.

Filippos takes no time to saddle the horses, and soon he and Rael are seated and ready to ride. I am relieved she won't have to walk, since she has been looking grayer and grayer as the days have worn on.

We haven't gone far when the company stops again. I scan the scenery, expecting to find an impressive stone wall looming before us, but it looks the same as ever.

"More trees," Belwyn says, equally nonplussed.

I blink at the scene and step forward, a quick inhale parting my lips when I understand. The walls of Ketsé are not made of rock but of many living things woven together. Large trunks bend first one way and then the other, snaking around each other to form a natural barrier as tall as the rest of the forest. They must have been trained from saplings to do so. Thick and woody vines fill the gaps between them. The wall extends into the forest as far as I can see to the left and right. It's so discreet that anyone looking at it from a distance would assume it was nothing but a denser area of forest.

The glint of a blade and a flash of rich brown winks at me from the top of the wall. I nudge Belwyn, but by the time he looks to where I'm pointing, the sentinel is gone.

Izra and Filippos approach the wall, and a large portion of it swings outward to reveal a shadowy passage through its depths. Two tall men clad in thick leather armor and cloaks the color of rich soil regard us, pulling Izra and Filippos aside for a tense, hushed conversation.

"Alright, friends." Holden spins around and looks at Belwyn and me in turn. "Bringing you in is going to take no small amount of diplomacy on Izra's part."

Belwyn rolls his eyes. "As if we pose any threat."

"I would not show any attitude if I were you. It's already nothing short of miraculous that Izra agreed to do this for strangers, especially strangers from the Vale. I advise you not to push your luck with him."

"And what if he is unable to convince the Nocil . . ." I stumble on the word, looking to Holden for help.

"The Nocilium?" His lips tense. "We will have to take our chances. It's Izra's hope that returning your weapons will demonstrate his implicit faith that you are not dangerous. But if you do anything rash"—he directs a meaningful look at Belwyn—"I cannot say what the consequences will be."

A defensive instinct wells inside me. Why can no one see the heart of the young man beside me as I do? He left everything behind for me.

But Belwyn hides his annoyance well. He nods under Holden's critical stare.

"Good." Holden's face breaks into his easy smile for an instant before he looks over his shoulder and receives a signal from Izra. "It's time."

Filippos leads his and Rael's horses forward, disappearing into the tunnel as it curves away. Izra follows. Holden motions for Belwyn and me to go ahead, and we enter the shadow of the living walls of Ketsé.

The passage within is long and earthy, supported by dark wooden beams. As we round the corner, the thick door swings shut and blocks out all daylight, but we aren't left in pitch black; colorful bolétis line the walls.

I stall, unable to make myself move forward, and reach out a hand to touch one of them.

"What is it?" Holden asks from behind. Belwyn stops and turns, his eyes trained on my face.

"Nothing. I-I haven't seen these since we left Utsanek." I try to swallow, but there's a knot in my throat.

I stand there a while, battling a confusing mixture of emotions. At first it's an aching sadness, but then I remember how, when the world seemed the darkest, those same glowing mushrooms gave me the courage to press through the shadows.

Holden clears his throat softly, and I remember to breathe. Blinking to rid my eyes of tears, I catch up to Belwyn. He holds his hand out, but before taking it, I reach into the pocket of my dress, pull out the argentilum necklace, and tie it around my neck.

8

SEYLA

How Tetyan would mock me if she knew I had risked everything to save a man.

My blade sighs across the whetstone with methodical rhythm, matching the shallow breaths issuing from that man sprawled across my cot.

He starts, moaning as his wounds pull tight.

"*Heshïn.*" The curse curls like steam from my lips.

His noise is too loud for this early in the day. I rest the khukuri on the rough table and hasten to check that none of his lacerations have opened again. I have not spent thirteen days and all my spare arlum on expensive balms, tinctures, and fresh linens to have him bleed out now.

I assess the carnage beneath the bandages. There were a half dozen gashes across his shoulders, sides, and legs when I found him, but only the one that wraps from under his left arm to his navel still concerns me. Whatever did this to him used a tearing force, leaving the flesh jagged and filthy. The healing process has been abnormally slow.

This man should have died from his wounds, and yet some external force keeps him going, warms him from the inside. I have never witnessed anything like it.

He starts and groans again as I peel the fabric back. The sutures are holding, but fresh blood coats the cloth. Another curse escapes as I fumble for a vial with one hand while pressing the wound with the other. I study his face as I tip a pungent, thick liquid into his mouth. He swallows without opening his eyes and mutters the same word I have heard many times over the last weeks.

"*My . . . my . . .*"

His brow folds in the middle, the mental turmoil proving more excruciating than his physical wounds. I imagine that crease would remain even if he smiled.

I blow a strand of black hair out of my eyes and rest a palm on his damp forehead even as my mind mocks me for such an obvious gesture of care.

"Your what?" I ask.

His eyes blink open, and I see them for the first time. They remind me of the waters of the loch on a clear Elberu afternoon.

"*For . . . give . . . me . . .*" he wheezes. Unconsciousness claims him once more.

My spine snaps straight, a chill mist of memory cloying the moors of my mind. How many times had my own mother said those words to me, only to reach for drink again, then invite a strange man into our home while I held Tetyan close in the byre so we wouldn't have to think about the questionable deeds that kept food in our bellies? She made me trust in the sincerity of her apologies, in her ability to fix herself, more times than I could count. I chose to forget her when I was sixteen, and twenty-three years later, the burn of hatred still has not diminished within my chest.

No. People don't change, but they are fashioned into harder versions of themselves.

A little more brusque than I need to be, I wrap the bindings around his chest. The bleeding seems to have slowed for now. He won't die from his injuries, but he might if I ever find out what he's apologizing for.

I have no idea what possessed me to rescue him.

The soft hum of voices shifts outside my tent. Heavy footfalls on crushed rock follow. I pull the blanket up to the stranger's chin and swipe a rag over my khukuri blade to dry it before sheathing it at my side. If it is Ordin, he will not respect my personal space. I would rather meet him on my terms.

Holding back the flap of my tent, I step into the open air. It is rich with the brackish scent of the Praeor Sea, even though the coast is more than a week's journey to the south. Desire to revisit the wild waters threatens to weaken my discipline.

Focus on the present, úramech, I tell myself. The longing burns away like dry rot.

As expected, my partner struts up the rows of tents with the commander of our Agmen regiment following closely behind.

A few úramech had seen me shoulder the stranger to my tent the day I rescued him. I should have been offended that no one thought it odd that I would bring an unfamiliar man home, but in that instance, I benefited from their assumptions.

If only Ordin could have kept that overlarge mouth of his shut. I saw the look in his eyes when I defied him, yet the reprieve gave me hope that he respected the threat I leveled against him. It appears the proud fool still thinks I am easily managed, though. The maddening thing is that he isn't wrong: I will always have to work twice as hard as anyone to keep my position in the Tarrivan Agmen. I must be twice as cautious of losing it.

Like my mother, I have used my body to purchase survival, but not in the manner she taught. She walked the edge of the night, and I walk the edge of a blade.

"Commander Verrek." I bow my chin, willfully ignoring Ordin's presence. I can feel him bristle from ten feet away. I resist the urge to smirk. "Is there something I can do for you?"

"Seyla Bréinth. Let me see him."

No pleasantries, then.

I step to the side and allow Verrek entry but lay my palm against Ordin's chest when he gets close.

"This will be the end of your úramech career." His words, spat out with a sneer, hold an air of warning

I drop my hand and let a smile flirt with my lips. "What a cause for celebration. Without me to offer you challenge, you'll finally have an opportunity to advance in the Agmen."

He glares at me for several heartbeats, a hideous vein bulging across his temple. I raise an eyebrow and hold his stare until Verrek emerges from the tent.

The commander straightens and folds his hands behind his back. His black eyes train on my face, but not with the accusatory glint of Ordin's. "Explain."

My mouth opens, but I falter, struggling to articulate something I don't even understand.

Verrek's straight brows lower disappointedly, and shame presses on my lungs with damning insistence.

"See? She might flip that blade around like a plaything, but sentiment will always be enough to get the better of her." Ordin's sharp laugh slices through all my soft places.

I narrow my eyes and lie. "It is not for his life that I saved him, but for the information he could give."

My partner snorts, but Verrek holds up a hand. "Let her speak, Ordin."

I breathe through my nose and shift straighter. "I have felt for a season that something is not right across the waters in the Vale, and—"

"The superstition of old wives."

"Ordin, hold your tongue or I will take disciplinary action against you."

Where I employed a blade, all Verrek needs is a subtle shift in tone to tame the man. My partner's face reddens as he bows his head and steps back.

"Continue, Bréinth. I desire to hear your suspicions," Verrek says.

I bob my chin toward my tent. "That man's wounds are something I have never seen before. I would guess they were inflicted by a great beast, or several."

Verrek's eyes flicker, but he says nothing.

I continue, clarity taking hold as I work through the situation verbally. "The way he was deposited in a boat so unceremoniously, cast off without oars or sail, suggests he is someone the Vale does not want."

Verrek's head tilts. "And yet someone took the trouble to save him."

"Yes, a foolish *girl* who realized tending to a man is the one thing that can complete her," Ordin interjects, spittle flying.

My chest inflates with indignation, but there is no need to let it burst. With a quick motion, the commander pulls out a small blade concealed in his armor, grabs one of the three hammered metal coins that dangle from matted strands of hair at Ordin's temple, and slices it off.

With his mouth opening and closing and the color draining from his face, Ordin looks not unlike a sucker fish plopped on the beach. Verrek stows the blade, pockets the coin, and acknowledges me as if I am the only other person present. "And yet someone took the trouble to save him." He motions for me to continue.

I must push the cold fact that our commander has removed one of my partner's ranks out of my mind before I can find my original line of thought. "Y-yes." I breathe in, confidence waning. "He was worth such a risk, which would mean that whoever he is or what he knows—"

"Could be significant." Verrek silences for a beat, and I try not to look in Ordin's direction as I wait for the commander's insight.

He paces a few steps, rubbing his smooth jaw with a scar-crossed hand. "If you had acted in this manner a season ago, I might have felt differently, but the ténesomni across the water has been changing. I have also witnessed it. And I have just received word that it is advancing toward us." He stares northward, his expression impossible to read.

To Ordin's credit, he manages to rein in his bluster. He stands a little straighter. "Advancing?"

"Yes. Growing, moving. Darkening our skies to the north."

A shiver runs over my arms.

Verrek turns to me. "Seyla Bréinth, you will nurse that man until he is able to stand before the Imperii and speak for himself. I will see to it that you have the supplies you need, and Ordin will ensure that no one gives you any trouble." Verrek eyes my partner, whose rosy complexion has shifted to the satisfying purple of barely subdued rage. "Well, úramech?"

"Yes, sir," he grunts.

"Good man."

As Verrek turns to leave, I rush to speak up. "Commander, there is another matter I wish to discuss."

He inclines his chin and clasps his hands behind his back.

"When I found the man, there was something else with him in the boat. A creature I have never witnessed in the Southlands."

The commander's eyes narrow. "Describe it."

"In many ways, it was like an abnormally large fox. Its tail flattened out at the end instead of coming to a point, but that was not what struck me most about it. It was the color. There was no pigment to it, like it had been drained of anything resembling life. It wasn't just drab; it was like a void. And yet I could find no wound, no sign of injury. It was curled up with the man as though sleeping, but there was no warmth left in it." I shake my head, grasping for any explanation other than the one I've settled on. "I think . . ."

"Out with it, Bréinth."

Ancestors, help me not to sound insane. "I think that creature gave its life energy to sustain the man."

An ugly cachinnation swells from Ordin, making me feel small, but I stand firm as it breaks upon the wall around my heart. It's weathered much worse.

Verrek's brows lower, and he paces. "Curious that you would mention such a thing. I would say that's not possible, knowing where the man came from, but what you're describing sounds like one of the Light Creatures of old."

"Surely not." Ordin balks, but his jaw snaps shut when Verrek spins on him.

"Oh? You would contradict me with your obvious wealth of knowledge on the subject?" he says, a dangerous bite to his words.

"No, Commander," Ordin mutters.

Muffled voices drift from the neighboring rows of tents. The Agmen camp is waking up, and the commander seems to remember himself. He tugs down the front of his uniform, lowering his voice to a calculated volume. "Strange events are occurring, and only a fool would ignore a single obscure detail."

Ordin tenses at the inferred insult, and for the briefest of moments, I feel for him.

Him.

How confusing.

Verrek faces me again. "You took a risk, keeping this man alive. Time will prove if it was worth it."

Distant thunder seems to expose a warning hidden in his words. If anything, this meeting has shown me that my commander is not as stable as I had imagined. He may be showing me favor now, but Ordin's missing medallion is a visible reminder that my standing is by no means secure.

Raising my eyes to meet Verrek's, I say, "Yes, sir."

"Until this stranger is well enough to travel and stand before the Imperii, he is under your care."

The commander motions to my partner. "I would speak with you in private."

Ordin gives me a look that could sour milk, and I wait outside my tent while he leaves with Verrek. Only when they are out of sight do I take a full breath and let my eyes drift to the storm clouds bubbling up from the southeast.

Despite the reprieve from having to sneak around, I do not feel relief. I have survived this long by hardening off places in my heart so I wouldn't feel pain, forcing logic and strategy to captain my emotions. The tactic has served me well, earning me a fierce reputation among men twice my size and ensuring I depend on no one but myself. But the moment that boat drifted into view, all my discipline came into question. A pebble broke away from my fortifications.

"*Heshïn*," I whisper.

Ordin is right. The reason I pulled the stranger from the water was a weak sentiment I can't explain.

9

BELWYN

KETSÉ'S LIVING STAIRCASES WIND into camouflaged houses in the treetops. Terraces and walkways weave a maze of roads above. Blossoms, herbs, and dangling fruit artfully work into walls, enough to make my mouth water.

These are all the things that would make deep impressions on Amyrah, the stewardess of all things lovely.

But they are not what stir me.

The people are what command my attention. Despite the differences in dress and the way they take light for granted, I don't find them much different from the valefolk. Idle gossips, busy mothers, pushy merchants. The young women, several of whom stop what they are doing to return my appraising glances, line their eyes with black strokes instead of the reflective paint used in the Vale to enhance features. The well-to-do pass us by with their chins up and their eyes on more important matters.

As we walk through Ketsé's midst, advancing farther into the hidden forest kingdom, we begin to attract more attention. Children are yanked indoors; whispers pass behind cupped hands. Eyes narrow at my sheathed sword, our different garb, and Amyrah's glowing necklace.

Why did I encourage her to wear it? I have to do better than that if I'm going to keep her safe.

Our procession halts as we come to a small river churning with ivory water. A group of women clog the stone bridge that spans it, disdain clear on their faces and in their postures. The woman closest to us crosses her arms, causing the wooden bangles populating her wrists to clunk together with hollow sounds. She assesses us, her heavy brows coming together at an extreme angle. Being well-acquainted with Izra's commanding presence, I am impressed by her nerve.

"Let us pass, Anit," Izra growls.

Anit tilts her head and laughs. "And why should I do that, husband? You've come back a moon sooner than anticipated, using the South Road, with strangers who carry weapons and tamper with light." Her eyes flick to the star necklace.

I edge closer to Amyrah.

"And you usher in traitors as if they are dignitaries." Anit's shadowy gaze lands on Rael, still seated on the horse, with Arlyn holding its reins in a fist. The tendons of his forearms stand out.

I hear Holden's feet shift back and forth behind me.

"Please, love." The term of endearment is made a farce by the spite in our leader's tone. "You don't know the fullness of the situation. And you are not Ketsé's gatekeeper."

"True, yet I have eyes, Izra."

"But not sense. The Nocilium holds the right to judge my actions, not you. Although you are always welcome to pretend."

The women gathered about Anit gasp, but Izra's spouse remains calm as she steps to the side, her ténesomni-black hair slinking over her shoulder like a forbidding waterfall. Her disgruntled companions follow her lead.

"I don't pretend," she says as she motions with an elegant hand to the bridge. "But if you require irrefutable proof of your folly, then I won't stand in your way."

As we cross the bridge, Izra holds back and approaches the woman. "Anit, there is more going on here than meets the eye. Please, trust me."

I glance at them as I pass. Anit scowls but doesn't pull away from her husband's touch.

"You make it hard at times, Izra Morlaine."

Izra presses a rough kiss to her forehead before falling in line behind Holden.

We pass the beginnings of a deep ravine that appears to be hand dug into the ground between the trees. Half of the trees' thick roots are exposed where the earth has been cleared away, forming a natural latticed roof above the wide crevice. A cobbled path is laid below a flight of slate steps, sloping downward into darkness. Huge slabs of stone line the sides of the passage to support the substantial weight above.

I look up at the platforms suspended above our heads, trying to make my mind appreciate the multiple levels of life the woodfolk have engineered within this forest. It's like they have constructed three cities within the space of one. Their similarities to the valefolk melt away in my mind. I doubt Utsanek could ever show this level of ingenuity.

Distant noise and savory smells emanate from the entrance to the lower level. The latter is a cruel reminder that we've had nothing but stale travel provisions in the last few days. Ahead, Amyrah stops to gaze down the ravine path, her interest equally piqued.

"What lies down there?" she asks.

I want to know as much as she does, but that desire lessens when Holden is the one who jumps to respond.

"That path will take you to the caves. There isn't much down there other than a few simple markets and some older neighborhoods."

"And the people Ketsé would rather pretend didn't exist," Rael says.

It is the first time I have heard her speak since we rode in the cart together. She shifts in her saddle and catches Holden with a look, challenging him to contradict her.

I glance behind long enough to see Holden's shoulders tense and his lips press together. The corner of my mouth drifts up in a satisfied grin as I look ahead again.

"I won't deny it's a bit of a rougher area."

Rael makes a disgusted sound in her throat and looks away. "What else would you expect? That's what happens when you don't give people another option. They start to believe they are trapped, and nothing invites darkness like desperation."

"No one is trapped." Holden mumbles something that could be an expletive but says no more.

"Whatever the case, Amyrah, you will find a much different version of the city down those paths," Izra says, smoothing the conversation.

We continue walking.

So Ketsé has its secrets too.

I shouldn't have assumed that people living outside of the ténesomni would be out of its reach. As much as I'd like to idealize a world where people haven't had to resort to taking a life to obtain light, I'm beginning to wonder if we're all the same no matter where you find us.

Does Amyrah realize this as well? Her need to discover her mother's history, to find some form of closure, could blind her to everything else happening around her. Could make her a danger to herself.

I jog a few paces to catch up, leaning close to whisper, "Why does it feel like we aren't that removed from the Vale?"

Her lips tense as her hand moves to cover the rays of her pendant. "We are so far away from there, Belwyn."

Her chin lifts and I follow her gaze. Above, a toddling child on a balcony dumps a small sack of what looks like seed into a bowl on a wooden stand. In a matter of moments, a flock of sparrows descends on it. The boy giggles with delight as the wind from their flapping wings tousles his hair.

"We are worlds apart," she says.

I stay close to Amyrah's side as we approach the meeting place of the Nocilium at the center of Ketsé. The raised platforms of the council hall loom above us, built into the branches of a truly gargantuan tree. More guards clad in rich brown are stationed at the broad stairway that winds around its base. They eye my bow and sword with grim expressions. Izra pushes ahead of us to speak with them on our behalf, and as I strain to hear what they say, Amyrah turns to me with a look of pure anxiety painting her face.

"I don't know if I can do this."

I have watched her rush into light-starved forests, approach wild creatures, and stand before an angry mob without so much as a second thought. What about these stuffy people could scare her?

But I decide it's best to keep these thoughts to myself. "Of course you can." I smile encouragingly. "And I'll be with you."

Pressing her necklace between her collarbones, she watches Arlyn helping Rael from her horse. "I don't know what they will expect of me." Her gaze shifts to the tree towering above us. "If what I did back at the cabin is revealed to these people . . ."

My gut twists. I'm the one that ensured her gift was exposed. I start to apologize, but she holds up a hand.

"Stop. I'm not blaming you. It's what had to happen. The ténesomni needed to be stalled, and I needed to know if I *could* do it. But I don't know how much more I can help." She clenches her hands a few times, shaking them out as if she can feel her Luvesti power in her fingers. "Or if I should even be intervening at all." Her breathing shudders and she shakes her head too fast. "Without *him*, I don't know who I'm supposed to be anymore." She fixes me with her cool gaze, and the tears that have been gathering along her lower lashes spill onto her cheeks.

I reach and brush one away. It's warm on my skin. "There has never been a time I did not know exactly who you are."

"And who is that?"

"You are bravery and kindness. You are a bringer of light and truth." A disbelieving exhale slides from her lips, but I persist, bending a little to meet her eyes at their level. "You are, even if you never intended to be. You don't have to be all those things at every moment, though. When it's too much, I'm going to do my best to be there for you."

I reach for her honey-brown braid and rub the soft ends between my thumb and forefinger. The string that held all her wild hair at bay unravels in my hand.

"Sorry," I mutter, stuffing my hands in my pockets before they do something else I have not sanctioned.

Amyrah's laugh dispels my awkwardness, and she combs out the waves with her fingers. I am relieved to see her hair take its usual form, because if there is one thing Amyrah should never be, it's restrained. Her smile softens on me, and I find I can't exhale.

"I'm not sure what I did to deserve you, Belwyn Kovah."

My heart dances, and I wish we were alone so I could make hers dance along with it.

Holden's unwelcome frame looms into our space, and he motions toward the stairs. "It looks like we're going in now."

I close my eyes, biting my lip to keep from snapping at the interruption, and turn my attention to the guards. One of them leads Rael to a railed landing attached to long ropes looped through pulleys in the branches. When she's seated on the narrow bench secured to the floor, the guard signals to two more men stationed on the next platform. They turn a large, spoked wheel, lifting her into the air foot by foot.

The guard turns around and motions to the formidable stairway. "After you," he says.

Arlyn and Izra begin the long ascent, but Amyrah waits for Holden to go first.

"Remember," I say, my eyes dipping to her necklace. "Don't be ashamed of who you are. They only want answers, and we haven't done anything wrong. We are just two lost valefolk who chased the light together."

The corner of her mouth twitches skyward.

We begin to climb together, but one of the guards plants his palm in the middle of my chest. "I have been instructed not to let you pass," he says firmly.

"Excuse me?"

"You are not permitted to enter the Nocilium."

Amyrah pauses on the steps and frowns at the man.

"Like Ikktar I'm not," I spit.

The guard stands straighter and thrusts the butt of his metal spear down so that it clangs against the stony earth. "Son, don't test me."

I fling a hand in Amyrah's direction. "You'll let her go in, but not me? We came together. I can help the council understand the Vale's situation."

The man's thinly mustached lip curls into a sneer as his cloudy eyes take me in from nose ring to boots. "You're useless here, shadow rat."

The snake of anger coils inside my belly. Venomous, desperate to strike. I clench my jaw to keep its cage secure. But I *want* to let it loose.

Amyrah's soft voice stills me. "Belwyn, it's fine." Her pale hands hold tighter to the strap of her satchel.

I gape at her, all my resolutions to stay by her side, to keep her safe, crumbling to dust. I shake my head. "No, it's not. I should be there with you."

The guard grabs my forearm when I step forward, pain screaming under each of his fingertips. I try to pull away, but he grips tighter. His face moves so close that I can almost taste his hot breath. I refuse to back away, though, because this feels like a battle I can't lose.

Until she makes me.

"Really. *Please*. I don't need you in there with me."

I shoot her a look, and the hint of embarrassment on her face makes the fire in my veins turn cold.

The guard must sense the change because his hideous grin erupts like a split in old leather. He relaxes his hold, and I jerk away from his touch.

"Fine. That's great." I laugh dryly, flinging my hands. "I'll go for a pleasure stroll, then. Go have a visit with *your* people, Amyrah."

Her mouth falls open, but I turn away before I can witness the full impact of my words.

10

AMYRAH

"THE LOGIC BEHIND YOUR ACTIONS baffles us, Izra Morlaine."

Almost a dozen men and women line the platform on either side of a regal, middle-aged woman, affirming her statement with solemn nods. All are dressed in Ketsé's understated finery, but I look at none of them closely.

Instead, my mind is clouded with the image of Belwyn's crestfallen face. The boy who escorted me to safety after Myrzeth's beasts attacked my father, who dropped everything in his life to be by my side as I search for answers to questions I can't bring myself to ask, who had to leave his own family in a light-hostile land . . . I told him I didn't need him.

The book within my bag weighs on my shoulder and my conscience like a gravestone. I adjust the strap with one hand and clasp my argentilum pendant with the other as an uncomfortable realization grips me:

You are shutting out the people who love you, just like your father did.

"I acknowledge that I have broken several—"

Disdainful laughter interrupts Izra's defense, breaking into my distraction, and I force myself to take in my surroundings. An arched roof of colorful material stretches between the branches, shielding the council hall from the sky. It flexes with the bending of the giant tree's boughs in the wind, and the sunlight filtering through the translucent panels lends an ethereal quality to the space. No walls surround us, but low banisters made of live tree branches indicate where the polished floor of the hall drops away. Beneath swaying banners embroidered with intricate crests and woodland scenes, a woman perches with strict posture upon an elaborate, living chair, silver hair crowning her in a graceful sweep. For the moment, her scrutinizing gaze is fixed in front of me on the large form of Izra.

"'Broken' doesn't begin to describe it. Opposed, discarded, *flaunted* would all serve better in its place." Her voice, threaded with age and reserved in tone, carries well in the cooler air of the treetops. Eight other stately men and women flank her, turning their faces to regard their spokeswoman. She taps her long fingers on the chair's woven armrests. I lose count of how many rings she wears. "Yet you would claim your actions serve the interests of Ketsé?"

Izra inclines his head. "I would, Elder Veridree."

The woman doesn't move for several breaths, except to quirk an eyebrow. I stay still for fear that she will notice me sooner than she needs to.

"Well then." She adjusts her posture, dispelling the tension with a flick of her hand. "Proceed."

I glance at Wehna's parents, who are waiting along the edges of the circular council. Arlyn's jaw is set, as if facing an inescapable storm. His wife stands straight and fierce at his side, all evidence of her physical weakness and exhaustion vanished.

"As you know," Izra says, "my company left for a scheduled trade run to bring back loads of grain, produce, and oil from the eastern shores. Not two days into our travels, we came upon the man who was supposed to be stationed at the mountain pass."

A contagious murmur works through the Nocilium.

"Torr Kalnix," an aged man to Veridree's right hisses, his wrinkled face plunging into a deep frown.

"Yes, it would seem some ill-placed sense of loyalty—"

Rael snorts.

"—led the watchman to abandon his responsibilities and hide like a coward in the wilds of East Tothlen Forest," Izra finishes, unbothered by Rael's ire.

"Are we calling compassion *cowardice* now?" she bursts out.

Izra doesn't even turn to acknowledge her. "He swore to protect Ketsé, not hide deserters who care nothing for it." His accusation surprises me. I never picked up on any animosity between them before.

Veridree rests her elbow on one of the chair's arms, shifting her weight to the side. Her lips press into a thin line as she studies Izra. "However ill-advised it was for them to leave three years ago, Izra, this has now become a case for mercy. I believe that decision cost them a great deal."

Clearing her throat, she turns her attention to Arlyn and Rael. "You left our domain and lowered yourselves to the level of the shadows we despise. You knew doing so would result in unmatched prejudice should you ever return, though your motives were born of a love for the lost."

Several of the elders shuffle in their seats. I wonder if Veridree's refusal to punish them does not sit well.

She continues before anyone can protest, her voice heavy with empathy. "Tell us, friends. What has happened to your children?"

"We did not mean to—" A sob chokes Rael's voice, and for the first time since the day I met her, she cracks. Swallowing, she closes her eyes for a breath. "We were forced to leave without them. And Torr . . ." She presses a fist to her lips, unable to continue.

Sorrow ripples across Arlyn's brow as he watches his wife hug her arms around her abdomen, fighting for composure. He rests a hand gently on her shoulder. "Torr should not be held in derision for his actions," he says, not taking his eyes from Rael's profile. "When my wife and I emerged from the Vale, we begged him for shelter. He showed us compassion, offering what little provisions he could spare to help us." Arlyn's gaze drifts around the council. "It was never our intention to come back to the Grovesha—your conditions were clear upon our departure—but we were forced when a kaligorva wounded Rael." He squeezes his wife's shoulder. "Once she was stable, we had every intention of re-entering the Vale."

Veridree leans forward. "Had? Do you mean to tell us you tried and were not successful?"

The ceiling appears to breathe above us, and Arlyn's eyes travel to it, perhaps to distract himself from his emotions. "There seems to be something preventing anyone who is not born of the ténesomni from entering its domain."

Worry etches Elder Veridree's face. She opens her mouth to speak, but Arlyn's gaze returns to her.

"And it's growing."

Silence shrouds the Nocilium like a cloud pregnant with rain.

"What does that mean?" a tiny woman wrapped in bright green robes asks in an uncertain, watery voice.

Izra laughs without mirth and gives his head a terse shake. "Exactly what he said. The domain of unnatural darkness is moving past the boundaries it has kept for a hundred years. This troubling news is why we agreed to accompany Arlyn and Rael back into Ketsé."

Veridree clears her throat. "Can anyone else bear witness to this phenomenon?"

I shift on my aching feet.

"No one you would trust, but yes," Arlyn responds, a motion in my periphery suggesting he is gesturing to me. "This young woman has seen it, as has the other young man whom you saw fit to bar from this council."

The subtle dig at the Nocilium's supposed wisdom does not go unnoticed. Veridree holds Arlyn's stare, nostrils flaring. Her eyes flick to me.

"You, girl."

I bite the inside of my cheek.

"Can you confirm what Arlyn says?"

Izra steps aside, exposing me to the full scrutiny of the Nocilium. Keeping my gaze down, I nod.

"What is your name?" Veridree asks, her tone shifting into something gentler.

"Amyrah Cantar."

"And where do you come into all of this?"

As if I know, my mind retorts. I lift my face and keep my fingers curled around the necklace under my throat. "I am from the Vale." The looks thrown my way are almost enough to make me want to run from the Nocilium. I press on before courage abandons me completely. "And I am seeking whatever information you can provide about my Luvesti heritage."

What had been expressions of wariness morph into full exhibitions of distrust, carried to me on a torrent of words.

"*Impossible.*"

"The Luvesti do not set foot outside of their kingdom."

"She claims to be both raised in ténesomni *and* one of the light-favored?"

"*Liar.*"

Holden paces off to my right, never taking his eyes from me, his hands clasped in front of him. I am certain he knew what I was long before I voiced it. Although he might not condemn me like the others, he doesn't offer a word in my defense.

"*Silence.*" Veridree's commanding voice stills every tongue. She glares around the circle, then turns back to me. "Can you offer proof of this heritage, child?"

I can think of nothing else other than to reach into my bag to retrieve my mother's book, which my father sought to get rid of thirteen years ago. Her initials are scrawled inside, and the librarian in Utsanek's hidden community assured me it did not originate from the Vale. It may be a futile hope that it could convince the Nocilium I am what I say, but I have nothing else. As I dig through my bag, I let my other hand fall from the necklace.

"*What is that*?"

"See how the argentilum glows?"

I glance up, confused. Elder Veridree's eyes are fixed to the pendant, and she approaches, holding out a hand to prevent me from covering it again.

"We need no more proof than to see the way this precious metal responds to your nearness, child."

I search her face, disarmed by the awe in her eyes and the slight upward pull of her lips.

"For it is said that it will only behave so in the possession of those who are of true Luvesti lineage," she whispers.

A rotund elder with a thin strip of black hair encircling his puckered lips jumps to his feet. "*Light whores.*" He flaps a meaty hand, contorting his fingers into an odd shape.

In three steps, Holden reaches my side. "Leave the obscene gestures for the Low Market, Ephson," he says, a growl in his tone.

Ephson glares at Holden like he wants to retaliate, but with a curl of the lip, he denies the impulse and smooths his midnight-blue robes over his bulbous midsection.

"Must I remind the members of the council that it was the Luvesti who won freedom for our lands from the kaligorven a century ago?" Elder Veridree angles away from me, observing her fellows with a slow, scathing rotation, her long, maroon skirt twisting around her feet. "If it weren't for them, we would still be battling with those fell beasts."

My breaths catch in my throat. The Shrouded, this far from the Vale?

Ephson retreats to his seat, his slouched posture and tight mouth belying his mutinous thoughts. He huffs. "They then graciously left us the endless task of defending the borders ever since."

"Yes, it is clear how much you have suffered for it," Holden remarks, prompting a chorus of stunted chuckles.

Ephson's corpulent face reddens.

"You may hold your own opinions about the Luvesti's actions," Veridree says, extending both hands to signal a temporary truce between the men, "but as they are a nation who sequesters themselves in the northernmost reaches of Atsun, we must face this problem on our own."

What little blaze I had urging me on—the timorous hope that somewhere in Ketsé lies the knowledge of who my mother was—flickers dangerously close to puffing out.

"What do you mean?" My voice is higher than usual, and I clear my throat and try again. "Are there no Luvesti living in this city?"

All eyes fix on me, some showing hints of amusement, others, pity. My cheeks burn.

But from Veridree, there is no scorn. "No, I am afraid there are not. You are the first to pass through our gates in well over ten years. You have no doubt seen the hatred most woodfolk hold for anyone from the Vale, but I assure you, the Luvesti provoke more."

She turns away and crosses the polished floor to retake her seat, seemingly unaware of how my hope lies trampled beneath her feet.

"Council," she says, her voice taking on a more official tone, "what course of action would you suggest we take following these tidings? Surely, we can agree that reinforcements need to be sent to the ténesomni's borders at once."

The Nocilium members voice their support, some of them thumping their armrests.

Veridree gestures at Izra. "Your actions have proved to be prudent. I trust you to assemble a contingent of soldiers to warn the smaller forest settlements. If the border of shadow is indeed moving, then we should begin evacuations of the southern forest sector immediately."

Izra does not require any further convincing. He spins on his heel, motioning for Holden to follow, and leaves the hall, the crisp sound of his boots fading away down the stairs.

Holden stays where he is.

Elder Veridree addresses her equals once more. "But what of our former neighbors?" She extends a hand toward Rael and Arlyn, as if offering them a hold in a tempestuous loch. "Given the information they have brought to us, I see no reason to expel them from the city. All who are willing to extend welcome, raise your right hand."

Arlyn pulls Rael close, and she holds her chin high.

Nine hands travel upward.

"And those in favor of welcoming the two valefolk into our midst?"

I look at each face in turn, certain someone will protest my existence within their perfect city. The response isn't as immediate as with Wehna's parents, but to their credit, all hands raise into the air, except for the meaty one belonging to the man with the thin goatee. If this small sampling of acceptance is representative of the rest of Ketsé, it will be enough.

"Excellent. It appears that this council has accomplished its purpose. Until we can gain a better understanding of what faces us in the coming days, we must do everything we can to prepare ourselves. Council members, return to your respective districts and keep a finger to the pulse of the woodfolk. We need to be cautious of anything that could stir up a panic within the city. As it stands now, not much is known and there is no need to spread false rumors." Elder Veridree takes the time to glance around the circle. "This session is concluded."

As the council members exit, leaving me a conspicuous amount of space, I have never felt so alone. I stand in the center of the floor as the hall empties, fingering my book within my bag, trying to process everything I have heard.

I recall the feeling of freedom that intoxicated me when Belwyn and I stepped out of the ténesomni and into the light-inhabited lands. At that moment, I didn't care about what had transpired to get me there. I forgot the fear, the grief, the despair of failing to free the Vale from the ténesomni. I believed we had moved beyond evil's grasp, but maybe its reach is farther than I realized.

My fingers trace the book's spine. I could tell Elder Veridree about it, ask if she knows who wrote it or where it came from, but is exposing its existence to the head elder of the council worth the risk? What if she confiscates it and I lose the last tangible connection I have to my mother? I already marred it irrevocably when I ripped out several pages to use for kindling. I don't know if I can bear to part with it in its entirety.

Holden loiters at the top of the stairs, as if he is still unwilling to leave, but eventually, he does. The platform continues to empty until Elder Veridree and Wehna's parents are the last people left other than me. The former watches me with an expression I can't interpret, like she knows I haven't been entirely forthright with her.

I pull my hand from my bag, empty.

"Elder Veridree," Arlyn says, stepping away from his wife, whose face is crimped with uncertainty. "There is more that you need to know."

The elder's delicate eyebrows raise in an invitation for him to continue.

"The change in the ténesomni coincides with the arrival of someone in the Vale."

"Oh?" She leans back in her seat. "And who would this person be?"

"Myrzeth."

I know my uncle's name has a peculiar effect on me, but I never expected that it would do the same with complete strangers.

Veridree's fingernails scrape across the armrests, and she angles forward. "After all these years . . ." A sound not unlike a cat's hiss passes between her gritted teeth. "We were witless to think we had seen the last of him."

The tension is a momentary lapse in self-control, and she straightens, her expression growing confident as if she anticipated this news all along. "It appears stirring up discord in Ketsé didn't satisfy him, then."

"Where has he been for five years?" Arlyn rubs the back of his neck.

"This lengthy absence almost worries me more than his presence would have."

Standing, Veridree dismisses the notion. "No, he would have done much more harm if he had stayed. Do you not recall how easily he won people over?" She runs her palms down the front of her robe, straightening the wrinkles, and crosses the platform floor.

"You, child. What do you know of this man?"

I purse my lips and force out a slow exhale. How much should I reveal? If the simple mention of my uncle could cause such a poised woman to forget herself, then what will my fate be when she knows I am related to him?

Keep it simple.

"When he arrived, he claimed to have superior knowledge of the kaligorven and encouraged the valefolk to take their devotion to them more seriously." I shiver at the thought.

Her eyes narrow. "In what way?"

I study the skillful dovetailed joints of the floor. Can my testimony make the pieces fit a fraction as well? "Leaving gifts for them, persecuting those who would hold on to their belief in Elyōn. Showing the Shrouded that they were welcome and honored in Utsanek."

A scoffing laugh escapes the elder. "How did he manage to convince the valefolk that this was a wise course of action?"

"He promised them power and prosperity in return." A stiff breeze picks up and rustles the leaves, reminding me of the gale force winds that would so often accompany the kaligorven's arrival in Utsanek, heightening the fear of their presence. As much as I want to accuse the valefolk of being weak and fickle, I can't condemn them for the generations of superstition and hardship that made them desperate.

"All of Utsanek was terrified, and they wanted their children to be free to walk the streets in safety. Myrzeth was so confident, always carrying with him a book that he let no one else touch." I swallow, realizing that I have been the same with my own tome.

You are not him, I tell myself.

"It—it gave substance to his claims, and with it he commanded the shadow beasts," I say.

Veridree's eyes narrow. "Curious."

"And . . ." I sip in a breath. This is the part I am most wary of sharing, but if it could help them understand what has caused the ténesomni to spread, it needs to be told. I raise my gaze to meet the elder's. "And then he chose a person to sacrifice to them."

The elder presses a hand to her lips, and my gaze sinks to my feet.

"*Highest*," Rael breathes.

"Did—" Arlyn jerks his head with disgust and wets his lips. "Did he succeed?"

Every eye is on me, and I have forgotten how to form words. The air is heavy, pressing in on my eardrums, my chest, and all I can manage is a minuscule bob of my chin and a prayer that they don't ask me to elaborate.

"Then his evil has grown beyond what it was when he was last in Ketsé," Veridree says gravely. "I do not recall him being in possession of this book you mention. I wonder at its significance." Her voice trails off, thoughtful silence taking its place.

Exhaustion bears down on me, and I am both disappointed that I did not learn more of my mother and relieved that this interview seems to be over.

Clearing her throat, Veridree snaps to the present. "No matter. What is important is that we know this is not a random occurrence. There are forces at play here that should not be underestimated."

She addresses Rael and Arlyn. "As I said before, you both have complete amnesty. The Ketsans tend to cling to past hurts, often to their detriment, but with the warning you have brought and what you sacrificed to do so, I believe you will find peace here."

I wonder if she hears Rael's mirthless huff.

Turning to me, she asks, "Now, what shall we do with you?"

My vision blurs, and I blink to clear it.

An arm slips around my waist, drawing me in tenderly. "Come, Amyrah," Rael whispers, addressing me and ignoring Elder Veridree. "Come with us. We will find a place for you—for us all—to stay. You belong with us."

It takes the last of my resolve to hold in my tears as we descend the stairs.

II

BELWYN

THE PUGNACIOUS GUARD INSISTS on following me as I leave.

Shades.

With difficulty, I resist the urge to give him the slip. If I am not trusted enough to join in their meeting, then the last thing I should be doing is acting like I have something to hide.

I stick to the only road I'm familiar with until I come to the side passage carved deep into the earth. When I duck down it, the guard chooses not to follow me.

I guess he doesn't care what kind of trouble I could cause down there.

The ravine path is cool, soothing my angry mind as the sound of my footfalls echoes between the stone walls. I move like a shadow underneath the lattice of roots, keeping my eyes averted as curious woodfolk shuffle by on the other side.

What am I doing here?

Amyrah would have left the Vale with or without me. So why did I come? She's proven that she's more than capable on her own. I was a morvus to think she needed me. That *anyone* would.

Rhun would have been better off without you.

Guilt splinters through my core. No, he needed me in a way I was too self-righteous to understand. And what about my mother and younger brothers? They were still in the billows of grief when I left them.

I *left* them.

"*Heshïn.*" The filthy word is exhilarating as it leaves my mouth. My father never permitted me to degrade myself with such vulgar language, since I was the son of the Foremost. I was always so afraid of the repercussions that I never dared to test him.

I'm no longer bound to that fear, and it feels right for a shadow rat to curse.

Consumed by these thoughts, I realize that somewhere a while back, the path must have stopped descending. I am now in a sharp tunnel cut out of black rock. An herbaceous and meaty smell wakes me as though from a dream, and I look around. This area of the city seems less like Ketsé and more like the Vale I know so intimately. Ordinary shadows press in on all sides, but they begin to thin farther ahead.

Is it so surprising that I didn't notice the darkness? It's part of who I am.

I emerge into a cavern that stretches so far, the torches lighting the space look like distant stars. It is festering with people of a different walk of life than any I saw on the city's ground level.

This is the Ketsé they wish to hide.

I welcome this new distraction and weave myself into the fabric of Ketsé's unwanted. The unmistakable sharpness of mildew and sewage mingles with the aroma of food. I try not to breathe through my nose. The chatter of the merchants is all but consumed by the rumblings of an underground river worming through the heart of the market. There are no guardrails around it, and the slippery, river-sprayed rocks could make for an untimely departure.

The crowd is rougher here, more boisterous than those milling above ground. Many of the people seem either on the edge of lunacy or unfettered rage, and it's relieving to find that no one notices me here. I visit a less crowded booth, where a dozen grimy pots balance over small fires. When I let down my guard and catch a whiff of the blue smoke rising from one of them, my vision goes black around the edges. I stagger forward. The hunched woman on the other side of the pots grabs my shoulders, cackling as I sway and gasp for breath.

"Never sniff an old hag's brews, darlin'. Didn't yer ma ever teach you that?"

I blanch at her as she releases me, and she laughs again until a fit of coughing takes her. It sounds wet and painful, and my disgust melts into pity.

"Thank you for the lesson. I'll remember it next time," I say, leaving her to recover and fuss over her dubious concoctions.

Without any arlum in my pockets, I prove a grave disappointment to the avaricious merchants, and they let me know it. My vocabulary of curse words grows exponentially, and I am no closer to sating my hunger. I slip into a narrow gap between two stalls and rub between my eyebrows with shaking fingers.

A quiet laugh makes me drop my hand and look around.

"I know. It's a little overwhelming down here."

A girl with glossy black hair teased into perfect waves watches me from across the way. She seems shockingly normal, and that's what draws me to her. Or maybe it's the way she raises an eyebrow and considers me, suggesting that she is more level-headed than the others I've encountered in the cavern. She pushes her heavy hair over a shoulder, revealing a swirling black tattoo that peaks from under her dress at her collarbone, and leans forward to arrange rows of glass bottles shimmering with an obsidian substance.

"That's one word for it," I say, approaching her counter and picking up one of the bottles. It's filled with liquid, but there's another quality to it that makes it slosh a little differently than it should. It's something both frightening and familiar. "What is this?"

She flashes a mischievous smile. "Drink it and find out."

I snort a laugh and set it down. "No, thank you. I almost passed out from an unknown substance once today."

Her responding giggle is clear and teasing. "I promise you, this isn't dangerous. All it will do is give you a brief sensation of—" She pauses, raising her chin and searching my face with a scrutinizing look, dangling her explanation before me like she's baiting a cat. She grins. "*Power.*"

The liquid swirls angrily behind the glass, as if trapped. I hold up the bottle and stare, recognition descending on my mind like nightfall.

"Ténesomni," I whisper.

Surprise flickers in the girl's gray eyes. "You are acquainted with it, I see. It's curious to find someone who actually recognizes it."

I say nothing but finger the cool glass, not sure what to think. We left the Vale and its creeping shroud behind weeks ago. It feels like a different world, a different lifetime. Yet here it is in my hand. "How . . . *why* would you have this?"

The girl lifts a nonchalant shoulder. "Why does anyone do anything? For the thrill of it. And to irritate some *key* people." Her eyes trace my frame, and she leans forward and says with breathless anticipation,

"What is it like?"

My eyes find hers, an ill-premonition grounding me. "What's *what* like?"

"Living in the ténesomni. *Breathing* it in."

"I—I don't know." I withdraw my hand from the bottle.

I was a fool to think that a people spared a life of darkness would never allow themselves to be tempted by it. Is it possible there will always be a little shadow in everyone?

The girl watches me, a knowing smile on her lips. "Yes, you do." She lays a warm hand on my forearm, and something inside me twists at her touch. "Go on. This one's my gift to you."

She picks up a bottle and uncorks it.

Amyrah wouldn't like it. This is everything I left behind. Then again, hasn't today proved that her and I are not as united as I once thought?

The blow of being treated like I am useless, of failing in my attempt to look out for Amyrah, of realizing how pointless leaving the Vale was flares painfully. *You're a shadow rat, aren't you? There's no harm in acting like one.*

Unwilling to give my conscience a chance to intervene, I grab the bottle and tip it back, drinking it down in a few gulps. It's malty and sweet, but it leaves a bitter taste. I cough, and the girl tosses her hair and laughs, a note of triumph in her voice. A sensation of warmth grips my belly, pooling heavily. I imagine the strange, black liquid eager to join the shadows that flow through my veins. Shocks of cold race up my core, then down my arms and legs. They reach my head, and it's like I have been doused in ice water. I gasp, dropping the bottle. It shatters on the slate ground.

She's right; I do feel something odd inside me. It's like splitting a stubborn log, or seeing cruel words hit their mark. It's like winning in a battle of the wills. Intoxicating, addicting.

A smooth voice purrs into my soul. *You were the eldest son of the Foremost. It's time you act like it.*

That feeling. It reminds me of being . . .

Home.

I shiver and leave the girl to her poisons and her cave of misfits.

12

AMYRAH

"WAS IT EVERYTHING YOU HOPED it would be?"

Belwyn waits at the bottom of the grand staircase, arms folded, hair disheveled, sooty shadows dancing under his eyes. His cloak, satchel, and weapons are piled on the ground. I slow at the last step, alarmed at how sour his tone is, how changed he seems within such a short length of time, like something pernicious is coursing through his broad-shouldered frame. He is quick to look away when I study him.

"Not really," I say, attempting to sound unaffected though my heart is still sore from the disappointment of learning I have no connections in Ketsé. I wish I felt like I could tell him about it.

His gaze, which I'm relieved to see still holds a fraction of its familiar warmth, meets mine. "Oh. I'm sorry."

Wehna's parents catch up with me, Rael's arm hooked in Arlyn's elbow as she keeps the weight off her bad leg and conquers each step. I wonder if her show of weakness in the Nocilium was enough for her, if descending the stairs instead of being lowered down by the Ketsans is her way of proving she is the master of herself once more. I move aside to let them pass.

Once on firm ground, Rael looks between Belwyn and me. "How strange this place must seem to the two of you." She clings tighter to her husband's arm and glances up at the leafy canopy glowing warmly in the sunset. "I can't deny how beautiful it is and how much I've missed it." Closing her eyes, she inhales.

I follow her example, and the smell transports me back to the Vale's forest. The air is thinner here, but not in a way that makes me hungry for oxygen. It feels less difficult to draw into my lungs, making me wonder if the shadows roaming the Vale affected more than my ability to see. The ténesomni is something that can be touched and held and felt, but how else can it affect a person?

My gaze dashes to Belwyn. All the relief he seemed to gain when he stepped into the true light of day appears to have been stolen away while I was busy with the council.

"The Ketsans' privilege has caused the woodfolk to forget their fellow humans, taking the blessings from Elyōn's hand and scorning the pain of others." Rael's finished thought pierces through mine.

Have I scorned the oppression of the Vale?

I think of my mentor, Orlagh, and my chest constricts. At this moment, I can picture her propping up swollen feet and holding a mug of spiced tea, fighting to recover the strength to face another long, lightless day. How much freer would she be without the ténesomni bearing down on her?

Was I right to run away from the Vale, to abandon her and Wehna and Arvo to a night that lusts after their souls?

"I can see why you left," Belwyn says with unfeeling coldness, and I give him a quizzical look. He makes a point of ignoring it.

Arlyn's jaw tenses. "They are as lost as the valefolk, son," he says, his tone stern.

Belwyn exhales and looks away.

What is wrong with him?

After an awkward moment, Arlyn brightens and motions to the roadway. "Enough of this standing around. I'm eager to get off my feet, as I'm sure you all are."

"Let's hope we still have some friends in Ketsé," Rael says under her breath, offering us a weak smile and following her husband.

"Is your position here so tenuous?" I ask. I'm no stranger to being a social pariah, but I wasn't anticipating that treatment to continue outside of the Vale.

"If we had slipped in without notice and Torr's actions hadn't been discovered, perhaps we wouldn't have anything to worry about, but the manner of our arrival has cast us all in a much unfriendlier light," Arlyn says.

Belwyn grabs up his gear, and we fall in step behind them, the silence between us anything but comfortable. After a while, though, he releases a deep breath, and I seek out his hand. His fingers are cold, but he folds them around mine.

"What happened?" I ask, stealing a sidelong glance at him.

His jaw tenses, but he shakes his head, a single, mirthless laugh escaping him. "Nothing. I wandered a bit and found a questionable market. Not some place I'll visit again soon." He looks at me, his face pale and his expression unreadable. "I'm sorry you found the council disappointing."

A regretful half-smile pulls at my lips. "It was a stretch to think I'd learn anything, but at least it wasn't a complete waste. The city has been warned of what's coming, and they're going to send out aid to the smaller settlements. I would never have dreamed that people living outside of the Vale would be so wary, so thoroughly plagued by fear."

He's quiet for a few steps, but then his hardness relents with a sigh. "I guess the sky is always lighter past the horizon."

I ponder the odd saying, which was a common phrase used by the valefolk. Even though all they understand is ténesomni, it's like their souls know it is not what Elyōn intended for them. But acting on those longings requires an incredible amount of faith.

Faith like Belwyn has displayed by staying by my side.

I stop, gripping his hand until he looks at me and stops too. "I want to . . . I've never thanked you for what you are doing—what you *did*." My throat closes, making it difficult to swallow. "If you hadn't been there . . ."

Compassion burns away the coolness to his gaze, and my own flood of emotions releases in response.

"Belwyn, my father threw himself in the kaligorven's path to save me." My breaths come in lurching waves, threatening to dash me on the shoals of my grief. "How am I supposed to live with that? He had been in such a horrible mental place for so long, and when a spark of hope ignited within him, when I thought that he could—*we* could . . ." I bite my lip, fruitlessly willing myself to remain in control. "*Oh, Elyōn,*" I groan.

Belwyn hesitates only a moment before wrapping me in a firm embrace.

"I know. I know." His voice has shifted into something kinder. Gently, he slides his fingers under my hair and guides my head to rest under his chin, then secures his arms around me again.

I heed the steady rhythm of his heart and let out a long breath once my sobs have stilled.

"You witnessed something awful, but it's not your fault it happened that way."

He rubs my back with his other hand, just like how Orlagh held me every time the clouds of my father's recurring depression took hold and made me feel so hopeless, so alone.

"And you never need to thank me. Not ever."

"But why, Belwyn?" I say into the soft leather of his jerkin, glad I can't see his face. "Why would you give up everything to be with me?"

I feel him draw in a breath to respond, but I can't let him. These are words that need to be said. I lift my head and look at him. "I've been thrust into a world I never could have anticipated. Discovering my gift, learning of my mother, meeting my uncle." A shudder passes through my chest. "Then you were there, a complete stranger, yet familiar to my soul. I-I clung to you because it was all I could do. But how much do we really know each other? Would we be like this if circumstances beyond our control hadn't forced us together?"

The words sound so callous, and I cringe.

Belwyn releases me and places his hands on my shoulders, inserting a little more distance between us. His eyes trace my features, but there is no hurt in them. "I have never experienced a desire for anyone like I feel for you, Amyrah. At first, it was because I longed for something new. You were an escape from expectations, from the crowd I'd fallen into." An ashamed smile breaches his face. "You helped me work through my grief over my brother's death, and I learned that you were so much more than a pretty girl who makes her own clothes." He fingers a lock of my hair, brushing it back over my shoulder. "You aren't a distraction, a task, or a fantasy I want to play out."

Tears threaten to spill from my eyes, and I cannot breathe.

"I *chose* to come with you, Amyrah Cantar, because my heart would bleed if I didn't."

My thoughts turn languid as his hands leave my shoulders to cup my face, as he leans in and pauses before brushing his lips over mine.

His kiss is like the unfathomable seal of a promise I don't deserve, could never earn. My mind screams my unworthiness as I drink in the impossible gift.

Something deep within me releases like a rich, dizzying wave, and my heart thunders in my chest. When he draws back, I bite my bottom lip and let my tears fall freely. He brushes them away with his thumbs and smiles.

A clearing of the throat prompts me to turn away. My cheeks warm when I find Arlyn standing ahead, distracting himself by staring at the trees above. Belwyn drops his hands from my face and adjusts his pack and quiver, as if that can disguise what we were doing.

"Rael sent me back to find you. We were worried you had gotten lost." Arlyn looks between the two of us, a hint of a knowing smile flashing across his face. It fades quickly, and he motions for us to come. "We were able to leave our home here to people we trust, and they are eager to welcome us back. For the moment, at least, we have a place in Ketsé."

We hurry to follow him.

I rub at my face to dispel the heat, still feeling Belwyn's lips on mine. I wonder if he feels as foolish as I do.

When he catches my hand in his and rubs his thumb along the back of it, I shiver and know he has no regrets.

Arlyn and Rael's house dwarfs the humble cottage my father and I owned in the Vale. Suspended about ten feet from the ground on thick platforms braced between four enormous cedars, its three stories look on us with a benevolent glow emanating from many round windows. I glance at Rael, finally able to account for her and her daughter's elegant, albeit time-worn, clothing. They came from considerable wealth.

We ascend the stone stairs and enter through a lavish doorway. "What a beautiful home," I say, stepping into an expansive entryway.

Pride brightens Arlyn's features as he gazes at the arching room. A short woman with loose red hair and an apron tied around her full waist comes around the corner, her joy uncontainable. She greets him with an immediate, tight hug.

"Oh, it's so good to see you. I knew you said never to expect you again, but I couldn't help asking Elyōn a few times to send your family back to us," she admits, like it's something to feel guilty about.

Arlyn laughs, although the sound holds a sad cadence. "It's fine, Sabine. Elyōn's purposes always prevail, no matter how we endeavor to thwart them."

"Yes, but that doesn't mean I won't be a persistent nuisance to him in the meantime."

What can only be described as a small army of children of all sizes and descriptions sweeps between her and Arlyn, hollering and shrieking. Arlyn staggers back, and Sabine swats the last straggler with her apron as he skitters past, giggling like a lunatic.

"Speaking of a nuisance," she huffs, her eyes alight with good humor, "we may have picked up a few more in your absence."

Rael comes from a room down the hall and rests a hand on one of the polished wood walls. "And I'm so glad. This house was always too big for us. Leaving it to you and Elyōn's sweet ones is exactly what we wanted. How beautiful to come back to it and see it bursting with life." Her smile is small but not false. It's the impossible joy that exists within the unrelenting weight of sorrow.

Sabine reaches and gives her hand a squeeze. Then she looks at Arlyn, her mouth turning down. "I am so sorry to hear about your children." Tears well in her blue eyes. "We'll keep praying that Elyōn will keep them safe until you can be reunited."

Rael thanks her in a barely audible whisper, her mouth tight.

"Sabine." Arlyn's tone quickly shifts the conversation. "I regret that we may have caused trouble for your husband. The Nocilium was unimpressed when they found out he had abandoned the Askonnet Mountain Pass." His forehead creases. "Have you heard from him?"

Sabine bobs her head. "Don't you worry about Torr. He managed to sneak into Ketsé and let me know what was going on after he left the cabin to your care. I sent him to visit our relatives farming out at the Northern Flats while he waits this out."

"That was a prudent plan, but Izra Morlaine rather unluckily came upon him in Tothlen Forest before he made it there." Arlyn rests a hand behind his neck and gives it a firm rub. "But I don't believe there will be any further repercussions. If it wasn't for his generosity, we would never have been able to bring news of what's happening at the Vale's border."

Concern shadows Sabine's face.

"Arlyn." Rael steps close to him and rests a hand on his forearm. "Perhaps you can catch Sabine up after we have had a chance to settle these two into their rooms. They are in need of rest, as we all are."

"Absolutely." Sabin fixes her watery gaze on me, her face brightening. "What's your name, dear?" she asks as she waits for me to come forward, slipping her hand behind my back when I do.

"Amyrah," I answer, throwing Belwyn an apologetic look before I let her shepherd me away. His cheek bunches in a resigned smile.

"Well, Amyrah, consider yourself welcome here for as long as you like." She leads me up a winding staircase lined with a thick rug and into a hallway lit by candles hanging from sconces along the wooden walls.

"Second door from the end on the left is the bath. I had filled it in preparation for the little'ns wash time, but you might as well get first crack at it. And this is where we'll put you." She stops at the last door and unlatches it, motioning for me to go in first.

The room is spacious, with a wide bed opposite a cozy stone fireplace and a little desk tucked under an oval window overlooking the rooftops of smaller dwellings.

A swell of emotion makes it difficult to breathe. I step inside, pull off my cloak and satchel, and sink down on the soft linens.

"You'll find plenty of soap and towels in the bathroom. Take your time. You look like you could use a good soak. Give us a holler when you're done, and I'll send in the first rascal."

She turns to leave but stops herself. "I apologize for the thumps and bangs you'll hear. The children have the run of the upper floor." She chuckles. "They are dear souls, but they do tend to make a racket."

"Thank you," I manage to say, and she gives me a kind smile and bustles away.

The bed calls out to me, but I drag myself first to the bathroom where I find a huge tub, much bigger than the one I used to bathe in at home. I sink underneath the steaming water, not bothering to stifle the groan that shunts out of me.

I don't want to think about anything from the last few weeks, but the warm welcome from Sabine, the tender care from Rael, and the protective concern from Arlyn have all seeped into my guarded heart.

Before my tears can begin to fall, I slip under the surface, where I can pretend they don't exist.

After longer than was strictly necessary, I return to my room and find a large bowl of pearl grain stew and a generous slice of bread topped with a slab of butter as thick as my pinkie finger waiting for me on the side table. Two sets of clothing are laid out on my bed, along with a note.

These are for you. You can set your traveling clothes in the basket outside your door, and I'll take care of them. Breakfast is whenever you like it. Follow the sound of the children and I'm sure you'll find the kitchen. —S

Letting the note fall to the floor, I inspect the clothing selected for me. Sabine has thought of everything: fresh undergarments, a soft nightgown, and a simple white chemise with a drawstring neckline paired with a sleeveless overdress the color of twilight leaves.

The dress is far too big for any of the children I saw downstairs and too narrow for Sabine, despite the lace of strings down the back to make it accommodate a range of sizes.

Is it Rael's? I wonder. Or maybe it belonged to a younger version of Wehna.

I bite my lip, waves of memory and regret assailing me with more force than they have all day. This unknowing reminder of loss slips past all the walls I had erected after my father's death. I was never sure what I hoped to find outside of the Vale, but it certainly wasn't unmerited generosity.

Donning the nightgown, I ignore the food, crawl under the covers, and cry myself to sleep.

13
BELWYN

AFTER WHAT SHOULD HAVE BEEN a wonderful night sleeping on an actual bed instead of the ground, I make the mistake of stumbling into the kitchen, where eight pairs of curious eyes and an overwhelming volume of chit-chat greets me. I'm about to abandon the scene and wait for a quieter moment to grab breakfast, when Sabine turns from the fire.

"Ah, Belwyn. You're finally up." She wipes her hands on her apron and jerks her chin toward the table. "Go on, sit and have some kip."

Begrudgingly, I obey. The children, who range from just-able-to-talk to somewhere around my brother Shem's age, bombard me with questions. My inconsiderate head throbs, the loud voices ringing through it like a blacksmith's hammer striking an anvil. I was stupid for downing that terrible beverage yesterday. How could it actually be made of tenesomni? It could have done something much worse than give me a headache and a sour mood.

I make an effort to concentrate on the children instead of these disturbing thoughts.

"What's it like outside the city?" a little girl asks.

I reach across the table and select a crumbly biscuit from the half-empty platter, hoping that if I take too long to answer, she'll forget about me.

No such luck. She taps my shoulder doggedly until I look at her. When I give in, I almost laugh at the exasperation squeezing her freckled face.

"It's not so much different than inside it," I say into my biscuit. A chunk falls into my lap, and the little girl slouches into her seat and scowls with disapproval.

"What kinda boring answer is that?"

A safe one. I shouldn't stray from the delicate line Amyrah and I seem to be walking in Ketsé.

"Now, now, Etta. Don't forget your manners. This young man is a guest in our house, so you will kindly keep that sass under a lid. Gravy, Belwyn?" Sabine overshadows me, ladle hovering above a large black pot.

"No, thank you," I say, provoking several tiny gasps.

"But the gravy ith the betht part," says a tiny boy across the table, a missing front tooth bestowing him with a significant lisp.

If I thought I understood what pressure was before, I was wrong. Nothing can persuade a person to do something more thoroughly than a ring of opinionated children. I set my biscuit on my plate and sit back to let her serve me. She slops a lumpy gravy on top and continues making her way around the table.

At first, I'm put off by its gray appearance, but the aroma makes my mouth water, and I scoop a mouthful with my fork. Its meaty, salty, creamy flavor is amazing with the buttery biscuit.

"I told you it wath good," the boy whispers sagely, and I almost choke on my food, trying to hold in a chuckle.

"What's that sticking out of your nose?" another boy with russet hair asks, his head tilting to the side.

Sabine lobs me a glance as she returns to the stove, almost as if she's warning me to tread carefully. If I had known I was going to be interrogated, I would have never come down for breakfast. Swallowing my food, I take a cautious sip from my mug. I'm not sure what's in it, but it's bitter and bracing and unexpectedly delicious.

"It's called a nose ring," I say, which causes the boy to look more confused.

"Does it go right through the skin?" he prods.

I nod, which prompts a collaborative "*ew*!" around the table.

"Did it hurt?"

"What about bogies?"

I set down my fork, a heavy sigh escaping me.

Her laughter is a welcome escape. I glance toward the doorway and find Amyrah wearing a different style of clothing than I've seen her in, her hair in rebellious waves over one shoulder. She leans against the frame with her arms crossed, an elusive smile dancing in her eyes.

Help me, I mouth.

She grins fully, turning to leave before the band of children can spot her. I snag another biscuit and an extra fork as I stand up. "Do you mind if I take my breakfast with me, Sabine?"

She bursts into a bout of chortles. "Absolutely, Belwyn. *Stars know* I can manage their prattle on my own."

Voicing my thanks, I escape amid a chorus of disappointed groans.

Outside the house, I catch up with Amyrah and settle down next to her on the front steps. "Here, I brought this for you."

She takes the proffered biscuit with a look of gratitude, breaking off a small piece. "I see you found a new crowd to run with," she teases, popping the bite into her mouth.

I let out a breathy laugh. "Trust me, you came at the right time. I think they were about to ask me *why* I got a nose ring, and that is a story I'm certain Sabine would not have appreciated." I pass Amyrah a fork. "You should try some of the gravy."

She accepts the utensil and lifts the smallest amount from the plate. Watching her eat, I grin when her eyes find mine and her cheeks flush pink.

Swallowing, she lays the fork down and resumes eating the biscuit in her previous fashion.

"So, what's the story?"

The smile abandons my lips.

"Sorry," she whispers, flicking a crumb from her deep-green dress.

"No, it's fine." I set the plate down on the stones between us and take a few steadying breaths, thankful that the quiet street and fresh air have soothed my headache into something less excruciating. "Things have always been a bit complicated for me when it comes to my father. He's the reason I did it in the first place."

Amyrah's face tilts toward me, but I don't think I can look at her right now.

"He has always demanded so much, right from the moment he became Foremost. I don't remember anything other than him manipulating me to be so much 'better' than the common valefolk. He accomplished that by hiring a private tutor to handle our education and making sure every spare moment was filled up with some arbitrary activity to make us look better."

I stare at the trees that line the other side of the roadway, their many terraces lacing them together like the clasped hands of lovers. "A couple years ago, I got sick of the pressure. I slacked in my studies, ran off, and found a group of friends to fill my time whenever I could slip away. It was freeing, in a way, but only when I wasn't at home. Behind closed doors, my father owned me."

Amyrah's hands lie limp in her lap, her biscuit half finished. I risk a look at her face, surprised when I see sadness pressing her brows close together.

"It was a horrible way to live, dodging him and earning his fury while losing myself to whatever distracted me. My mother was the one who made me see how selfish I was being, what kind of example I was setting for my brothers. I knew I had to start showing up for my family, but I wanted to remind myself that, although I was choosing to obey him and act like the son he desired, I was also my own person."

Rhun's face, preserved in perfect detail from the last night I saw him, eclipses my thoughts. I almost can't breathe thinking about how my lack of care left my closest brother as an easy target for the kaligorven. Did I ever show up for him?

I swipe a rogue tear from my cheek.

"So you pierced your nose?" Amyrah asks, oblivious to my internal battle.

I run my hands through my hair and let my gaze fall to my boots. "I know it's kind of pathetic, but I'm stuck with it now."

Her fingers find my wrist, and when I look at her, a ghost of a smile graces her lips before she resumes eating her biscuit. "It suits you."

Time passes in a seamless rhythm within the House of Hope, as Sabine calls it. Every morning, when the sun bleeds its rays into the corners of this unfamiliar place, I press down the feeling of surprise that I no longer need to stumble around in blindness. I can't seem to get used to it. My gloomier thoughts try to convince me it's because the ténesomni within me will always crave that familiar dwelling of shadows.

Maybe that's why I am in the cavern marketplace now, staring at the angry black bottles. I can't shake the strange ténesomni beverage's appeal, though it made me sick, because it reminds me of who I once was. I had forgotten how intoxicating the old feeling of anger and self-gratification could be, and the liquid brought it all rushing back like a bracing wind. That high used to be what I lived for before the solas returned, Rhun was murdered, and my whole life was rearranged.

But is that who I want to be now?

The young woman is not anywhere in the cavern, and I let out a shaky exhale. I'm almost relieved that this disgusting craving has no chance of being satisfied.

While I still have the willpower to do so, I flee the cavern as if a kaligorva stalks my steps.

When I return to Sabine's, determined to never speak a word of where I have been, one of the smaller girls with an explosion of freckles and two auburn braids meets me outside. She tugs on my arm, her eyes brimming with hope. "Belwyn, can you give me a horsey ride?"

I crouch, looking both directions before answering in a conspiratorial tone, "Just a little one, as long as you don't tell the others."

She giggles as I spin and offer her my back.

The children have become a welcome diversion from the strange realities that have led me here, although they remind me often of my youngest brothers.

We go up and down the street twice before I lower the girl back to the ground. She repays me by hugging my waist. "Thank you for"—she hunches and makes sure no one is listening—"for our *secret*," she finishes in a whisper.

As she skips inside, oblivious to the cold hard realities of life, I think of Shem. He is only nine years old. Has he held on to his boyish innocence?

And what of the rest of my family? Has Mother managed to keep her grief at bay? Was Father's sudden change of heart permanent? Is Korvin taking too much on his twelve-year-old shoulders?

My chest aches, and I focus instead on Amyrah. I wish I knew what's going on in her head. She isn't the type of person who can be content with merely existing, yet here she is, helping with chores and engaging in polite conversation. I'm not sure she knows what to do with the children, though. A soft laugh breeches my lips, then evaporates.

I know the loss of her father must be weighing on her, despite how strong she tries to appear.

She steps out of the house now, clutching that ever-present book, and her face brightens when she sees me. I slip my hands in my pockets and let her presence loosen my tangled emotions.

"Hello," she whispers when she steps onto the ground, her eyes meeting mine and darting away shyly. I don't bother holding back a smile.

We walk until we come to the end of the rows of houses, where an area of forest has been preserved within Ketsé's limits. Paths inlaid with glowing rocks, used for adornment instead of illumination, wind through the trees and between manicured patches of enatuberry bushes and fanning ferns. The heartening sound of a stream tempts me with a feeling of contentment.

Amyrah bends to study the low-lying bushes, plucking a few purple berries from the stems and popping some into her mouth. She straightens and holds the rest out to me.

"Enatuberries are always the best at the beginning of Zomré," she says.

I take them with a grin and enjoy how their sweet-sour flavor bursts on my tongue.

"That's one thing my father always loved to do. Every year, we would grab as many baskets as we could carry and scour the forest until we had filled them all. He was practical when it came to food, rarely doing anything in excess. Then berry season would hit, and he would get this strange look in his eyes. We would spend the next weeks feasting on them, setting aside a tiny fraction of what we collected for Orlagh." She slides down against a tree.

I join her on the ground. "I still regret that I've only had one of Orlagh's cheese loaves," I say between mouthfuls of berries.

Amyrah laughs, but it turns stale. "How do you think they are doing in the Vale, Belwyn?" she asks, turning her gaze on me.

Her eyes are a striking color of blue, like the sky the moment before the sun spills over the mountains. I love that I know what to compare them to now. But her question presses on my heart.

"Honestly, I have no idea." I rest my forearms on my knees and clasp my hands. "I'm trying not to think about it too much, but the Foremost was quite agitated at how his plans for you turned out."

Amyrah hugs the book to her heart. "I wish I knew why my uncle is doing this."

"It's because Myrzeth is a demented specimen of—"

"No, Belwyn. There must be a reason." She shakes her head until her waves spring from behind her shoulders. "When I was alone with him in the forest, he told me his parents were the ones who messed him up."

I watch her for a moment, clenching my jaw. "I get that you want to understand him, but Amyrah . . . he's . . . *evil.*"

"He may be," she says, pausing to take a few breaths. "But how can I know who *I* am without understanding those who came before me?" She rests the book in her lap and runs her fingers across the words embossed into the cover: *avis ténesomni luvem*. "This book is the last connection I have to any of that."

I hold out a hand, palm up, and she raises an eyebrow before relinquishing the book. Stretching out my legs, I flip through the pages reverently. "What is all this?"

She chews her cheek thoughtfully. "Most of it is like a love letter to Elyōn. It talks often of his character, his past deeds. I'm certain it was written by many authors over many years. You can tell from the different handwriting and how the ink has aged. Praise poured from some pens like water, and with others I can feel the pain inked into the words."

She flips a few pages and points to a verse opposite an angular drawing that resembles her necklace. "Here's a section that references the beginning of this world and the stars he set in place. It's all so beautiful and poetic, and it stirs my heart to praise the Highest."

Her words fall heavy on my soul, though she speaks them with such lightheartedness. Studying the ancient deity was not something deemed appropriate for the Foremost Family. We were supposed to be loyal to none but the kaligorven. I frown away the memories and keep flipping. The book slips open to a section with a few missing leaves.

"Was this what you sacrificed so I could start that fire back with the wolves?" I ask.

Amyrah bites her lip. "Yes, but I had those pages memorized."

When I look at her questioningly, she stands and dusts herself off. I hasten to follow. We walk along the strange, iridescent path.

"It was a song that my mother sang to me—at least I think so. I don't remember her voice, but I know the words, and my father was never much for music."

Before I can ask her to sing it, she's already begun. Her voice is unique and haunting, and it fills me with a strange feeling of sorrow. No, sorrow isn't the right word. It's more like a longing for something *beyond*.

By the time I start paying attention to the words, she's on the third verse.

Lo, there will be a coming day
When bird, beast, man shall see,
For all the darkness will fade away
And all of the Vale will be free.

Thus grows the ever-brightening day,
From the fields to the ne'er ending sea,
And the Light of Life will shine on all,
For rich and whole we shall be.

When the song is through and she closes her eyes, it's as if I am hearing creation's music for the first time: the wind in the branches, the birds calling out to one another, the stream attempting to drown it all out.

She turns to me, her cheeks deepening a shade. I open my mouth and find I'm at a loss for words.

"That was beautiful," another voice says.

We turn around to discover Holden standing behind us, ogling Amyrah like she's sprouted a pair of wings. I feel my neck grow hot, and my reaction has nothing to do with shy embarrassment.

"It's been a while since we've seen you," I force out through a jaw that refuses to unclench. A dry laugh lurches from me. "Are you following us now?"

He shakes off his stupor and looks at me, his eyes clearing. "Why would I do that? Sabine told me where you went." His attention shifts to Amyrah. "I went with Izra to check on the ténesomni's border, Amyrah." The muscles around his lips grow taut, as do mine. Why wouldn't that be information I want to know?

"And?" Amyrah asks, stepping closer to him. "Is it holding?"

Holden's expression darkens. "I'm afraid not. It's already passed the boundaries of the Tothlen Forest."

Amyrah blinks. "My efforts have proved pointless. Again." Her cheeks flush, and her face grows pained.

I move in front of her, grabbing her by the shoulders. She doesn't see me until I give her a little shake. "*No*. This isn't on you, Amyrah."

Her eyes widen insistently. "Isn't it, though?"

I want to contradict her, but am I one to chastise her for claiming illegitimate guilt?

Holden strolls away, wisely choosing to leave us alone, but it doesn't matter. Whatever moment we were sharing is over.

14
WEHNA

GOLD, BURGUNDY, WOOD, BURGUNDY. Gold, burgundy, wood, burgundy. *Gold* . . .

The tedium of stringing tiny, glowing beads always gets under my skin at first, but as the peaceful rhythm takes hold, it thwarts the anxiety that gorges itself on the rotten places in my mind. That's part of the reason I took up making jewelry three years ago.

I let the monotony do its work, and for the first time in a week, the throbbing pain in my temples subsides to a dull pressure. My thoughts line up in orderly fashion, and I slip them onto the cord with the beads, one by one.

Gold. *The solas returned to the Vale*. Burgundy. *Amyrah's gift awakened*. Wood. *The kaligorven retaliated*. Burgundy. *My parents opposed them, and they are gone*. Gold. *Myrzeth intends to show the Vale the power of the kaligorven*. Burgundy. *Amyrah is gone*. Wood. *Arvo does not need me anymore*. Burgundy. *Myrzeth has threatened those who oppose him*. Gold. *And nobody but me knows*. Burgundy. *I should tell someone*. Wood. *It would be so much easier if I was on his side—*

"Whatcha doin', Wehna?"

Small fingers jab at my ribs from behind, wriggling madly, and my hands jerk, fumbling a whole necklace's worth of beads. They slide off the strand, tick-tick-ticking as they hit and bounce all over the flagstone floor. An angry curse slips between my teeth, snatching the smile from Arvo's smooth features as he comes into view. I press my knuckles to my lips and then my temple, where a knife-like pain shatters my mental solitude.

"Mada says that's a bad word." His bottom lip quivers. I shut my eyes, at a loss to understand what is wrong with me.

"She's right," I say, calling myself much worse words in my mind. "Please, never repeat it."

I feel one of his hands press against my temple, and the other rests on top of mine. "Your head still hurting you?"

Opening my eyes, I feign a smile. "Only a little."

I have lost track of the lies I have told him over the past weeks. Or months. I don't know how long it's been anymore.

Arvo studies my face, chin tilting to the side. He looks down at the mess of beads. "Sorry I scared you, but I'll help clean them up."

"No, Arvo," I say, but he's already scrambling around the floor on hands and knees. I rest my wrists on my thighs, watching him for a moment, and my smile loses its falsehood.

Getting down with him causes my head to throb again, but I bite my cheek and let the swell of nausea subside.

By the time we've finished, something like life pulses through my body once more. A welcome change, though it hurts. I lean against the outer stone wall of the Peren house and Arvo clambers onto my lap.

"You know, you're getting pretty big for a fledgling." I hug him, hoping to dispel the emotions my sore heart has no capacity to hold. He squirms but soon gives up and leans into my embrace. My breaths tangle with the soft fragrance of his head. It hasn't changed at all since he was a baby. "We'll be alright, you know. I promise."

"'Cause Elyōn won't steal you from me like he stole Mada and Pada."

Those words are like charred edges on a sweet confectionery. I clasp his shoulders and push him back to see his face.

"Who told you that?"

He bites a lip. "Pada always said that nothing happens that Elyōn doesn't control." His brows shadow his eyes. "And if he was telling the truth, then Elyōn planned to take them from us."

I open and close my mouth like a beached fish gasping for air in a place I have no business expecting such luxuries. "Arvo—"

"Was Pada lying?"

I snap my teeth together, suddenly angry. Furious. Raging at my parents for leaving us, at Elyōn for sanctioning it. At the Perens for taking us in when they don't have the room, no matter what they say or how they rearrange their lives to pretend they do.

Arvo shifts to his knees and raises himself higher, eyes level with mine. His frown isn't a challenge so much as it is a plea to help him understand, to fight for faith in an all-knowing, all-powerful, everywhere-present deity on his behalf.

You need to be strong, Wehna, my mother's voice echoes.

But I've never been strong.

"Pada wouldn't lie to you, Arvo." My voice emerges hardly above a whisper. "It's what he believed."

Tears collect on Arvo's thick lashes. "Why, Wehna? Why would Elyōn want that for us?"

Grabbing his hand, I turn it over so his palm is flush with mine. I study the colorful bracelet—the one that used to be mine. Its line of purple, green, and blue glowing birds forever circle his small wrist.

"I don't know, Arvo." I can't begin to understand why, let alone explain it. A tear splashes the back of my hand—*his*. I look up and lean forward. "All I can cling to is that one day, we will." Another tear hits between my knuckles—*mine*.

As I watch Arvo's face and how he processes the weak response I've given him, it occurs to me that this is the moment that could define his faith for the rest of his life.

If I have caused him to stumble, I will never forgive myself.

He wipes the dampness with the back of his sleeve and crawls once more into my lap, whispering, "You sound like Mada."

My heart has no time to crack before Elodie throws open the door and dashes into the front room.

"Wehna, come quickly," she says between gasps, taking a moment to flick her hair out of her face. Her eyes are wide and though the ambient light is weak, I can see how white her face is.

A dreadful sensation thrusts my stomach down to the soles of my feet. I can't feel them as I stand.

"Arvo, I mean it. *Stay. Here.*" Grabbing him by the shoulders, I plant him on a chair with more force than I mean to.

Hurt quivers his lips and draws tears from his eyes. "But, Wehna—"

"*No, Arvo.* You will not leave this spot, understand?" My raised volume causes pain to radiate around my skull, and I let it add force to my anger. "Don't you dare run off on me again."

Unwilling to give him the opportunity to protest, or to allow myself to feel guilty for how I treated him, I follow Elodie outside.

At first, I don't understand the source of her panic, but then I realize that I am standing in Ellithïm, not some random Utsanek alleyway. This neighborhood is supposed to be defined by the myriads of glowing bolétis above its streets, yet now it is as shadowy as the rest of the Vale. A swell of ténesomni creeps above me, swallowing the bioluminescent mushrooms whole. They sway on their strings and dim to faint smudges.

Elodie's shivering hands find my forearm. "Is one of those *things* here?" she hisses into my ear.

My mouth has gone dry; my mind is blank with confusion.

More people step out from their homes, from the library and tea shop, and gape at the oily billows. A toddling boy begins to wail, his mother handing him off to her daughter to take him indoors. That's when their panic starts to set in.

"Wehna—"

"Please be quiet, Elodie. Keep still," I whisper harshly and rest a hand on hers.

Glancing up and down the street, I find no evidence of a kaligorva nearby. Myrzeth, with his colorless hair, is nowhere to be seen. My heartbeat slows a fraction.

The darkness sliding along like liquid night lessens my fears instead of heightening them. Immersed in the Vale as I have been since we moved here, I have forgotten the non-threatening behavior of real shadows and started to believe that ténesomni is the same as nightfall outside of the Vale.

But staring up at this thing that moves of its own accord and consumes the goodness of Ellithïm, I know two truths:

It is evil. And it is alive.

For some reason, those facts make it less debilitating. If it is evil, then good can oppose it. If it is alive, then it can also die.

From farther down the street a collection of voices echoes, laden with the strident tones of alarm and fear, but a deeper voice rises above them.

"Steady, *steady*. Do not panic. It is nothing that we have not seen before." Bryn shuffles between the onlookers, their worried expressions easing with his nearness.

"Pa." Elodie releases my arm and trips into her father's embrace. He rubs her back in small circles, eyes fixed on the upside-down sea.

The sharp pain behind my eyes intensifies as she and Bryn approach together.

"We saw something like this a few days ago," Elodie confesses and I bite my lip, anxious about him hearing of the danger I led his eldest daughter into. "It-it was ténesomni like I've never experienced," she continues, oblivious to my discomfort. "I was so afraid, Pa. The Shrouded passed right in front of me and—"

That pulls Bryn from his dazed stare. Abruptly, he faces his daughter. "Where did this happen?"

She has the good sense to close her mouth.

Bryn frowns, but he makes a great effort to moderate his tone. "Who have you been wandering the city streets with, El?" He brushes a strand of hair away from her face. "And why in all of Atsun would you think doing that would be a good idea—*now*?"

Before she can burst into tears, I rush forward. "Please, Bryn. It was me. I'm the one that couldn't bear to stay in Ellithïm. She was concerned for me." The lie tastes rancid, but I gulp it down. It's not her fault she's thirteen and restless.

Bryn straightens, pinning me with a disappointed look. "You, of all people, should know how dangerous the city has become, Wehna." His lips press together so hard they almost disappear until a resigned sigh cracks them apart. "But we can talk about that later. Right now, I need you to tell me what you saw."

I blink a few times, trying to detach my brain from the roiling guilt and focus on the facts. My gaze hitches on my shoes. "The kaligorven are openly prowling the streets of Utsanek now. One of them passed within several feet of us in the poorer district east of here. It didn't notice our presence because it was fixated on the sola bone lighting the street. It was tr-trying to touch it, but it could do nothing to weaken it."

My voice is foreign, monotone and quiet and something that should not issue from my mouth. I look up to find Bryn watching me intently. His eyes are dark yet comforting.

"The Foremost was following the beast," I say, shivering as I think of the encounter, "and he said something strange. It sounded like Atsunic, but I've never heard the word before. When he spoke it, the sola bone seemed to lose its power. Not its illumination—that was still as bright as ever. But it was like it lost all ability to fight the monster's hunger. The kaligorva drank in the light. Extinguished it."

"*Elyōn*," Bryn whispers, and it isn't a curse. It's a plea.

Tress approaches the three of us, carrying a lit lantern. She holds out an arm to Elodie, who welcomes her embrace. I notice the people from down the street quietly coming closer.

Folding his thick arms in front of him, Bryn rests his chin on his chest, deep in thought. "So Myrzeth is not content to offer only the solas' blood to the kaligorven. He has found a way to strengthen them with the illumination he promised to the valefolk." He shifts his weight on his heels, then lets out an exasperated grunt and regards his wife. "I wish we understood what his purpose was or where he has gotten this knowledge, this control over those beasts."

Elodie lobs me a panicked look, and her father doesn't miss it. He turns to me, waiting for an explanation.

"I might not know exactly what he wants." I twist the front of my tunic. "But I can tell you that he threatened all those who are faithful to Elyōn."

"He has done that before, Wehna." Bryn says, disappointed.

I shake my head. "No, not like this. It felt like he was certain he would have success against us. Like he . . . like he knows where we are hiding."

That's enough to clear the cobwebs.

"Bryn, if what she is saying is true, then we are no safer here than anywhere else in this city," Tress says, stepping forward, her voice remarkably calm for such a realization.

Her husband tilts his face skyward and watches the wave of ténesomni as it finishes blanketing the entire street. He is quiet for a maddeningly long time. The crowd thickens, and I hug my arms around myself.

Finally, he breaks the silence with thoughtful tones. "Darkness like this, in this potency, is something I have never seen in the Vale. Perhaps this is what we need to convince more valefolk that Myrzeth's intentions are not good." Grunts of agreement chase his words. He makes eye contact with Tress. "But, yes, my dear. If it has found us here, then I am sure the kaligorven will not be far behind. It's time the fidrélas stop lurking in the shadows and step into the light."

I blink and Tress laughs softly at my confusion. "What my husband is trying to say is that we have always known this place of escape, of safety, would never last. It was meant to be a temporary reprieve from the crushing weight of Utsanek's oppressors." She pulls Elodie closer, and Arvo's curious face peeks from the window behind them. "And that is exactly what it has been, but Elyōn's people were never meant to hide. He intends us to go into the world and be its light. Maybe it's time for us to realize our calling. In doing so, Elyōn will hide us in full view."

Can she really mean what I think she means, that these few broken souls should welcome the hardship that will come with open arms?

While I'm still sifting through my own confliction, my own dread of tribulation, Bryn turns to the dozens of people hemming us in. "I know it feels contrary to what is right, but we must open our gates and let the rest of Utsanek in. It would be unwise to invite unnecessary persecution, however, so let us at least make this neighborhood appear like any other in Utsanek." He glances at the bioluminescent glow only just visible within the roiling ténesomni. "We will start now by taking down all of the bolétis that illuminate our paths."

There is not even a pause for consideration before the fidrélas grab the mushrooms within reach and yank them down. Someone produces a stepladder for the higher ones, and within what feels like only a handful of heartbeats, the entire street's worth of light lies mounded in woven baskets.

"Take them into the fenced forest area to be dispersed among the ferns and bushes. We must disguise the entrance to Ellithïm's garden once all the bolétis are accounted for. I hope the kaligorven will not notice its existence."

Elodie surprises me by determinedly grabbing a basket and hurrying toward the camouflaged forest entrance.

I have been a resident of the Vale for three short years, and these people have struggled within it their whole lives. Yet here they are, willingly disposing of all the light that they possess because a man who has no claim to authority told them to. Why? Why would anyone ever concede to toss away something good with no assurance that the sacrifice will bring them something better?

Faith, Wehna. It makes a person strong when she is weak.

I don't know if they are my mother's words or if they come from my own mind, but I find in them a piercing accusation.

Ducking my head low to avoid attention, I slip inside the Peren house and motion for Arvo to come. Before the door swings shut, Bryn's deep voice calls out, "Unlatch the hidden passageways. It's time for Ellithïm to open its doors for good."

I am not sure of much anymore, but I know this: Arvo and I have no place among these people.

15
SEYLA

IT WAS EASY TO CONVINCE MYSELF I could not see the black wall edging closer while I was under the apathetic gaze of a new moon.

Now that dawn has broken and the sun reveals what night had veiled, I recognize the lie.

The ténesomni is so close, I could wade out into the water and touch it. Something inside me wants to . . . like it's . . . it's *calling* me.

"*Sea's fury*. The rumors are true."

I start at Ordin's voice, even though I have kept watch with him the entire night. He has been uncharacteristically quiet in my presence since Commander Verrek robbed him of one of his ranks. I am too relieved to feel bad for him. His badgering had grown more than tiresome.

"It won't be long until we no longer have a beach to patrol." I squint at the billows. "Tell me, Ordin. Do you see shapes in the mist?"

He screws up his face but shakes it loose with a barked laugh. "The watch must be getting to you, woman. There's nothing in it but your own superstitions."

My hands move to the belt across my torso of their own accord, unfastening my baldric and dropping my sword on the ground. It lands with a clatter on stones smoothed by the loch's lapping waters, and I repeat the process with my khukuri and its sheath.

"What in Elyōn's name are you doing?" Ordin asks, holding his palms out wide from his body.

Ignoring his incredulous mutterings, I slip off my arm bracers and step into the water. Even though the air has grown humid with Zomré's heat, the water still carries the memory of Vestri's ice. I wade until the waterline has made it to my armpits, then flatten my hands together above my head, arms straight, and dive.

"Come back, morvus." Ordin's voice is lost in Loch Skythe's muting waters.

After a few long, steady strokes, I reach the ever-hungry border to the shadowlands. Adjusting my position with deft arm movements, I tread water with my legs and hold up a hand to the black. A slow, stuttering breath inflates my lungs. I hold it in, pray to my ancestors for protection, and reach toward it.

Bubbling shadows bulge and cave underneath my palm, cold like ice and just as solid. I cannot penetrate it a hair's breadth.

"How in Atsun—"

Something dark, all scales and claws, shoots out and wraps around my forearm. Its frozen touch is like a blast of a northern gale. My scream is halfway formed as my head is yanked below the waters. I fight to see what has me in its clutches, but the shadows have just as much dominion in the water as they do on land. My attacker remains concealed, its strong grip never faltering, entombing me in the loch's depths.

But I was never one to give in.

In a mad attempt to break free, I kick against anything, everything my feet might find. There is nothing except this imprisoning wall. I try to pry the thing off with my other hand, but its grip constricts and pain tears through my wrist. A silent scream bursts out in quivering bubbles. Red trails leak from my skin, thinning into pink gossamer strands.

Random images fire through my brain as my lungs convulse for air. My sister's raven hair in a braid like a fish tail. The uneven sutures I managed to sew with my left hand above my right elbow when I was seventeen. The stranger's brow as it presses together when he whispers words I have never heard and names I do not understand.

Until the darkness surrounds me. Consumes me. *Is* me.

At least I will see Tetyan again.

A guttural wail shakes through the water, lurching my heart within my chest. The crushing claws release their hold. I open my eyes to see a meaty hand reaching through the shards of crystal light, grabbing me by the languid braid drifting above. Dragging me backward, upward. Away.

Throwing me on the beach as I cough up a sea's worth of water.

"*Ordin*," I splutter, pushing my hands and knees under me.

"You ridiculous, impulsive, morvus of a woman," he growls, collapsing on a driftwood log and rubbing his hands over his glistening face, shoulders rising and falling like the shifting plates of the earth itself.

I rest my head in my hands and, for the first time since I was sixteen, wish I remembered how to cry.

Ordin bandages my wounds without a word, and with a little loosening of the leather bracer, I manage to hide my mangled forearm.

The entire journey back to camp, Ordin stays silent. He did not mention anything about my indiscretion to the two úramech who replaced us—an unprecedented show of restraint for him—and he says nothing about the beast that grabbed me. I wonder if he even saw it.

I try to deny the chill that has grafted itself to my bones, but to no avail. I can still feel the monster's claws tearing through my flesh. *These are the monsters Tetyan and I used to fear.* And they are very, very real.

When the rows of tents are within sight, Ordin steps into my path and crosses his arms. "Don't you think that I will ever do anything like that again."

I refuse to look him in the eyes.

His fingers trap my chin and angle it up. I almost spit at him but stop when I see his face. Time has formed it into something hard and ugly and scarred, but underneath there is a glimpse, a mere fleck, of something sad. Something raw.

"How am I supposed to keep my promise to her if you go off half-drawn, without a stitch of armor . . ." His voice dies in his throat, and he grits his teeth.

Her? My mind struggles to find purchase. I search his haggard face, the spidery wrinkles, the age-spotted skin. There are days when I feel the limitations of my age bearing down on me. Aches and exhaustion that never used to plague me before. It scares me, and I am only thirty-nine. Ordin, however, is at least twenty years older, and he has always been like an immovable force.

The realization hits me like a ram's head to the stomach. *He knew my mother.*

I rip his hand from my face and glare with ignati burning in my eyes. "Don't worry. You will never find yourself in that position again. *Ever.*" I spit on the ground at his feet and step around him, flinging my damp braid over my shoulder as I pass.

I am deaf to the early morning encampment sounds. Noise, color, and shape swoop around me in a meaningless blur.

Was that monster one of the kaligorven? The name sends a thrill down my spine. I have accepted that my people patrolled the shores of Loch Skythe for good reason, but there has never been anything to report, no records of contact with any of the shadow beasts since the Confinement a century ago. There was certainly never any hint that they could swim.

My forearm throbs with a sharp pain, heat crawling past my elbow. The wound, which has a hideous, torn appearance, will need tending as soon as I get back to my tent.

The stranger's injuries were similar. Did he encounter one—or perhaps several—of these daemons within the Vale? He could hold a wealth of information, as Commander Verrek hopes, but so far, he has been incoherent, barely clinging to life.

I shake out my arm, urging my brain to forget the pain, the terror of this morning. The ease with which I accepted my fate. Death was never an acceptable option until that moment.

Have I become so weak?

Letting out a frustrated growl, I allow a more uncomfortable question to take precedence. What did Ordin mean when he spoke of the promise he made to *her*? He can have only been referring to my mother.

A burst of air hisses through my gritted teeth.

Could someone have loved—no, that is too strong a word—*cared* for such a woman as Fehlan Bréinth enough to make her an honest vow? Men often promised her many things, none of which they honored. At first, I believed her portents of ample, rich food and fine linens to come, of a delicious garden where Tetyan and I could spend sun-drowned afternoons. Soon, I grew wise to these whispered apparitions and gave up hoping for anything beyond the bare minimum to keep my body functioning.

Perhaps Ordin knew her in that same manner that drove me and my sister far from home night after night.

My stomach convulses. Is it possible he's my . . . my . . .

Ancestors, no. I won't entertain the thought. Nothing in me could ever reflect anything in that man.

I pick up my pace, ignoring the judgmental looks and forcing my mind to bury the aftermath of the morning in the realities of the present.

Darkness is looming. The Shrouded are reaching. My arm requires tending. The stranger needs—

I come to a sudden stop. My tent flap is unlaced, waving in the western breeze.

Not how I left it.

My hand darts to the hilt of my khukuri, drawing it in a quick motion as I assess my surroundings. Two young úramech across the pathway hone their blades in silence, glancing my direction and exchanging disdainful looks before returning to their tasks. Arrogant, but not guilty. I resist the urge to make a rude gesture at them. They cannot fathom the mountain of life experience I hold over them.

Even with Verrek's approval to house the stranger, I have sensed the animosity growing toward this man's presence among the Agmen. The gossip has ignited the encampment's action-starved minds like a lightning strike to Morpa's dry plateau grasses.

I lift the door flap to peer inside.

The cot is empty, my table upturned.

No.

Sheathing my blade, I hurry down the narrow row of tents, peering inside some of them, not allowing myself to process what kind of danger that fool of a man could be in, or how much unnecessary grief he could cause me.

I skid to a halt, and my eyes rake the low, rugged hills that tuck in our camp. I plead with my pulse to still.

If he is wandering the Boretel Forest, if he makes it to the Southern Moors, I'll never find him.

If someone came and grabbed him, he could already be dead.

"*Heshïn.*" I curse in defiance of the despair that constricts my throat and force myself to listen.

A break in the camp's monotonous rumble reaches my ears: crude laughter and a muffled cry.

I follow the sounds, senses heightened, and round a corner into an open area around several spent cook fires. In the middle of a circle of soldiers, the man—*my* stranger—lies with his face pressed into the dirt, a burly úramech youth standing above him with the heel of his boot digging into his back.

My panic dissolves, resolve taking its place. I stride forward with firm steps, fingertips brushing the leather tassets covering my thighs.

The soldier tosses his head, stringy blond hair flicking out of his face. "Ah, here comes your little woman."

A couple of the men part for me, but it would be lying to say the action is chivalrous. I feel their gazes like a slimy touch, but I will not let them cow me. I cannot.

When I dare to look down at the stranger, I see a tear slicing through the dirt on his face.

"Come to save him again, sweetheart?"

My mother's crooning voice whispers through my mind, as if in response to the disgusting pet name. *Don't you dare let them see who you really are, sweetheart. Let them only know the role you're willing to play.*

Emboldened, I move within spitting distance of the young man, whose lips spread in a smile devoid of warmth. In one swift movement, I draw the thin blades hidden in the tassets, cross them in front of each other, then slice outward into the unprotected flesh above the young man's elbow. He hollers and staggers back, a string of hideous names flying with the spittle from his lips. Red spills between the fingers he presses to the wound.

Imitating an appearance of calm, I stand over the stranger, hold the knives out from my sides, and stare every soldier down. "This man has earned Verrek's seal of protection. Those who would oppose their commander, come forward, and I will show you how 'sweet' these blades can be."

"*Please*, don't," the stranger wheezes.

Hard expressions unchanged, no one makes a move. I bite my tongue, needing the shock of pain to keep me from acknowledging how my heart thunders within the cage of my chest.

"What pitiful excuses for úramech."

I cringe at the gravelly voice. *Not again. Not a second time in one day.*

Ordin muscles his way into the circle, resting the flat of his unsheathed sword atop his right shoulder. "Could've sworn it was a bunch of old biddies having a good old Xitus morning gossip." He swings his weapon down and around, taking a moment to admire the way it glistens in the late morning glow.

"The vixen cut me," the blond-haired soldier sputters pathetically, hunching over his arm.

"Is that so?" Ordin's eyebrows peak and he clicks his tongue. "Well, that's too bad. Terrible." He flips his longsword so its tip penetrates the earth and drapes a forearm over the top of the pommel. "Unfortunately for you, she speaks the truth. If you don't leave now, you'll have something much worse than claw marks to deal with."

With muttered frustration, the rabble disperses, leaving Ordin, me, and the stranger alone. I wipe my blades on the edge of my tunic, ignoring my trembling hands, and bend to hook the man under the elbow. He groans and catches his bottom lip between his teeth as he struggles to find his feet.

I wedge my shoulder under his armpit. His weight sags so heavily against me, I am not sure he is fully conscious.

My partner sheaths his sword and eyes the man.

"Well, are you going to stand there?" I snarl.

Sighing, Ordin approaches. "Half-drawn, yet again, Seyla," he says under his breath. But he silences as he grabs the man around the back and awkwardly helps me take him back to my tent.

The aroma of warm oats fills the small space as I drop a generous amount of enatuberry preserves on the three fist-sized cakes. I would not waste such a precious luxury on myself, but the man teetering on the edge of my cot needs all the nourishment he can get after weeks of being bedridden.

I hold out the dish, and he stares at it with apathetic disdain.

"You must eat."

When he doesn't respond, I set it on the bed and fold my arms.

"What is your name?" I question, my tone harsher than I intended. My patience is clearly nearing its limits.

A lazy blink is his only response.

I flick a braid behind my shoulder and lower myself to a small, three-legged stool beside my table. Mercifully, none of my bottles shattered when my fellow úramech upended it in their haste to apprehend the stranger.

Even after weeks of tending to him and fighting for his existence, the man remains a complete mystery. If he doesn't start talking soon, my frustration will get the better of me.

Instead of glaring at him, I occupy myself by loosening the bracer from around my right forearm and sliding it off. A small gasp parts my lips. The bandage beneath is soaked with crimson.

"That looks bad."

Glancing up, I discover the man's brows furrowed in deep concern. The hollow spaces around his eyes and below his cheek bones momentarily cause me to forget my injury. He would be handsome, I think, if he weren't so emaciated.

Swallowing, I give my head a small shake. "It's nothing but a mark of my foolishness."

He watches me unwind the fabric. The bleeding has slowed, and I dab a potent tincture to the angry scours in my flesh, the same medicine I have applied to his wounds so many times.

When I look away, fumbling to reach a fresh roll of bandages, a warm palm presses to the back of my hand.

"Let me."

I cast him a dubious glance as he scoots forward on the cot, leaning over to acquire what I could not reach.

I hope he does not fall over.

With careful movements and a touch as soft as old linens, the man binds my wounds.

"You're a healer, then?" I ask, expecting him to ignore me again.

His jaw tenses. He secures the fabric with a careful knot, the gentle tug causing pain to lace up my arm. "Nothing so noble. I was a mason."

A breath of weak laughter hides my discomfort.

His shoulders hitch up, then drop. "It takes more delicacy than most people realize." He clears his throat and looks at my bandaged arm, some uneasy thought causing his brows to crease further. "Was this wound caused by a-a wild beast?" he asks, his voice catching.

I sit back, holding my sore arm up to my chest with the other hand. "I have wondered the same about yours."

His hand travels to his side and his eyes take on a vacant look.

Sighing, I jerk my chin. "Here, let me take a look."

A guarded expression shadows his features as he pulls away.

"Please. Do you think I haven't seen you without a shirt on yet?"

Still, he hesitates and my ire rises. "Listen, I've spent too much time on you to have my efforts wasted." I stand up, grabbing the tray of food and setting it on the stool. "Now, *lie down*."

Though I can tell he would rather not, he acquiesces, turning his face away when I push up his tunic. *Thank the ancestors.* The bandages have remained in place, and I find no fresh blood or indication that the wound has soured. When I lower his shirt and discover his eyes trained on mine, heat traipses up my cheeks.

Weeks of caring for this man in every capacity possible, and *now* I feel uncomfortable? I force my embarrassment away with a question. "Do you recall what happened?"

He struggles to sit, and I hasten to support him and tuck a pillow behind his back. He leans against the robust canvas of the tent, taking several deep breaths. Seeing his chest rise and fall with such ease fills me with relief. There were days when I doubted he would make it.

He is quiet for so long, I give up waiting for a reply. *I hope to the seas Commander Verrek has more patience than I do.* After today's altercation and the barricade of shadow pressing in on us, I have a feeling it will soon wear thin.

Straightening, I turn away and begin tidying up the spent bandages, the tincture, and the preserves, until his soft voice arrests me.

"I-I couldn't let them have her."

My hands still around the little pot, and I resist turning around. "Who?"

He doesn't answer.

The lid of the pot closes with a *snap* between my fingers. Does he speak of a friend, a daughter . . . a lover? A strange emotion creeps up in my chest. I give it no quarter in my heart. I know every item that came with this man, and there was nothing to indicate he was bonded to anyone. Casting a neutral look over my shoulder, I watch his calloused hands clench around the bedsheets, and his trembling lips thin into a line.

I finish my task and sit on the bed at his feet.

"What were you protecting her from?"

He jerks his head furiously, freeing the tears that had gathered along his lower eyelids to course down his cheeks. He swallows a few times before turning his blue eyes on me. "Please, tell me. Where am I? How did I get to this place of . . . of light?"

I angle my head, frowning. "How can you not know?"

He blinks dumbly.

He may not be as useful as Verrek hopes. Dread of what the Imperii will do with me—with this man—if he finds we've wasted his time clings to my thoughts. With a grimace, I focus on answering the question. "I found you in a boat along the southern shore of Loch Skythe, all but torn to pieces. Something propelled you here from within the lands claimed by ténesomni."

Confusion washes over his face, but he remains quiet.

"There was a strange creature with you in the boat. It was dead."

His eyes narrow, and he scrapes his shaking fingers over his jaw. "The last thing I remember was seeing her face before the . . . the . . ." His mouth puckers like he has tasted something sour. "The kaligorven attacked me."

My heart climbs to my throat as I recall the cold, sharp claws holding me under the black surface of the loch. "Is that a normal occurrence in the Vale?"

He stares at the ceiling of the tent. "Not until recent days, and before that, not for thirteen years."

A heavy silence falls between us. I close my eyes, fighting disappointment. Learning anything from him is going to take time. Can I give it to him?

Or will the black walls reach us first?

"It doesn't matter. We don't need to do this right now." I smooth my expression and hand him the plate of food again. "What is most important is that you recover your strength. I can't promise the coming days will provide much opportunity for that."

He regards me for a few beats, then exhales and docilely accepts the plate. "Thank you . . ." His voice travels up in an unasked question.

"Seyla," I answer with a small smile.

Taking a bite from an oat cake and settling back against the tent wall, he closes his eyes. "Enatuberries have always been my favorite."

I raise an eyebrow. The other úramech would mock me for keeping a supply of such a costly little luxury as enatuberry preserves, but it is one thing I have never been able to keep myself from splurging on. It was

Tetyan's favorite and—

"Mine too," I breathe.

The man's eyes open and he regards me with something close to understanding.

"Téron," he whispers.

The tension in my back eases the smallest sliver. "What?"

"My name is Téron."

16

AMYRAH

WITHIN A WEEK OF HOLDEN'S RETURN, an entourage of refugees arrives with their possessions strapped to their backs and piled on top of oxen and donkeys. They draw out what must be the entire city's population to witness their arrival as they trundle up Ketsé's main road, stopping to rest at the base of the Nocilium Chamber's steps. The weary picture exhausts me to my bones.

"We saw the ténesomni coming less than half a day before it reached us." A middle-aged man wheezes from under a load of kitchen chairs lashed together with rope. He lets it slide to the ground and straightens, bracing his lower back with the heels of his hands. Many of the other travelers follow his example, their soft groans filling the air.

"No one thought to touch it," the man says, "to see what it would do when it reached us. We were preoccupied with gathering firewood, stocking our shelves, and making certain our lanterns were well-supplied with oil."

"You were just going to let it swallow you?"

I can't see who asked the question, but the disdain is clear in his adolescent voice.

"Qortehr is our home," states a woman with sagging skin under her eyes and hair knotted in a long, graying rope. She straightens her neck, raising her chin. "Although it may not be much compared to Ketsan finery, it is *ours*. Could you so easily abandon what you know?"

"I wouldn't have given up without a fight," the young man retorts.

"Let the people speak." Veridree steps into the clear space before the refugees, her tone carrying a practiced diplomacy. Her silver-blond hair is down today, a complicated pattern of thin braids woven over it like a net.

The haggard man slips his arm around his equally haggard wife. "We were willing to shelter in place until it passed, if it ever would."

The young man scoffs. "Well, *I* would never accept having to live like those valefolk shadow rats."

It is an unfortunate moment for Belwyn to join the throng and hear the conversation. His hands curve into fists, but I snag his arm and tug him back before he can push past me. "Ignore him."

The man's continued narrative hushes Belwyn before he has a chance to object. "All our preparations proved to be in vain. When the wall reached our fences, it began to digest Qortehr like a slithering reptile, swallowing our homes and belongings, our crops and cattle."

"Our livelihood," the woman adds, gripping a large sack against her breast. A pair of chickens cluck pensively from a woven branch cage at her feet.

Veridree's face sobers. "Are you saying the ténesomni pushed you out?"

"I still don't see why you wouldn't put up a fight—"

"*Silence*, fool," Veridree snaps, whipping her head around to stare down the freckle-faced teen. "Keep your unfounded opinions between your ears." Smoothing her hair, she turns back to the group and gestures for the refugee woman to continue.

Her face flushes and she nods fervently. "Yes, it pushed us out, but there were a few people whom the ténesomni accepted, who could walk in and out of its blinding wake. At first, this gave us hope we could all find passage through the boundary." She goes quiet, her mouth snapping shut and eyebrows arching up in the middle.

The man rests a hand on her shoulder and continues where she cannot. "But something . . . something found them." His tongue darts out to wet his dry lips. "There were terrible screams, hideous snarls. And then silence."

My attention hitches on a young girl, eight or nine years old, with straight brown hair that reaches her middle. A shaggy dog stands watch at her side, a loop of rope around his neck. She crouches and scratches behind his ears, blissfully unaware of the surrounding conversation. She throws her arms around the canine and hugs it tight. A long tongue lolls out of its happy mouth. When she looks at me, though, her joy evaporates, and her eyes strike me like an arrow-fletched accusation. She stands and tucks herself into the woman's side, her gaze locked on my face.

It's as if she knows I could have stopped their home from being consumed.

You're being ridiculous, Amyrah. This girl has no connection with you. Didn't your last encounters with Myrzeth and the ténesomni's border prove that you are useless?

That's what my head tells me, but as heat floods through my palms and my eyes fill with light, I know it is a liar.

But I stopped it. Back at the cabin, I stopped the ténesomni. I could have done the same for them. I could have tried.

My heart burns within my chest.

Belwyn's fingers grasp mine insistently. I turn to him, watch his eyes widen.

"Amyrah." He leans in and whispers into my ear. "Be careful. You're . . . you're *shining*."

Alarmed, I shut my eyes. *Contain this*, I coach myself. There is something alive within me, something hungry to escape, and my mounting panic fuels the phenomenon further.

"I-I can't help it." I swallow a yelp.

"*Shades*," he hisses. "Let's get you out of here." Belwyn pulls me through the crowd, and I let him lead me without opening my eyes.

How can I hold this light at bay?

The answer settles on me like a cold night mist.

With darkness, daughter.

My eyes spring open. Where did that thought, that *voice*, come from?

"Amyrah, it's getting worse."

Belwyn pulls me behind him, his grip so firm that my knuckles begin to ache.

Thank Elyōn, the woodfolk are focused elsewhere. I don't know where he's taking me, and I don't care. The burning flame presses on my thin exterior, consumes my thoughts, begs to be shared. Belwyn picks up his pace. I struggle to keep up as we run down what would be a dark stone passageway if it weren't for the light pouring from my being.

We emerge into an open cavern, but I can't risk keeping my eyes open any longer to assess our surroundings. Belwyn guides me by my shoulders until I feel a hard, concave surface behind me, like a cleft in a rock. Like the one I crawled into for shelter when a kaligorva pursued me in the forest outside the Vale a lifetime ago.

"Breathe. J-Just breathe."

The warble in his words breaks me, even as it offers a breath of clarity for me to cling to.

Broaden your mind. Hold the light at bay with the darkness.

The voice comes again, implanting itself into my thoughts, setting my teeth on edge. Yet it also reminds me of something Myrzeth said about him and my mother. *We could call and banish the darkness at will, as all the Luvesti are able.*

Belwyn's hand presses to my forehead. His voice pierces through the screaming that has filled my skull. "Amyrah, you're burning up."

Gritting my teeth, I draw on all my focus as I did on the mountain. Only this time, I don't call to the light.

I call to the darkness.

And it answers like a ravenous wave.

"Amyrah, *shades—*"

The fear in Belwyn's voice prompts me to open my eyes, and my breath is stolen away.

Inky shadows exude from my palms, crawling up my arms and sliding over my skin. I choke on a blackness that is eager to replace the blinding illumination. Uncontrollable shivering seizes my body as ice replaces fire. Belwyn's hands drop from my shoulders, and he stumbles back. Away.

No, I didn't want this. A wordless prayer of pleading, of penitence, groans from my soul.

And Elyōn answers.

Life flows through my veins once more, displacing the fingers of death I had unknowingly welcomed. The air loses its chill, its weight, and I can draw breath again. I search for Belwyn's face, stifling a sob when I see both horror and relief plastering it.

"What did you do, Amyrah?" he asks, voice morphing into something stern.

"That"—I curl into a ball around my knees, barely able to croak out —"that was ténesomni," before breaking into hideous, remorseful tears.

Belwyn's arms circle me now like the night I had summoned, but I do not recoil from his touch.

"It's alright." His gentle murmur weaves in all my frayed edges. My sobs slow under the steady influence of his thudding heart. "I know something of what you're feeling right now."

How is that possible? I want to ask, but instead I just let him hold me tight.

When calm has been returned to me, Belwyn shifts to sit by my side, leaning against the rock wall. I finally look around at the expansive cavern, alarm thudding in my gut when I see market booths wheeled not ten feet before us.

"Belwyn, *no*. This is the *worst* place you could have thought to come." I moan into the shirtsleeve pulled over my fingers. "How many people saw?"

He grunts dismissively. "No one cares about what happens down here."

I toss him a misgiving glare. "How do you know that?"

"You remember Rael talking about the place Ketsé keeps their unwanted?" He flicks a loose stone with the toe of his boot. "Well, this is that place."

I take in what I can see of the room. We are sitting off to the side, tucked away from the main thoroughfare. "You've been here before?"

The deep roar of a fast-moving body of water fills his pause. "Yeah, a couple times. For some reason, it reminds me of . . . of home."

My heart squeezes with longing, and it catches me by surprise. I have spent every conscious moment since we left the Vale acting like I no longer have a home. Have I been deceiving myself the whole time?

Maybe home isn't the place we wish it would be, but it's the place that formed us. Whether it used a cruel or a gentle hand doesn't matter, doesn't change the fact that it's where our hearts first learned to beat.

"Do you think . . ." Struggling to finish the question, I lift a hand to my argentilum necklace and let its eight points ground me. "Do you think I was right in leaving?"

Belwyn doesn't ask me to clarify. He rests his elbows on his knees and watches the milling customers. "I've been battling the same thoughts." He grows pensive for a while, his expression slipping into something uneasy. "But I don't think it was safe for you to stay. Whatever Myrzeth had planned for you"—he shakes his head—"wasn't good."

"But that's *why* I should have stayed. He's not going to relent because I'm no longer within his reach. I bet he's taking his anger out on them right now."

"Amyrah, the fate of an entire city doesn't rest solely on you."

I make a sound somewhere between a sigh and a moan. "You don't get it. When I discovered my gift, I was certain, *so certain*, that it meant I was supposed to be the one to break the darkness. I believed it was up to me to complete the purpose that my mother had failed to realize. When I stood up to my uncle's weaponized ténesomni, it melted like snow in the season of Niatev. Wasn't that proof that if anyone is supposed to stop his progress, it's me?"

I can feel Belwyn's gaze, but I can't bring myself to return it.

"I should have been able to stop Qortehr from being consumed." The little girl's wary expression haunts my mind like a night owl's call. I look down at my hands, still expecting to see the shadows staining them.

But now I'm too afraid to try.

"We could go back, you know," he says, the words nearly stolen away by the river's chatter.

I allow myself to look at him. His eyebrows pitch downward, but his eyes hold a pained understanding. He laces his fingers through mine. "Nothing's stopping us."

As I open my mouth to respond, someone rounds the corner from the long passageway, almost stepping on us.

A beautiful girl around Belwyn's age titters a laugh, her glistening black hair disappearing against her form-fitting, gray dress. "Ah, it's *you*. I was wondering if you'd find your way down here to see me again."

She only has eyes for Belwyn. I clear my throat, indignation and betrayal wrestling within my chest. Her brows lift in surprise, as if she hadn't noticed me sitting a hand width to his right. "Oh, I'm sorry. I didn't realize you'd brought someone with you."

"You know this person?" I ask Belwyn, my tone flat.

He gets to his feet, brushing grit from his pants and offering a hand to help me up. I take it only because I'm not sure what else to do.

"Belwyn—"

"You're right, Amyrah," he breathes. "Coming here was a mistake."

"We never did have a moment to ask each other's names." The girl cocks her mouth in a coy smile and adjusts a small wooden crate filled with clinking bottles on her hip. "I'm Jaki. Nice to *finally* meet you, Belwyn." Eyes that match her dress seek out the necklace below my chin. "I believe you've already had the misfortune of meeting my parents."

I narrow my gaze to hide my confusion.

"Izra and Anit. I do believe you've met, yes? My father speaks very . . ." She cocks an eyebrow and tilts her chin. "Well, no, he doesn't waste words on you at all."

My lips part and I struggle to come to my own defense, but Belwyn is more than done with this conversation. Refusing to acknowledge Jaki, he lays a hand between my shoulder blades and urges me away from her.

And I submit because I haven't yet established the degree to which I am furious with him.

17
WEHNA

SOLA VINARI'S HORN SOUNDS AGAIN, a triumphant roar greeting what must be another lifeless Light Creature as it is carried into the Vale on the backs of the hunters. Like every time before, Elyōn's faithful ignore the summons to the Reckoning Grounds, where the valefolk will trade sola blood for peace with the kaligorven. Arvo and I do not attend, staying instead in Ellithïm to shiver in the dark, eat simple food, and petition the Highest for forgiveness while the rest of Utsanek feasts for the seventh night in three weeks.

I stay with them because it's the right thing to do.

So this is how Myrzeth intends to steal the sola brossa's luminescence without causing a stir among the valefolk. With such an abundance of glowing bones and a surplus of rich food to distract them, the greater population does not care how many bones are going missing, or why.

He's brilliant.

Ten of us, including Orlagh Bekyr, sit in the unfeeling shadows, hands joined around the Perens' too-small kitchen table. Even the height of Zomré's heat can't challenge the chill that fills this room of unanswered prayers and waning hopes.

"Highest, strengthen us to stay faithful to you when our hearts quake within our chests. Give us courage to stand against wickedness," Bryn whispers.

Orlagh's soft hand clasps mine tighter, and pressure builds behind my eyes.

Since we opened Ellithïm to the rest of Utsanek, it has felt like I have been holding my breath, waiting for that first scream to rend the night. None has come, although I swear I've seen kaligorven crawling through the shadows outside my window when I should be sleeping. I'm not sure whether it's my constant headache, Arvo's bony limbs, or fear that has kept me awake.

Despite my unflagging exhaustion, it's impossible to keep my eyes closed as we pray. I let my gaze move around the room, taking in the serene faces caught up in silent longings. A pair of bolétis sits in the center of the table, providing all the light we can risk on Reckoning Ceremony nights. Their illumination just reaches around the circle.

I watch Elodie's lips purse in earnest agreement with her father's words, which I don't bother paying attention to. Our mutual encounter with the kaligorven and Myrzeth, coupled with the loss of Ellithïm's secrecy, has had a sobering effect on her. Although it's a relief she's no longer pestering me about finding a mystery boy or making me arrange her hair only to pull half of it down, her subdued state feels all wrong. She's thirteen. She *should* be fussed about relationships and her appearance, not hiding in fear.

My eyes drift to Tress seated on the other side of Elodie. The woman is benevolence itself, bending to all the tasks set before her without a hint of resentment and graciously accommodating the dozens of people her husband shepherds through their lives. Yet she is firm with her daughters, ensuring that they are competent and self-controlled individuals, even in the middle of what I consider exceptional circumstances.

I wonder if she locks her anxieties away or if she truly doesn't have any.

Subtle movement farther down the line of chairs draws my focus, and chagrin seizes me when Arvo's pale eyes latch onto mine. A spiral of hair springs loose and falls over his forehead when he cocks his chin. I feign embarrassment, mouthing the word "whoops" as I dramatically close my eyes.

Acting, acting, always acting.

"*Elyōn erit agértu,*" Bryn says with more volume than the rest of his prayer. Everyone repeats this declaration.

Except me.

With a babble of subdued conversation, the basket of bread and a platter of goat shanks swimming in a red sauce makes its way around the circle. I pass on the latter, not at all in the mood to eat. When I go to hand the basket of baked goods to Lissi on my left, Orlagh keeps her hold on it. I frown.

"Do you want more?" I ask dumbly.

She clicks her tongue. "Child, no good will ever come of starvin' yerself." Her chin dips toward the small, fragrant loaves. "Feelin' sorry for yerself cheapens the trials of others, and I'll not thank yeh for scorning my hard work."

Thus chastened, I take one, and she lets go of the basket, which I thrust at Lissi.

Under Orlagh's watchful eye, I take a bite of the herb-infused bread.

My stomach responds by cramping with the hunger I've refused to acknowledge. Tears threaten, and I find it difficult to swallow past the emotions corking my throat.

Grabbing a pitcher, Orlagh pours water into my earthenware cup. I stare at it before taking a long drink. When I set it down and gasp for breath, Orlagh's kindly face spreads into a smile.

"There yeh go. Now." She smears a generous dollop of butter onto a roll of her own. "Tell me what's eatin' at yer soul."

The quiet chatter buzzes around me, and although I try, I can't coax my voice to join it.

Orlagh takes her time eating, the silence between us easing into something less awkward when she hums a quiet tune. The knot between my shoulders loosens.

"I don't see the purpose of it," I blurt hoarsely.

"Purpose of what?"

"Of existing in this place."

She chuckles. "Oh, is tha' all?"

When she notes my stormy expression, she makes an effort to hide her mirth. "And where else d'yeh think we are supposed to exist?"

I bite my lip, that old tug of responsibility staying the words I want to say. When my parents brought Arvo and me here, they insisted that I should never speak of what lies outside the Vale. *These people have a long history of turmoil, Wehna. There's no way of telling what they know or what information could prove harmful to them. It's not our goal to remove them from their circumstances. We are here to bring light for their souls, not their houses.*

As if sensing my inner conflict, Orlagh pushes her plate aside and rests an arm around my shoulders. "Yeh might be surprised by the things an old widow knows," she whispers. Her soft touch is enough to unspool my apprehensions.

"Orlagh, there's . . . there's more out there. A world of light where people don't have to fight or kill to get it. That's where me and my brother—where my parents—come from. *Came* from." I loop a finger under the braided bracelet Arvo gave me and twist it around my wrist. "I don't understand why anyone would choose this place, or why it would be bad to break this delusion they're all living under. All these people could be *free* if they woke up." Slipping my sleeve over my fist, I erase my errant tears with a rough swipe and seek out what Orlagh thinks of my confession.

Her face is about as placid as the wrinkles netting it will allow. "Yeh think tha' evil is contained in this dark place, tha' it doesn't roam beyond the borders of the ténesomni?" She nods solemnly when my eyes widen. "Tha's right. I am fully aware these shadows aren't a thing of Elyōn's intention."

"So why don't you say something to them?" I grab her hand and hold it between both of mine. "All we need to do is convince a few people that this"—I look up and all around the darkened room—"is not natural. It's not a life worth living."

Orlagh's expression, which had been a bittersweet mix of sad and wistful, twists with grief. "Wehna girl, tha's exactly what my husband thought all those years ago, and he convinced me of the same." Her arm slips off my back, and she claps a shaking hand on top of mine. "And I don't deny he was right. All the old tales and songs and books spoke of the 'ligh' of day' as if it were an unapologetic truth, not a thing tha' only the dreamers believed in. This idea took hold o' us. Perhaps, though, it was fear tha' drove us to it. The Shrouded were attacking so many, righ' in the streets, and the blood of a hundred solas couldn't satisfy their anger. Even my own three boys were caught up in it, but I don't blame them for their hope." She closes her eyes and holds her breath for a time. Tears that reflect the silver-blue bolétis crawl down her channel-engraved cheeks.

I recall the story the librarian told me about the great exodus that ended in a massacre, and regret cinches my insides like a noose. "Oh, Orlagh, I'm sorry. You don't have to put yourself through this."

She pulls her hand from mine and holds it out to stop me. "Nay." After giving her head a quick shake, her eyes open and she smiles through her tears. "It's not a bad thing to feel."

A peal of impish laughter, followed by a stern chorus of shushing, interrupts the heaviness of the moment. I watch Arvo and Téah hide their giggles behind their hands, Elodie leaning forward and scowling at the pair of them.

I blink a few times, trying to refocus my thoughts as I turn back to Orlagh. "What—what happened?"

Withdrawing from me, she leans back in her chair and reaches trembling fingers to the edges of her frayed shawl, tugging it around her shoulders. "Ennis was such an earnest soul. He had a way about him, made people trust him. Within a for'night he had convinced a great many folks to leave the Vale, myself included. We had such complete faith that Elyōn would see us through the ténesomni unharmed." Her voice catches, and her fists clench tighter around her shawl. "But he didn't."

How like him.

Wild images of carnage fill my mind in Orlagh's silence, and I don't bother counteracting the thought.

Something silky tickles my leg, startling me and staunching the flow of these terrible thoughts. I pick up Lissi's white kitten, making sure to keep him below the table so Bryn won't scold me for breaking one of the Peren's dinnertime rules. The tiny thing rumbles contentedly in my lap as

I stroke its long fur with the backs of my fingers.

"I'm so sorry, Orlagh," I whisper.

She makes a visible effort to break free from her tortured recollections. "Nay, say nothin' of it, m'dear. It does my soul good to recall what led me to where I am today, though it brings me so much shame to think of how I raged at Elyōn for so many years since then. Fifty-five turns of the six seasons. Highest, has it been that long?"

Nell and Anwen, the youngest and the third oldest of the Peren sisters, interrupt our conversation. The former barrages Orlagh with a tight hug and the sort of grin my heart could feast on if it hadn't lost its appetite for loveliness an age ago.

"Tanks, Miss Ow-lah," Nell says shyly, looking at Anwen for approval.

"For?" her sister prompts.

"Fo baking wif me," the sweet toddler declares, jabbing a finger at her pudgy cheek.

Anwen winks at her. "We want to help you again, if you'll let us."

Delighted, Nell bounces up and down. "Bake now?"

"No, Nell. Mada told us to clean up dinner, remember?"

Nell gasps, holding out her hands expectantly.

"Ah, well. Yeh'd best not dillydally," Orlagh replies, entrusting her plate to the little palms. "Hold tha' tight, sweet girl."

Anwen takes the rest of the dishes from us, patiently moving around the table behind Nell, collecting the rest. She is very responsible for an eight-year-old. I was still an only child at that age, with no idea how privileged I was. And yet, watching Anwen happily help her baby sister, I can't help thinking that their life isn't as terrible as my traitorous heart would lead me to believe.

Chairs scrape the floor and feet shuffle about the room as everyone else gets up. Tress wipes her hands on her apron as she glances at me and Orlagh, then shepherds everyone out, including Arvo, who doesn't look my way as he scampers from the room.

I used to be so concerned about losing him that I tried to never let him stray from me, but he doesn't seem to want much to do with me anymore. And there's always one of the Peren girls around to keep an eye out for him.

Orlagh sighs longingly in the quiet. I try to imagine her as a young mother of Tress's age, but with a busy household of sons instead of daughters.

"When I watched my dear Ennis and my boys get ripped from me," she continues, as if there hadn't been a pause in the conversation, "I declared in my heart tha' I'd never do the Highest the honor of acknowledging his name again."

Oh . . . What inconceivable horrors this poor woman has suffered.

A rueful chuckle bounces her shoulders. "Yet all that did was rob me of the foundation beneath my feet, and I feel like I've been fightin' sand ever since."

I look down at the kitten but see, instead, the nightmarish image of my parents lying on the roadside. I swallow. "Well, I can't blame you. I don't understand how something like that could be acceptable to an all-powerful deity."

"Oh, child, no. Don't think such things of our Elyōn. Don't you think for one moment tha' this pain 'n destruction doesn't rip his heart out. This world—all of it—is broken, and I have faith Elyōn will stoop to breakin' himself to set it to rights."

Keeping my eyes fixed on the kitten, I shift in my seat. My father and mother used to say similar things to me, yet their faith didn't save them.

I clear my throat and look at Orlagh once more, attempting to steer the conversation out of such painful waters. "If what you say is true and there is no safe way for a large group to leave the Vale, then there truly is no escape."

Not for everyone, but maybe there could be for Arvo and me.

"Ah, now yeh've hit upon the one regret I haven't been able to shake for fifty-five years. I wish to the heights that Ennis and I could've seen how stayin' here in the Vale, though sure to be difficult, could still be good. If I could talk to him now, I am almost certain he'd agree tha' the absence of trial is not what makes a life worth livin'."

A sob tumbles from her thin lips, and she stifles it with her fingers. "Perhaps I'd have little grand bairns of my own gathered 'round my feet," she says after lowering her hand, her voice thick with emotion. Her muddy eyes find mine. "But then I wouldn't be so invested in the sweet souls Elyōn has led my way for guidance, would I?" She cups my cheek. "Yours included, dear."

The first genuine smile I have felt in longer than I can remember pulls at the corner of my mouth. And, weak though it may be, it lifts an entire house's weight of stress from my mind.

Dumping the kitten unceremoniously, I stand, wincing when my temples pound from the motion, and offer a hand to Orlagh. She accepts the help, letting out a soft groan as she struggles to her feet.

"How can you see light when there is only darkness?" I ask, my tone easy, though the question is anything but.

Orlagh leans into me as we exit the room and walk down the hall. "Because, Wehna. Darkness is everywhere we go, in every heart tha' we meet, in every corner of this world. I choose to trust the One who is capable of bringin' beauty from the corruption."

For a fleeting moment, I almost glimpse the purpose behind why my parents brought our family to this place. It wasn't out of a sense of duty to an exacting deity or because they valued other people's lives more than their own family. They had faith that through their sacrifice, they would witness the Highest's work firsthand.

Why couldn't they do that outside the Vale? I question petulantly.

Why can't you do it from within? another voice counters.

The thought is so ridiculous, I want to dismiss it, but Orlagh's words give me pause. Could Arvo and I find peace here too?

But there is a sinister presence that governs this place, fighting tooth and claw to steal all that is good and bury it deep. It seizes my hope, rending it with a piercing wail that splits the night.

Fearing the worst, I yank my arm from Orlagh's grip and rush into the dismal street.

I blink and strain my useless eyes, wishing to the stars that there were still bolétis to illuminate the path. Another scream fills the air, sapping the strength from my legs. They threaten to buckle, and I struggle to stand.

Close to the end of the street, where the clever gate that used to protect Ellithïm now stands open, the ténesomni collects into a frenzied cyclone. I lurch when I see a small shape beneath it, a cry tumbling like shattered glass from my lips.

"Arvo!"

Pinned against the side of a building, my brother cowers before a towering, hideous creature. Shadows leap and dive from its bestial frame as it arches its back, hackles raised. A sepulchral moan cracks through the cool air, and my splintering shriek rises to challenge it.

"Plea-ease, *no.*"

Not him too.

"Shadow beast." A voice commands its attention, and it freezes with ragged claws held high. Bryn steps into the center of the street. "Who gave you dominion over the fidrélas?" he bellows.

Footsteps echo behind me as Tress runs up, braid whipping forward when she skids to a stop and presses a hand to her mouth.

The kaligorva lowers itself to grip the earth with elongated claws. Bryn's provocation takes hold, and the beast turns, its glowing red eyes fixing onto a more tantalizing target.

Arvo whimpers. It takes everything in me to resist running to him, but I know I must not move. I can't risk drawing attention to myself or to him.

A laugh peels from Bryn's mouth, the mocking sound incongruent with my terror. He disappears between two buildings, and the Shrouded gives chase, pulling the ténesomni with it like a cloth whisked away from a table.

Tress scrambles after them while I spring to Arvo, gathering him into quaking limbs.

"Wehna," he sobs into my shoulder.

"*Shh*. You're fine. *We* are fine. It's gone. It's gone now. *Shh* . . ."

A roar. A scream.

I whip my head around to see Elodie staring at the place her father and mother disappeared, arms limp by her sides. Fighting for courage, I find my feet and carry Arvo to her.

"Here, Elodie."

She turns and stares at me in a glazed stupor.

"*Take. Him*," I say through gritted teeth.

She blinks several times, pulling Arvo to her abdomen in a daze when I set him down. "My Pa—"

"Knows what he's doing." Another roar shreds the night. Placing my hands on the girl's shoulders, I give her a little shake until she looks me in the eyes. "You need to be strong, Elodie."

Biting her lip, she gives a tiny, determined nod.

I follow the sounds—of what, I can't tell, wish I didn't have to find out—and extend my arms in front of me as I crash through the opaque black. I haven't gone far when a light bursts from up high, as bright as the sunrise spilling between the Askonnet Mountains. A sensation like stepping out from a waterfall and into a hot spring arrests me. I shield my eyes, trying to see what is causing it, but I can't make anything come into focus.

Instead, I search for the source of a keening wail that bounces between the buildings, dreading what lies ahead.

A woman kneels on the cobblestones, gathering the limp form of a man into her lap. Not just any woman. *Tress*. She moves her hands from Bryn's chest to his face, a trail of blood following the touch of her fingers. For a terrible moment, I think he's dead, but his chest lurches and he coughs out a mouthful of blood. Tress wipes it away with her skirt, bending over him to kiss his forehead.

The kaligorva is gone.

My pulse hammers in my throat, in my ears. "This—" I gasp, swallowing the bile that has crawled up my throat. "This is my fault."

I slacked in my responsibility to watch Arvo, and now someone else is hurt.

If this is what believing in Elyōn leads to, then is he worth trusting at all?

Shaking her head forcefully, Tress gulps in two, three breaths. She takes care to rest Bryn's head gently on the unforgiving street.

"No. *Myrzeth*." The name exudes from her like ténesomni as she crawls, shaking hands finding a low wall to help her find her feet. "Foremost or not, he is the one who must answer for this."

Three high-pitched chirps call out from the roofline, and this time I recognize the shape of a small, incandescent bird as it flutters away.

Leaving us in complete darkness.

18

BELWYN

"TALK TO ME, AMYRAH."

She brushes past my shoulder, refusing to meet my eyes, like she has been doing for two days. I've given her space, but my patience is frayed and I'm struggling to hold on to the strands. I stand in the corridor of Sabine's house for a breath, curling my fingers to quell the anger that could leap so readily in response, before turning and following her out the front door.

The air outside suffocates with its humidity and warmth. "Believe me when I say that nothing happened between Jaki and me. I didn't even know her name."

She laughs without humor and doesn't slow, her hair bouncing as she runs down the steps.

I pick up my pace, almost tripping in my haste. "*Please*. Stop shutting me out like this."

She spins around, her clear blue eyes wide and cold, like an ice-cloaked loch. "When you said we were meant to face what comes together, did you mean it?"

I pull up like I've hit a wall. "Of course I did. Do you think I would have left everything behind if I didn't?"

She fixes her gaze to a point past my ear. "I find it interesting how 'together' means you and me and *Jaki*."

"Amyrah," I groan. "*Stop*."

"Stop what?"

"Insinuating something has happened here." I catch her hand, squeezing it tighter than I intend, and her eyes flick up. I ease my grip. "I am here for no one but you." Lifting her hand between us, I fold it in both of mine and hold it below my chin. "And nothing is going to change that."

Shining tears fall down her freckled cheeks. She shakes her head and looks away.

I brush a thumb over her knuckles. "What are you really upset about?"

For a moment, she softens. "I-I don't know. Nothing." A sigh. "Everything." When she pulls her arm, I let it swing free. Raising her chin, she looks at the sliver of sky peeking between the trees. "I have no purpose here."

"That's not true."

Her gaze drops. "Isn't it? Ketsé has already been warned about what's coming. My attempt to stop the ténesomni only delayed it for a while."

"But it helped, and I'm sure you'll be able to do it again if you try."

She blinks, dismissing the suggestion. "And you?"

"What about me?"

"I know you have your own regrets for leaving the Vale. You shouldn't feel like you're shackled to me."

"That is *not* it at all," I say, but I'm unable to keep a twinge of doubt from my voice, because I can't think of my mother and brothers, and even my father, without some regret that I am here and they are not.

Amyrah, perceptive as always, angles her chin and watches me with a soft sadness on her face. "I can't comprehend why you would leave them and come with me when it caused you so much pain."

"You needed . . ." I stumble over my words and fight back a groan.

What is happening? *Why is she choosing to bring this up now*? She's unsettled, on edge. Ready for a fight or trying to push me away. The last thing she will want is me dictating what she needs, so I switch tactics. "It was to protect you."

"From what? My own ineptitude?"

When I frown, she presses her hands to her face and closes her eyes. "I couldn't challenge him, Belwyn. I had done it before, and I should have been able to when it mattered most. I could have stopped him."

"No. Don't do that. Don't take that blame on yourself. It's possible you could have been a match for Myrzeth, but there was no hope against dozens of kaligorven. Your father chose to save you in the best way he knew how, and he did the right thing."

She shakes her head adamantly.

"And I pulled you out of there because, well, when I saw you standing on that platform with Myrzeth prowling around you like some feral animal . . ." Hesitantly, I guide her hands away from her face and touch my forehead to hers. "Amyrah, I was scared I would lose you."

She stifles a sob and we pull together, sharing air, oblivious to those who pass us by. After a moment, Amyrah angles away, biting her lip. "But that's it. We *don't* belong to each other, Belwyn, do we? Not really. We're two strangers who happened to be thrown together."

Something collides deep inside my core, sending spider web cracks racing through my thoughts. My fingers slip from her wrists.

She pales, her eyes widening. "I-I'm sorry. I'm sorry."

I turn and pace a few steps to collect myself.

"You should have left me," she whispers. "I don't deserve you, and I don't deserve to be free from the ténesomni."

Shelving the sledgehammer of her words to deal with later, I blink and run a hand through my hair, staring at her. "What are you talking about? If anyone was made for the light, it was you."

Amyrah takes a small step back, wrapping her arms around herself. A rectangular shape bulges in the front pocket of her green overdress—likely the book she won't go anywhere without.

"My gift is not what you think, Belwyn," she whispers. "It scares me. My uncle told me that the Luvesti are not only skilled with light, but also with shadow. What he is, what he can do . . . What if that is what *I* become? What if I end up adding to the shadows I was so sure I was meant to destroy?"

"No. *No*. I don't believe you could ever do that."

She throws her arms out wide. The star pendant bounces at her throat. "You saw it back in that cavern. I let the darkness in once already. It jumped to my call, and it was easy, *so easy* to invite it. That was the only way I could keep myself from burning up, yet it felt like I sacrificed a piece of my soul to do it. What if there comes a moment when I need the ténesomni again, and I don't have the strength to keep it from consuming me?" Her arms drop. "What if it hurts someone?"

I step forward, intent on bringing some sort of assurance to end this whole disorienting argument. "I *won't* let that happen."

"It's no kaligorva, Belwyn. Do you expect a sword will do anything against it?"

"*Shades*, Amyrah." My voice swells to a dangerous timbre. "Why can't you let me protect you? Will you not let me try?"

She hides her face in her hands and sobs. "Because I can't let you get hurt too."

My vexation eases and I pull her hands away from her face, waiting for her eyes to seek mine again. "Getting hurt is a part of living."

She scowls. "It shouldn't be."

I lean closer. "You're hurting right now. Don't you think it breaks my heart to see it?" My gaze dips to her freckles, to her lips. "It would be my privilege to bear your pain with you, Amyrah Cantar. That's what I want to be for you, but I can't do that if you refuse to let me."

Slipping her hands out of mine, she pushes away. "It . . . it's better this way."

I trap a breath in my lungs and try to hold back my frustration, but my words come out forceful and exasperated. "No. We're better *together*."

"Are you two alright?"

I cringe. It's just like Holden to show up right when I'm on the verge of losing myself. My back tenses and I keep it turned to him as I answer through gritted teeth. "We're fine, thanks."

He walks into view and stops beside us, hands buried in pockets, brow knit with concern. "I was coming to ask you something, Amyrah. If now is a good time, that is."

I open my mouth to tell him off, but Amyrah swaps the pained expression she's worn this whole conversation with relief when she regards him. The rage within me grows. I take a shaky breath, trying to rein it in.

"Look, just . . . don't throw me out completely," I mutter, refusing to look her in the eye. "I'm sure you can find some use for me if you try."

I whip around, knocking a shoulder into Holden and throwing him off-balance as I leave.

19

AMYRAH

"ARE YOU SURE YOU'RE FINE?" Holden asks.

I shake my head to fling my own hurt, confusion, and remorse far away. "No. *Yes*, I mean." I press my fingers to my forehead and take a calming breath. "We were only talking."

He gives me an appraising look, and I refuse to let it convince me to confide in him. Dropping my hand, I force my features into something more open, as if my heart hasn't cracked in two. "What did you want to ask me?"

His eyes narrow, but he motions his chin toward the street. "Walk with me?"

We go in awkward silence to the nature preserve area Belwyn and I had visited before.

My thoughts are barbed as they slink through my mind, but I can't halt their progression or stop them from tearing me to shreds. *Why did you treat Belwyn like that, Amyrah?*

There isn't an answer that absolves me of my guilt. Just one that makes no sense whatsoever.

If I can convince myself I have never had him, then I can't lose him.

Turning away from the paths below the trees, Holden heads to a narrow flight of stairs carved around a thick trunk, waiting for me to ascend ahead of him. Whatever he has to say, he must be eager that no one will overhear it.

I squash down my apprehensions and climb, gasping by the time I reach the top. Embarrassed by being so easily winded, I decide not to wait for Holden to catch up and walk out onto the suspended walkway to catch my breath. The slats beneath my feet jerk to the side, and I throw out my hands to catch guardrails made of twisted vines.

"Don't worry. You'll get your bridge legs yet."

Heart in my throat, I shoot him a dark look over my shoulder. "Bridge legs? Really?" I continue to cross with more caution, noticing a couple women walking with ease across a similar walkway on the other side of the nature sanctuary. "I suppose gallivanting in the treetops comes as second nature to Ketsans."

Holden does not respond.

Thank the Highest, I make it to a large viewing platform with comfortable seating lining the railings. My footing no longer quakes beneath me, and my muscles unspool.

"I've been wanting to talk to you for a while," Holden says, gesturing toward one of the benches. I sit, and he follows.

"Really? What about?" My abdomen tightens nervously. Several things jump to mind, starting with either my Vale upbringing or my Luvesti heritage. I don't want to talk about either.

Scratching his neck, Holden seems to struggle to find the right words. He resolutely avoids my eyes, his gaze settling on the angular bulge in my dress pocket. "What's that?"

"Oh." I hesitate, wondering if such a precious thing should be shared. I search Holden's face and find nothing but genuine kindness. And something familiar I can't name.

His features aren't like anyone I recognize: rich green eyes, a sharp jaw, and hair that toes the line between blond and auburn. He seems a fair amount older than me, but not as old as my uncle. Perhaps in his early twenties? Something about him puts me at ease, and when one of his eyebrows tips up and his mouth stretches into a grin, I pull out the book and rest it on my lap.

"It belonged to my mother." I brush a finger across the gilded title. "I brought it with me from the Vale because I thought it could give me some insight into who she was, and I hoped I would find someone who could interpret the things written in it."

"May I?"

I consider stuffing it back in my pocket, but that instinct to trust him grows. Slowly, I hold it out to him.

Holden accepts it and flips through the pages.

"Do you recognize anything?" I can't keep the pathetic note of hope from my voice.

He's quiet, pausing to read a few lines. A frown creases his brow, casting his deep-set eyes in shadow. He swallows, smoothing his features.

"No." He tilts his head, eyes narrowing at the missing pages. "I can't say I do. It's beautiful writing, though."

Hope snuffs out inside of me, but I hide it with a false smile. "I was wondering if it had originated from Ketsé."

Holden glances up. "This? No. Definitely not. It's much too poetic for them—us," he corrects.

My eyebrows arch at the slip.

"Trust me. It's more like . . ." He shakes his head. His eyes find mine, and he avoids the question in my gaze. "What did your mother tell you about it?"

I clear my throat and try to move past his evasiveness. "She . . . well, I don't remember much of her. She died a long time ago."

Narrowing his gaze, Holden looks inside the cover at the initials. "How long?"

"Thirteen years."

His frown deepens, and I wish I could interpret the meaning behind his expression.

"Was this what you wanted to talk to me about?"

"No." He blinks several times, passing the book back. "No, I wanted to ask you about that song you were singing the other day."

"The song?"

He leans back against the railing and takes me in. "You know, the one I caught you serenading Belwyn with."

Warmth rushes to my cheeks. "That was *not* a serenade."

Holden smirks. "Whatever you want to call it, fine, but I heard enough to know that it was a *moment*."

My cheeks burn. To think of me singing love songs to a boy.

Not any boy. *Belwyn*.

I try to rub away the heat, to no avail.

Holden laughs, getting to his feet and walking to the boundary of the platform. "I feel like I recognize the tune, and it made me curious."

Thankful that I have a moment without his scrutinizing eyes on me, I swallow and take a slow breath before joining him at the railing.

"Where would you have heard it?"

He watches the leaves fluttering around us. "I'm not sure. It reminded me of something from long ago. It felt familiar."

I slip the book into my overdress pocket and exhale. "The words used to be in this book, until I tore it out." I wince at the wrongness of the confession.

Abandoning the view, Holden squares his shoulders with me. "Wait. That song was written in there as well?"

"Yes." I frown, then my eyes grow wide with hope. "Is that important?"

As he opens his mouth to answer, a bright flash from below catches my attention. I grip the rail and lean out as far as I dare, peering at the forest floor. Holden's hand grasps my forearm tentatively.

"Did you see that?" I whisper.

"See what?"

I brush my hair out of my face. "For a moment I thought—"

Liquid luminescence spills through the trees for a heartbeat more, blinding and bouncing and as stunning as I remember. It disappears again, and I press a hand to my mouth. "A sola."

The smile in Holden's voice dies. "Solas don't come to Ketsé."

But he is wrong. He *must be* wrong.

I slip out of his grasp and hurry across the bridge, no longer frightened by the way it sways.

"Amyrah, wait."

Heedless and much too reckless to be safe, I descend the steps, stumbling when I get to firm ground.

The brilliance explodes again, and I squint against the discomfort in my eyes.

"You should stop and think about this," he calls, his footsteps sounding behind me.

"It looks like a rabbit of some sort." I run the best I can through the low-growing foliage, fixing my eyes to the darting form.

Holden curses, chasing me with crashing steps.

I was right. It *is* a rabbit and most definitely a sola. The little hare bounds through the ferns, jumping nimbly over branches and ducking under brambles. My pulse quickens, my feet scrambling to match it. I can't explain why I am so desperate to catch up with it, except that my heart yearns for something familiar, something *pure*, in this kingdom of unknowns.

The sola loops around before halting near the boundary of the preserved forest area. I make myself slow, ragged gasps tearing through me as I struggle to keep quiet. I can't bear the thought of scaring it off, and I cringe as I think of Holden bumbling through and ruining everything.

But it turns out he's skilled at being quiet when he wants to be.

Taking two, three careful steps and nudging my toes under the ground cover before putting my weight on them, I creep forward. The beautiful creature noses under a fern, casting striped shadows across my dress, even though plenty of daylight streams between the trees from the midday sun. When it is within reach, I crouch and hold out my hand, gently lifting the fern away. Curious, the sola stands to its hind legs and twitches its twinkling nose in the air. Warmth embraces me as though I am seated near a hearth, and I catch my lip between my teeth. Spiraling lines of brighter light ripple through its glossy fur, dancing like wind across meadow grass.

"Hello, my friend."

A harsh whistle breaks the moment's spell, and the resulting alarm causes me to fall into the soft loam. I gape as the rabbit sola jumps into the arms of a girl with black hair and a charcoal dress girded with a belt.

As soon as her fingers touch the rabbit's fur, its glow dies.

"Did you seek to steal my pet from me?" She laughs as she straightens, the sound devoid of warmth. Holding the rabbit close to her chest, she runs her hands over the length of its ears. "No doubt you believe every single light-bearing creature belongs to you."

Shaking my head, I push myself off the ground. "I only wanted to see it, Jaki."

"I'm not a morvus, Amyrah. You don't know what it's like to have been brought up in a world that's been distorted by the Luvesti's actions. They abandoned us to guard a volatile border that should never have been created in the first place. They can't be bothered to dwell with the problem they created, yet they still think they alone have the right to wield light." Her gray gaze pins me. "But you and I know that's a ridiculous hypocrisy."

"What do you mean?" Holden asks, coming to stand several feet to my left. I've never seen him so tense.

"Oh, she knows. The line between light and darkness is remarkably thin, isn't it?"

Shame forces down my throat, weighing uncomfortably in my stomach. Jaki must know what happened in the Low Market. It was ridiculous to believe the gossip about what happened—what I *made* happen—wouldn't spread like wild ignati.

I feel Holden's probing look. Does he know? He makes me want to hide the truth of my dark side from him. I raise my chin, disguising my guilt. "I wouldn't know."

She barks out a derisive laugh. "A liar, like the rest of them. I didn't expect anything different."

Holden points a finger threateningly and leans forward. "Careful."

"And why should I be? You aren't any better than her."

It's my turn to shoot Holden a glance and his turn to pretend he didn't see it.

I spin back to Jaki. "What do you mean?"

She keeps her eyes fixed on him and angles her shoulders. "No one knows much about you, Holden. There's no word on your parentage, and I don't think anyone remembers you as you were growing up. Ketsé isn't *that* big, is it?"

"I'm good at keeping out of city affairs," Holden replies in a low tone.

"And I'm good at seeing things from the shadows." She drinks in his steely response like a cold beverage. "There's also the question about how someone so young has been accepted into the Watch with so little information about his history. These people should be aware that there's a snake in their midst."

Holden's jaw clenches, but he doesn't defend himself.

Who is he?

"But that's not why I arranged this little meeting." Jaki sinks her weight into one hip and holds the rabbit higher, looking at it adoringly. "I would rather discuss the absurdity of most Ketsans. So many of them can't grasp that we don't have to be devoted solely to light *or* shadow. We can dabble in a bit of both."

I slip my hands into my front pocket, feeling the grounding edges of the book's pages beneath my fingers. "They can't dwell with each other. It's not what Elyōn designed."

Jaki cocks an eyebrow. "One could argue that *you* have disproved that theory. And maybe Elyōn isn't the only player in this game."

"You do realize you're cursing the ground you stand on, right?" asks Holden, his face growing pale.

She shrugs and shifts to address me, not him. "It might seem like you're welcome in Ketsé, but that's a necessity while the idiotic Nocilium tries to figure out what's happening out there. If you stay here long enough, though, you'll find what people like me think of you."

My arms tremble, threatening to give out beneath me, but I will my voice to be firm. "What do you think of me?"

Her smirk changes into a scowl. "That you're an insipid example of goodness that no one will ever be able to compare to."

From the cover of the trees, three others emerge, their hoods washing their faces in shadow.

"Figured the best way to reel in a Luvesti would be with a sola," the one sneers. He is tall and skeletal. Limp, yellow hair escapes from his hood. The other shape snickers and cracks his fingers.

The third is nothing more than a rounded silhouette prowling behind them.

My skin crawls as if invisible insects cover it. I rub my palms over my arms to smooth away the sensation. Holden steps close, pressing a hand to the space between my shoulders, the tension in his fingertips like sparks.

"What is this?" His voice is low, forbidding.

"A lesson." Jaki does not acknowledge the presence of her cohorts. "We think you need a reminder that there is darkness in everyone."

With a swift motion, she grabs something from her hip. Too late, I see that it's a small knife. She flicks it across the rabbit's throat, sending a stream of sola blood to dampen the earth. It shines brighter than the sun. With a twitch of her lips, Jaki tilts her chin and lets the animal slip out of her hands.

"*No*," I sob, tearing from Holden's grip and falling to my knees before the slain animal. The brightness of the rabbit's lifeblood swirls in my tear-blinded eyes as I stroke its cold fur. "W-why did you have to do that?"

Insidious laughter twists around us from the three shadowy figures, but Jaki remains silent. I feel Holden brush past me, hear him slip a dagger from its sheath, smell the strange yet sweet tang of the sola's blood. The three strangers flee like cowards.

"You've made your point." Holden's words travel to me as if from a great distance. "What more do you want?"

"A visible reminder."

I'm dimly aware of Jaki turning around, bending to pick something up, but I am too defeated to care.

Until a black, foul liquid pours over my head. I scramble back, shrieking as it stings my eyes, dribbles into my mouth. I cough and choke and paw at my face, my hands coming away black.

"*Wretch,*" Holden shouts.

The sound of shattering pottery erupts, and a venomous curse follows it. Quick footsteps approach through the bracken, barely audible above my sobs. For a breath, a hand rests on my shoulder. Then it slips away.

"Get back here," Holden shouts, but Jaki's lilting laughter echoes between the trees, fading, leaving the forest silent.

My dress lies in a crumpled heap in the corner of the bathroom, stained beyond saving. The substance Jaki dumped over me was an acidic dye, and it has not left me unscathed. My skin is bright red and raw. My eyes, blurred and stinging. All traces of the incriminating black have been scoured away, except for what clings to the thick band of hair that hangs in front of my face. Scrunching the section in my hands, I try to squeeze out the inky stains, but the water comes out clear.

Jaki wasn't lying when she said she'd leave me with a visible reminder.

I pull myself from the tub, each limb weighing more than it should, and curve into a dripping ball in front of the hearth. Even the fire cannot counter the chill that has claimed me. Grasping a thin sheet, I wrap it around my naked, shivering body.

I want to forget the image of the bleeding sola, to erase Jaki's words and convince myself the whole incident didn't happen. The longer I dwell on it, though, the more I realize I can't.

Because she's right. My heart holds the capacity for both light and dark, good and evil.

A shudder takes me. I can still feel the exhilaration of the ténesomni as it flowed through my veins in the cavern, thrilling to douse all goodness. I am capable of so much more corruption than I thought.

It frightens me.

I pull my hair over a shoulder and comb through it with my fingers, shaking it out in front of the ignati's heat.

What was the purpose of that elaborate ambush, other than to convince me I am no better than anyone else? That's a lesson I thought I knew intimately.

No, there had to be more to it than that. Holden said it was an attempt to intimidate me because Jaki feels threatened, because she fears what she does not understand.

But I think she wanted to provoke me into using the Luvesti abilities I have not yet fully tapped.

The question I have been asking myself for two days screams to be acknowledged: if I am equally divided between light and darkness, why should I cling to either?

I don't know. *I don't know.* It would be so much easier to let my soul swirl with gray, but I'm afraid that if I surrender to the ténesomni for even a moment more, I will lose myself forever.

Sighing, I slide the book away from my ruined garments and hold it in my lap. I'm so relieved the stain did not mar it. Thumbing its pages, I let its promises pass over me until my eyes land on a single sentence.

The light shines in the darkness, and the darkness cannot overcome it.

Confusion cramps my chest. How can this be true when I stand in such contrast? I want to believe that darkness trembles in light's presence, kneels before it in submission. I want to believe that light will always pierce through, no matter how insignificant.

But, oh, it is so hard.

There is one thing I do understand, though. Luvesti or not, I am in a battle that will either be won or lost within the conflict of what I want to do and what I can't stop myself from doing.

"Elyōn, help me," I plead. Silence answers.

"Amyrah, it's Belwyn."

I jump at the soft knock, scrambling to my feet and wrapping the sheet tighter around me. I feel exposed even though a locked door stands between us. "W-what do you want?"

I hear him exhale heavily, as if he's relieved to hear my voice. "Holden found me and told me what happened," he says.

There's a pause, like he's waiting for me to respond, but I don't know what to say.

"Are you . . . are you alright?"

I rest my forehead against the rough-hewn wood. "I think I will be."

More silence. I close my eyes, fearing that he left, but a gentle sound, like a hand sliding down the door frame, brushes my senses.

"Can I come in?" he asks softly.

Swallowing, I straighten, discard the sheet, and pad to the clothing draped over a chair. The linen of my old dress has become supple, sliding over my skin like a gentle caress, folding me in familiarity. I grab an earthy brown shawl and wrap it around my shoulders, easing into its warmth.

When I open the door, Belwyn is halfway down the hall. He turns when he hears the hinges squeak, his brow knit with worry. I can't meet his gaze, knowing how badly I've treated him. Closing the distance in three long strides, he grips my shoulders and pulls me into a tight hug.

All my anxieties unspool in his embrace.

After an eternity, he steps back and lets his eyes trace my features. When they catch on my half-dried hair, my cheeks warm and I reach to tuck the marred section behind my ear. His hand captures my fingers, pulling them away.

"Don't. You are always beautiful. Nothing in all Atsun could ever change that."

He threads an arm through mine and leads me down the hall. I rest my head on his shoulder and decide that no matter what comes in the following days, I'm done hurting him.

20

SEYLA

"BLOCK THE BLOW, BRÉINTH." Commander Verrek's tone slices far deeper than a blade. He rarely oversees the training exercises, yet now he's here, breathing down our necks, witnessing our exercises in person.

And he seems inordinately focused on *me.*

A frustrated grunt tears through my clenched jaw as I hold the sword at an angle across my body, taking the full force of an úramech nearly twice my size. This is nothing unusual, since I am the only woman in this Agmen regiment. Normally I can stand my ground, but today, the blows jolt me through my bones.

I have grown weak in my days of caring for Téron and neglecting my own training.

My opponent, the stringy-haired youth whom I humiliated the

other day, comes at me without mercy. He swings down his blade with a shout, and my legs buckle.

"A stalk of wheat would offer more resistance before a sickle blade." The young man cackles triumphantly, the sound fueling my rage.

Curse this unwieldy thing.

Using his distracted gloating to my advantage, I grab the khukuri from the sheath at my waist and lunge, sliding underneath his sword and launching back up to level my weapon at his throat.

"Th-this is a sword fight," he splutters, red creeping up his cheeks. But he drops his blade and holds his hands out in surrender.

I lean in so he can feel my breath hit his face. "Be sure to tell that to your real opponents before they slit your throat."

Our heated sparring has drawn a crowd around us, and they break out in chuckling and reluctant clapping. Satisfaction surges through my battle-warmed blood.

"Enough."

Both of us turn to regard our commander, who has stepped into the ring with an air of authority. I do not let my khukuri fall as his shrewd gaze travels from the youth's face and slides over my tight muscles.

"As much enjoyment as you get from taunting the men with these *wily* tactics"—Verrek's lip curls in a sneer that coats me in shame—"Lonn is correct. Were you not instructed to train in sword combat?"

The khukuri sags in my grip, suddenly heavy, like it is wrought from gold instead of hammered steel. "With respect, Commander, does it matter *how* I win?" I can feel my legs beginning to shake from the tension, and with a quick breath, I force my body to turn that weakness into strength. "I would think you would understand—"

My words are cut short by Verrek's quick advance. His eyes are lit with internal fire, and his hand juts out to clamp around my wrist. I bite my tongue to keep from crying out.

"Have you forgotten your place, úramech?"

The khukuri clatters to the packed earth, and I do not dare take my eyes from Verrek's feral glare.

"You have no idea what kind of man I am."

The other soldiers make no attempt to conceal their chuckles. Heat climbs up my collar.

Verrek peels his fingers from my wrist and steps back, his ire replaced with his usual cold, calculating expression.

"Pick up your sword, Bréinth, and fight in the instructed manner."

I work to keep my features neutral. What has brought on this change in demeanor toward me? Verrek may be harsh, but he is usually fair. Yet I did witness him rob Ordin of one of his ranks just for interrupting. I can't afford to provoke him into doing the same to me.

Straightening, I turn to face Lonn's smug visage again. "Yes, Commander."

The fighting resumes after we have both retrieved our swords, Lonn bearing down once more while I use my speed to my advantage, dodging most of his swings. But the man is ferocious, and when his steel crashes down with a sickening crunch on the bracer protecting my wound, a traitorous cry springs from my lips. My weapon drops from my hand.

I fall to the ground, pressing my screaming forearm to my chest and holding the other above me. "Stop," I plead.

Lonn's eyes are wild, his mouth stretched into a wicked grin.

"Excellent." Verrek bobs his chin at Lonn, who sheathes his sword and struts out of the ring.

I drop my hand and curl forward, the pain in my arm excruciating now that I can give myself a moment to feel it.

"Now, you."

Bewildered, I look up to find Verrek motioning another soldier, no less intimidating than Lonn, into the circle. The commander stares at me, and I do not understand.

"Up, Bréinth," he shouts, the air cracking around him.

He's punishing me for something. It's the only conclusion I can draw, even if it doesn't make sense. I do as he says and stand.

Verrek walks a few paces, clasping his hands behind his back. His plated armor clinks as the entire camp seems to hold its breath. "Show no mercy, even to the weak."

It's one thing to acknowledge my own weakness. It's another to have it proclaimed over me like an immutable fact. How have I ever shown that I am weak?

"To underestimate an opponent based on size or sex is to lose the battle."

The young úramech glances at me, doubt dancing in his eyes. "But, Commander, she is hurt."

Verrek pivots. "An injured animal is no less dangerous. Will you let that be your excuse when she stabs you in the back?" When the úramech is unable to make an intelligent reply, Verrek thrusts his chin toward us. "Fight."

I adjust my grip on the sword, compensating for my weakness with my non-injured hand. The young man faces me, issuing a jarring shout to shake away his cowardice.

I cock my mouth in a grin, as if this is nothing more than an amusing game, while my mind panics.

Ancestors, help me.

But they do not hear, and it only takes a few additional strikes for me to admit defeat.

I drag in ragged breaths, my lungs burning as I get to my feet again and look to my commander, but it would seem he is intent on breaking me completely. On and on the punishment goes, Verrek sending in a new opponent as soon as one has dropped me, until the simple effort to hold my sword above my waist draws tears of pain from my eyes.

All men are the same, Seyla. They can't stand when a woman holds power over them.

My mother's wisdom comes to me yet again, but I can't make sense of it. What power do I have over Verrek?

"Do not be taken in by a fair face, men," Verrek calls. "Let nothing stand in your path to victory."

I bite my tongue until I can taste blood, the sharpness of the pain distracting my mind from my fatigue, from my rage at how he's making an example of me. Why, I do not know.

From the corner of my eye, I see a bald pate edging through the crowd, and I fight to hold in a groan. Ordin. Has he come to belittle me, like he used to love to do, or will it be the version of him that seems to care for me? If he were to intervene on my behalf yet another time, I would never forgive him.

This is your *battle, Seyla. Fight it.*

But my strength is gone, and all I have left is words.

"Commander," I wheeze, the effort to project my voice more difficult than it should be. I force my spine into a soldier's posture, sweat slipping down the bridge of my nose and trickling between my shoulder blades, and look him in the eye. "Permission to speak?"

Verrek regards me with an icy gaze, then inclines his head.

I take a breath to collect myself, afraid that if I am not careful, I will fall apart at the seams. There is one chance to speak, one chance to be heard. If I do it wrong, it could be the end of my career.

Which might as well be the end of my life.

"The only thing you have accomplished is training us in excessive brutality." I will my voice not to waver. "I was defeated four opponents ago."

Verrek's eyes darken. "Yet you still have the ability to stand against me."

I swallow, knowing I am dangerously close to suffering a worse punishment than Ordin received.

At my silence, he circles me, then looks out at the rest of the regiment. "Make no mistake. Even a man one blink from death can be a threat to the Southlands."

There it is. He is making sure no one will even entertain the idea of repeating my action by rescuing enemy strangers.

Verrek turns to me again, a pitying smile flashing across his lips. Indignation threads through my thoughts. "We should not be surprised that you resorted to an entreaty to spare yourself pain. Just like a woman."

Laughter swirls around me, hitting harder than any of the strikes from my comrades' swords. I want to tune it out, to let it bounce off me, but for all the armor encasing me, I feel naked.

"No, Commander." I lower my eyes, hoping my deference appears genuine. "I only desired clarification."

The commander strides forward, stopping when he is an arm's length away. His face is impassive as he leans and speaks in a tone meant for my ears alone. "I am no longer certain you belong among my ranks. You seem to make a better nursemaid." Our eyes lock. "Or perhaps you are more suited for your mother's vocation?"

My modest breakfast sours in my stomach.

Verrek straightens and raises his voice so all can hear. "I welcome any and all questions you may have. You need to be as confident in me as you are in each other, and that means vicious transparency." He motions toward me, his eyebrows disappearing into the sweep of his hair. His voice takes on a mocking lilt. "And how fortunate we are to have a woman among us who can lend understanding on the more sensitive side of battle that we men are so often prone to miss."

I wince as chuckles lick my ears like the tongues of adders, as my cheeks blush in a way they haven't since I was four years old.

And I.

Can't.

Breathe.

Relishing the men's laughter for a moment, Verrek waves to dismiss his soldiers. "That is enough for today. Report to your detail."

I stay where I am, letting everything blur until only Verrek remains. His gaze travels in my direction, and I wonder if the question burns in my eyes the way it does in my mind. *Why? Why commend me for saving Téron, then cut me down like this?*

A sneer curls his lips. "As useful as this stranger could prove, Seyla, did you think you could challenge our laws and show mercy to the enemy without repercussions?" He laughs at my gaping mouth, my wide eyes. "You've completed your duty, bringing the man back to health, but now that he no longer depends on you to keep him alive, it seemed prudent to remind you to *never* oppose the Imperii's orders again."

I am dangerously close to tears.

"Your life is not your own, Seyla. It belongs to the Southlands. And as long as you are one of my úramech, it belongs to *me*." He comes close, glaring at me from above. I blink at his chest plate and my whole body shakes. His rough hand shoots to my chin and jerks my face so I look into his eyes. "Do not challenge me again."

My tent is empty and I do not care, do not care, *do not care* where Téron is. Maybe he ran away. Maybe he left me like everyone else.

It would be better.

My breaths come in high-pitched gasps, and everything is too tight. I loosen my breastplate, my nail beds bleeding from ripping at the stiff straps. Muffled sobs fill the dead air of my tent as I work the armor over my head and throw it to the side. The khukuri follows with a smash.

Can't breathe. Can't breathe.

Every piece of armor, every weapon lashed to my body burns, and red blooms to the surface of my skin where my nails rip it all away. My clawing fingers snag my braids. I tear at them until my hair covers my shoulders like a curtain, like the wall of black itself.

Why did you do it, Seyla? Why did you work so hard to get where you are, then risk everything by using your brain? Opening your mouth? Unlocking your heart?

Why did you ever think you could be something more than your mother?

I free my body from the boots, the bracers, the padding beneath my armor, and it still isn't enough. I rip off my tunic, my pants, every outer garment until I am hugging my knees on the dirt floor, a pillow shoved between my thighs and my tightly bound chest, screaming into the softness until my throat is raw, until I can't scream anymore.

21
TÉRON

THESE BONES ARE BRITTLE. These muscles, weak. My pride used to hinge on my strength, on my ability to protect and provide for my wife and daughter. But what am I now? An empty shell, a spent husk. A useless man.

My feet carry me on an aimless path between the tents and through the gnarled bushes surrounding the camp. The rhythmic sound of steel-on-steel rings through the air, but the camp is mostly empty. Even so, a few disdainful looks track my steps like arrows. Why should they find their mark? These people only aim at the outward man, not the bruised and festering soul within.

Despite the animosity, there is an ease I didn't expect to find in this land of glaring lights. Each breath is unchallenged, slipping over my tongue like honeyed wine, and the colors that cling to the most pitiful weeds are so vivid, they deserve much better names than blue, green, and yellow.

What is this world?

I turn my face to the sky, begging its crystal purity to wash over me, to clear away the fool I once was. The fool who believed that justice for my grieving heart would be found once I doused the light.

Will every false truth I trusted in be exposed, one speck at a time?

Highest, I hope so. It never did anyone good, did it? Not for my wife, and especially not for my daughter.

I stop quickly, my bare feet kicking up a spray of sand.

An incredible body of water pulses along a quiet shore, reflecting the mellow tones of the sky's forever blue, but a shifting cliff of darkness bears down upon the loch in the distance, swallowing its far banks in the jaws of a predatory beast.

A shiver creeps across my skin, and I close my eyes for a beat. *I am out. I am out. I am out.* I release a labored breath, willing myself to expel the last traces of ténesomni from my existence.

Do I struggle to accept the truth even now, with all this evidence around me? Can I still not make my soul believe that I have been delivered from the Vale?

This doesn't feel like deliverance.

I rub my eyes, half hoping the image will have faded when I look again. Yet there it is, the unfeeling division between dark and light, between my world and one I don't belong in.

A bitter laugh tumbles out. What kind of man cannot admit he was wrong when the evidence lies right before his eyes? And what kind of man would not storm the very gates of Ikktar if there was any chance he could be reunited with his loved one?

A foolish, cowardly one who spent thirteen years hating the thing his own wife loved and refusing to acknowledge who his daughter was.

Legs threatening to give out, I lower myself to the ground, swallowing a groan. I stretch out one leg, folding the other in so I can rest my forearm across the knee. My other arm wraps tightly around my ribs, and I wince when it presses too hard against the wounds concealed beneath my shirt.

I stare at that strange juxtaposition between sky blue and deathly black.

Between me and my daughter.

You could run, Téron. You could flee all you fear and leave these brutal people behind. There must be a place where you can disappear, where no one will know your history. Where you could be forgotten.

Where you could forget.

It is a tempting thought, and if it weren't for my injuries, I might consider heeding it. But how can I know where Amyrah is or if she escaped Myrzeth's plans? What if she is close, and running away now would ensure I would never see her again?

There is also the matter of the woman with hair that shines a soft blue in the morning light, whose tongue is a blade, who possesses a healer's practiced hands. That sharp, hard apparition protects me, tends to me. She is fire buried under a grave's depth of ice. Her armor is impenetrable, and it binds her heart in calloused plates. She fights for everything yet shares costly enatuberry preserves with me.

And before her the whole of who I am has been laid bare.

No, I cannot repay her kindness by leaving without a word. Surely she'd bear the punishment if I did.

Passing a hand roughly down my face and leaving it pressed hard against my mouth, I let my eyes lose focus somewhere between the gentle rise and fall of Loch Skythe and the ténesomni's barrier. I count my heartbeats as they thump in my chest. They are proof that I am, against all reason, still a living man.

The last memory I have from the Vale is of my daughter's face. Defeated, horrified. Then I remember pain—cold, ripping, burning pain —and a hungry blackness like I've never known.

But more details cling to the edges of my recollection. My eyebrows knock together, and I beg my mind to focus. Seyla's account of how she found me has unlocked my memories, like a key in an old chest. There was . . . there was someone else with me on the day I finally woke up and protected the one I loved, taking the wrath of the kaligorven. Soft hands, weak and strong. How could they be both? A voice seasoned with age and humble wisdom.

And there was an . . . an animal?

Every thought is more ridiculous than the last, and I growl my frustration. Dropping my hand to the shore, I select a jagged rock to fling into the waters. The sound it makes when it hits is as disappointing as the sad distance I managed to throw it.

I wish I could have forgotten my name, who I was. I almost did. It would have been easier to accept the broken thing I am if I did not have all the specters of the people I've lost and hurt screaming at me from morning to night.

Movement to the left catches my eye. A man in impeccable armor emerges from the low bushes and paces the shore, his eyes fixed to where the bank on the other side of the loch should be. At least half a dozen coins fastened to thin braids dangle at different heights along the side of his jaw. He must be of considerable rank, perhaps a commander. I hunch low, grateful that he has not noticed me poorly hidden behind a large driftwood log. Another soldier appears, then another. The three hold a tense conversation, the commander motioning to the loch, to the beach, as if he is trying to work something out. He grips his chin, eyes probing the ténesomni again. I am too far from him to see his face, but everything about his posture, his rapt attention, communicates not the wariness I would expect but something much more *eager*. After a while he departs, the soldiers bowing in deference and taking up a patrol along the shore.

An uneasy feeling turns my insides to rot.

Téron, get off this beach.

I wait for them to move the other way, holding my breath to lend some support to the lacerations across my chest and abdomen. It takes everything in my power not to cry out as I get to my feet. I duck my head, moving quickly into the bushes before they have a chance to turn and see me. A faint "*hey*" chases my retreat, but my course is no longer aimless, and I have already passed through the bushes and re-entered the outskirts of the camp.

I cannot be certain which tent belongs to Seyla, and panic supersedes my attention-hungry pain. When I wandered, I did not have the presence of mind to think about getting back. Was it my intention to slip away all along?

It doesn't matter now. The fact remains that I have nowhere to go, and I do not feel right about abandoning the one soul who has shown me kindness here.

The training session has been dismissed, the sharp sounds no longer ringing from the clearing to the west of the camp. I walk up and down the tent rows, my steps quicker than my weakened body can afford. If I'm caught wandering around, what could it mean for Seyla? I should have thought of that before I left. Sweat seeps through my tunic. I grit my teeth against the pain and attempt not to draw attention to myself.

When I emerge into a vaguely familiar row and spot a fire pit more neatly kept than the others, I dare to hope I have found my way back. Seyla is always orderly, precise. I reach for the entrance flap and try to think of something clever, or perhaps opaque enough, to keep her from peppering me with too many questions. Or a believable excuse if I barge into a stranger's tent.

Did she care at all that I had run away, or was it a relief to be spared of this burden? Warmth wicks up my neck. Why does it devastate me to think the latter is the case?

I push the flap aside, then pull up short.

Pieces of armor congest the dirt floor, and the sharp scent of perspiration hits me.

This must be the wrong tent.

My gaze passes over the mess once more, but my retreat halts when I spot a curved shape crammed into the foot of space at the end of the cot.

Seyla.

"Stay away from me," she snaps when I take a tentative step inside.

Her eyes are wild, her hair a tangled mess about her shoulders. She is wearing nothing but a threadbare undergarment, and her olive-toned arms are patterned with the shadowy hues of fresh bruises. Bright red blood splotches the bandage around her forearm.

Anger thrums in my chest when I see the desperation in her expression. I do not recognize it on her. The thick ice around her has cracked, and what lies behind it is not at all what I expected.

I hold out a palm and lower myself to the cot, careful to keep an acceptable distance between us.

Seyla rubs the back of a hand across her damp forehead and barks out a laugh. "If you are well enough to go on a pleasure stroll, then why come back here? Unless you also can't resist the opportunity to laugh at my weakness." Her voice has an abnormal rasp to it.

"Seyla, I would never . . ." Confused, I shake my head. "No. That's not why I'm here."

"Isn't it?" She snorts and rolls her eyes away to the tent's stained canvas. "That's what men do. You would not be the first, and ancestors know you won't be the last."

Is she trying to push me away, to make me think she is hardened to me? But her pain-laced words are as thin as a moth's wings. Her arms constrict around her pillow, knuckles going white where she clutches the fabric.

My heart pumps angrily, and I gesture at her bruises. "Who gave those to you?"

"No one." Her eyes flick to mine, as if daring me to challenge her.

My gaze travels over her rows of carefully labeled jars and bottles, to the crisply folded tunics and pants in a small cubby beside the cot, then lands on the disaster on the floor. She keeps every aspect of her life under careful watch; someone must have caused this worrying act of chaos.

I choose my words carefully. "This doesn't seem like you." I look at her bruises. "And those were not made by your hands."

She grimaces, another dry laugh escaping her. "I'm an úramech, Téron. A few bruises are to be expected, aren't they?" Her voice warbles, and she catches her lip between her teeth, her expression growing forbidding again. "And you know nothing of me, stranger."

I ignore the label she tosses, ignore the impulse to insist that after all she has done for me, we are much more than strangers.

"True." I pass my hands through my hair, noting my greasy scalp. "I can't say I know much of anything anymore."

Lips pressing together until they all but disappear, Seyla gets to her feet and drops the pillow on the foot of the bed. She bends to collect the strewn pieces of armor, placing the smaller items in the cubby below the folded clothes and hanging the breast piece on a pair of hooks on the tent's ridgepole.

I watch her thoughtfully, noting how her brow is now smooth and the tears have dried completely from her cheeks. The fracture in her casing has iced over once more, and the only remaining evidence of weakness is her disheveled hair and minimal clothes.

She is very dignified for someone in her undergarments.

"You can let your guard down in front of me, you know." I speak the words as loud as I dare, unsure of whether she will brush them off, mock them, or explode with defensive anger.

I don't care what she thinks.

"I won't think less of you." I rub a hand lightly over the lacerations across my abdomen. She has seen me in a worse state, and I owe her everything. That includes the truth.

Unchanged, Seyla continues to tidy up with the air of someone who wasn't just discovered cowering in a corner.

The awkwardness thickens between us until I am weary of it, and I begin to feel the consequences for my excursion catching up with me. Exhaustion presses down on my shoulders with firm insistence. I notice Seyla's hands shake as she slowly pulls a comb through her waist-length hair. She must be even more depleted than me.

I groan and stand, avoiding Seyla's shrewd eyes, which fix to where the bandages hide underneath my shirt. "Here. Have your own bed tonight." I don't wait for her to protest, bending as far as I dare to retrieve the quilted roll tucked under the cot. With a flick, I unfurl the mat parallel to the cot and carefully lie back, slipping my interlaced fingers beneath my head.

Seyla must respect the determination on my face, or perhaps she doesn't want to risk aggravating my wounds further by making me get up off the ground. She doesn't argue, and instead blows out the lantern and lies on her own cot after she finishes plaiting her hair into a single, thick rope.

The sounds of night settle around us, and as tired as I am, I cannot find sleep.

"Why didn't you run?"

Her whisper is soft, almost plaintive. It could be mistaken for the voice of a stranger.

"It didn't seem right," I say, and they are the last words spoken between us.

When her breathing deepens and I am certain she is asleep, I prop myself up on an elbow and look at the strip of her face illuminated by the moon through a gap in the canvas flap.

The urge to comb a loose strand of hair from her cheek comes over me. I don't fight it.

Even if I did leave, the only place I could go would be back to the Vale, and I am too much of a coward for that. What if all that awaits me is more heartache, more loss? What would I do if I found my daughter had been taken from me like Ellehra was?

That would be a blow I would not recover from.

I withdraw my hand and think of the Seyla I caught a glimpse of earlier, the one I doubt she has let anyone see before.

This world might be foreign, and I might not belong in it, but maybe, if Elyōn is willing, he could use me here for good.

22

WEHNA

UTSANEK'S MARKET SQUARE IS THE LAST place I want to be. Loud. Overstimulating. Seething with an inordinate number of valefolk. Yet here I am, gripping Arvo's hand as tightly as I can without hurting him, being jostled by people who smell like smoke and sweat and a hundred potent occupations.

"Excuse me." I tap a middle-aged woman's shoulder and try not to shrivel under her glare. "Do you know why the market is so crowded today?"

"Foremost called a meeting, didn't he?"

I pull back and let a sharp retort spill out. "I don't know. Would I ask you if I did?"

The woman adjusts the scarf pulled over her gray-streaked hair and leers at me. "Got quite the mouth, I see."

My face goes hot, but I keep my lips pressed together. She shakes her head and slips away into the crowd.

"Wehna, I wanna go with Téah," Arvo whines, leaning his weight into my arm and returning me to my senses.

I have been lenient with him for too long, and I'm not about to let him escape me again. Chafed from getting rebuffed by a stranger, my irritation spills over to him.

"Téah is staying home with her sisters, remember?" I yank him close as two young men bustle by, not caring who they knock out of the way. Looking down at Arvo, I paste on the most hypocritical smile. "And I wanted some time with my baby brother."

He rolls his eyes—a mannerism I am certain he's picked up from the abundance of sass in the Peren home. Mada would never let him get away with it. With the performance I just gave, though, I'm not in a place to call him on it.

I exhale and focus not on the shrine to the Shrouded, where all attention seems to be directed, but on the dirty-blond braid pushing through the crowd ahead of me. Dread clings to my throat as I watch Tress approach the fanum. I have never seen a person more determined, as if she is ready to burn Utsanek down.

"Let me go with Miss Tress."

I bite together, speaking through gritted teeth to keep myself from shouting at him. "No, Arvo."

He gives up pulling against me, fight spent.

I press my free fingertips to my temple and take a breath. "You're staying right here with me."

"I didn't know a kavigorban"—he stumbles through the pronunciation—"was gonna come," he whispers, and I almost don't catch it amid the noise of the people.

Shame fills me for being so sharp with him. He went through a traumatic experience too, and I'm not being fair.

"No, I know you didn't," I say in a softer tone.

"I didn't mean for Mister Bryn to get hurt."

Something wilts inside me. I stop tugging him along and spin around, crouching to his level. "Listen to me. Nothing that happens here with those monsters is your fault. Never. You got that?"

He bites his lip, his eyes as round as bolétis caps. "But if I hadn't—"

"Don't let your mind do that to you. When we start thinking about all the ways things could be different, we stop trusting Elyōn with what he *has* given us."

My own words slink through my mind like a lochfish, trailing guilt in their wake. Do I believe them, or is it more regurgitated rhetoric? Because I have been fixated on nothing but what things *should* have been since the night my parents left and never returned.

"Is he *really* good, Wehna?"

I lean in closer to hear him better. "What?"

"Elyōn. Tress says he is, and I remember Mada and Pada telling me that too, but . . ."

"But what?"

"Well, we love him. And he watches over us, right?"

"Always."

"Then why does he leave us here?"

I grasp his shoulder, my lips parting to answer, but I am interrupted by a loud clanging ringing out over the din of the square. Silence falls, thick as sap.

"Listen, little fledgling," I say as loud as I dare, rushing to get this out before I am stopped again. Before I lose my nerve. "I know it's hard sometimes, but we must hold on to the goodness of Elyōn when doubts circle in. Especially then."

Arvo sucks his lips in and gulps.

I brush a curl from his forehead. "I'll keep reminding you of that, and I need you to remind me of it too."

He gives a tiny nod.

Standing, I guide Arvo into my side and hold on to him firmly, not only because I'm afraid of losing him, but because I want him to believe that I am here for him, that I love him.

And if I had the time or the strength, I would assure him beyond room for doubt that the Highest loves him, too, though I have wrestled with the same question a thousand times over.

"Good people, how wonderful to see your happy faces," Myrzeth croons.

Though this prompts a few valefolk to chuckle, the chill mist of his voice coats my skin. I shiver.

The Foremost stands at the top of the shrine's steps, feet shoulder-width apart and a benevolent grin quirking his lips. He has dispensed with the frayed black tunic he was wearing when he first appeared in the Vale and now dons a crisp coat of new linen dyed a smoky gray, with thin straps looped around offset black buttons down the front. His gaze passes over the valefolk's hungry gazes.

"I commend you for your noble efforts to worship the kaligorven."

He waves a hand to the space above the people. Only a couple sola brossa would serve to illuminate this whole area, yet many strings cast their diseased glow over the throng. It's as close to real daylight as I have ever seen in the Vale, even if the hue makes my stomach churn.

"As you can see, we have had good fortune with the Hunts. The kaligorven have never been so well-pleased with our offerings. As we anoint them with the blood of sacrifice, they grow ever stronger. As they grow stronger, *we* grow stronger."

Disconcerted murmurs sweep around the square.

"How does what they do make us strong?" a person asks in a trembling tone.

"Our children are afraid to leave our homes because the Shrouded now walk the streets," someone else speaks up. "Fear is not strength."

Myrzeth spreads his hands, appealing to the people. "Their presence is a true mark of how far we have come, don't you think? It wasn't long ago that they kept to the forests beyond Utsanek's borders, preying on those who wandered from the city. Now, such is your relationship with them that they desire to live among us."

Unable to stand watching him politicking any longer, my attention wanders to a girl with straight, fair hair who looks to be around my age. She stands off to the side of the fanum steps, removed from the rest of the people. Her eyes never leave the movements of the Foremost, and a greedy smile dances across her red mouth. My stomach twists further with her adoring glance. The dress she wears is a deep-wine hue, and I think how strange it is to be seeing color to its full potential within the ténesomni's reach.

"How can that be a good thing?" a young father asks, a child perching on his shoulders.

Bobbing his head, Myrzeth addresses the man like a tutor with his pupil. "It is a matter of protection, of loyalty. While they are here, they will defend us from any force that would seek to weaken us, will they not? If they identify with us, they will come to our aid should we need it."

By the whispers that still shift around me, I know the people are not yet convinced. *Good. Let them question every word that spills from his wicked lips. Let* me *question them too.*

A thin smile loosens Myrzeth's pale features. "I understand your apprehension. It must be difficult to abandon the fears that have sustained you for so long, but I challenge you to look at their behavior among us. Have there been attacks? Was there an instance where they proved, beyond question, that they intended to destroy us? They certainly would have the capability if they desired." He laces his fingers behind his back and paces the length of the steps. "And yet they restrain themselves. Is this not proof of their noble intention toward us?"

A frown ripples my forehead. This is an easy argument to counter if the kaligorven have continued to behave in the manner I have witnessed, but no one speaks up. In fact, many of the faces relax as if Myrzeth's words are a soothing balm on a stinging wound.

"He's right," I overhear a woman say to another. "They haven't touched a soul."

I almost jump into their conversation but decide silence would be safer at this moment.

"He is a *liar*. Don't believe his smooth words. The kaligorven mean to harm us."

My throat constricts as Tress calls out, climbing the fanum steps with boldness I can't comprehend.

"Tress, *no*," I whisper.

The people go quiet.

"My own husband"—her voice cracks, and she takes a moment to sweep her eyes over the crowd—"was attacked two days ago within the streets this man claims the Shrouded protect."

The women close to me exchange apprehensive glances.

Myrzeth looks down at his footwear, his shoulders raising and dropping dismissively. "I do not claim that they will not turn violent if provoked."

"Provoked?" An incredulous laugh slips out as Tress folds her arms.

She looks Myrzeth straight on. "Yes, I suppose you could say my husband did drive the beast to it, but I am confident almost everyone within this city would do the same if they came across the Shrouded stalking a child."

The valefolk gasp, and I hold Arvo tighter. His shoulders shake under my palms. My fears swell, but not for him.

What will the girls do if something happens to Tress?

Bryn lies in a bed in their home, unresponsive. The streets of Ellithïm stand empty, dark, and open to whatever may prowl its way. And five precious daughters wait within a lightless house with no idea how close they are to losing it all.

Myrzeth regards Tress for several painfully long breaths, his gaze as unyielding as stone until he begins to circle the top landing of the shrine's steps.

Resolve solidifies within me like a red-hot blade plunged into oil. It emerges flaming, blackened and rough, but hard and sharp enough to dismember the fear that binds me.

"Be strong, Arvo." My heart thuds madly beneath my ribs, and I push through the throng, pulling him behind me.

Ceasing his pacing, Myrzeth looks at Tress again. I sidle between strangers' shoulders, losing sight of him for a moment.

"Interesting," he says. "I am surprised to hear this, if you have been behaving toward them like the rest of those gathered here."

No reply comes from Tress.

There are only a few rows left between me and the front.

"Tell me. Was it your child whom the kaligorven cornered?"

Silence still.

"There must have been something about them and your husband that the kaligorven did not like. The Shrouded are skilled at sensing the intentions of people's hearts."

I glance at Tress's face, alarmed to find she doesn't appear to be the least bit intimidated.

She's going to do it. She's going to expose her connection to the fidrélas in front of all these people. She's going to leave her children motherless.

I cut through the last row, Arvo struggling to stay with me.

"It-it was my fault, Myrzeth," I nearly shout. Sweat beads on my brow, trickling down my temples.

The Foremost's predatory gaze swivels to find me, his features remaining impassive.

Arvo's little hands hug my waist, and he peeks around me.

"I have angered them with my worship of Elyōn, and that is why they pursued my brother." There is no time to ponder whether this lie will earn me consequences beyond this world. I push my apprehension aside and gesture toward Tress. "This woman's husband saw and stepped in to protect him, for which I am grateful, but I can't forgive myself for letting a stranger come to harm on our behalf."

Tress's eyes find mine, fear dominating them at last.

I clamp my jaw shut and turn my attention to Myrzeth.

Don't interfere, Tress. Please don't. Please, please . . .

A bout of laughter exudes from the Foremost, sending a shock of weakness through my legs. But I *will* stand.

Oh, Elyōn, help me to stand.

"I should have known to expect your involvement, but didn't I send you away with a warning to take to your people?" He casts Tress a dubious look.

I lift my chin, willing my heart to slow. "I . . . I was afraid. Instead of going back, I chose to hide myself and my brother far away from them." I pause to drag in a shaky breath. This next lie is so much closer to the truth, it almost doesn't feel like a lie at all. "It was selfish of me to think only about protecting my own."

Myrzeth descends the steps and stands in front of me, elbow resting in a palm and his other hand cupping his chin. Ténesomni swirls in his irises.

"Is this true? You do not know this woman?"

I shake my head and pray that Arvo and Tress do not ruin it all.

Dropping his hands, the Foremost slaps his thighs and bounds back up the steps. "Well. It appears we've found our infidel," he says, turning around at the top to look out at the valefolk again. "If we are to keep our balance with the kaligorven, then all adherents to the faith of Elyōn need to be punished."

The crowd, which had been utterly silent up until this point, divulges into restless chatter. I wince, thinking at first that they are agreeing with this man of shadows, but after a moment it becomes apparent that their voices are tinged with protest.

"She is but a child herself, Foremost."

"Are we condoning violence to children now?"

"This is *wicked*."

The crowd behind me reaches an instantaneous boil. Myrzeth's gaze detaches from mine and darts back and forth as a shade of apprehension clouds his face. I make use of his distraction and slink back into the froth, pushing Arvo behind me into the safety of the jostling bodies.

"*Silence*," the Foremost shouts, but no one listens. My eyes seek out the other side of the steps, and I am relieved to find that Tress has also taken the opportunity to escape.

I continue to backpedal, hoping no one will notice or care about my presence.

"Sweet daugh'er, what have yeh done?"

Soft fingers find my forearm, and I turn to witness Orlagh's wrinkled face a breath from mine. She reaches up and clutches my cheeks between her palms.

"Yeh brave, foolish child. Yeh are just like your mother."

"Orlagh, I—"

Holding a finger to my lips, she silences me. "Yeh need to listen to me. Go to the northwest corner of Utsanek, where a channel of water flows into the city. Follow the stream. Take tha' dear boy of yours and follow the stream through the woods. It will lead yeh to a safe place away from prying eyes." Her hands fall and she rests one on Arvo's springy hair. "I pray that Elyōn will keep yeh safe there. Now go. *Go.*"

Taking a moment to clutch her in a tight, quick hug, I pick up Arvo and plunge through the heart of the square and into the streets, hoping against hope that salvation and rest lay outside the borders of Utsanek.

But not ten feet into the forest, the monsters find us.

Grating howls chase my heels, spurring me to run faster than I have ever run in my life. I slip down the bank of the stream, teeth piercing my lip and drawing blood as I try to keep myself from crying out. Arvo's heels dig into me so hard, I can already feel bruises forming.

Follow the stream. Follow the stream.

The words become one with my heartbeat, with my footsteps, with Arvo's hot puffs of breath against my neck.

Crashing sounds fill the air from both sides of the stream, sending a chill through my veins. The frigid water cackles around us, heedless of our peril as I cut through its heart. Arvo whimpers and I hold him tighter.

Realizing much too late that running upstream like this has us hemmed in, I look for a way of escape, but the ténesomni is impenetrable and I can see nothing, not even the bolétis. The banks are so steep that I can't risk climbing them without giving up precious ground. We are being herded like cattle by wild beasts that thirst for our souls. I can only keep plunging my feet blindly through these waters of life.

I am on the verge of exhaustion, and strangled, aching words only Elyōn can interpret crack from my lungs.

Highest, can you see us?

From the heights, the dawn awakens, and a peculiar song rises to greet it.

I come to a splashing stop, a gasp parting my lips.

It can't be.

Snarls encircle me and Arvo, the gale of the kaligorven's presence whipping my hair around my face and my sopping dress around my ankles. I fix my attention instead to the burning star descending to earth, its song increasing as it draws near.

Closing my eyes, I call out above the tumult, "Hold on to me, Arvo. Just hold on."

Shrieks and song battle each other to be heard. Hot and cold twist in violent arms, the epicenter of a tempest I cannot fathom, am too afraid to witness. Sinking to my knees, I press Arvo's head under my chin with a shaking hand.

And then it's over. My garments and my hair fall limp, and uncanny warmth embraces me. Blood red shines from behind my closed eyelids, and Arvo's grip loosens.

"Wehna, *look*."

I open my eyes, squinting through the smarting brilliance.

A celestial body sits on Arvo's extended hand, fluttering delicate wings and cocking its tiny head.

A deep, resonant trilling pours from its beak.

"Elyōn sent it to save us," he whispers, not flinching at its brightness as he draws it closer to his awe-filled face. The bird—is it a wren?—goes quiet but does not startle at the movement.

I glance around the stream, passing my eyes over its banks. Nothing but resolute trees and low leafy greens witness this unspeakable moment.

Trembling, I set Arvo down and get to my feet. The wren stays on his finger, balancing with ease while Arvo's hand sways and tilts. I take his free hand, and together we climb the bank on the right side.

When we come to the level ground, a quaint cottage with stone walls and a sloping roof greets us. Several fluffy chickens peck the ground out front, and the bleats of goats reach us from a small shed to the left.

Was this the place Orlagh meant?

Refusing to let Arvo go, I take advantage of the tiny sola's light. We explore the homestead without fear. The shed houses four hungry-looking goats, one of them a small kid. Traces of feed litter the ground around a torn-up sack, and their cries grow frantic when they see Arvo and me.

How long have they been locked up in here?

I find another bag of grain on a high shelf, out of their reach. Directing Arvo to step aside, I pull it down and untie it. The feed spills out and the goats leap to consume it.

"Steady, friends. You'll be fine now."

I check to make sure they have water, finding a clever gutter system that feeds up to the shed's roof, where rainwater collects and fills their trough.

Outside, the chickens seem to be caring for themselves well enough, so we leave them alone and approach the cottage. The door creaks with a solemn ballad of disuse. Along the far wall stands a beautiful stone hearth with a bouquet of drooping, crispy pink flowers set atop its wooden mantle. The water in the vase has long since dried up. There are two comfortable-looking beds draped in woven wools, a small wooden table, and a section of shelves piled with baskets full of nuts, flour, and preserves. Dried herbs hang from the rafters. The sola chirps.

"Wehna, can we stay here?" my brother asks, but I can make no reply. How can we know who lived here or if it is right for us to stay without being welcomed?

I tug Arvo out the door and to the side of the house where a lean-to stands. When I unlatch the door and it swings forward, my brother gasps and a cheerful sight greets us.

Jars cover the narrow shelves within, filled with a rainbow of colorful mushrooms. Most of them have lost their bioluminescent properties, and some are shriveled up. Enough of them still glow, though, to show me that these are not the regular variety that grow close to Utsanek's borders.

Who would be brave enough to scour the woods for a collection of rare bolétis?

I don't have to cast around long for an answer. *Amyrah.*

"Yes, Arvo." I squeeze his hand, offering a silent word of thanks to Elyōn "I think we can stay."

23
AMYRAH

RAEL'S GENTLE FINGERS TUG the front section of my hair while I close my eyes and sink into her touch. Belwyn has tried to convince me my stained hair doesn't look bad, but I hate seeing it in front of my nose, a symbol of all the ways I have failed and could fail if I give in to the temptation of the ténesomni.

"There. What do you think of this?" Rael hands me a looking glass, holding a similar one off to the side so I can see. She has managed to incorporate the braid into my hair so that it looks like a waterfall of black dripping down from it, softened by my deep honey-colored waves. It winds from my right temple and around the back where it disappears into my lengths.

It looks lovely.

I set down the mirror and turn to her. "Rael, it's perfect. You'll have to teach me how to do this."

A subtle smile bunches her cheek. She uncorks a bottle and tips a small amount of fragrant oil into her palms, rubbing it between them. "First, I need to show you how to take care of your waves."

Fingering my locks, I feel my cheeks warm. "I've never done much with my hair, except given it a trim occasionally. My father didn't ever develop a knack for arranging it."

Grabbing the bulk of it, Rael smooths the oil over the ends. "You've got the basics. It could use a bit of extra moisture, and I can show you how to handle it when it's wet, so it won't turn into a frizzy disaster."

We sink into companionable silence as she finishes up.

I pull my sleeves over my fists. "Is this how you do Wehna's hair?"

Rael exhales, wiping her hands on a cloth. "She needs a lot more than this, starting with a decent detangling. We always make an evening of it, sitting on cushions in front of the fire and eating our weight in goat cheese, honeyed nuts, and kifa crackers." She goes quiet, and sadness pervades the air as thoroughly as the oil's fragrance.

"Wherever she is, I'm sure she's safe," I say, trying to forget how on our last meeting she was hit over the head in an Utsanek alley.

"But we can't know that, can we?" She turns her dark eyes on me. "The only thing I have to go on is hope." She tucks hair behind her ear with a shaking hand. "And I'm finding mine dangerously close to running out." Taking the chair across from me at the table, she slides her fingers around a mug of tea. "If there was any possible way, I'd be back in Utsanek before the sun rises in the morning."

I reach across the table and rest a hand on her forearm. "Wehna is strong, Rael. She knows how to persevere. And she was so devoted to Arvo, I know she'll take good care of him."

That's when she cracks.

"*My boy.*" A sob racks her lungs, and she presses a hand to her lips to hold it in. "We should have never left him like that, never put such a responsibility on Wehna's shoulders. She's only a girl, but I have treated her like a grown up since she was twelve."

My own childhood is brought to mind, and for the first time, I truly understand how it was stolen from me. All I have known is responsibility and the next task to be accomplished. I wonder if the reason Wehna and I bonded so quickly was because we connected on a level that we didn't have time to understand.

Sabine breezes into the kitchen and collapses onto a chair, combing her fingers through her red waves and fastening them in a loose knot at her neck. "I'll tell you what. Those children sure do know how to tire a body out."

Without being asked, Rael stands and fetches another mug, filling it to the brim with tea. "Take a break, Sabine."

"Oh, I shouldn't. I only popped down here to fetch a snack for the little 'uns. Joph is holding them captive at the moment with a tale of his own making. That boy is quite the story weaver."

"Sounds like he has everything under control, then." Rael hands her the mug, which Sabine doesn't hesitate to accept.

If I hadn't just witnessed Rael's pain, I wouldn't believe it had emerged a moment ago.

A tired exhale escapes Sabine. "What were you girls up to?"

Rael takes a sip from her mug. "Catching up. It's been a challenging few weeks."

"You don't have to convince me. Everything has felt askew since Torr showed up, then went to hide in the Tothlen Forest. And before you say it again, I will have no more apologies from you for that." She fixes Rael with a firm look.

"Fine, fine. I won't apologize." An eyebrow arches mischievously. "This time."

I run my thumb over the smooth side of my mug, lost in my thoughts.

"Something bothering you, Amyrah?" Sabine asks.

"*Hmm*?" Blinking away my daydream, I find both women's eyes on me. I swallow and pull my tea closer. "Oh. Not really."

Except for Elder Ephson's disdain, the three shadowed people in the nature preserve, Jaki's desire to make a fool of me, the unbearable tension between me and Belwyn . . .

I hook my toes around the chair legs and hold my tongue.

Sabine sits back, resting an elbow on the backrest. "Well? Out with it. I don't have all day," she says, winking.

Resigned, I press my lips together and think. "Why is there so much prejudice against the Luvesti? Growing up in the Vale, I would have never fathomed that a life without ténesomni could still be so difficult. It didn't even cross my mind that people here would take offense to someone like me." My fingers go to my black-inked braid.

Rael gives Sabine a look as if to say, "this question is yours." Her friend does not balk at the challenge.

"It's a bit baffling to me as well, since it's because of the Luvesti that our lands are free of the kaligorven." Sabine shakes her head, then takes a careful sip of tea. "But time has a way of eroding the truths we once held."

She sets the mug back on the table. "I suspect the battle between all the peoples of Atsun and the kaligorven was more brutal than anyone can recall. It made our nation eager to remedy the horrors of the past. The problem with that sentiment is that, unless someone is willing to retell the old stories of evil and risk stepping on toes, people have an astounding tendency to forget what their forefathers fought for."

I don't have to look far from my own experience to understand this. It was difficult for me to learn anything about the true nature of the solas within the Vale. Knowledge of the kind of life that existed in the Grovesha had faded from memory for most valefolk.

"How long ago was that?" I ask.

"Oh, let me think. I'm sure it's been over a hundred years now. Can you believe that, Rael? A century since Ketsans, the Luvesti, and Southlanders worked together to contain the kaligorven's corruption and the spreading ténesomni. I'll wager there is no longer anyone with a living memory of those days. We've all been brought up on stories that have rapidly lost their potency, wandering into the domain of myth and fiction."

I frown. "But how could they forget? There's a living wall of darkness south of here. Your own people have set watchmen and protectors to keep guard over the Vale."

"Out of sight, out of mind," Rael says with a sad smile.

"That's exactly it. We're fickle, Amyrah, and we've grown comfortable behind our fortified walls, basking in our light-filled lives. When I was a girl, though, people still held to the belief that the kaligorven were evil. The attitude toward them has shifted in recent years, and it makes my blood run cold." Sabine shivers, glancing at Rael. "You've felt it too, haven't you?"

Rael nods. "Arlyn and I had grown more and more concerned with the trend before we left, and it's worse now. It did make it an easier decision to move our family to Utsanek, though. It wasn't like we were stealing some idyllic childhood from Wehna and Arvo. We were exchanging one land of broken souls for another, with the faith that we could share Elyōn more effectively to a people starved of hope." Her eyes glisten and she looks at her friend. "And, oh Sabine, we did see such growth. The valefolk clung to the Highest's goodness and purpose in a way I could never have been prepared for." A shadow falls across her features. "But we let it blind us to the needs of our family."

Sabine takes Rael's hand. "There's grace for you. That I know."

Tears shining on her cheeks, Rael sniffs.

All three of us are quiet for a while, sipping our beverages and navigating our own squalling thoughts.

"Oh, *stars*. I didn't answer your first question yet, did I?" Sabine drums her fingers on the table. "Let's think. Why is there animosity toward the Luvesti? Well, I suppose it comes down to the fact that many have begun to doubt the necessity of the Confining at all, claiming the kaligorven were natural predators in this habitat. They say we have upset the balance of things by restricting them to a single area of Atsun. And, therefore, the wisdom of our actions, which were largely prompted by the Luvesti, is called into question."

Distractedly, Rael rubs her leg. The beast that chased her and Arlyn out of the Vale, that marked her future with pain, was anything but natural. "It doesn't help that the Luvesti retreated to their northern kingdom not long after the Confining. They show up from time to time to check on things, but for the most part, I believe the Ketsans feel abandoned by them." Her gaze finds me, dips to my necklace. "And there is that flashy trick they have with light that leaves the rest of us wondering why we weren't so fortunate to be blessed."

I fight against the thought that she's accusing me, even though her eyes hold nothing but compassion, and finger the argentilum pendant at my throat. "I wish I knew how to use it."

There is no time to dwell on such thoughts. A resonant gong peels through the morning quiet, setting my pulse galloping. The women are instantly on their feet, racing to the doorway. Sabine holds back at the stairs, raising her arms to stymie the wave of children that comes stampeding down in a panic.

I follow Rael outside, my arms and neck covered with chill bumps. "What is it?"

She descends the landing steps swiftly, as if her leg is perfectly fine. I struggle to keep up.

We are almost at the ravine passage when an out-of-breath Belwyn finds me, a sheen of sweat on his brow. "Have you heard?"

"Heard what? The gong?"

He grabs my hands and tugs me down South Road. "The ténesomni has breached Ketsé's walls. It arrived much sooner than they were predicting."

I plant my feet, panic gripping every nerve of my body, and cling desperately to Belwyn's hand. He glances over his shoulder, an unasked question raising his eyebrows.

"We should leave." Dizziness rushes in.

His eyes narrow. "Amyrah, what are you thinking?"

"*No*. Listen to me. I can't do anything for these people, like I couldn't do anything for Qortehr or the Vale." My voice holds a ragged edge. "Whatever power I hold, it isn't enough. It will never be enough."

Unless you give in to the ténesomni.

A shiver travels up my spine.

Belwyn extricates himself from my grip and holds me by the arms. "That's not true at all. I watched you freeze it in place on the mountaintop, remember?"

"And what good did that do? The shadow still caught up with us." My teeth catch my lip. "I only made it speed up in the end. I'm worse than useless—I'm *dangerous*."

"Hey." Belwyn draws me in, his voice lowering to a husky tone. "I don't want to hear you say those things about yourself." Tucking a strand behind my shoulder, his eyes pass distractedly over my new hairstyle, curiosity and affection tinging his expression.

My stomach twists.

His eyes return to my face. "I believe in you, Amyrah Cantar." A smile slants his lips. "You were born for a moment like this."

Gulping, I nod.

Hand in hand, we race down the street to the scene of the commotion. Belwyn's confidence unfolds inside my chest like a late-blooming dahlia, combating my doubts. The trickle of woodfolk becomes a river the closer we get, and soon the reason becomes clear.

A consuming black wall, higher than the trees, rolls forward at an unfeeling pace, and my skin goes cold. At the base of the blackness, a huge crowd of harried people staggers, some of them pushing against its folds of shadow to no avail.

"*Get out of your houses*," Izra shouts, going from building to building and banging on the doors. He ducks inside one and yanks a person out by the tunic on her back, chucking her onto the road. The elaborate vase she had been clutching shatters, and her cries of surprise morph into venom-tipped accusations.

"Silence, woman." Izra points to the ténesomni as it approaches her doorway. "What do you think would happen if that wall moved into your home, blocking your escape while you were still inside hunting down your useless treasures?"

She blinks, but when her gaze travels to the stumbling mass of people losing ground before it, her face blanches.

I taste bile as I consider what he's implying. Have there already been casualties from this unnatural thing?

Dropping Belwyn's hand, I fight my way through the throng and approach Izra. "Let me help."

He laughs in his throat and pushes past me to the other dwellings.

Embarrassment warms my cheeks and I stay where I am, too stunned to do anything until Belwyn finds me.

"Ignore him, Amyrah. He doesn't know you." His fingers thread through mine. "Let's go prove his judgments wrong."

I let him lead me to the frontline.

People look at me askance as I approach it with trembling, outstretched hands. I force myself not to care, to only think of the monstrous task that lays before me. The crowd is too thick, and the jostling ruins my concentration. My next attempt results in the same failure.

"Give her space. Come on, move back. Make room." Belwyn waves his arms behind me, shoving people back as they stare at him dumbly. "Give her *space*," he bellows, and finally they comply.

Sucking in a breath and letting it escape through my nostrils, I close my eyes and focus, fingers outstretched to the darkness. The noise around me fades to a dull hum.

Elyōn, my mind breathes. *Can you use such a weak effort as this?*

When I was on the mountaintop facing this foe before, the action I needed to take against it came instinctively. I cried out to the Highest, felt his power flowing in me, enabling me to oppose the ténesomni. I didn't have to consider *how* to challenge it.

But now something else festers within me: a diseased branch snaking through my thoughts, leaving black trails on each one it touches. I am no longer a vessel untouched by blight. Doubt gutters the flame of my borrowed confidence.

Can I still be useful if I am tainted?

The despairing question clouds my focus, implores me to give up, but one pure thought springs free as the confusion churns through my mind.

I'm not sure it has much to do with deservin' anythin'.

Orlagh's words, which quelled my fears not so long ago and ignited hope where defeat had thrived before, offer me a lifeline.

Yer of a different race.

Calling upon the Highest to honor the heritage to which I was born, if not me as a person, I rest my efforts in him.

And he answers. Warmth flows through my fingers, pushing against the ténesomni. I open my eyes, watch the wall's advance slow to a crawl. I hear Belwyn laugh from somewhere behind me.

But it's not enough, and the effort of holding it back burns through my chest with a scorching heat.

"I-I can't do this on my own." A painful sob lurches from my throat.

"You aren't alone."

A man steps beside me, his calm words meant solely for me. *Holden.* My eyes dart to him, uncomprehending. His features are pulled into a resigned grimace as he focuses on the ténesomni. He mimics my stance, holding his palms outward.

Holden is . . . Luvesti?

There isn't time to ponder this, to let the ravenous questions distract me. I look back to the void of black and channel my efforts once more.

With Holden's bolstering presence beside me, I command the luminescence in my veins toward the ténesomni. Light begins to pour from my fingertips, then Holden's, shifting along the ground and spreading steadily up the shadowy curtain until the shadows lose their advantage.

Shuddering, slowing.

Stopping.

Relieved cries spring up from the woodfolk, and I catch Holden's triumphant smile and let down my guard as I dare to allow the victory of the moment bubble within me.

Let it out, let it out, let it out, let it out . . .

With a shudder, the whisper melts my bones. I am not prepared for it, and my defenses weaken a fraction. The seductive call of the ténesomni grows almost to an audible level. Coils of smoke wrap around my arms, extinguishing my light, and oozing from my skin toward the greater darkness beyond.

The whispering shifts.

Let us in, let us in, let us in, let us in . . .

I grit my teeth, trying to hold back the ténesomni originating from somewhere inside me, but I am not strong enough and the terror is paralyzing.

"Amyrah, what's happening? What are you doing?" Belwyn asks, words tinted with alarm.

"I can't help it!" The answer emerges shrill, like the screech of a wild animal.

The curious woodfolk closest to the wall reach out, and their hands pass with ease through the barrier.

Holden's tense voice reaches me. "Keep holding it, Amyrah. Don't give in."

Sobbing, I call the shadows back. They do not listen. The tendrils slink away, and when they graze the black wall, a ripple moves outward, like the epicenter of a boulder dropped into a pond.

A rush of wind hits me, carrying the ténesomni with it. My hands drop and I lose the connection. Holden drops his hands, too, his chest heaving.

Furling and unfurling my fingers, I stare at them with wide eyes. The inky ropes dissipate into the air. *What have I done?*

The answer comes as a grating voice, as a hundred grating voices. At first, I wonder if I'm the only one who can hear them until I see the Ketsans cover their ears and cower.

You've freed us to roam the Grovesha and the Southlands. All Atsun will know the strength of the kaligorven.

Crumpling to the ground, I bury my face in my knees as the ténesomni shrouds the day, released from its bounds for the first time in a hundred years.

If I struggled to admit it before, now I know for sure. The only way I can help those I love is to take myself far, far away from them.

24
BELWYN

I'M LOSING HER.

Maybe that's a selfish fear to have when a moving blockade is crushing people in their houses. Maybe it's despicable to be so wrapped up in myself while Amyrah's giving so much, but that's all I can think when shadows claim the girl who woke me up, who always exudes such pure light.

I'm losing her. Oh, Elyōn, I'm losing her.

Like waters from a dam, the ténesomni breaks its boundaries, diluting the daylight with mud-churned shadows. They don't block out the sky entirely but reduce the visibility to a dusky soup.

The woodfolk cry out, but nothing in me can be roused to feel surprised. A heaviness presses on my chest, and I give in to the inevitability of this moment.

I was never going to be free from the darkness.

My brooding breaks when Amyrah slips to the ground and covers her face with her hands. I rush to her.

"Holden, what was that?" My anger needs an outlet, and he is the perfect target.

Kneeling beside Amyrah, I put an arm around her and brush her hair from her back, but I can't seem to rouse her from her despair.

Walking over as if in a daze, Holden inspects his hands with a creased brow. "I don't know."

"And, *shades*, who are you?"

As the sky continues to grow darker, his face blanches.

"She's spent all this time thinking she's alone out here, searching for answers, giving up hope, and you could have helped her."

Color returns to his features and his jaw clenches. "You know nothing about it."

I'm on my feet and in his face before I think about what I'm doing. "That isn't my fault, is it? I'm just one of the pathetic shadow rats you kept in a cage to feed the kaligorven."

"I had nothing to do with that," he growls.

"No, how ridiculous of me." I force out a chuckle. "You're Luvesti. Far be it from you to actually get involved."

"Careful." Holden brings his face a handbreadth from mine. "You are beginning to sound like the ténesomni sympathizers who catch unwitting fools with their clever conspiracies."

I shake my head. "Did you ever consider that they wouldn't be drawn to the shadow if people like you didn't make belonging to the light seem so insufferable?"

Holden laughs grimly, shifting his feet into a wider stance. "I'm beginning to see why the Confining was necessary in the first place.

Atsun was better off without your kind being allowed to roam free."

"My *kind*?" Grabbing Holden by the collar, I pull back a fist.

"Stop!"

We freeze at Amyrah's shrill command. She wedges in between our chests, pushing us apart with her palms.

Holden is the one to break eye contact. I back off and rake both my hands through my hair.

"Please." Amyrah's voice warbles as she wraps her arms around herself. Beads of moisture glisten on her face, and her freckles stand out in bold relief against the ghostly pallor of her skin. My rage cools.

"Don't do this right . . . I don't have the energy for . . ." Her words are breathy, and her eyelids flutter as she pitches forward. Springing before Holden can beat me to it, I catch her as she loses consciousness.

"Look what you did," I say through gritted teeth.

"Me? You're the one who—"

An inhuman shriek echoes from beyond where the misty wall used to be, and the hair on my arms stands on end. Holden's eyes meet mine.

"The kaligorven?" he asks, his fury with me displaced by a sober grimace that yanks at his mouth.

"What else could it be?" I ask impatiently, as if the sound hasn't turn my blood to ice too. I slip my arms behind Amyrah's back and under the crooks of her knees, hoisting her up. Her head falls awkwardly, and I curse as I fold her in and rest her forehead under my chin.

Grabbing his ever-present longbow and nocking an arrow, Holden faces the thicker shadows spilling into Ketsé's central road.

"You got a sola in that quiver?" I ask over my shoulder.

The tip of his arrow dips, and his voice is terse. "What?"

"It's the only way you're going to beat them." Not quite true. I did kill one with my sword before Amyrah and I ventured out of the Vale, but that was because the wolf-sola had already weakened it. All I did was stand between the kaligorva and Amyrah, praying one stab through the chest would end its life.

"We'll do what we can," says another voice. Izra emerges from the shadows, bow drawn alongside the stout, sword-brandishing Filippos.

Frowning, I glance at the panicked Ketsans running through the streets. "You should get these people inside. Tell them not to go anywhere alone. It's going to feel like a nightmare, but they can weather it if they band together."

To my surprise, Izra offers no argument, nodding curtly before issuing out my instructions.

"You heard him. Women, children, and the elderly, go to your houses. Bar your doors. Ignite your lanterns and stoke your fires. It could be a long night." He turns to the men who remain. "Anyone who has skill with a bow or spear, gear up. We are going to make sure Ketsé's walls cannot be breached."

Good. That should keep Holden busy for a while. I look around, relieved when I can't see him anywhere.

"What about you, lad? Do you have any skills to offer?" Filippos approaches me.

I know he is aware of the weapons I brought into Ketsé, but I dip my eyes to Amyrah's ashen face. "Even if I did, that's not where I am most needed tonight."

He doesn't chastise me but slaps me on the back before running down the street.

Careful and as quickly as I can, I carry Amyrah to safety.

25
HOLDEN

FOUR YEARS IN THIS CLAUSTROPHOBIC PLACE, ingratiating myself to a foreign society, and all of it has shattered in an instant.

You were supposed to be what your siblings were not.

Slinging my bow to my back, I fling out my hands to try to rid them of the feeling of the ténesomni. They shake and I curl them into fists.

I was the Luvesti's finger on the Grovesha's pulse, never meant to be recognized for what I was. Didn't I accomplish that?

But no longer.

Not caring who sees me, I move through the streets in the opposite direction of where Izra led his men, letting my aura flare for the first time since I arrived. It feels alarmingly good. What does any of the secrecy matter anymore? I can relax and force the ténesomni to rush away from me, as it should.

Blazes. What did Amyrah do? What does any of this mean?

The temptation the Luvesti face to employ both light and darkness is unique to our race, but I have never seen ténesomni manifest physically in a person before.

Never except . . . But I was so young then. Can I trust that memory?

Belwyn was right; I should have stepped in sooner. My honesty could have prevented this from happening, but I was so wary of upsetting the tenuous balance I had struck in Ketsé, of disappointing the Luvesti, that I chose to keep my identity a secret.

It doesn't matter anymore—who I am, why I'm out here. I couldn't help the people of the Grovesha, and I couldn't find the one person I was sent to look for.

I need to leave as quietly as possible.

"And where are you going, Holden?"

The mature, feminine voice arrests me. I slow, glowering as I pivot around.

Elder Veridree steps from a passageway, arms crossed, ringed fingers tapping her elbow. She eyes my bow. "Luvesti or not, you're a skilled archer. You are to be helping defend our borders. Or was your commitment to the ways of Ketsé a farce from the beginning?"

I fold my arms and crack my neck with closed eyes. "You know it wasn't. I have proven many times over that I am for these people as much as my own."

"There lies the truth, doesn't it? We are not your people."

Eyes shooting open, I level a scrutinizing gaze at her. Father said I could trust Veridree with my identity, insisting she was supportive of our ongoing presence in the Grovesha. I regret ever confiding in her now.

"And that bothers you, doesn't it?"

When she doesn't respond, I forge ahead. "But why now? You've never had any problem lying to *your people* on my behalf."

My anger surprises me, showing how precarious the façade I had been maintaining was. *So much for respecting my elders.*

Veridree's eyes go round at my snappishness, but she masks her surprise with a pious raise of the chin. "Because I understood that one day it might prove useful to have help from Luvesta that wouldn't be hindered by the woodfolk's prejudice."

"Then don't expect me to respond like a Ketsan, and don't shame me for acting according to my Luvesti intuition." I turn to continue on my way, hoping I look like I know what I'm doing.

"Holden, stop."

It takes an enormous effort to heed her.

She catches up and lays a cold hand on my forearm. "I do not wish to own you. I apologize for calling your loyalty into question."

Sighing, I turn and regard her lined face.

"But I confess, this new development has shaken all of us. We are lost at sea here, Holden. Is there nothing that can be done?"

I pace away from her, pinching the bridge of my nose between thumb and forefinger. "Possibly, but I need to return to my kinsmen and seek their counsel."

Veridree looks disappointed, but she agrees. "Yes, if you have nothing else to offer us, then I believe that would be best." She withdraws her hand. "But I will ask you to do one more thing."

What would it be like to be in command of my own life? I stuff the thought down and grunt. "What would that be?"

Hiding her hands in the gaping sleeves of her robes, she lets out a long exhale. "Take Amyrah. I have already lied to her once about there being no Luvesti here, and that was on your request, but I fear for her now. Although it is clear she was trying to help, I do not think the woodfolk will be as lenient as I have been."

Regret returns in full force. Yes, my choice to keep her at arm's length was what failed her. I may have been alone out in the Grovesha, but I always knew I had a people, a home, waiting for me. What did she have to hold on to except a fleeting hope that she could learn something about her mother? She has been wandering this new land with no knowledge of any other Luvesti beyond herself.

Facing the elder again, I grant her a terse jerk of my chin. "I can try, but promise me that you will keep an eye out for the man I spoke to you about."

I did not think it possible to rattle Veridree until this moment. Her olive complexion pales to a sickly hue, and her mouth moves, no sound emerging. She blinks a couple times, a frown crimping her brow. "But have you not heard? It is he who has caused all this."

My mouth gapes, but the look in her eyes confirms it.

"Yes, Holden. Myrzeth is the one who has transformed the Vale."

Not allowing myself a chance to react, to let the elder see my shock, I redirect my path to Sabine's house.

Whether or not I can convince Amyrah to accompany me to Luvesta is irrelevant. I need to return there as soon as possible.

26

BELWYN

Safe inside the House of Hope, Sabine discovers what anyone who has spent time in the Vale knows: fire makes little difference against the ténesomni.

"*Stars*, what next?" She whisks a hand towel away from the hearth as it starts to smoke. "You'd think I didn't know my way around a fire."

Arlyn enters the room, carrying a lantern and dropping a massive, lumpy shape on the table. "It's not you, Sabine. It takes time to get used to the ténesomni." He glances at the cup and plate in my hands. "How's Amyrah?"

I lift a shoulder. "She's worn out but awake now. I think she'll be fine, but what happened out there was . . ."

What? Too much? Terrifying? Something I should never have pushed her to try?

"It was a lot," he says, looking at the floor. "More than any child should have to bear."

I want to tell him that she's not a child, but Amyrah is the same age as his daughter. I glance at the heap, which I now recognize as a travel pack. My eyebrows pop up. "Does this mean—"

Resolve firms his features. "Rael and I are going back to the Vale as soon as we are able."

An intake of air sounds behind me from the direction of the washbasin. A quick look over my shoulder finds Sabine aggressively scouring the pots, keeping her back to us.

Turning to Arlyn, I search his face. "Are you sure? The kaligorven could be more volatile than ever. The Grovesha haven't yet purchased peace from them." I cringe as soon as the words are spoken. Sola Vinari is wicked. I know it deep within my being. How can I suggest that peace is something we could ever gain from killing Light Creatures? "I-I mean, we don't know how they will behave here or within Tothlen Forest."

"What's to say they are obeying those 'rules' within the Vale anymore? Belwyn, we don't know what's happened there. Why has the ténesomni grown like this? Why wouldn't it let us back in?" He shakes his head in irritation, in dread. "There's much we need to understand, and we aren't going to do that cowering here."

If I give these questions any ground in my mind, they will undo me. I straighten my shoulders, refusing to let them gain a footing. "There's a difference between hiding and being smart."

"What do you know about it?" Arlyn snaps, slamming the heels of his hands on the table and trapping me with the expression of a man barely holding on. My children are living in that Ikktar as we speak, and now that the ténesomni is no longer keeping us out, I have the chance to go rescue them like I should have long ago. How can I stay here?" His head sags and his chest heaves. "What kind of father abandons his children?" A low moan escapes him. "A wise man would never have brought them to a land of night."

I am stricken both by his brokenness and by my own conscience, because I also left my own family. I curse my careless mouth.

Who am I to speak? As much as I have tried to be supportive of Amyrah and stayed by her side during her unspeakable grief, my ineptitude and lack of knowledge about her heritage and what it means for her has left me feeling powerless. For weeks I have been fighting down fears that I could never be worthy of her, and my stamina is running out.

Face it, Belwyn. You are not made for anything but darkness.

Grimacing, I attempt to move past Arlyn, but he straightens and runs a hand over his whisker-covered chin, closing his eyes and exhaling before looking at me again. "We've been praying for a way back in to fight for those who need us, and we'd be stupid not to risk it all now."

Those who need us.

The knot twists in my stomach. Grabbing the plate and cup I prepared, I leave the kitchen.

I find Amyrah sitting up in bed, a blanket wrapped around her shoulders. Several yellow candles crowd together on the desk, and a fire glows in the hearth. Her eyes flutter to mine, and I note the shadows skirting them, prominent even through the soft glow of her light.

"You didn't have to do this," she says, taking the items from me and setting the plate on her lap.

I raise an eyebrow. "It's just toast with dûrum nut butter and milk. Really creamy milk, though."

"Perfection." She offers me a weak smile and takes a bite. Her face relaxes as the simple fare works its magic.

Careful not to sit on her feet, I perch on the end of her bed and rest my elbows on my knees. She eats in silence while I stare at nothing in particular.

"I'm going with Holden," she says finally.

Those soft words tear through me like a kaligorva's claws. *You always feared she would choose him over you.* Ignoring the thought, I face her. "What?"

She sets her cup and plate on the small bedside table, shifting so her bare feet slip from the covers and touch the wooden floor, and raises her eyes to mine. "I'm going with Holden to Luvesta."

Unable to keep still, I stand and pace the room. "And when was this plan formed?"

Blinking, Amyrah steels herself with a quick inhale. "He left not long before you came up here."

Fingernails biting into my palms, I walk to the window and watch the darkness that lies beyond. "I was toasting bread while he was up here sweet-talking you away."

"It's not like that," she whispers.

Despite the pain in her voice, I wheel around. "Then tell me. Tell me what it's like, Amyrah."

Her lips press together, the silence prodding my mind dangerously close to the flames of anger. I let out a long breath and begin pacing again.

Her soft whisper finds me. "I'm afraid. I'm so afraid of what I did . . . what I let happen through me."

"And being with him will help you overcome that?"

"I don't know." She rubs her temples. "I feel unstable, and no one here can help me gain control."

I turn to her, my volume dropping to an earnest tone. "And you think Holden can do that for you?"

Shaking her head fervently, Amyrah groans. "You're not listening to me, Belwyn. Not Holden. The *Luvesti*. What better place to understand this than among the people I belong with?" She cringes and I let the words bite.

A tense silence falls for a while. "Look outside," she says finally, gesturing at the window, but I don't need to see it again.

"*That* is because of me." She thumps her breast with a fist. "*I* am the one who let it out to flood Ketsé."

Compassion curbs my anger. I cross the room and kneel, taking her hands. "Amyrah." She is so, so cold. "It would have been so much worse if you had done nothing. As awful as it was, you had to try."

"You don't understand." She bites her lip. "I could have forced it to hold its position, but something in me wanted to let the ténesomni out. *That* is why I need to seek someone who can help me control this thing." A sob shakes her shoulders. "I don't want to become like Myrzeth."

"Hey, listen to me. You will never become that. I won't let it happen."

She swallows and refuses to meet my eyes, so I grip her hands tighter until she acknowledges me. My voice softens to barely above a whisper. "No matter what you do, I'm here for you. You know that, right? You haven't been alone through all of this, and you don't ever have to be."

Sighing, she frees a hand from mine and lets her fingertips graze my cheek. "I know. You have done more for me than I deserve." A twinkling tear slips off thick eyelashes. "I couldn't have known how much I needed you."

Her eyes trip across my face as her fingers comb into my hair, sending shivers scampering across my skin. I try to remember how to breathe under her gaze. She tugs me closer but stills when our breaths tangle.

"I need to figure this out, Belwyn." Her cold, bright eyes meet mine.

Pleading. She lowers her hand to the tunic over my chest. "And going with Holden is my best chance for that right now."

Flooded with fiery jealousy, I straighten, my hands circling around Amyrah's waist. I pull her forward, to the edge of her bed, and the blanket falls from her shoulders as my mouth claims hers. She sucks in sharply, her body growing tense. Uncertain, but not forbidding. I kiss her softly, tasting the salt of her tears, the flavor of light. Slowly, she responds, her trembling fingers finding where my skull meets my neck and twisting into my hair. Her kiss deepens. An insatiable hunger fills me, a need to bind her to my heart, and my hand slides between her shoulders. I press her in, gently at first, then firmer as she melts into my arms.

I will drown all apprehensions about Holden from my mind. I will drown in her.

"Stop, Belwyn," she gasps suddenly, her words a cold wind. She lays both hands flat against my chest and pushes me away, shaking.

Surprised, I relinquish my hold. Doubt pins me when I see her pained expression, when I feel her fingers tremble against my collarbones.

"Sorry," I murmur, pulling farther back, my breaths leaving my chest in lurches. "What did I do?"

"Nothing," she says, brushing a spiral of hair away, but her troubled face communicates otherwise. "I-I can't think rationally when you—when we—" Her cheeks flush and she looks down, biting her lip. "It frightens me."

A stab of guilt twists my stomach as I realize how close I came to giving up control, to pressing for things that the old Belwyn would not have thought twice about. I reach for my hair and find my own fingers shaking. A bitter laugh spills out between my breaths. Yet again, I was one lapse in judgment away from becoming the very person I thought I had put to death. "Me too."

Expression softening, she grips my hands between us. "I don't want to lose myself. Each time we have been together like this, it's gotten more difficult to find the divide between what I want and what is right." A reflective tear trails over her freckles, then clings to her jawline. "I need to figure myself out first, though all my heart desires is you." Her eyes climb up to mine, stirring that desire to draw her in to my embrace again. Although my chest aches with bitter disappointment, I cannot be angry with her. She's right. How can we be the best for each other if we haven't learned to be that for ourselves? She is stronger than I will ever be.

Yanked through desire, disappointment, conviction, then admiration, my addled brain latches on to her last whispered words.

Taking her face in my hands, I touch my forehead to hers and close my eyes. She slides her fingers around my wrists, keeping me there.

We stay like that until my knees ache, and she draws away. I climb off the floor and sit next to her on the bed. She hooks one foot behind the other and rests her head on my shoulder, her fingers finding the spaces between mine and slipping in. I exhale slowly. No, it's not me she's denying; it's the passions that could so easily blind us if we gave in to them.

I find myself wishing we could stay in this moment forever, but my earlier conversation with Arlyn pricks at my thoughts.

"Arlyn and Rael are going back to the Vale," I say.

Straightening, Amyrah fingers the star pendant. "Wehna," she whispers. "Of course they are." She rests a hand on my forearm, sending shivers racing upward. "And what about you? I know you've been concerned for your family, however you try to hide it."

I open my mouth, wanting to deny it, but I can't. "Yes, I am. I'm dreading what the Foremost has done while we've been gone."

"You should go to them." Amyrah's fingers press, her eyes widening insistently. "I will be fine with Holden, and they need you."

The snake of resentment darts through me once again, and I force my jaw to relax. "Come with me, Amyrah." I angle my torso toward her, tuck a stray hair behind her ear, and fight the desire to kiss her again.

She shakes her head. "I can't, Belwyn. I need—"

"Yes, I know. *Your* people. But isn't there more to kinship than blood and heritage?"

When she has no reply, I let my eyes fall to her necklace. Once it was a reminder of the vicious wound I inflicted on an innocent Light Creature, but now it is a beacon in the black, guiding me through unseen dangers. My voice melts into something softer. "I don't agree with your insistence that you are going to turn into an instrument of destruction."

Her lips part, stunned, and I resist the urge to brush a thumb across them.

"The heart within you, the heart I have come to love . . ." I swallow, my throat inexplicably dry, and turn my gaze to our hands clasped between us. "That person cannot change so drastically. You have always been determined in your convictions, and I hate seeing you doubt yourself now."

"You think better of me than you should, Belwyn."

Quiet passes between us like an unfeeling river, carrying away our unspoken words. It is difficult to escape its insistent pull.

I look back at her face, at the freckles crossing her nose like a constellation of firelights. "Your light is needed there. Not in some distant kingdom where they have so much of it that I'm sure they can't fathom what darkness really is."

Her thoughts play out over her face. She exhales, a slight lowering of the brow shadowing her eyes before she closes them.

"Come with me." It's more of a prayer than a request, albeit a selfish one, because I can't comprehend going back into the heart of darkness without her.

Amyrah opens her eyes and fixes me with a firm look. "Yes."

Surprise trickles over me, but her transition from apprehension to determination was so swift, I struggle to trust it. "Really?"

Reaching for her plate again, she picks up the toast and takes her time chewing and swallowing a bite before answering. "Because you asked me, I will. And because you would do the same for me."

Twisting emotions force an odd laugh to bubble from my chest. I put my arm around her shoulder and breathe my words into her temple. "Why do you always have to be so maddeningly noble?"

She curls into my side, munching on her food. "I wish that were true."

Choosing to forgo my cloak, I adjust the bow and quiver on my back before slipping the satchel over my shoulder, making sure my sword hilt is still accessible.

"Ready?" Arlyn glances at me, holding the reins of a sorrel gelding in one hand and a lantern in the other. Rael sits in the saddle, the pack I saw earlier tucking her in from behind.

"Almost." I grab my lantern and bound up the house's front steps.

Amyrah waits at the top, fingers curled around the sleeves of her dress. I slow, glancing around the landing. "Where are your things?"

"Belwyn, I . . . I can't."

A cold fist clamps around my throat, trapping the air in my lungs. "Can't what?"

Her lips pinch together, like she is afraid of letting the truth out, but I already know it.

"I-I can't come with you."

My shoulders climb upward as the anger I have worked so hard to tame gnaws at its bonds. "I don't understand. You agreed—"

She takes a quick step forward, swallowing the space between us and pressing her fingertips to my cheek.

I look away from her apologetic gaze.

"I know I did. I know. And, oh, Belwyn." Her voice catches. "This is the last thing my heart wants."

It's difficult to swallow, to breathe, to do anything but stare at my feet and try to make sense of these idiotic things she's saying. My hands twitch, longing to fill my arms with her and whisper words that will sway her, that she cannot refuse. I want to hold her close and never let go, but instead of telling her how my soul is shredding within me, all I do is blink and stuff my hands into my pockets. "Then why?"

Amyrah lets her hand fall and clutches her arms around her abdomen, raising her face to the cloaked sky. "How can I go back when I don't understand what I am? How can I face the people I failed to save, walk where my father walked?" She presses the heel of her hand to her lips and closes her eyes.

I let out a slow breath. *Always so maddeningly noble.* Setting down the lantern, I slide my hands up and down her arms, trying to impart a small measure of assurance. "You don't do it alone."

Her chin lowers, her voice along with it. "There's a part of me that you'll never understand. I need . . ." She looks anywhere but my face. "As wonderful as you have been . . ." Her gaze hitches on mine. "Belwyn, I need answers that you can't give. It frightens me how, when I'm with you, I start to not care about the rest of this. The pain I've caused, the purpose I'm failing to understand. All of it."

My emotions walk the ridgepole between anger and pain. I stoop to pick up the lantern again, to give my words a chance to decide on which side of the roof they'd rather fall. "I'm sorry I've been so distracting."

Anger, then.

Amyrah's face flushes with hurt, and I despise myself for doing that to her. For feeling satisfied that I did.

She closes her eyes, brows crimping. "Stop that," she says, looking at me after regaining herself. "That's not what I said."

I shake out a brittle laugh. "It's what you meant, wasn't it? That you can't really be *you* when you're with me. That I'm preventing you from achieving what you were made to be." My voice snaps like a spark catching in old wood. I drop my gaze to the pendant resting between her collar bones and let everything else blur around the edges.

"No. *No.*"

She grabs my chin with both hands, as if to make sure she has my attention. Doesn't she realize that she's had it since the moment I first saw her? I swallow the longing, the anger, and try to empty myself so I can weather the gale of what comes next.

"But I don't know if it's the best time for us to be together. Maybe we need to find who we are apart from each other." Her eyebrows arch up, pleading with me to accept.

I want to give in, to agree and let her know she's right. We're alright. We'll make it through this. That I understand. But all I can manage is a weak, terse nod.

"Your family needs you, Belwyn. You. Not me." The hope melts from her face as she whispers, "Please be safe."

I thumb a tear from her face, pressing it to my lips. "You too," I mutter, turning to descend the stairs without a look back.

Wehna's parents and I are three houses down when I hear rapid footsteps behind me, barely audible above my drumming heart. I turn in time for Amyrah to barrel into my side, arms wrapping me tightly, fingers digging into my shoulder blades.

"We need to find each other again, Belwyn. We *will.*" A sob shakes her smaller frame. "I don't want this world if you aren't in it."

Stunned, I take a moment to make this statement fit together with everything that preceded it, but her words are an empty promise, a vain assertion. Silent sobs continue to shake her, though, and I am just standing here like an idiotic, unfeeling pillar. Resigning, I melt into the ruin of this last embrace and kiss the top of her head with closed eyes and a fragmenting heart.

"Elyōn watch over you," I say in a rough whisper. My fingers catch on the knot of her necklace.

And I let her go.

She was never mine to keep.

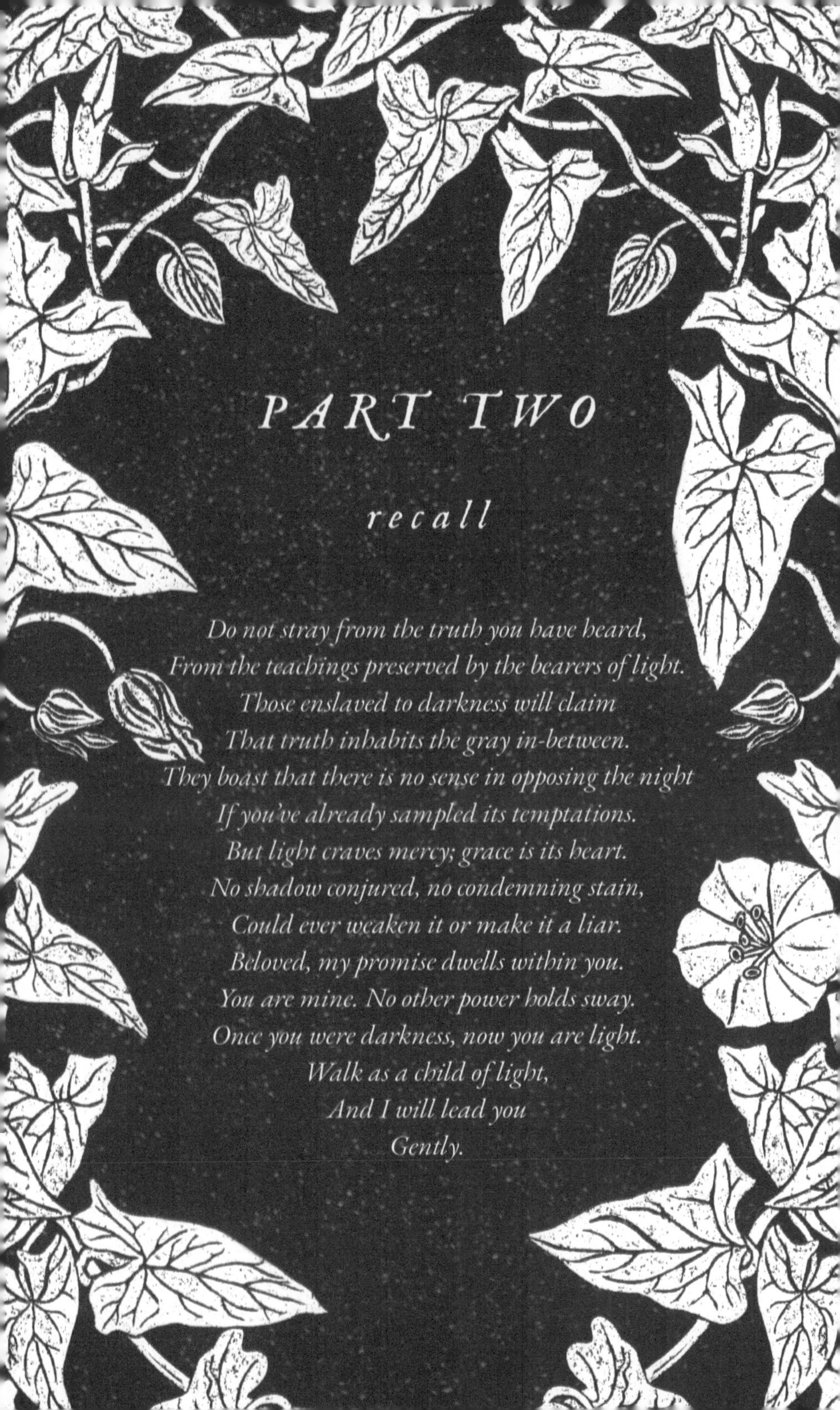

PART TWO

recall

Do not stray from the truth you have heard,
From the teachings preserved by the bearers of light.
Those enslaved to darkness will claim
That truth inhabits the gray in-between.
They boast that there is no sense in opposing the night
If you've already sampled its temptations.
But light craves mercy; grace is its heart.
No shadow conjured, no condemning stain,
Could ever weaken it or make it a liar.
Beloved, my promise dwells within you.
You are mine. No other power holds sway.
Once you were darkness, now you are light.
Walk as a child of light,
And I will lead you
Gently.

27
SEYLA

Seyla.

The whisper escapes the wind, entangling with the twilit air all about me. I spin, watching the strands of my name weave together, materializing into a hazy shape. A hand finds me. My wide eyes follow an arm as it forms into being, up to a delicate face framed within wide cheekbones and a strong jaw. Slanting brows, almond-shaped eyes with midnight irises and thick lashes. A high nose bridge. It's like looking in a mirror, except that my own face would never reflect such naivety.

Tetyan?

My younger sister's eyes sparkle and she laughs, tugging me to follow her through the moor's bracken. Her hip-length hair, unbound and black as ever, slides over our clasped hands.

I try to make her slow, but she is stronger than I remember. Tripping and stumbling with every step to keep up, I can't seem to find my feet.

Tetyan, wait. Please. There's something I want to s—

Heavy clouds, crackling with energy and bursts of lightning, overshadow us. My next step buries my right leg up to my knee in the earth, and the other follows. I pitch forward, my sister's fingers ripping from mine.

I dig at the ground like an animal, but it's as unyielding as stone. Terrified, I plead with Tetyan to help me.

Her face moves from side to side as the sheets of rain fall, blurring the sharpness of her features.

I'm sorry, Seyla.

Sorry for what? I ask.

I'm sorry you couldn't save me.

A shudder jolts through my chest as if someone grips me, shaking me back and forth.

She walks forward, crouches before me. I smell the eucalyptus balm I would rub on her chest on nights when she couldn't breathe. Looking up, I am horrified to discover the rain erasing her bit by bit, until she is a collection of loose threads only just holding together. Her eyes, though, are still intact, still brilliant though this obsidian tempest consumes the world.

If you wake up, you might be able to save yourself, she says weakly as she stands.

I struggle against the ground until my joints pop, but I cannot escape, cannot get to her in time.

Seyla, she whispers over her shoulder, her hair rising in the wind to embrace what's left of her face. *It's time to wake up.*

As I scream her name, she fades completely.

"Wake up, Seyla. *Wake up.*"

When I open my eyes, the darkness is thick and I can make out nothing, but heat radiates from someone hovering over me. With a cry, I grab the khukuri from under my pillow and launch off the mat on the ground, using my momentum to knock the man over and reverse our positions. Straddling his hips, I flip the blade and press its point under his jaw.

"Easy, *easy*. It's Téron." He holds his hands up in surrender. When my eyes finally confirm his identity in the gloom, I toss the blade to the side and scramble off him.

He rolls away, coughing and holding his midsection as he carefully sits up.

"Sorry," I mutter, trying to still my reverberating heart. "Do you need me to check that?" I motion to his injuries.

He grunts and lifts his shirt, then lowers it and shakes his head. "Though, I would be grateful if you reminded me never to wake you again."

I laugh weakly. "I doubt you'll forget."

Adrenaline dissipating, I stand and adjust the knob on the lantern, but the flame does nothing to lessen the gloom. Disconcerted, I level a look at Téron. "How long did I sleep?"

Resting his head on the cot, he stares at the tent ceiling. "It's mid-morning."

A chill runs through me. *How in Atsun . . .*

"To attention, úramech." Commander Verrek's voice thrums in my chest from outside the tent.

"*Heshïn*," I hiss, scrambling around for the missing pieces of my uniform.

"That would be why I was attempting to wake you." Téron tilts his chin toward the door flap, his mouth turning up at the corner.

"Seyla Bréinth." The crunching footfalls halt outside my tent as I slip on my second bracer. I duck out the flap and snap my spine straight.

Verrek's chest is right in front of my nose, and it's a good thing because otherwise I would not be able to see him. The air is thick with a disorienting darkness, and for a beat I forget why I have stepped outside. This is not like anything I have ever experienced before. A physical *presence* that seeps into my thoughts.

I gasp as I realize what this is: *ténesomni*.

Perhaps it is a combination of the terrible dream and the lack of ability to see the sky, but panic overwhelms me in a potency I have not known since the night Tetyan was lost to me. Grinding my teeth, I make my eyes meet Verrek's.

"What is it, Commander?"

He turns to the side. "Bring me light."

One of Verrek's underlings hands him a lantern. The flames within are reddish, like the moon on a night when smoke chokes the air. He holds it higher and points his chin at my tent. "How is he?"

I school my features into neutrality. "Fine, no thanks to my comrades."

Verrek does not make a response but assesses the line of soldiers instead. The hard creases of his face deepen as he strolls down the row. My eyes, somewhat adjusted to the lack of light, follow the glow of his lantern.

"Guards of the Southlands, this is the moment you have been training for. The boundary we have patrolled for a century is no more, and we can no longer count ourselves better than the denizens of the Vale."

A shiver passes through my body.

He turns on his heel at the far end and makes his way back, assessing every úramech as he passes them. "We no longer have the advantage. In fact, the upper hand is theirs, for they have lived a lifetime adapting to the ténesomni. Arm yourselves and take up your positions along the border. We will not let a single soul past our defenses without our knowledge. Understood?"

A chorus of affirmations launches skyward.

"*We have no one*," Verrek shouts.

"*Let no one have us*," the regiment answers.

The words rasp my throat like sand. I have never struggled to say the phrase before. It always seemed an appropriate motto for someone to whom life has dealt a poor hand. I made it my identity.

But it's easy to scorn the world when no one depends on you.

Verrek's chin dips. "First watch, to your posts," he says, halting in front of me as he waits for everyone to dissipate. In my peripheral vision, I see Ordin taking an extended amount of time to check his gear, but I keep my chin high and my attention fixed on the commander.

"Now, Úramech Bréinth," Verrek says to me in a low tone, "it is time to see if your healing abilities rival your quick blade."

My insides quiver. I knew this day was coming, when this man I risked everything to save would be sent to Tarriv as nothing more than a tool, a means to glean information. I have told myself countless times not to let myself get attached, pretended that giving him such meticulous care was a calculated move that could bring me advancement.

But maybe I'm not as skilled of a liar as I thought.

"My men will come for him shortly," Verrek says with an air of finality, motioning to his attendant as he turns to leave.

Desperation rises in my throat like acid. The day I rescued Téron from that boat, I didn't do it so he could be a pawn in the Imperii's game, so he could be discarded to rot in the Tarriv refuse pits.

"I will be ready," I say before the ténesomni has a chance to erase the commander completely.

He stills, and I can feel Ordin's eyes boring holes in my profile.

"You already have a posting, do you not, úramech?" he asks, not bothering to turn my way.

"Yes, sir, but—"

"Then that's an end to it," he snaps.

My eyes widen and my mouth opens to fire back a retort, but one glance at Ordin dissuades me. His expression is severe in a way I do not recognize. Less like he is critical of me as a potential insult to his manhood and more like he is concerned that I will do something foolish.

"Commander, if I may be so bold to ask you to give me an audience?" Ordin steps forward and bows his head in subservience. No doubt he still smarts from the loss of one of his ranks.

The long pause heightens my anxiety until Verrek squares his shoulders to him, clasping his hands behind his back. "Speak."

"Úramech Bréinth is not respected within this regiment, though she is equally as capable—if not more—than half of the men stationed here."

I inhale a sharp breath. Did he pay me a *compliment?*

Ordin fingers the straps of his leather overcoat, his face puckering as if he has burped up something foul. "But a soldier without respect is a soldier alone, and a soldier alone is a chink in the Southland's armor."

Verrek clears his throat impatiently. "Your point?"

"I was getting there, sir," the old man growls.

It is difficult to suppress a grin. Ordin's quick mouth doesn't irritate me half so much when he isn't using it to color me with insults.

"I suggest the best way she can be of use to the Agmen," he continues, putting on an attitude of humility with painful effort, "would be to escort the stranger to Tarriv. Seyla is already on familiar terms with him, and if he proves hesitant to comply, I believe she could be an asset in making him see reason."

The recent nightmare rises before my eyes, and again I watch Tetyan's sad features unraveling in front of me.

I will not be guilty of failing to save yet another person.

Please . . . please make this work, my mind begs. In the event that the ancestors don't answer, my fingers twitch toward my khukuri. Rash actions have always served me better than these futile entreaties, anyway.

I freeze when Commander Verrek's gaze darts over me before returning to Ordin's heavyset frame. His eyes narrow, as if confirming something to himself. "Neither of you would be my first choice against the enemy, so I accept your suggestion on the condition that you also accompany her to Tarriv. It will free up my other men for more important duties."

Ordin's countenance falls, but he straightens. "Yes, Commander."

Verrek beckons me forward, motioning to my tent. "Bring him out. I wish to speak with him before you leave. Ordin, see to securing the horses."

With a dip of the head, my unexpected ally departs, and I slip into my tent.

Téron is on his feet, fastening a battered leather jerkin over a threadbare tunic. I managed to trade from my dwindling supply of tinctures for both. It is fortunate that a stubborn case of armor itch has been plaguing the encampment.

Animals. Did their mothers never teach them to bathe?

"Looks like it all fits well," I say, risking wearing my commander's patience thin with small talk. Verrek may have the right to issue commands, but I prefer to leave Téron with his dignity.

"It does. Thank you." His eyes graze mine, and I find myself grateful that I committed their piercing blue color to memory before the ténesomni could hide them.

Seyla Bréinth, what has gotten into you?

He points to a jagged seam on his pants. "Your sewing skills could use some refinement, though."

My ire starts to rise, but then I catch the hint of a smile on his face.

I swallow my own.

"Seyla, I do not have all day."

Though the irritation in Verrek's tone is gratifying, I am wary of pushing my luck any further. "My commander wants a word with you."

"I heard." Téron fastens the last button of his jerkin as I hold the tent flap open. "Let's get this over with," he says as he ducks out.

I take up my lantern and follow, my heart swelling with a strange sense of pride when I see him stand straight and tall before a leader known for his calculated moves and ruthless punishment.

Verrek's eyes narrow for a moment, and a hard grin splits his face like a seam in a rock. He holds out an open palm. "I am long past due for welcoming you to the Southlands."

My hands stiffen at my side. Hospitality is not usually one of the commander's strengths.

Téron's brows lift in surprise. His posture relaxes as he reaches to take his hand. "Thank you—"

With alarming speed, Verrek makes a fist and propels it into Téron's midsection. I taste blood as a guttural moan spills from Téron's lips and he curls forward. Verrek moves to catch him, whispering into his ear loud enough for me to hear, "You have been allowed to heal only so you could be whole for the Imperii. Be grateful that my loyalty to him has kept me from interrogating you myself." He straightens, looking down his crooked nose at Téron, who meets his eyes with unfathomable calmness.

It takes everything in me not to go to him.

"Do not think for one moment that your stay will be anywhere near as comfortable as it has been." Stepping back, Verrek lets Téron slump to the ground and pins me with a severe look. "Deliver your pet to the capitol, úramech, or may you perish in Ikktar's heat." He motions to his attendant, then strolls away, taking the light with him.

I hate him. I hate that cruel man and his need to make sure everyone around him knows he's the one in control.

When he is out of earshot, I feel safe to assess Téron's side. My shaking fingers slip under his jerkin, feeling hot blood soaking his tunic. I help him slide back so he can rest against the tent pole, undo the jerkin's buttons, and lift his shirt. A gentle probing of his wound confirms that his stitches have popped.

A humorless laugh whistles between Téron's clenched teeth. "It looks like you'll have the chance for more sewing practice."

I gape at him, then let a wry grin emerge, thankful there's no way he can see it.

28

AMYRAH

"WITH A LITTLE INGENUITY AND PATIENCE, you don't have any reason to fear the ténesomni."

All of Sabine's adopted children press around me in the quiet street while I craft a quick bolétis lantern. They are cautious to stay within the boundary of my illumination—at least I have not lost all my good Luvesti qualities—as they watch my movements with rapt attention. I knot the twine that will secure the willow branches, then work aside a couple of the bars near the top to make a gap wide enough to slip four bioluminescent mushrooms through. When finished, I hold it up for the children to see.

"But they don't do anything," a boy says, doubt wrinkling his freckled nose.

"When they are held up against a flame, yes, they are pitiful."

Raising an eyebrow, I beckon him and another boy closer. They step over warily.

"Take both of these lanterns and walk twenty paces down the street."

"But what about the monsters?" the other boy whispers, his hair falling over one eye.

I do my best to smile. "The Watch has made sure Ketsé's borders are secure, remember? We're safe within these walls. Do you think you can help give these other children the courage they need?"

They look at each other, then stand together, walking to where I instructed.

"Good. Now—Joph, was it?" There is enough light from the ignati to see the freckled boy nod. "Blow out your other lantern."

The children gasp when the flame flickers out. A tiny girl finds her way under my arm. "I wanna stay with you, where shadows can't get me."

"It will be fine," I soothe, giving her a gentle embrace. "Just watch."

It doesn't take long for the faces of both boys to come into clear, cool blue focus. I let out a chuckle at the children's astonishment.

"Do you see? The ténesomni doesn't regard the bolétis' glow as a threat, and it doesn't try to crowd around it like it does with flame."

The boys return, both staring in wonder at the mushroom lantern.

I take it from them and place it in the middle of our gathering. "If you train yourself to see with them, you will always have a source of light at hand. You don't have to worry about burning yourself or setting something ablaze."

The little girl peels from my side and wastes no time constructing her own lantern cage from the piles of supplies I had Holden help me gather this morning.

Holden, not Belwyn.

A soft ache grips my chest.

After making sure the older ones understand my instructions and can help the rest, I stand up, dust off my dress, and watch the children go about the task. All indications of fear have vanished from their concentrated faces for the moment.

"You are so good with them."

Sabine stands outside the front entrance of the house, a metal lantern dangling from her crossed arms. I ascend the steps to join her.

"The ténesomni is so intimidating, especially for young ones. The least I can do is help them find small ways to fight the shadows."

Sabine grips my shoulder. "You have done that." Her mouth curves down. "Amyrah, are you certain I can't convince you to stay?"

I sit on the top step and observe a mild dispute over who gets what color of bolétis. This place has been a balm for my soul in many ways, but guilt shivers through my thoughts. They wouldn't have to be making bolétis lanterns at all if I hadn't released the ténesomni in the first place.

I shake my head. "No. If I'm here, I could be a danger to everyone. I've already done more harm than good."

So, so much harm.

Sabine lowers herself beside me with a small grunt. "Now that simply isn't true, Amyrah. You give much more light than you realize." She dismisses my skeptical expression with a wave. "And I'm not talking about the kind we can see. What you brought to Ketsé was a chance for us to gain some compassion for our fellow man. It was so easy to think of the Vale as a place where dark things prowled instead of a prison to souls every bit as human as ours." She chuckles ruefully. "Rael and Arlyn have always seen it, but the rest of us have needed more convincing."

"I'm sure that's not true. Look at what you've done with this house, these children. You're responsible for your own share of light, Sabine."

Her eyes mist over. "Torr and I have given them a home, yes. We've supplemented them with love, but what I wouldn't give for their situations to be reversed, to fix all the hurt that led them here in the first place."

Laughter reaches us as the children compare lanterns and play in the street without a care.

"This world is broken, Amyrah." Sabine swipes roughly at the dusting of flour clinging to her skirts. "Cracked and bleeding at the seams. It's so easy to pass over the wrong surrounding us when a much greater evil looms in the distance." She blinks and her eyes fix on mine. "What you did was remove that excuse for Ketsans. We no longer have them to point at and say, 'look how much worse they are.'"

Finding I can't hold her gaze, I rest an elbow on my knee, cup my chin in my hand, and look ahead.

"You removed our pretense, Amyrah, and now we will be made to see the darkness that lies within our own hearts."

We shift into speculative silence, observing the children as they swiftly abandon their apprehensions, laughing together. I close my eyes and let my heart soak in the sound of freedom.

After a while, Sabine stands and offers me her hand. "Well, if you're set on it, then I'm going to see to it you and Holden are well stocked with provisions."

I let her help me up, then follow her through the ill-lit house and into the kitchen. The table is already laid with foods of all kinds. Several small loaves, three blocks of cheese, a lumpy brown package tied with string.

"You knew I wasn't going to change my mind, didn't you?"

Sabine raises an eyebrow. "Please. A girl who faces a wall of ténesomni when she doesn't know if she can make a dent against it is not someone who is going to give up her convictions." She points at the cheese and hands me waxed cloth. "You can help by wrapping those up."

In little time, the provisions are bundled together in two even piles.

"You'll want to be careful with that cheese. My best guess is it will have to be eaten within the first few days. The meat will keep for a while. It's been salted, smoked, and dried. Save that for the end."

"You shouldn't have gone to all this effort," I say as I fill my own satchel and a second that Sabine gave me.

She waves me off. "Nonsense. Caring for young ones is what I do best."

"Miss Amyrah, that man is here for you." I look to see Joph standing in the kitchen, pointing outside.

The other children race in, bolétis lanterns held high. They bombard their matron, each clambering to show her what they made. Rosy glows cling to their cheeks, lifting my heart's weight.

"Listen, you rascals." Sabine laughs after showing the appropriate amount of recognition to each creation. "Make sure you thank Amyrah for teaching you how to make them. And give her a good ol' squeeze. She's setting out soon."

After warding off their questions and farewells, I manage to escape their clutches with the two satchels and my cloak. It is much too warm to wear it now, but I will need it for the nights and the inevitable rains. Right before I reach the door, however, Sabine calls me back.

"Take care, Amyrah girl." She pulls me into a tight hug. I let myself sink into her embrace, inhaling the fragrance of lavender and home cooking that clings to her hair. "Elyōn will watch over you. Remember that. Call to him in your distress." She pushes away and cups my cheek. "*Avis ténesomni luvem.*"

"After darkness, light." I nod, tears pricking my eyes.

Holden waits for me at the base of the stairs, his back laden with traveling gear and weapons. I falter a little when I see that he also has a circle around him where the ténesomni dares not reach.

A smirk pulls at his mouth. "What, you thought I didn't have the same fancy tricks as you?"

I shake my head. "No, it's just strange seeing it around someone else. Is this what I look like to other people?"

He steps back and squints at the space around me. "Yes. I think it's safe to say we are both equally anomalous." His eyes fall to the satchel at my side and the one in my hands. "Is that all you're bringing?" he asks, taking the second bag and adding it to his load.

"It's all I have." But that's not true. My hand travels up to my throat, feeling nothing but bare skin where the argentilum pendant should be. I frown. "Give me a moment," I say, dropping my gear and sprinting back to my room.

After a thorough search, however, I can't find the necklace anywhere.

Frustrated, I return to the street.

"Ready now?" Holden asks, one eyebrow arching.

Pasting on a smile, I slip my satchel over my shoulder and join him.

Holden speaks with the manager of the stable inside the Western Gate, handing her a small but heavy-looking pouch, no doubt filled with arlum. Moments later, the woman leads out a beautiful dapple-gray horse, taller and livelier than the one Arlyn chose for Rael.

Handing the lantern to me, Holden thanks the woman and takes the reins. The horse greets him with a snort and stamp of its feet.

"Yes, hello, my friend. It's been a while." Holden rubs the horse's nose, looks at me, and jerks his chin. "Come meet Zenith."

At my wary approach, Holden chuckles. "He's a bit spirited, but he won't hurt you."

"Is he yours?"

He feels over Zenith's legs, checks his horseshoes, and tightens the saddle straps. "A present from my father before I left Luvesta." He slips off his gear and ties it and the lantern to the saddle strings. Turning to me, he ignores the question on my face and holds out a hand. "Well? You're up."

A cold rush prickles over my skin. "You want me to ride that thing?"

He gasps with mock hurt. "Zenith, did you hear that? She called you a thing." The horse nickers. At my stern look, Holden drops the act. "How else did you think we were going to get there?"

"I . . . I don't know. Walking sounded like a reasonable option."

He puts the reins over Zenith's head. "You have no idea what kind of journey lies before us, do you?"

My cheeks warm. "Obviously not, Holden. It's not like I've ever seen a complete map of Atsun."

His face grows somber. "No, I suppose you haven't." He comes close and puts his hands on my sides, his expression neutral.

"What are you doing?" I squeak.

"Giving you a boost." Without allowing me a chance to protest, he lifts me and sets me atop the horse.

I swallow a yelp, choosing to give no room to the indignity, and focus on hoisting up the skirt of my dress so I can sit with a leg on either side of the horse. I reach for the reins, but Holden holds them tight and puts his left foot in the stirrup.

"Aren't you going to ride your own horse?" I ask dumbly.

He pauses and looks up at me. "This *is* my own horse, Amyrah. Do you even know how to ride one?"

When I can't supply a decent retort, he huffs a laugh. "Don't worry. It won't be as bad as you think." He pushes himself up in the stirrup, glancing at me. "Shuffle back, will you? I don't want to kick you in the face."

I might prefer being knocked out to having to ride like this, I think darkly.

But after he mounts and the West Gate is opened for us, Zenith's rhythmic gait settles me. I don't sense any tension from Holden, despite my own. No awkwardness as I am forced to slip my arms around his torso and cling to him. This is different. I feel safe with him, but still wholly in command of my thoughts.

They drift to Belwyn now, my stomach wobbling as I process yesterday's events. He caught me at a vulnerable moment, and my heart clung to his affection. Alarming desire ignited within me, whispering enticing words I almost didn't have the strength to resist. It would have been so, so easy to give in to the flame that twisted my core.

I draw in a sharp breath and hope Holden didn't notice.

Was that how it was between my father and mother? Did they feel this thrill, this fear that once the door is open, they would not be able to resist walking through it?

I swallow against the tears, wishing I had a mother to help sort through these tangled emotions and find the truth hidden at the center.

Bitterness flares within my chest. *Elyōn, how could you have left me so unprepared for life?*

But shame rushes to temper it. He gave me Orlagh, didn't he? And although her season for romantic love had long since passed, I can recall her soft words.

Be wary, sweet Amyrah, of awakenin' love before its time. Whenever yeh give of yer heart, the body will press yeh to follow. There is a time and place where tha' is good and right and beau'iful. But take care, my girl, not to awaken it before its time.

Was that the real reason I pushed Belwyn away? Or was it because I understood the best way I could honor his love was to trust that if we are meant for each other, there will be a day when longing turns to privilege, when we will be forged into two halves of a whole?

I bite my lip. Refusing to awaken love before its time is not the same thing as crushing it completely.

A shiver races down my spine, a rush of light-headedness chasing it, and I push out a breath to free myself from its guilt-ridden touch.

"So . . ." I clear my throat. "Your father gave you this horse?"

"Zenith was always mine, really. He doesn't appreciate many others riding him."

A squirrel, too high to see, chatters at us from above.

"What does the name mean?"

"Zenith?" he asks, as if needing to confirm that's really what I don't know. My silence is my answer. He adjusts the reins. "It refers to the moment when the sun is highest in the heavens, when all the world is bright and the shadows barely cling to the ground."

I gaze at the phantom-like trees. The Tothlen Forest outside of Ketsé is wild, untamed, and more mysterious now that ténesomni prowls it. I watch its ropes strain toward us, shuddering to recall the times I have let them course through me.

"Why didn't you tell me you were Luvesti, Holden?" I ask quietly.

I feel his back tense.

"I-I couldn't."

"Couldn't, or wouldn't?" I pull back indignantly, nearly losing my balance and clutching his tunic tighter as I wait in vain for his answer.

Releasing a breath, I let the matter drop with it. "When did you realize?"

Holden's face turns to the side. "Realize what?"

"That I was Luvesti too?"

He faces the path again, stretching his neck. "The moment I met you."

Tears prick my eyes, but I can't fight them any longer. Will I ever stop feeling like everyone is holding me at arm's length?

Everyone except Belwyn.

"You must understand, Amyrah. Our people learned long ago that our name is met with disdain in the Grovesha, and sometimes it has provoked persecution. Keeping our identities a secret was for our protection. I was shielding us both."

A heavy exhaustion grips me, and I lean my cheek on his back. "I still can't fathom how Ketsé could scorn the people to whom they owe their freedom."

"Freedom is a matter of perspective. For all you knew before you left the Vale, the whole world was infested with sentient darkness. If you had never ventured beyond its borders and learned what kind of life lay beyond, would you have ever grasped how trapped you were?"

The horse's footfalls fill the silence between us.

"Yes," I whisper after a while. "I would. I *did*." Something inside me has always believed in light I could not see.

"That's because you're Luvesti. Perhaps that wasn't the best question."

I worry my lip, pondering if every ambition, every hope I've had, can be explained away by my heritage. Is it an unfeeling fact that can't be denied any more than my need for food and water? Am I a witless piece in Elyōn's elaborate game, unable to alter my destiny if I wanted to?

That is not who I know him to be.

"We're all enslaved to something, whether we acknowledge it or not," Holden says. "The Ketsans recognize how little control they have, and it scares them. They resent Luvesta for it. They may have been spared having to live in the ténesomni for a century, but that doesn't mean their lives have been absent of turmoil."

"What about Luvesta?" Already uncomfortable, I shift in the saddle. *How am I going to travel like this for days*? "What false ideas of freedom do they hold?"

The trees have begun to thin around us, the path growing wider.

"That," he says, leaning forward and clicking his tongue to urge Zenith into a trot, "is a good question. It might be best for you to answer that one on your own."

"So, you don't know, then."

His response is a laugh, and the tiniest pinprick of hope fights my inner doubts.

29

WEHNA

In the stillness of Amyrah's cottage, the burdens I have clung to begin to unravel, thread by thread. It's as if this place has seen the most horrible trials and overcome them, and I am enfolded in an air of peace that goes beyond my comprehension.

But what I do understand is here, I can breathe. Here, I can weep.

I unclip a blanket from the clothesline, keeping an eye on Arvo as he attempts to train the kid to jump over an obstacle of his own construction. First, he demonstrates how to perform the feat, then he implores the tiny thing to take a leap. His efforts are met with an obstinate bleat, and I smile.

Arvo complained about the boredom at first, missing his playmate Téah fiercely, but now he has named and befriended all the goats and made it his personal ambition to remodel the chicken coop because "they deserve the best home for their babies." I decide not to tell him that unless he can find a rooster, he won't have to worry about that.

I feel like I have my brother again. And maybe, just maybe, he also has me.

"Arvo, lead the goats back into their shed," I call. "It's getting late."

His lip protrudes momentarily, and he snatches the kid and totes him to the shed. I glance upward at the brilliance that trails him before stepping inside the cottage with my load of fresh laundry.

The tiny sola cutting through the black fills me with wonder. Since we arrived, the wren has never strayed far from the homestead. Day and night, its lusty song permeates the atmosphere. Arvo seems to be a particular favorite, and wherever he goes, the sola isn't far behind. It has been a huge relief after fretting about him nonstop since my parents left.

No. Not since they left. Since they were murdered.

Dropping the basket at my feet, I settle on the edge of one of the beds and allow my grief to swell.

The way Mada and Pada left us used to spark a bitterness that burned as hot as a blacksmith's forge. I wanted it to tear through me, to consume all the pointless things that made me weak, to leave me like a sharpened blade when it was through. The fire didn't do what I'd hoped, reducing me to an unfeeling, jagged pile of bones that could neither bend with the blows of life, nor curve to embrace its beauties. Without those soft places to cushion me, I became brittle. I damaged all I touched.

This place is gradually turning my heart of stone into a heart of flesh once more. I'm no longer surrounded by what a family should look like; it's just me and my brother with a sola watching over us, set apart in our own little world with no expectations except what we choose for ourselves.

Tears dampen my cheeks and I feel no compulsion to whisk them away. What if it isn't the absence of pain, fear, and weakness that makes us strong? What if strength comes from how we endure in the storm of those realities?

Happy chatter drifts through the open door, and I dry my eyes before Arvo sees me like this. The last thing I want is to snap him out of this blissful reprieve from our troubles. Although the ténesomni prowls around the homestead, and more than once I have imagined smoldering eyes deep within its folds, we have been safe.

Stranger still, I have not doubted Elyōn once since we came.

I glance at the food on our table. Orlagh has visited us a few times, bringing a basket heaped with bread, biscuits, and spiced buns to share. Last time, she also brought a parcel of cheese, fresh herbs, and tomatoes from the Perens. She won't take anything in recompense, but she did let me slip a handful of eggs into her empty basket. For some reason, seeing the eggs laying there made her eyes tear up.

Sighing, I stand and tend the fire, which has dimmed into glowing coals perfect for cooking. I place a metal grate over it and lay several thick slices of Orlagh's bread on top. After toasting one side, I flip them and adorn each with two generous slices of cheese.

It isn't much, but it will have to do. I'm certain Arvo can't come up with a credible argument against cheese toast.

I allow my mind to drift as I watch the cheese melt.

When my brother's shrill voice reaches me, I scramble to my feet, my heart lurching, and run to the doorway. I cling to the frame, searching the yard for danger. The sola sits above the goat shed, preening its gilded feathers. I can't see Arvo anywhere, but I can hear his joyful prattle.

"Arvo?"

30
BELWYN

IF YOU FOLLOW THE STREAM, it will take you home.

Amyrah's words from a lifetime ago echo through my mind as I drag my feet through dewy grass, the sound of mirthful waters trickling to my right. I grip the star pendant in my palm and try to think of anything other than the girl I took it from. The girl who begged us to part.

I listen to the stream, its melody drawing up the memory of when I held Amyrah along its banks. Is it wrong to wish we could go back to that day?

Of course it's wrong. That only happened because she had witnessed the Shrouded tear her father to pieces, and I was the only one there to bear the weight of her grief. I let that realization sink in, and every other moment we shared comes into a cruel clarity.

Was it just coincidence that drove us together? Maybe my own grief, self-loathing, and loneliness truly did make me view her as something she is not, could never, be.

Do I love her?

My chest burns with the answer. *Yes, I do. With all my heart I do.* The next thought festers in my mind like a disease.

Does she *love* me?

I swallow, trying to forget the question, but it shadows me like a kaligorva.

"Do you see that?" Rael's soft voice pulls me from my brooding. It has been days since I have heard her speak, and I squint into the ténesomni and see nothing. My foot lands on a branch, cracking it loudly. I should be more cautious, but I am weary from the ten days' journey from Tothlen Forest, through the Askonnet Mountain Pass, and down into the Vale. We may have not come upon a single kaligorva, but I have been on edge, senses heightened, the entire time.

I will be home soon. The thought does little to console me.

"Yes, yes, there it is."

Arlyn's excited tone snaps me to alertness a moment before blinding light exudes from high in the trees. I step into the illumination, staring dumbly until my mind registers it as a tiny bird. A wren-sola, like the one that found Amyrah and me before we left the Vale, perches above a clearing. I blink away the spots in my eyes and look around us. A small cottage comes into view.

Amyrah's cottage, where she kissed me for the first time.

My lungs tighten with her absence.

With a startling cry, Rael throws herself from the horse and limps to the small silhouette of a boy. Arlyn follows with no less abandon, swallowing them both in his arms.

Grateful weeping washes away the silence. This is a sacred moment that I dare not disturb.

I look back at the cottage's open door, where inviting ignati light glows within. A shadow slides into view, and a feminine voice calls into the evening air.

"Arvo?"

Rael and Arlyn turn toward the sound. *Wehna*.

With all that I could face today, I can't bear to add another meeting that will dredge up more questions and more pain. I take advantage of their distractedness, tether the abandoned gelding beside a handcart and a dwindling supply of hay, and slip into the black with a lantern in hand.

My breathing tangles with the racket of my heart's quickening pulse as I traverse the woods that border the world I used to know. This might be the shortest leg of my journey, but it can't be over soon enough. Something snaps to my left, and I raise my lantern, cursing when the flame gutters out. The oil must be spent, and Arlyn was the one carrying the extra supply. When more crunching emerges closer than before, my palms grow slick. I open my eyes idiotically wide, forcing them to adjust to the absence of light, and spot a patch of bolétis. Hands shaking, I pluck them and cram as many as I can into the metal cage.

The wind picks up, carrying a twinge of foul odor and a hissing sound. Clumsily, I draw my father's longsword and hold it out. It glows blue in the bioluminescence.

This was what I dreaded as the three of us traveled, though it never came. I can't think of a reasonable explanation for why we didn't encounter any kaligorven on our journey, save for the prayers I overheard Arlyn uttering. Maybe the shrieks that rang out while we were in Ketsé were meant to frighten. Maybe they aren't interested in us.

Or maybe they are glad to welcome one of their own.

My back tenses. Returning is both a relief and an utter failure.

I listen for more sounds, struggling to control my breaths, but there are none. Sheathing the sword, I press on with my odd lantern raised. Though it feels a little foolish relying on mushrooms for illumination, I am surprised by how well they work. The light is enough to know where I'm setting my feet, almost as good as the fire had been in this intense black. Still, dread sticks to my mind like ash. I remember how thick the ténesomni grew the last time I was in the Vale, when the kaligorven had issued the command of darkness. There is no question it has grown since we left.

My steps quicken, and so does my pulse.

Concentrating on every movement, I don't think to raise my eyes toward Utsanek until the trees fall away behind me.

I come to a stuttering stop.

An odd glow arches over the city, a sickly dawn in a land that cannot know the word.

The kaligorven have not demanded complete darkness, then.

I pause and stare at the lantern in my hands, the sword strapped to my side, the satchel crossing my torso. What kind of upset will my reappearance cause? Is it wise to turn up looking like I've been on a journey?

After searching the trees near the edge of the Reckoning Grounds, I find a mound composed of a few boulders and a moss-covered log. I scoop out a cavity in the log, wrap my sword, bow, and arrows in my cloak, and place them as far within as I can. I start to do likewise with the satchel, but it belongs to my brother, Korvin. For some reason I don't care about not returning the sword to my father, but the thought of coming home without this tattered bag pains me. I settle for emptying the waxed fabric wrappers and any other clues to where I've been.

I risk leaving Amyrah's necklace wound around my wrist; it could easily be mistaken for a simple leather bracelet. And the lantern, once emptied of the bolétis, shouldn't draw any notice.

With a deep breath and a muttered prayer that I won't do something stupid, I enter the city that has been, and will always be, my home.

31
WEHNA

ARVO'S GLEEFUL NOISES STILL, but before I can figure out what excited him, the smell of something burning reaches me. I dash back to the fire to find my toast blackened at the edges.

"*Falling firelights.*" I grab a lifter and attempt to rescue our pitiful meal. The first piece flips off the grate and lands cheese-side down on the platter, but I manage to retrieve the others without mishap.

Shuffling noises reach me from outside, and I push a spiral of hair out of my hot face with the back of a hand. "Sorry, fledgling. The meal is a bit burned tonight."

"Burned or not, I'm sure it will be wonderful."

The platter slips from my hands, shattering on the floor.

Someone stands in the doorway—a man with hair like burnished bronze, hands that can fix anything in the world, and a laugh that can be heard three houses down.

"Pa-Pada?" I gasp.

My legs buckle and I crumble.

In three steps he is on the floor next to me, pushing the ruined food and pottery to the side. He grabs my face in his hands, glistening eyes drinking in every facet of it. "My girl."

I lean into his touch and raise a shaking hand to feel his cheek, struggling to believe that he exists. "H-how is this possible? How are you here?"

He lurches out a sob and pulls my head to his chest, stroking my hair and holding me so tight it hurts.

I blink, but there are no tears.

This . . . this is not real.

When Arvo enters the cottage, dragging my mother by the hand, I know it is, and it isn't relief that grips me.

It's anger.

I focus all of it on my mother. "Where have you been?" Pushing Pada away, I struggle to my feet. He stands and reaches to help me, hesitating when Mada speaks up.

"Wehna, it's—"

"*Where. Have. You. Been*?"

Her mouth closes, hurt crossing her features before being replaced with a hard look I recognize. The one that always accompanied the words, "You need to be strong."

"Wehna, watch your tone," my father warns.

"How can you tell me what to do? How can you tell me *anything*? For months, Arvo and I have been alone, and I have had to take all that weight on my shoulders."

"We've been fine, Wehna," Arvo says, lip quivering.

I glare at him, the degree of my fury frightening me. "Fine? Really? Is that what you think we've been?" It feels like something wild is chewing at my ribcage. "With you running off on me every other day and the kaligorven breathing down our necks? With no one to provide for us and the very real possibility that we could starve?"

"We had Miss Tress and Mister Bryn."

"And look what good it did them."

Arvo backs away, his eyes filling with tears.

My father lays a hand on my shoulder, and I jerk out of his reach. My whole body is in tremors, my throat screaming with the pressure of unshed tears.

Mada watches me, Arvo clinging to her side and hiding his face in her shawl. Her voice is quiet. "Did you think we wanted to leave you like that?"

"I didn't know what to think, except that you were dead."

She presses a hand to her mouth and closes her eyes. "Oh, my girl."

I bite my lip and hug myself, as if I can ward off her compassion. My shaking intensifies.

Father beckons Arvo to him with a jerk of his chin, and my brother does not require any further convincing to leap into his arms.

"I knew you'd n-never l-leave us," he says through sobs, tucking his head under Father's chin as tears continue to stream down his cheeks. Father sits on a bed and holds Arvo close.

I shut my eyes and fight the urge to cry. To scream. To laugh. To lose it all.

"Wehna," my mother whispers, now close to me.

My muscles tense when her fingers find my arms. I refuse to look at her.

"You have been so strong."

My chest heaves.

Tender but firm, she pulls my arms down so they are no longer fastened like armor over my aching heart. "You always were, you know."

She tucks a coil of hair behind my ear, and I am five years old again, snuggled up in her bed after a nightmare, not sure if I can trust that I am awake.

"But you can unravel now." Her arms slip around my back as a sob slips out of me. "Because we found our way to you."

I work up the courage to look her in the face. Every hint of hardness has been eased away, her features smoothed and shaped by the waters of suffering. Her brows cinch and tears shine on her cheeks.

"And we should have never, ever left."

She pulls me in, and together we fall apart.

32
BELWYN

PASSING THROUGH THE CITY without using the main streets is impossible. It's been a while since I was here, and I don't trust myself to find my family's new abode in the poorer district without taking them. Many sola brossa hang between the buildings, making my eyes ache. I turn my chin down to avoid their glare.

"Bel, where in Ikktar have you been?"

A hearty slap to my back follows the incredulous voice. I grimace. I should have known my reappearance was never going to go unnoticed. Feigning a bemused expression, I turn around.

One of my former friends greets me with a wide grin and a self-important bent to his posture.

"Flip." I pass my gaze over his lanky frame and clothes. "I've been busy. You look like you've done well for yourself, though."

He touches his crisp black shirt and beams. "Foremost has been looking to refresh his men. Guess who was his first pick?"

I attempt a surprised laugh. "I don't believe it. Flip Rigez, right hand to The Man."

"You mock, but you can't argue that Myrzeth doesn't have style. Turning over that sola-loving wench was what secured it for me."

My blood runs cold, then hot.

Insensible to my rage, recollection claims Flip's face and his smile dries up. "Weren't you two kind of a . . . thing?" One of his hands travels to the other wrist, as if it still smarts from when I grabbed it and forced him to his knees when he had been troubling Amyrah. He frowns, shifting a bit taller.

Careful, Belwyn. Although every impulse in my body screams to lash out at him, I can't afford a confrontation right now.

"You can't be serious," I say, impressed by the disinterest I've managed to achieve in my voice. "We'd never met before that day. I only intervened because I assumed you were being your usual idiotic self and taking a joke too far." A guilty smile stretches my mouth. "And you know I've always been drawn to a pretty face."

The words make my gut twist because that *is* the person I used to be.

He blinks a few times, eyes narrowing before breaking into a sharp laugh. "You always have. Nothing's changed, has it?" His grin is too wide for his face. "Except for Flip Rigez."

"Right, right." I chuckle and lay a hand on his back, hoping he can't feel the disgust radiating through my fingertips. "Good to run into you, morvus."

He shoves me away, chuckling. "Get out of here. I'm sure you've got some other girl's bed to warm. Someone a bit more enticing than that wild-haired flake, I hope."

I draw in a breath and trap it in my lungs. *Not. The. Time.*

He doesn't stick around for a response, and that's better for him. Every muscle in my body uncoils.

I continue threading through the streets, keeping my chin down and avoiding any further attention as much as possible. I come out at Utsanek's central square, where the market is livelier than it used to be on an average Vindéré evening. I take a moment to absorb it, wondering at the prosperity that seems to have befallen the Vale.

"Nice lantern."

Ketra, one of the young women I used to boast knowing, emerges from between two stalls and raises a dainty eyebrow.

So much for avoiding recognition.

I give my fist an uncaring shake. "It's just an ordinary lantern."

"I'm curious why you need it." She steps closer, arms folded across her ribcage. "It's been a while since our paths crossed, Belwyn." Her eyes, which are a deep brown I have never seen to their full potential, narrow. "You haven't been venturing anywhere *questionable*, I hope?"

I take a moment to study her. It feels like a lifetime since I was in Utsanek, and longer still since she and I were in each other's affections. She's changed. The playfulness has vacated her eyes, and her features, though still perfect, are frigid in a way I've can't explain. It's like the Ketra I knew died along with my brother.

Is . . . is it *my* fault?

"Something came up, and I've been busy." I motion my jaw toward the lantern. "My mother loaned this to a friend, and she sent me to retrieve it. It's dark in the poor district, Ketra, if you haven't noticed." I wince, hoping that still holds true.

She walks a slow circle around me. "Funny. I didn't think your family had friends anymore."

When she sees my hard expression, she laughs and runs a hand up my arm. "*Bones*, you're tense." Standing on tiptoe, she kisses my cheek. My fingers stiffen around the lantern's handle. She pulls back and giggles. "Relax. I'm only teasing."

I release a breath. "Good. You know how protective I am of my family."

The smile dies on her lips.

"Yes. I do," she whispers, backing away. She sweeps her gaze over me again, landing on the necklace wound around my wrist. I trap the pendant against my palm. A slight frown passes over her brow, but she blinks it away. "It's good you've found something that's finally worthy of your time."

Her words bite. My absence hasn't improved matters for either of us; she's still bitter and I am still the cause. For once, I'm willing to own it. I lick my lips, my voice softening. "And what about Myrzeth?"

She raises her chin, her expression impassive. "What about him?"

I sip in a breath, ready to shatter her perception of the world, but as I take in her meticulous appearance—hair arranged in a complicated style, a vivid dress that becomes her olive complexion, understated jewelry, and light-reflecting makeup—my anger melts. I thought these were things she had chosen to express herself, and I have never desired to look beyond them. I didn't think she wanted that. For the first time, I'm getting a glimpse of the soul that lies beneath. It was there all along, and I never cared enough to recognize the mask she wore to protect her own, fearful heart.

My eyes trace her face, noting how her angles are sharper, how shadows pool in places they never did before. And peeking out from the cuff of a sleeve, I spot a mottled green bruise.

"Is he worthy of you?" I ask in a low tone.

Her face blanches, but she soon recovers and tosses out a confused laugh as she brushes past me.

"Since when did you care about me?"

She slips into the crowd.

I need to get home. It's more than a thought; it's an all-consuming desire.

Outside of the main arteries of Utsanek, the ténesomni chokes the air with ghastly billows. Not a single bone is strung to light the path in this area, which makes no sense when so many of them hang over the more affluent neighborhoods. When my father was Foremost, he made sure all sectors of Utsanek received at least some scrap of light after taking a generous share for himself. This lopsided distribution makes me wonder what Myrzeth's goal is. Is he hoping to lull the city into a false sense of security by making the places where people gather seem brighter? To me, it seems he has only increased the distinction between the prosperous and the less fortunate.

This divide reminds me of Ketsé, the ill-reputed market in the cavern, and Jaki tempting me with a drink poisoned with ténesomni.

A shudder runs through me.

Was the real reason I came back because something in me craved the intoxication of these unnatural shadows like it craved that beverage?

As I traverse the streets, I have to stop and regain my bearings multiple times, squinting through the black to find any notable detail to ground myself. Lanterns languish in some windows, but they only help if I'm a few feet from them. Perspiration beads along my hairline as the carrion of doubt circles my thoughts.

Conspicuous or not, the bolétis would be a huge relief right now. I huff out a growl. What can I do but press forward and hope I come out on the other side of this?

After taking more guesswork turns and arriving at yet another intersection I do not recognize, the slouched form of a man emerges from the shadows ahead. He is the first person I have encountered in these poverty-ridden alleys. I swallow my pride and approach him.

"Excuse me."

When the man lifts his lazy head and turns it to regard me, light from the lantern at his side limns his face.

Dark circles frame his eyes, and his hair has grown into short, tired waves. The defeated posture may be uncharacteristic, but there is no mistaking him.

"Father?" I manage to say before the air turns to stone within my lungs.

He blinks, confusion shadowing his brow like fog over the Askonnet Mountains. He staggers to his feet. "Belwyn?"

I stare, uncertain how to respond.

"What're you—"

A commotion from the open doorway behind him drowns out his slurred words.

"Shem, get off your backside and help me for once." Korvin's irritated voice twists around my throat.

"Why? I don't have to listen to you."

"Yes," Korvin says with forced patience. "You. *Do*. Belwyn said so, remember?"

"Belwyn isn't even here."

"Forget it. I'll do it myself, since I'm the one Mother depends on. Like always."

"You are *not*."

The door swings open and both boys tumble out, Shem struggling to take a basket of wet laundry from Korvin's arms, Korvin jabbing his elbow into Shem's chest to prevent him. In their distraction, they fail to notice Father and the lantern on the ground. One wayward step and Korvin kicks it over. The glass shatters and the ignati goes out.

Father roars a jumble of unintelligible words and grabs Korvin by the wrist. My brother cries out, dropping the basket. The linens spill everywhere.

Impulsively, I wedge myself between them and glare into my father's glassy eyes. I smell his acidic breath, feel the bewilderment emanating from his pores. His jaw tenses and his back straightens, but I set a palm against his sternum. "No."

He glares, chest rising and falling with unspent rage. As quickly as it flared up, it fades, exhaustion falling over him, dragging his shoulders down.

"So," he says, dropping Korvin's wrist and staggering back a few paces. "You're back."

Hunching over once more, he stoops away into the night.

Bewildered by his changeable behavior, I turn to my brothers.

"Are you—"

"*Bel*." Korvin rushes into my arms, making no attempt to stifle his sobs.

Shocked, I stand with my arms out, staring at the top of his fair head, which reaches past my chin now. My gaze flicks to Shemai, who looks like he is facing a specter.

"Is it really you?" he whispers, eyes wide.

I swallow. Why did I never consider how they would be affected by yet another brother's absence?

Shemai needs no confirmation. He leaps forward and I trap him in my arms too.

I hold them for Rhun.

After helping shake out the wet clothes and clipping them to the line strung in the narrow gap between our house and the one next door, I let my brothers lead me inside.

The drab little dwelling that I remember with apprehension has been transformed. Several lanterns dot the perimeter of the room, making a respectable dent in the gloom. Bundles of herbs hang from the rafters in the kitchen, and the modest hearth has had a good scrubbing. There are several new pieces of furniture, obvious cast-offs from wealthier people that have been brought back to functionality.

I gape at Korvin. "You've been busy."

A reluctant grin angles his lips. "You told me to take care of them."

Inhaling sharply, I bid my emotions to stay under control. "Didn't expect you to take that to heart like this."

Shemai crosses his arms. "It wasn't *all* you, Korvin. The herbs were my idea." He points above us. "I'm drying them out and making spice blends to sell at the market."

Grabbing him by the shirt collar, I drag him over and tousle his hair. "Excellent idea, Shem."

He fusses and ducks out of my reach.

"And what about Father?"

Korvin stuffs a hand into his pocket, looking down. "Think he's been finding jobs in the trade district, working with the builder's guild or something. We don't see him that much, and when we do, he's not . . . *here*."

Disgust rears in my chest, and all I can afford is a small clearing of my throat. "At least he's doing something."

I turn away, several colorful shapes above the fire catching my eye. Welcoming the distraction, I walk over to investigate.

At least a dozen paintings in all shapes, sizes, and hues line the mantle. Some have been applied to the smooth insides of bark, and others make use of broken platters and old cedar shakes. The style is not precise, the thick splotches of pigment painted with a loose hand, but I am impressed with the feeling and motion they invoke. A lot of the scenes depict various interpretations of the forest that brackets Utsanek along the north side. I notice how they all take liberties with the amount of light in the scene, whether it's with the hints of bolétis dotting the forest floor or the reach of the lantern's glow. My eyes fix on one that reminds me of a sunrise shining between twisting boughs.

Korvin has always been the most creative member of the family. I regard him. "Did you do these?"

He shakes his head. "No, that was Mother."

My mother, taking up a hobby?

I look at the dawn painting again. How can she know what the sun looks like, having never set foot outside the Vale?

Perhaps the knowledge of true light is engraved on all our hearts.

"W-where is she?" I stutter through my wonder.

"She hasn't been feeling well." Shem kicks at a chair, glancing at me with a wince when it clatters to the floor.

I turn to Korvin for an explanation.

He bends and quietly rights the chair. "That's why we've been doing so much. She keeps to her room most days."

I let out a frustrated moan. "I knew I shouldn't have left."

Korvin holds out a hand. "She's alright, Bel. Really. Shem and I have been making sure she eats—"

"At least a little," Shem says.

"And when she's with us, she's *with* us. I think she just can't handle too much anymore. When that happens, she paints."

Slipping off the satchel, I hand it to Korvin. "Thanks, Kor. This was useful."

His expression brightens when he sees his tattered old bag, and I do too. It may be a small thing, but it feels like the first step in setting the world right.

My gaze travels to the uneven stairs leading to the second level. "I'm going to go see her."

Nodding, Korvin offers an encouraging smile. "She'll like that."

The door at the top is fastened tight, and I hesitate before rapping it with my knuckles.

What should I say?

All I can think of is her gaunt frame haunting the windows of our old, luxurious house as she kept an endless watch for the son that would never return.

But she got better, didn't she? I saw her come out of that haze and reclaim a tiny part of who she had been before. That's why I thought they would be fine if I left.

Breathing in deeply and pushing aside my own guilt, I knock on the door.

"Come in," issues her soft reply.

Candles fill every surface of the small space, the warmth of the room almost unbearable. In the center of the glow, my mother curves away from me, wrapped in creamy linens and engrossed in a project. Her bare feet are propped up on the crossbar beneath the stool, and her long, blond braid trails down her back like a woodland road. A dozen more paintings crowd the room, tucked behind the candles, resting on the floor, and leaning against the dresser, walls, and bed frame.

"I'm almost finished with this one, Korvin. I'll come down for some kip when I'm done."

"Take your time," I say.

Her head snaps up, and the brush falls from her hand, clattering to the floor. When I see her shoulders heave, I question if I should have surprised her like this.

"Belwyn?"

My name is a wish, a prayer, a temporal dusting of snow at the end of Elberu's harvest. She turns on the seat and presses her fingers to her mouth.

"Hello, Mother."

Shaking as she fights for control, she lowers her hands, swallows hard, and holds out her arms. Slowly, I cross the room until she is within reach.

Hand trembling, she touches my chin and the hair that has flopped in front of my forehead. The shock drains from her eyes, warmth and joy replacing it, spilling over the rest of her features.

She seems both older and younger than when I saw her last. Tired. Heartsick, yet clinging to a childlike breath of hope.

I catch her hand in mine.

A smile transforms her lips. "You have changed so much."

"Have I?"

She nods. "I can see it in your eyes. You've become your own man over these past weeks."

My insides swirl. Is that what I am? My own? I feel like I'm still being dragged from one event, one revelation to the next, caught in a vortex of what the world expects of me and who I want to be.

The shame grows too heavy and my gaze shies away from hers.

She frees her hand and grips my face tenderly. I look at her again through tear-blurred eyes.

"My brave boy, you are home now. This is the place where you can let your walls down." She brushes her thumbs across my cheeks. "Tell me everything."

33
AMYRAH

THE TÉNESOMNI LOSES ITS POTENCY the farther we travel. I wasn't certain at first, but now I'm sure that the eight days we've been together have grown marginally brighter.

Holden clucks to Zenith, slowing him to a walk. "There aren't enough kaligorven to fill Atsun yet. That's a relief. It was impossible to know while we were still in Tothlen Forest, but it is more obvious out here." He gives the reins a quick tug. "Hopefully we will come to the end of the ténesomni soon."

We have been out from the suffocating trees for two days, and I'm frustrated that I haven't been able to see any of this new terrain. "Do they create the shadows, then?" I slip off Zenith and press my palms against my aching lower back, stretching it out. Holden tosses me a questioning look. "The kaligorven, I mean."

Dismounting, he brings the reins over the stallion's head. "Not exactly, but the ténesomni always increases to match their presence. It is rare to find one without the other."

"Don't you find it strange that we haven't encountered any of them?"

Holden shrugs. "They were all confined within the Vale's borders until recently, and even if they have been freed to roam Atsun, it will still take time for them to move through the mountains or go around them."

He digs through his bag for what remains of our provisions and hands me a stick of cured venison. "How did people respond to them in the Vale?"

I wince. "With a decent amount of terror. Most people kept out of their way, and they believed there was a way they could live in an uneasy truce with them."

"Would you say the valefolk served them?"

"More like they were in bondage to them."

"That's the case for the kaligorven too. They are bound to something more potent than they are."

I chew on both his words and the tough meat. "What could compare to their wickedness?"

"Érechlys."

A chill chases the unfamiliar name, and my stomach sours as I wait for Holden to explain.

"The Luvesti teach that she has been given dominion in Atsun for a little while, but that a day is coming when her darkness will come to an end."

"Who is she?"

"A daemon, once a servant of Elyōn, who grew to envy his power and light and sought to steal it for her own. She did not understand that light can never be taken, only shared. When her attempt to obtain it left her humiliated, she vowed to cover the world in shadow." Holden shrugs. "Or so they say."

I rub my palms over my arms, but I cannot shake the cold. Is Érechlys's voice the one I've been hearing when tempted by the ténesomni? I search Holden's face with a desperation I don't bother to hide. "And you say that her end has been prophesied?"

"That is what our people believe, yes."

The words of the sola's song come to my mind. *For all the darkness will fade away . . . And all of the Vale will be free.*

"That promise feels so far away," I whisper. I stare above at the streams of curious shadow, willing it to dissipate, when a diamond of brightness shines through a gap. As I watch with my breath trapped in my chest, the oppressive ténesomni slips away, one filthy limb at a time. The firelights peer down at me with unchanging assurance, as if to chastise me for my disbelief.

A low laugh exudes from Holden.

The end of the darkness. I close my eyes, but I cannot share in his joy, nor feel the stars' distant warmth. Perhaps I wasn't the one who cursed the whole world to a lightless existence after all, but I certainly helped.

Releasing a shaky breath, I open my eyes and turn to Zenith. "Do you want to take the first watch, or the second?" I ask, beginning to untie the saddle strings to retrieve my cloak. Anything to distract myself from my incriminating thoughts.

Holden strides away a few paces, hands on his hips. "Neither."

"What?" My voice is tinged with panic.

There is no way I can stay awake all night.

He beckons for me to join him, pointing to the distance when I oblige. A moment ago, there would have been nothing to note but formless black, but now the moon bestows milky light over the plain, outlining each blade of grass in bold relief.

We stand upon a gentle slope that angles away until it is broken by a glimmering silver ribbon.

"That is the Eldyn River. We have come a little farther south than I intended. I was wondering why this journey has taken us so long, but it will be to our advantage. The river is shallow and calm here. It is the perfect place for us to cross."

"It still looks so far away," I say, unsure if my aching body can stand to be jostled by a horse again.

"Zenith won't mind a midnight run." Holden's white teeth reflect the moonlight. "And I would feel better putting the Eldyn between us and the Shrouded."

I raise an eyebrow and hide a yawn behind my hand. "I thought you said there weren't many out here."

"And I'm probably right, but, Amyrah . . ." His hand finds my shoulder and grips it tight. "Once we're over, it's going to feel like I'm almost home."

I hold his gaze, waiting for his excitement to spread to me. Although I'll never know what it feels like to return home, I know it means something to him. Weariness infusing my bones, I follow him to Zenith. "You think camping across a shallow river will offer us safety?"

"Believe me. The Sighing Woods is one of the safest places in Atsun."

Holden mounts the horse, then leans and offers me his hand. Grateful for the extra help and bone-weary, I don't think twice about clinging to him anymore. The only question plaguing my mind is how I am going to keep myself from falling asleep.

"Hold on," he says, as if I don't know how to ride a horse after over a week of traveling on one. I roll my eyes and shift in the saddle.

With a few commands and a kick of his heels, he sets Zenith to running at such a frightening gallop that all drowsiness is chased from my mind.

"Is this necessary?" I shriek into his shirt, fingers digging into his ribcage.

He repays my terror with a loud *whoop* that echoes over the plains.

My fear melts, whisked away by Holden's good humor, the staggering power of the stallion beneath me, and the fresh, purifying hue of moonlight.

The mad race slows as we approach the Eldyn. Zenith needs a little encouragement, but he soon treads into the water. It barely reaches my toes, and in little time, we have made it across.

Exhilarating though the ride was, my exhaustion is quick to reassert itself. I am desperate to feel hard earth beneath my feet. Before the horse has come to a complete halt, I slide off and stumble through a narrow gap in the strange boulders that line this bank to the aspens on the other side.

"Amyrah, wait."

He need not have shouted my name, because I have already spotted the gigantic bear lumbering toward me.

"Keep calm," Holden whispers behind my ear.

"I *am* calm," I say through gritted teeth.

The bruin snorts and huffs the low bushes crowding around the roots of the trees. It is monstrous, larger than any bear I have ever heard of. Our noise—or perhaps our scent—reaches it, and it raises its huge head, alerted to our presence. I am about to implore Holden to nock an arrow when the sun itself collides with us. It bursts from the creature's fur, throwing the wood into a golden haze.

I almost laugh in my relief, but when the bear turns to regard me, fear flares in my chest. "I thought you said these woods were safe."

"Safe from the kaligorven, yes."

I steel myself, closing my eyes, though that does little to hide the bear's magnificent form. My eyelids might as well be made of paper.

It's a sola, Amyrah, I chide myself. *You're comfortable with them.*

But being approached by a deer, wren, or fox feels very different from a bear taller than a horse.

"Solas can sense intention. She will know we aren't a threat if we remain calm."

"She?"

Holden ignores the question. "The Sighing Woods are one of Luvesta's defenses against outsiders. Only one of our own may pass through it safely."

A laugh born of pure terror escapes me. *What about someone who has touched the ténesomni, who has helped Érechlys further her domain?*

Opening my eyes, I suppress a shudder as Holden sidesteps me, holding out a hand.

"Easy, girl. We are not your enemies."

"Holden." I try to snag his cloak as he passes, but my fingers grasp air. "I don't think that's a good—"

The words dissipate on my lips when the bear comes forward and presses her head to Holden's palm. He casts a glance over his shoulder, a challenge in his eyes. "I told you, Amyrah. We have nothing to fear from them." His hand drops and he jerks his chin. "Now, you."

Despite his assurance, I struggle to trust the sola. The blind confidence I possessed in the Vale that led me to approach the deer, stand against the kaligorven, and take an unfamiliar boy's hand to comfort his troubled heart, is no longer mine.

The tears that trickle from the corners of my eyes evaporate in the sola's supernatural heat.

I don't know who or what I am.

Surely the sola must feel the tumult in my soul.

Holden's eyes meet mine, an eyebrow cocked bemusedly. "What's wrong?"

I knot my arms protectively in front of me. "You say they are capable of sensing intentions."

His brow relaxes. "Yes."

"But what of our past deeds? What of compromises that have painted the Grovesha black?"

Before he can answer, a rumbling growl meets us, carried on a wave of warmth.

The bear pads toward me on great, clawed feet. Bursts of light rush outward at each footfall. I fight the urge to back away, to retreat across the Eldyn and into the Grovesha where the shadows will welcome me with open arms.

When she is a mere handbreadth away, the bear sniffs the air, then rises onto her hind legs.

I am terrified; I am in awe. She lets out a roar that slices me to my marrow.

"Elyōn," I whisper in a voice that isn't there, closing my eyes and bowing my head, "I know I am not worthy."

The blow I am expecting, that I deserve, does not come. Instead, warmth anoints my forehead and courses through me. I feel the sola's snout and her hot, fragrant breath as it pours over my body, bidding my eyes to open.

The Light Creature looks down on me with compassion brimming in her eyes. Her head tilts and she gives her body a tremendous shake. Illumination sprinkles through the air, hitting with the sound of tinkling glass against the fluttering leaves.

"See?" Holden's gentle timbre is difficult to hear above my thundering heart. His arm slips around my shoulders. "You are one of our own."

We take shelter along the inside of the boulder wall for what remains of the night. The sola roams the thin beginnings of the Sighing Woods that stretches away in grassy knolls. My chest no longer drums when I look at her. I slide down against the jagged rock and hug my knees to my chest.

"No sense in starting a fire tonight." Holden finishes hobbling Zenith, eyeing the bear as he comes to sit next to me. I can still feel the warmth of her at a distance.

"How did you know it was female?" I ask.

He drinks from his water flask and hands it to me, wiping his mouth with the back of a hand. "There aren't many bear-solas. We call her 'Little Cottla,' the Guardian of the Woods. She likes to give people a good fright."

I quench my thirst, then rest my chin on my knees, watching her ponderous movements. The spiraling patterns that ripple over her thick coat make me dizzy. I blink and return my attention to Holden.

"Do you know them all by name?"

He laughs heartily. "Far too many solas for that, but there are a few recognizable ones."

"It's curious that solas can be found in so many familiar forms and yet be so different from the creatures of Atsun."

"A gift from Elyōn to protect his people from the ténesomni."

I raise my chin. "*His* people?"

"The Luvesti."

I think of Wehna's parents, who were so committed to Elyōn's calling. Of Orlagh, who speaks of the Highest as if he is an intimate friend. Of Belwyn, who has embodied what sacrificial love looks like. Have they all been rejected by Elyōn simply because they were born to the wrong family?

"Are you saying that the Highest has chosen them alone?" I ask.

"*Us*, Amyrah. And yes. It's what is taught in the oral tradition, which I don't expect you to know. The Luvesti were once spread all over Atsun, as were the solas and the kaligorven. Light and dark forever challenging one another. Some think that there was balance in that—"

"Like Jaki believes," I interject.

He bobs his chin. "People like her do not acknowledge—or perhaps they do not know—the destruction and souls lost in the crossfire, nor how seductive Érechlys was. Her lies poisoned more than the sky. She moved in the shadows, capturing the hearts of all who heeded her."

I finger the buttons down my dress and bite my lip.

"The Confining didn't only restrict the kaligorven and all who served them." Holden's eyes hitch on the surprise in mine, and his mouth curves downward. "It drew Elyōn's people together in one place. With so many losses, they chose to band together and remove themselves from the scene of their sorrow."

"Leaving the rest of the world to fend for themselves," I say, bitterness turning my words brittle.

Holden gazes at the stars. "That is one view of it, yes."

"If what you say is true, then the Confining didn't just lock away the darkness; it robbed the rest of Atsun of the solas' light." I snap a twig between my fingers, wishing I had something much more substantial to break. "How could Elyōn allow that?"

A cloudy silence gathers between us.

"I don't know." Holden takes a slow, sobering breath through his nose. "There are those who view this removal as a crime, believing Elyōn's people were not intended to keep to themselves."

"Yet the knowledge of the Highest has still made it to the Vale," I say quietly, awestruck by this simple fact. That must be proof of his heart for all, Luvesti or otherwise.

My throat constricts thinking of those still living in Utsanek, unaware of all that lies outside the valley's borders. Has Belwyn made it back to them?

Was it right to choose my heritage over my heart?

I understand, now, why all knowledge of the Grovesha has been scrubbed from valefolk history. If the people who were confined with the kaligorven were adherents to the teachings of Érechlys, knowingly or not, they wouldn't have wanted to admit their defeat. Better to propagate the lie that a kingdom of twisting shadows was all there was. Better to forget that the world outside existed.

A heavy exhale leaves me feeling spent. "What now?"

"*Hmm*?"

I watch the sola's combustive glow slip into the distance, feel the cold from the stone at my back creeping through me. "I have released the ténesomni, Holden. The kaligorven are free to roam unchallenged. I have undone the work our people prize so highly." I turn my gaze to him. "Will I be welcomed in? Or will they cast me out?"

Holden tilts his chin, thinking. "The Luvesti have been lying to themselves for a hundred years, believing that evil can be neatly contained and good easily preserved. If one stray Luvesti can shatter that whole system . . ." He grabs a stone and hurls it into the whispering trees. "Then I say it was about blazing time."

Not for the first time, I wonder at this young man with whom I feel a strange connection. I'm unsure if it is our shared heritage that bonds us or something else. I tug my cloak closer. Am I betraying Belwyn by getting to know Holden like this? When I think of the night we parted, my stomach flutters. I can picture the band of gold in his hazel irises, the auburn hair falling over his forehead. His half-smile creasing his cheek. My heart aches, and I sigh.

No, I am certain nothing romantic exists between Holden and me, but how else can I explain this familiar pull?

My eyelids become heavy, and I can feel myself slipping . . .

Sometime in the quiet before morning, I start awake and sit up, fear drumming my pulse. Darkness has resumed its natural course and the night-chill clings to my limbs. Heavy breaths rumble from within the trees, and I realize with relief that the sola has not abandoned us. It has merely reserved its glow.

I never considered that their light might exhaust them too.

Glancing around, I find Holden wrapped in his cloak, propped up where two of the boulders meet. Sleeping, as I should be.

After a week of looking over our shoulders and trading off watches, it is strange to see him so at ease.

I settle back down, using my pack as a pillow, and drift into conflicted dreams of sola creatures fighting the kaligorven, of light meeting the shadow in an endless battle.

Through it all, I cannot tell which will win.

34
SEYLA

I PULL AT MY SHIRT COLLAR, my chest constricted as if bound by thick ropes. The birds fill the air with their hateful songs, and I want to hunt down the lot of them.

What do they sing for? Can't they see that the ténesomni still poisons the sky?

Tetyan's unraveling face claims my sleepless nights, my waking thoughts. However I try, I cannot make the threads of her weave back together.

Oh, *beshïn*, am I going to lose my memory of her too?

I pass my fingers over my brow, finding it clammy to the touch. At an assessing glance from Ordin, I drop my hand. I haven't been able to take a full breath since I awoke from my nightmare four days ago, and whether the lingering fear or the ever-present ténesomni is to blame, I cannot tell. I dare not question whether my partner feels the same, to allow him to see how pathetic I am for struggling. He already has suspicions of my weakness, I'm sure. I'd rather not confirm them.

Téron could help me sift through this, but my pride keeps me from asking him. If it is the ténesomni that is affecting me, then he will think me a coward. If it is my dreams, and he learns that I am a woman haunted, then I will appear weak.

Either scenario is unthinkable.

Thank the skies, the shadows have thinned the farther we have traveled from Loch Skythe. Until I see a dawn, though, I will not believe we aren't trapped like the valefolk are.

Ancestors, how can they stomach it?

"Scourge of the Vale," Ordin mutters under his breath, kicking at a swirl of ténesomni as it crosses the roadway. It curls away from him, resuming its brazen snaking once he has passed. "Where are those blazing light whores when you need them?"

I grasp at the diversion from my pernicious thoughts like a lifeline. "If I didn't know better, I'd say the darkness is toying with you, Ordin."

"Aye? You might be right, but it's a coward's game." He spits at the ground. "We'll soon be out of its reach, I think. Then, to Ikktar with it all."

"Thank the Highest."

The soft voice contrasts Ordin's like a sea breeze cutting across a torrid plain. I glance at the wagon that trundles behind the stout horse. "I did not think you were awake, Téron."

"Awake and sick to death of being carted around like goat feed." He pushes himself up against the wooden rails with a grunt and rubs his bedraggled beard.

My mouth tips up and I turn ahead again. "If you think you won't slow us down, you are welcome to jump ship."

"Slow us down? That's rich." Ordin barks a laugh. "We've already been anchored by this fat excuse of a mule. Traded two fine steeds for that worm-ridden thing and the cart to haul your weak backside around. Can't even ride the beast."

Despite his bluster, Ordin pulls back on the packhorse's lead and brings the cart to a rolling stop.

Téron slides across the slatted floor and lowers himself to the ground with careful movements. He takes a few shaky steps and stretches his back. "Ah, yes. This is better."

"How is that side of yours?" I ask, narrowing my eyes at the off-balance hunch to his shoulders. I suspect that Commander Verrek cracked some of his ribs with his blow.

"Better, I think."

He sucks in a sharp breath mid-stretch and clutches his torso. I lift an eyebrow. "You might be a bit too optimistic, but I do agree that walking would serve you well for a span." I motion to his shirt. "Let me see."

When he hesitates, I approach him and grab his tunic, lifting the hem and probing the bandage. His warm exhales collide with my cool forehead, and I back away as a shiver grips me.

I clear my throat. "It looks to be almost mended."

"Get a move on, ya old beast of burden."

Téron's face swivels to my partner, eyebrows arched in offense. I turn away, glad for the chance to conceal both my amusement and my befuddling embarrassment.

"And you too, Merl." Ordin gives the old mule a slap on the rump.

Téron laughs.

Adjusting my pace, I allow him a chance to feel out his feet and see whether he can keep up. Every breath causes his forehead to pinch. His face glistens with a sheen of sweat, but he is moving on his own.

Thank the ancestors.

Ordin's prediction proves correct, and we soon outpace the last feeble bands of ténesomni. Without its presence, the dark before the dawn gives way to subtle pink and orange strokes, teasing away the pressure from my chest. Relief floods through me. I breathe in the woodsmoke-tinged scent of the Southern Moors.

Tarriv is close.

The last few days, we have passed only a few people on the road through the coniferous Boretel Forest. Ordinarily, a steady flow of traders and supplies would be moving to the Loch Skythe Agmen encampment, but it appears commerce has been halted with the advancing darkness. A lone figure approaches us now, leading a mule piled to the skies with goods. He's young, and a wariness clings to his spotted face.

I know what it is to approach the unknown with nothing more than feeble hope.

"Have ye need for anything, good folks?" The merchant eyes our odd entourage curiously.

I remind myself to hold my head high, though I'm aware that it is not normal for the úramech of Tarriv to travel like common folk. "No. Be on your way."

"And what can we expect to find along this path?" The young man peers into the sable mists curling at our backs, his widening gaze betraying his misgiving.

Ordin snorts. "Well, what do y'think? It's no meadow picnic." When the young merchant's face blanches—he really is no more than a boy—Ordin softens. "But think of it as twilight, lad, and you'll be fine."

The boy nods, the tight braids on his half-shaved head waggling. He urges his mule forward, and the tired beast issues a hideous racket as they leave us.

"I haven't had a chance to thank you both for what you have done for me," Téron says once we are out of earshot.

"What are ya thanking me for? If I'd had my way, your bones would have been picked clean by bottom feeders by now."

Téron's eyes widen, and I raise an eyebrow. "Well, it's true. Ordin would have tossed you back into Loch Skythe had I not intervened, but he was brought to see reason before he had a chance."

"Brought to see the edge of your blade, more like." He breaks off into unintelligible muttering, which relents when I clear my throat.

Téron looks down. "Again, thank you."

My heart skips with his humble gratitude.

Don't be so weak, Seyla. What would Tetyan say?

I distract myself by loosening the straps of the bracer on my right arm and peeling it away. "I hope you are prepared for what awaits you in Tarriv."

A forced expression that I assume is supposed to mimic excitement crosses his face, but it's more like indigestion. "More creative interrogations?"

My grimace kills his attempt at humor. "You would be fortunate to avoid at least a couple—"

"More like several."

I glare at the back of Ordin's wrinkled head. "*Several* beatings."

Téron rubs his eyes, as if exhausted by the thought. "What has made your people so fierce?"

Ordin wheezes, amused. "I never knew these valefolk were so adorable."

I prod my forearm. The wound has knitted back together, not exactly neatly, but it will hold. The skin around it is less angry than it was. Replacing the bracer, I look toward Tarriv's torches blinking demurely in the distance. "Warring clans, the occasional ship of marauders from the Praeor Sea, and a weak barrier between the monsters that fuel frightfables does that to a people, you'll find."

"Aye, that. And being abandoned by the ungrateful Luvesti."

A white pallor washes over Téron's features. "Luvesti?" he croaks.

"Don't tell me you are one of those sorry saps who sympathizes with their actions?"

Téron is silent.

Shaking his head, Ordin huffs out a pitying chuckle. "You have more than several beatings coming your way, I'll wager."

A cloud seems to settle on Téron's spirit, as the ténesomni settled on mine. I move closer to him. "What do you know of the Luvesti?"

Blinking, Téron casts his eyes around as if frantic for something to anchor his mind. "N-nothing. Nothing at all. What do you mean by 'marauders?'"

Oblivious as ever, Ordin bumbles into the moment. "Right. Forgot you've been tucked into the Vale your whole life. Must be nice not to have to worry that your homes will be burned while you are sleeping."

Téron tenses, his posture shifting taller. "What?"

"That's right, Vale man. Sit up and take notice of the world that lies around you. It's wide open and full of dangers that no wall of shadow can shield us from."

"Are you insinuating that life within the Vale was better than it is out here?"

"Nay, that's not what I'm getting at. I'm suggesting that if the valefolk had half a collective brain, they would've sorted it out. Couldn't be bothered to ask what kind of horse droppings your little predicament landed the rest of us in, eh?"

"Quiet, Ordin," I say through clenched teeth, concerned that

Téron's agitation will affect his healing wounds. "You have no idea what life is like in the Vale, and we can't blame him for what has happened beyond it."

"That so?" He sneers over his shoulder at Téron. "Well, then. Forgive me, Seyla Bréinth, for voicing what everyone who learns of this man will think."

I pluck a small blade from a sheath on my thigh and spin it on my palm. "They can bring their speculations to me."

"We didn't know."

The blade stills. "Didn't know what?" I ask.

Téron presses a fist to his forehead, as though his thoughts bring him physical pain. "That the world was so big. That the darkness would end. That our shadow-stalked existence wasn't what defined all of creation."

"Bah." Ordin dismisses him with the flap of his hand. "You're saying you never once felt there was something missing?"

Téron's shoulders sag. "No, I . . . I knew. My wife . . ."

My stomach flips and I grit my teeth. *Seyla, you fool.*

"Well, I knew there was no possibility that she was a product of that black land, but she never spoke of what lay beyond except for a city called Ketsé. She said she was from there, and I assumed it was a place not so different from Utsanek. I had no desire to see it." He withers, the crease between his brows deepening. "I am glad, at least, I told my daughter to go there. I pray she has found the light I always knew she was meant for."

Wife. Daughter. This man has built a life beyond anything I could ever imagine.

"Ketsé, you say?" Ordin scratches his chin with a yellowed fingernail. "Those tree dwellers aren't much better than the Luvesti, in my opinion. Did she tell you anything else?"

Téron's arms go rigid at his sides, and as if in reflex, he answers,

"No." But then his chest stoops forward and he exhales heavily. "I-I don't know. It's been so long since she died."

Sorrow and relief twist inside me, and I flatten a palm against my stomach and curse its instability. This man has lost everything, and I feel glad? I wet my lips. "I am sorry for your loss," I say, wishing I had more to offer him.

"Why did she not tell you the truth?" As ever, Ordin plows ahead with little consideration for the feelings of others.

"I think . . ." Téron shakes his head. "I think she knew it would not go well, and I do not blame her. The people were combustive enough as it was. Or maybe she tried to tell me, and I refused to listen."

Quiet falls over us, broken only by our footfalls, the lowing of cattle, and the tinny sound of cowbells. Téron's gait lags. Glancing at his troubled face, I whistle to catch Ordin's attention. He eyes me but still slows the horse. Turning reluctantly toward Téron, he crosses his arms above his rounded belly and waits for him to get out with it.

Téron studies the ground. "I know it has been costly for you, and I acknowledge that I owe you both my life. Whatever comes, I will accept it with humility. I have been as good as dead for thirteen years, anyway." His eyes raise to meet mine. "But if the Highest wills me to survive this, can I make one request of you?"

I press my lips together and incline my head.

"Take me back to the Vale."

Ordin snorts. "Not a chance in Ikktar, Vale man." Chuckling to himself, he moves off with Merl.

Learn from my mistakes, sweetheart. Do not shackle yourself to a desperate man.

My mother's dimly recalled words unseat me, so loud in my mind that I must fight the impulse to look around for her.

Why here? *Why now*? It has been years since anything about her has crossed my mind, long enough that I can't recall her face in sure detail. And now I hear her voice multiple times within a matter of weeks?

Téron's gaze is unmoving, his irises like the weeping rains of Tiosh. Is this the kind of man she was talking about? My own heart warns against him, but not, I think, for the reasons she meant.

I should heed her. Oh, *beshïn*, just this once, I should heed her.

But my feet stay planted and my right arm crosses my chest, fist pressing against the thick leather over my heart. "I swear."

Tarriv's main gate, the sole beautiful thing in the capital of the Southlands, looms before us. Its ancient timber structure has avoided being set on fire by the warring clans, by some miracle. A snarling beast with horns, fangs, and twisting joints is carved with angular lines into the left door, its arms of shadow clawing toward the center. On the right door, a winged creature with a razor beak and taloned feet rears to oppose it. Its lines are flowing and precise, like rays of sun radiating as straight as the arrow's flight. On either side of the gate, spiked, black walls made from fire-treated logs curve away and encircle the entire city. Long poles angle out from the top with tattered banners hanging beneath them, limp in the morning's calm.

The gate opens and I shift closer to Téron, trying for all the world to appear worthy of my rank and not like a wandering trader as a contingent of soldiers approaches. Ahead, Ordin also alters his stance so his face angles away from them.

I finger my single ranking medallion, a shade of remorse twinging my conscience. He is concealing the visible symbol of his demotion, possibly subconsciously. I had been consumed with nothing but hatred for my partner for months, believing he was harboring the same dislike for me, but he has proved to be the opposite of what I thought. Even though he isn't exactly a friend, he may be someone I can rely on—connection to my mother aside.

And he will now have to bear scorn because of me.

Ignoring my guilt, I turn my attention to the soldiers' strict march, weathering their scowls and lascivious glances without flinching.

"*Noéth ignat u ténesomni*," I shout, pounding my fist against my chest, then raising it high. The heavy gates bang closed in the breath that follows, and disciplined úramech that they are, they jump to respond in kind.

"*Ïth kuvrï ut luvem*," they shout, mimicking my actions.

I do not miss the apprehension and disdain rimming their eyes.

Téron looks at me questioningly when they pass. "What did that mean?"

"It's the Tarrivan war chant. 'We burn the shadows and bleed the light.' Now, be quiet."

"And I thought valefolk were the only ones who slaughtered solas," he says, lifting his eyes to a banner embroidered with a gilded sun sinking into the Praeor Sea.

My steps falter. "What do you m—"

"Declare yourselves, úramech."

Two guards stationed at the gates stare us down, blood-red streamers tied beneath the heads of their sharpened spears.

I lean in close to Téron and say in a terse whisper, "The only way they will give you entry is if you are under my watch. So, stay close." I put a hand around his elbow and feel his tendons tense beneath my thumb.

"I'm not going anywhere, you know," he says, a broken snag to his the cadence of words.

"Good. You would be a fool if you tried."

"G'morning, Parnesh." Ordin addresses the dark-skinned úramech who addressed us, handing him a folded yellow paper with a black seal.

"Is it?" Parnesh's voice is low and rich. He studies Ordin, then frowns beyond him. "You act as though you haven't just emerged from an unnatural bloom of shadow." The broad man takes the paper, his wizened face impassive as he breaks the seal and reads the script.

The other soldier leers at me as he leans against the right door. His filthy amber eyes, like soured cadmot leaf, rake over me. "Weren't expecting you to return to us so soon, blossom. Must have missed me."

I angle my chin and choose one of my more maddening smiles. "Why, yes, I have, Yanim. How have I slept at night without the satisfaction of having turned you down *again*? No fingers to snap back, no groin to knee." I shift my weight into one hip. "It's been unbearable having to do without your whimper."

The smile vacates his face, a firm scowl replacing it. "Keep talking like that, Bréinth, and I'll treat you like the dog you are."

Téron jerks beside me, and I dig my fingers into his arm to keep him where he is.

Yanim's brow arcs. "Or perhaps you've found another beast to satisfy you?" He pushes off the gate and saunters close, circling us. The smell of the pungent oils he rubs into his curled beard makes me want to gag.

"Looks like you've already broken this one," he sneers.

"That's enough, Yanim. You would do well to shut your mouth," Parnesh barks. He hits the paper with the back of a hand and holds it for Yanim to see. "They have come on Verrek's business."

Yanim tears his eyes from Téron's and glances at the commander's seal.

"And with a gift for the Imperii, no less." Parnesh scours Téron with a flint-hard gaze.

This is going to be a difficult week.

Yanim eyes the three of us, then looks toward the billows of shadow beyond. "What did you boys do out there to kick up such a fuss?"

I clack my teeth together, subduing the urge to spit on the polished toes of Yanim's boots, though I can't say why I shouldn't. I am used to being underestimated, even lumped in with women who have sold their bodies to survive. That is much easier to rise above because I have had constant experience with it, but I will *not* have him ignore my womanhood. "That's cute coming from a man who cannot advance beyond opening and closing doors for a living."

Parnesh chuckles at his comrade's speechlessness.

"Why do you laugh? She insults you too," Yanim hisses.

"My friend, I have already broken my body for the Southlands. This is my comfortable retirement." The older man beckons us forward, handing the paper back to Ordin. He grabs the left door of the gate and waits for Yanim to do likewise with the other.

With a curl to his lip and a fiery expletive, Yanim obeys, but his eyes do not leave my face. "I've always thought you were an insult to the name úramech, but you are also a blight on the female sex."

The hairs on the back of my neck stand on end, but I keep my gaze forward as we pass between the gates, walking that precarious line between shadow and light, between Shrouded and sola, as the Southlanders have done for a hundred years.

35
BELWYN

JUST ONCE MORE, I beg of the sky, *I need to see the dawn.* I step outside the house and look up, hoping for light to cut through the ténesomni.

But like every other morning in the Vale, there is nothing but black.

Is this despair what Amyrah experienced when she lived here? Did she always have an insatiable, certain knowledge that this world is wrong, that it is not the life that Elyōn destined for her? She believed there was more even when she couldn't see it, but I only believe because I have seen.

No wonder she could not bear to return with me.

I hoped this feeling of inadequacy would fade once I was back in the place that made me who I am, but I have been shaped into something new in my absence, and I no longer fit here either.

"What are you doing, Bel?" Korvin yawns from within the house, stumbling over the threshold with no shirt on and a lantern dangling at his side. His eyes are puffy underneath, and his hair is a humorous mop sticking straight up on one side.

"Nothing." My attempted grin feels more feeble than reassuring. "It's a new day, brother. Can't you feel it? The air is alive with promise."

He stares at me with a blank look, like I informed him he has to go back to the maevotér and resume his schooling. "With . . . *what*?" His eyes widen. "What have you done with my brother?" he deadpans.

I laugh, but a dull pain flares within my heart. He looks so much like Rhun, and his question hits in a way I'm sure he didn't mean.

"Honestly." Korvin rubs the sleep out of his eyes with the back of his free hand. "I thought you were leaving us again."

"No," I answer in a breath. "I won't do that."

"You'd better not." The levity has fled his voice, and he sounds much older than his twelve years. "But why are you standing out in the ténesomni? It's like you're . . . you're different now. Not afraid or something. Didn't we tell you that the kaligorven are wandering the streets?"

I comb my fingers through my hair, shaking it out at the roots. "Yeah, I know, Kor. It's going to take me a while to get used to being here again."

Korvin slides down on the front step, and I sit beside him. We gaze at the nothingness, the lantern at our feet doing little to cut through the persistent black.

"What's it really like out there?"

I rub my forehead. "Hard to explain if you've never seen something like it before."

Korvin tilts his chin, unimpressed. "Try."

Leaning my elbows on my knees, I rest my chin on clasped hands.

"The daylight reveals all things. I don't think I can put into words all we have missed being raised in the Vale. The colors, the distance, the sky. It's all so exaggerated and makes you realize how vast the world is. Your concerns start to feel small."

"Is that a good thing?"

"To have your gaze lifted to something beyond it all? Yes. But as stunning as the Grovesha may have seemed, even without the ténesomni pressing in on every side, there was still a black that clings. It was just better at disguising itself."

Quiet befalls me as I remember standing on the mountaintop and looking down on the Tothlen Forest. If only I could have held onto that feeling of clarity forever.

"I bet it's still way better than this place."

"You'd think so, but it made me realize that wherever you go, people are the same."

"Do they murder Light Creatures to make them feel better about the darkness?" Korvin's tone is bitter, and I glance at him to see a sheen of tears in his eyes.

"No," I say gently. "But given the right circumstances, people will resort to doing anything."

He shakes his head as if he refuses to believe this. I don't want to shatter his worldview, but I need him to understand. I try a different tactic.

"Think of the best person you know."

He angles a dubious eyebrow.

"Humor me."

"Fine," he relents, closing his eyes.

"Got someone in mind?"

"If you're hinting that I've chosen you, you're wrong."

My chuckle surprises me. "I would never accuse you of such a thing."

He cracks open an eye. "So . . . is there a point to this?"

I nudge him with my shoulder. "Even though this person might be wonderful, and you can't ever imagine a time when you would not love them, there are still moments when they hurt you." My words catch in my throat. "When you hurt them."

"Belwyn." Korvin groans. "This is depressing."

"Stay with me. I promise there's a point."

He huffs. "Can I at least open my eyes?"

"Never said you had to close them."

Though the light is weak, I can see his skin tone deepen. He mutters something I don't catch.

I can't hold back a smirk. "The point is that even the best of us make hideous mistakes."

Silence pools between us like a murky puddle.

"Not you, Bel." Korvin says, his eyes flicking to mine.

I lower my hands and rub a thumb along the veins crossing one of my forearms—the veins I can imagine darkness running through at this moment. "Yes, me."

When Korvin does not relent his intense gaze, I offer him a weak smile. "And yet for those beset with faults, there are unsought moments of good."

My thoughts stray to the days when Rhun and I were boys, racing to the slough to play and build and climb away the pressures Father laid on us. It felt like we made our own light between the two of us. I think of walking in on my brothers making soup for Mother on their own initiative, of all the times a Vestri snow doubled the ambient glow and turned the city into a pillowy soft playground.

Korvin's shoulders slump. "We don't deserve them."

A breeze picks up as the first few drops of rain begin to fall from phantom clouds, splashing the ground and filling the air with petrichor. It escalates into a steady drizzle, but we are sheltered under the overhang above us. I couldn't tell it was overcast or that it was going to rain. Yet here it is, watering the earth, causing crops to grow.

A common thing, wholly unearned, falling on the dark and the light alike.

"Maybe not," I say quietly, holding a palm out to catch the droplets. "But I think the Highest must delight in showing grace to all, giving us glimpses of good when we fail. And that good is light of a different kind."

Korvin sniffs, staring at me curiously. I don't blame him. Have I ever spoken of Elyōn to him, or anyone, before?

"Take it or leave it," I say quickly, realizing I have no right to be speaking of things I clearly do not understand. I get up, offering him a hand. "But it gives me hope that someone beyond this messed up world is the author of good things, sending rain on both the shadow-tainted and those who call on his name."

Korvin stares at my proffered hand, his face smoothing into a soft smile. "Yeah. I like that thought too." He accepts the help and I pull him upright. He fingers the handle of the lantern. "I still want to see the Grovesha one day, though."

My lips slants into my cheek. "I think you will."

"Are you boys hungry?"

We turn to find the shadow of our mother looming in the dim kitchen, holding a lantern and watching us with her head angled curiously to the side.

"No, Mother." I enter the house, laying a hand on her arm as she reaches for a loaf of bread and a long knife. "You don't have to make anything for us. We're fine."

She tucks her arm back under her shawl. Although it's the morning and she's been in her room all night, she looks as though she hasn't slept.

Circles frame her eyes like watery ink stains, and her smile is wan. "It's so good to see you both together again." Her eyes assess my brother's disheveled state. "Korvin, put a shirt on."

Laughing at Korvin's incredulous spluttering, I take the knife and cut the bread into thin slices while my mother seats herself at the small table.

"Did Father come in last night?" I ask as I set the plate before her, then cross the room to get a fire going.

Her silence is all the answer I need. I let the flint take the brunt of my frustration, blowing on the sparks until the ignati crackles to life.

That man has only been home for a few moments since I returned. Always acting like a beaten dog, always reeking of strong drink. I wish I could find it in my heart to offer him a drop of kindness, but it's hard when he stands in such stark contrast to the father in my memories—not that I want that one back, either.

Korvin thumps down the stairs sulkily, pulling a sand-colored tunic over his head.

"You're going to wake Shemai with that noise," Mother scolds, though her voice is weak.

I straighten and brush off my hands, my gaze traveling to her pale face. She can't make a whole sentence without being winded.

"He's already awake," Korvin says, choosing a chair next to her and helping himself to the bread and a generous glob of honey.

Mother smiles at him and runs her hands through his hair, and he doesn't object. The freckle on his right cheek travels upward with a grin of his own.

"What's the plan for you boys today?" she asks.

"I was thinking of going to the market. Shem wants to see if he can get some arlum for his herbs," Korvin answers.

My throat twists like a wrung-out rag. Is this what I returned for?

Daily rhythms and the weary grind of surviving the ténesomni?

No, it's not. I came for my family, yes, but also to find out why the ténesomni has been growing. So far, I haven't unearthed a single answer, and it plagues me. Should I just convince my family to leave, to find somewhere else that's safe?

The stairs creak again. Shem slumps to the bottom step, wrapped in a fluffy blanket, and rests his cheek on the banister as he tries and fails to make his eyes stay open.

I grin, but responsibility soon weighs it down. Crossing the room, I inspect the archery gear hung on the wall behind the front door. "It might be a good time to teach these boys how to handle themselves with a bow."

My mother's breath catches audibly.

I return to her and crouch. "I'll take them no further than the Reckoning Grounds. We'll bring a lot of lanterns." My hands snag hers, lending them my warmth. "Father taught me and Rhun, remember?"

She inhales and bites her lip.

"All I want is to make sure my family is safe." I search her face for any hint that I have upset her. Her warm eyes are hooded. "If you would rather I not, I won't," I say, sincere. "But I also can't stand to let fear have its way with us anymore."

From the stairs, Shem seems to wake up. "You want to do *what* with us?"

Mother clears her throat, gulping like she has been held underwater. "Tomorrow. Can you wait until then? Can I have one more day with all my boys?" She brushes a stray flop of hair away from my forehead and searches my face, her affection mingling with incomprehensible sorrow.

Sighing, I trap her hand against my jaw. "Absolutely."

A soft, sad smile claims her lips. "You aren't the same reckless boy who left, are you?"

An uneasy quiet inhabits the Reckoning Grounds.

I can still feel the cold press of my mother's fingers on my jaw, bidding me to take caution. Giving her the chance to rest was only part of my motivation to get my brothers away. I thought it best not to tell her that the real reason I wanted to take them shooting was to retrieve my sword from its hiding place.

She believes I am not the same fool who left, and she's right. I'm a fool of an entirely different kind. What was the point of coming back if all I'm going to do is wait around in ignorance?

No more. I need answers, need to know that I can make a difference for my family, for everyone trapped here. I need to change this place or Amyrah might never return to me. And I'm not going to incite change if something doesn't shatter the lies that bind us.

Thus my need for a sword.

"You told her you wouldn't go into the trees, Belwyn," Korvin calls, apprehension clinging to his voice. I glance behind. He waits in the center of the Reckoning Grounds, relaxing the tension on his bowstring. Shem stands farther back, balancing his own bow on end as he waits for his turn. Three lanterns surround them on the grass, doing little more than marking where they are anchored in the sea of ténesomni. A stump is set on its end fifteen paces away, bolétis piled around it so the boys know where to aim.

"I know, Kor. I'll be quick." I turn back to the forest, holding another lantern out. "Keep shooting until you've used up all the arrows, then wait for me before you and Shem retrieve them."

I find the mossy hiding place without difficulty, relieved that my cache of weapons remains undisturbed. The fragrance of wet mulch envelops me. I unwrap the blade and the bow, shaking the leaves from the damp cloak and draping it over a tree limb to air out.

"Shem, Bel said to wait."

"But it's *my* turn now."

My brothers' arguing reaches me, distorted in the gloom. Irritated, I open my mouth to warn them not to be so loud, but the words clog in my throat when a repulsive odor cuts through the wet and the dirt.

The smell is more than decay. It is death.

Dread laces through my stomach, shooting out long roots that impede my breathing, my limbs. My mind. Something is watching. I can't see it, can't hear it, but I feel its presence lurking just out of reach. My heart drums in response. With shaking hands, I strap on the sword belt and pick up the bow.

A low sound like a moan forced from a drowning creature's lungs shivers through the air, making my arm hairs stand to attention. I back away, clumsy footsteps cracking twigs and announcing my location with unforgivable precision.

The moan increases into a growl.

Forcing my body to turn before terror immobilizes it, I let out a single, frenzied command—"*Run*!"—and waste no time demonstrating.

With a hiss, the thing pursues.

Korvin and Shem's alarmed faces slip into view between the swirls of ténesomni, and I wave my arms as I careen toward them. "Did you not hear me? Run. *Run*!"

I grab their shirt collars and drag them with me, ignoring how they protest. I don't dare acknowledge the scraping sounds and snarls bearing down on us.

Highest, save us.

When the sola bones and gates of Utsanek come into view, I plant my palms between each brothers' shoulder blades and shove them forward. They sprawl onto the stone roadway, yelping.

I spin on my heel and draw my sword.

The hideous beast rises to its hind legs and roars, shaking coils of ténesomni from its body to congest the air between us. The bones hung at the gate manage to reveal the monster in greater detail than I have seen before. Long yellow fangs snap an arm's length away, and a slimy black tongue lolls from a cavernous throat that glows red from deep within. My eyes shoot to the thing's face, which is elongated, fleshy, and covered with oozing sores. I make the mistake of looking into its soulless eyes, and for a horrible moment, I feel like I'm looking into the eyes of a human. But its piercing gaze is beyond either man or beast.

I raise the sword higher, tremors coursing up my arm, and aim its point at the center of the kaligorva's convulsing chest. This Shrouded is smaller than the one I faced on Amyrah's behalf, but I have no doubt it could tear me apart with its clawed feet, its rigid, muscle-roped limbs. Fear draws my strength through the soles of my boots, but the sound of my brothers rasping for breath, endeavoring to disguise their own terror, steels my resolve.

I grit my teeth viciously, and pain shoots through my molars. "You will *not* have them," I say, daring to take a small step forward.

Bristling hairs rise from the kaligorva's humped back, and its rattling breaths fill the air with that putrid stench. To my amazement, it does not attack. I grip the sword more firmly in both hands, holding it out as I take careful steps toward the gate. Saliva drips from the beast's fangs and it does not move, though the swells of ténesomni grow thicker and angrier around it, billowing like a sail.

Cold perspiration beads on my forehead. I can't look away from those eyes, straight from the pits of Ikktar. They will never stop boring into my soul. I will see them in every corner, in every dream. They will be with me always, tainting every moment of beauty as long as I live . . .

A whimper severs the connection, like a flame to old twine, and I suck in a sharp breath of stale air.

"Shem. Korvin," I say in a voice that sounds too calm. "Go into the city."

"But, Bel—"

"Go into the city and don't stop running until you make it to the market square."

"What about y—"

"*Now.*"

The kaligorva hisses. My hair stands on end.

There is a beat of silence, followed by the cadence of scuffling feet fading into the distance. I take a measured breath.

Step by shaky step, I back away, but the beast presses forward as if it intends to follow me into the streets.

Korvin said the monsters had started doing that, but I didn't believe him until now.

I am a boy who disturbed a hornet's nest. If I do manage to escape, the Shrouded would only find another target to bear its rage.

If it attacks people in the streets, their blood will be on my hands.

Shades. What have I done?

Anger answers my fear, blazing in the timber structure of my chest. This time, I let it catch fire.

It's a physical heat that I swear I can feel radiating right out through my fingertips. It calls to mind Amyrah standing against an impossible foe; the blur of Téron jumping to take her place; my father's dumbfounded expression when I proved to him for the first time that I *am* strong. I take hold of all these memories, all the feelings of inadequacy that I have been harboring for months, and let them pour through me in a torrent of fury.

"You will not have them."

The kaligorva seems to decrease in size, its long tail twitching behind great, lion-like haunches. That moment of doubt is the opportunity I need. I pull my sword back and lunge forward, aiming for the center of the kaligorva's crudely formed torso.

But the beast is quick and sparks fly as my steel deflects against its claws. I strike again and again, managing to catch it in the leg. The tang of copper mixed with sulfur fills the air. The monster screams.

And I scream back, "*I will not let you pass.*"

The kaligorva pulls back a razored limb, preparing to strike. Fury blazes from its eyes. My knuckles gleam white against the sword's pommel.

Incongruent laughter, more chilling than the kaligorva's hiss, carries across the clearing, and the world seems to freeze around us.

"Oh, well done. Well *done*."

A smudge of white pushes through the ténesomni, but I don't dare break my concentration on my opponent to look at it.

"I have only seen one other among the valefolk with such courage." There is a pause before a word I do not understand. "*Sedéré*."

One command and the kaligorva relaxes, lowering to all fours and bowing its head. The response is so odd, so subservient, that a disbelieving laugh pushes from my chest. I know who can command the Shrouded like that, and his presence is the furthest thing from humorous. Facing him, I drop the sword by my side. Its tip strikes a rock with a resonant *clang*.

Ténesomni skirts each quiet footfall, dancing around Myrzeth's limbs and darting away to greet the kaligorva's darkness like an old friend. The Foremost's sharp eyes assess me from head to boots, snagging at last on the weapon at my side.

"Curious," he whispers as he comes close enough for me to end his life, if I had the inclination. If I didn't need the answers that he possesses.

"I recognize that blade." His black irises meet mine, and I suppress a grimace. "That must make you one of Dravek's sons."

I wet my lips with my tongue and raise my chin. "Belwyn."

His smile makes my gut roil. "I wish I could say that he made a worthy opponent, but that would be untrue. Our battle was rather disappointing in the end. And to be related to such a weak man . . ." He shakes his head. "How unfortunate."

Ignoring his pronged words, I glance at the kaligorva. "Your hounds aren't very well-trained, Myrzeth."

The beast growls. Myrzeth reaches to it, his hand disappearing into its wiry fur, and takes a long inhale with his eyes closed. The shadows flowing around us rush toward him, disappearing into his nostrils and parted lips. When he turns to me again, black stains the whites of his eyes like ink. He blinks and they clear. "On the contrary. They serve their purpose well."

"And what is that purpose, Myrzeth? To pollute Atsun with shadows?" I snort a laugh. "Seems kind of basic."

"I wouldn't expect you to understand. The dark is just the beginning, my friend."

Chill bumps prickle my arms. "Then what's next?" I gesture around the clearing. "What keeps the people bending the knee to your reign if this is all you can offer them?"

Myrzeth lets his hand fall from the Shrouded and looks it in the eyes, then pointedly to where the trees are hidden. With a low, rumbling growl, the kaligorva lurches away, melting into oblivion. A howl echoes through the forest, and others return it from a distance.

The Foremost turns to me. "I offer them power. What pitiful, naïve people you were before I came back here. Crippled by your traditions, your lack of knowledge of what lays beyond. Yet at the same time, that weakness is also what will make you strong. Your hearts are already primed to accept the darkness, to do anything for survival." His gaze drifts to the city gates behind my back. "That is what I'm counting on."

"You're wrong."

Myrzeth cocks an eyebrow at me, amused.

"They will resist you." I can feel my whole body shaking—with rage or fear, I cannot tell—but my voice does not betray me. "I've seen it already, Myrzeth. You do not own the valefolk. Not yet."

He looks at me pityingly. "The seeds have already been sown, Belwyn. They go far beyond the Vale. Nothing can stop what I have set in motion."

Misgiving fills me, even though I cannot make sense of his words. I am losing my courage, sickened and exhausted by this conversation, by wondering if my brothers made it to Utsanek's market unharmed. Trying to appear casual, unbothered, I sheathe my sword and risk a wry chuckle. "Daylight isn't so bad. You should try it."

I regret the words immediately.

Myrzeth lunges forward, bringing his face close. A draft of cold rushes from his skin like wind off the Vestri-touched Loch Skythe. "Ah, now it is all made clear," he says. "I sensed my little Ketra's conflicted emotions the other day."

I stiffen at the mention of her name.

Oblivious, Myrzeth continues in a carefree tone that stands in sharp contrast to this confrontation. "She was out of sorts but did not wish to confide in me about what troubled her." His lip twitches like he is recalling an amusing joke, and something grows hot inside of me. "With the proper *persuasion*, she divulged that she had met someone whom she hadn't seen for a while, that she suspected had left the Vale for a time."

He straightens, his penetrating eyes taking mine hostage. "And that leaves me with one question. Where, oh where, have you been hiding?"

When I do not respond, he crosses his arms and grips his chin between long, white fingers. His brows lower, shadowing his eyes from the city's sola bone glare, but then he laughs. "Belwyn. Belwyn Kovah." His tone lowers. "I will be watching you."

He shoves past me, dragging the heavy mantle of ténesomni with him into Utsanek's streets, where it crashes against the stony buildings like Jaki's dark beverage. The weight of the air decreases, and I can breathe again.

I don't understand what that was, but there is one thing I am certain about. No matter how it terrifies me, Myrzeth must be stopped.

36

AMYRAH

The Sighing Woods are like a living, breathing organism. Four-footed Light Creatures peek from under bushes, observed from above by their winged counterparts, and every breath of wind that rustles the leaves is a warm exhale. The thin trees dance as if swept up in the night's melody, their branches erupting with adoring applause.

"We are almost through the woods," Holden calls. Heedless of how his simple pronouncement makes my stomach drop, he leads Zenith by the reins through a dense area of bush a fair distance ahead.

I slow and let my fingers touch the smooth bark of the aspen trees. This place has been one of reprieve for my soul, where I don't have Rael reminding me of the friend I left behind, where the woodfolk cannot cast me in suspicion, and where Belwyn isn't making my head spin. Here, I can pretend that something good has come from all the heartache.

An unbearable pressure grips my chest, and I can almost hear a crooning voice. *Lie down and rest, child. Here, you need not consider what was or what is to come.*

It sounds like wisdom, and I want so badly to heed it. If this is a place where I am never tempted to use the ténesomni again, wouldn't it be better for everyone if I stayed here?

I close my eyes and lean on a tree, weariness wrapping me in its compelling limbs.

Yes, stay, the voice purrs.

But as I give in to the whispers, a song pierces the sky, and my hands grow hot. I hold them up to discover light seeping from the lines in my palms. Panic seizing me, I curl my fingers in and press my fists to my collarbones.

"Elyōn, help me," I gasp.

The heat is unbearable, but it does not consume me as I thought it would in Ketsé. Instead, it burns through my drowsy thoughts, returning my clarity. The song grows in volume, and the purring voice shifts to a hiss as I resist it.

As swift as the heat began, it dissipates, washing up my arms and spinning itself around my heart. I stare at my hands, once again pale and ordinary in the starlight.

I turn my face to the sky as the song, barely perceptible yet hauntingly lovely, flirts with the breeze. It is like a whisper of a forgotten lyric, a melody just after the singer has grown silent.

A tiny bird takes to the sky like a shooting star, and all is quiet. The leaves swish overhead, like they, too, are breathing in relief.

Shame bears down on my soul for being so quick to let that strange voice sway me. It is frightening how much it sounded like wisdom, though I know it can't have been from Elyōn. Yet he intervened, keeping me alert and in command of my thoughts.

"Did you enjoy the song?" Holden smiles over his shoulder at me, as if completely ignorant of the battle I just faced.

"Y-yes. It was lovely."

I rub my palms on my dress and hurry to catch up. We walk in silence, and soon I can see the trees thinning ahead with open space beyond. I pass my eyes over the edge of the woods, wondering if the bird will be the last sola we see before leaving its borders.

Over the past days, we haven't been able to move fifty paces without being met by a new, fascinating sola. With their delicate crystal horns, doleful calls, and light-dripping feathers, the owls have been my favorite. The many deer are also lovely and surprising, since not all of them resemble what I have come to expect within the Vale. Some aren't much larger than a wild dog, with pronged antlers at sharp geometric angles, and others tower above Zenith with fearsome crowns covered in white flowers. I've only seen them from a distance; I shiver at the thought of standing next to one.

The beautiful creatures have grown in number the closer we have drawn to Luvesta. Not all of them have glowed at first. Many waited until Holden and I were near to share their brilliance with us, like the bear, Little Cottla. And some of the animals we've come across haven't been solas, either. Holden laughed at me for approaching an agitated squirrel. It took the little menace throwing nuts before I believed it wasn't a sola.

Despite that embarrassing encounter, I have gotten better at identifying them. Some are like regular forest fauna, yet they have peculiar differences, like exaggerated, curling tail feathers, or scales in places where they ought not to be. More than that, they conjure a feeling of familiarity that can't be explained.

After my encounter with the Guardian of the Woods, I no longer fear being seen by them.

"Why do they hold back their light sometimes?" I ask as a huge owl soars overhead with silent wingbeats, casting sparkling rays to the ground. A thrill reaches through me, right down to my toes.

Holden indulges in a noisy yawn. "They're sort of like people. Some are shyer than others. It takes a special Light Creature to enter an unknown scene, lights blazing."

"And do they all possess the ability to withhold their light?"

"Most of them. They can't help but reveal it when one of their own is near, whether animal or human."

"Can all Luvesti choose not to cast light as well?" I ask, discreetly checking my palms to make sure they haven't started glowing again.

Holden chuckles. "That's a lot of questions." He thinks, eyes narrowing slightly. "Usually, but it takes practice, and since they stay close to Luvesta, most of them don't. I've had to do it for years." A long breath escapes him. "It feels good to be able to let it out."

Stopping, Holden glances at me, then puts the reins over Zenith's head. "Come on. The night is almost over. We can't miss it."

"Miss what?" I ask, wrinkling my nose at him. Just as a person couldn't call it day in the Vale, it is laughable to call this night.

Holden smiles. "Dawn."

The trees part around us as we come to an open stretch of whispering grass curving upward in a gentle slope. In the northeast, a distant ridge overlooking the plain glows with a golden halo arcing above it. And from the west, a strange scent is carried on the wind. It reminds me of walking the shores of Loch Skythe on a stormy day, but with a briny note I can't place.

"What is that—"

"Smell?" Holden finishes. "It's the Vestri Sea. If we were to travel west, you could look at it from the cliffs of the Astellum Plain. It's much more impressive at sunset, though."

A twig snaps behind me. Glancing back, I spy a shy fox emerging from the woods with its light concealed for the moment. Unlike ordinary woodland foxes, its ears are large, and its tail is broad and flat at the end. I stagger and turn toward it.

"What's wrong, Amyrah?" Holden's voice struggles to pierce through the fog of recollection that possesses me.

I fall to my knees and extend my hand out to the sola. "I have met a creature like this before."

The fox sniffs the air, its paddle-like tail flapping and sending a puff of wind toward me.

My whole arm begins to tremble, and I can't free myself from the idea that I am back in the Vale and my father has pushed me off the platform moments before. I can feel the impressions his palms left in my ribs as he took my place.

I hold a shaking palm to my mouth to stifle the sob forcing up my throat. A sola identical to this one found me after he disappeared into the writhing swarm of incensed kaligorven. And I had whispered a prayer to Elyōn in its ear, a wild hope that my father would not be devoured.

Did it ever make it to him, I wonder?

Did he die alone?

Holden's soft tread ceases. The sola doesn't stir at his approach, or when he sinks onto his knees beside me.

"How is that possible?" he whispers.

I wipe my cheeks and blink through the hideous memories, focusing on him instead. His jaw is relaxed, but his eyes are narrowed, moving between me and the sola.

"W-what do you mean?" I stutter.

An odd look passes over his face before a breathy laugh escapes him.

"Sorry. It's . . ." He shakes his head, brows pressing together. "Your reaction to Little Cottla, the way you've been so enamored with every sola we meet. I was sure you can't have seen many."

"I haven't."

The fox takes a tentative step on a delicate paw, her ears pricking forward. She hasn't flared yet, and with the ambient light all around us, I am able to make out more detail than I have before. Each strand of fur is as though it has been spun of fine silver, and even without the sola glow, her body shimmers with an undulating pattern, like ripples on a pond.

"You don't understand," Holden persists. "I mean, you shouldn't have seen *any* before. I was confused how you immediately knew the dead wolf was a sola, why your mind went to the Light Creatures when you saw that rabbit in Ketsé." He turns his face to the fox, thoughtful. "They are rare enough in the Grovesha, and you were raised in the heart of darkness."

I frown. "But they come into the Vale, Holden."

He pivots suddenly from the fox. "They do *what*?"

"They—"

The fox's nose brushes my fingertips, and the creature bursts into a blaze of pure, white luminescence. It yips and bounds away, frolicking into the trees. I fall back, shielding my eyes with my forearm as my sadness breaks into nervous, breathless laughter.

Holden is unfazed by the fox-sola's theatrics. His deep-green eyes bore into me. "What do you mean about them coming into the Vale?"

My smile fractures in the face of his intensity. *Does he have no idea what the valefolk have done*?

A warning rises in my chest. If he doesn't know, the Luvesti may not either. My future here could be compromised because of the sins of my people.

My former people, I remind myself, although it's a hideous untruth that makes me feel filthy. Belwyn is one of them, and my heart is wrapped up with his. And could I really reject the heritage of my father?

No, the fox-sola has been a stern reminder that no matter where I travel, I'll never be far from him. And it's a reminder of why I can't give up now.

I push up onto my hands and tilt my head, almost afraid to broach the subject. "You have no knowledge of the Vale's customs, do you?"

Standing, he holds out a hand to pull me up. "Think about it. The Vale has been trapped in a border of shadow for a hundred years. There was no need to know anything about it at all. Only to contain it." His voice is pinched. Perhaps he is annoyed at having to explain himself to me or bothered by his own lack of understanding.

I accept the help, although my own irritation pounds against my skull. "And what of the people the Luvesti imprisoned?"

He releases my hand, his frustration tinged with uncertainty. "The Confining was supposed to affect the kaligorven alone. The people were free to leave if they chose."

"And you believe it was as easy as that?" A disbelieving huff shakes from my lungs, prompting a flash of embarrassment to cross Holden's face.

"You must understand. At the time the kaligorven were condemned to their fate, the people who were trapped with them were devoted to the ténesomni."

"To Érechlys." The name hisses through my mind, and I shiver.

He nods.

"How is it I have never heard of her?"

"I don't know. She's a deceiver." Holden throws down his hands and paces. "She thrives within the ignorance of man. The less people understand who is controlling them, twisting their thoughts to dark purposes, the more willing they are to do her bidding."

I pull my sleeves over my fists and press them under my chin. "Please don't get upset with me. I think I understand, but I also can't help reacting when the people I was raised among are painted with such broad, unfeeling strokes. There are good people there, too, and far more Elyōn worshippers within the Vale than you realize."

"Which is unexpected." Holden runs his hands through his hair, takes a few deep breaths, and looks at me. "But we were talking about the solas, not the people."

I cross my arms and incline my chin for him to continue.

"As far as anyone knew, when the Confining concluded, all contact between the Light Creatures and the Shrouded was cut off. With the kaligorven bound as they were in the Vale, there was no longer any reason the two would meet."

"But, Holden," I say, adjusting my pack and following him to the contented horse grazing on dewy grasses, "the solas have been coming to the Vale this whole time. Our entire culture centered around the ritual of hunting them."

He spins. "*Your* culture? Did you hunt them as well?"

"No. No, not me," I say with exasperation. "I hated the Hunt, at least what little of it I saw, but it hadn't happened for thirteen years."

Mounting the horse, Holden reaches to give me something to hold as I climb up. I settle into the saddle behind him, wishing I could put more distance between us to reflect the tension. With the gentle rhythm of Zenith's gait and the night persisting undeterred around us, it soon leeches from my mind like poison from a wound.

"The kaligorven may have been prevented from leaving, but the solas were never kept out," Holden thinks aloud, his voice no longer holding that accusatory edge. "Interesting."

"It would have been better for them if they had. Then the city would not be lit by the bones of the dead."

Silence befalls us as we cross the plain in the softly glowing moments before dawn. A sweet fragrance has permeated the air, mingling with the salty scent. I look down to find wildflowers thick and abundant about us, dotted with vibrant crimsons, lush purples, fiery yellows. They are so perfect and breathtaking that it feels like we have strayed into someone's garden. As Zenith tramples them under hoof, a bloom of blossoms rises into the air, and I gasp in bewilderment. No, they are not blossoms, but butterflies even more divine than the flowers. They flutter around us in a gentle vortex, and I hold out my open hand.

One brushes my finger with a silken wing, and its tiny body ignites into a dazzling sola glow. My mouth drops as others lose their cloaks of camouflage. Pinpricks of illumination erupt all around, flowing out like a rush of sparks, like starlight breaking through the evening sky to calm anxious hearts.

Holden reins Zenith to a stop as we watch the field transform into a floating, sparkling constellation hovering above the surface of the earth. I follow the progression of the living wave until I notice a forlorn shape nestled in the center of the field.

A small house.

"Who lives there?" I whisper, fearing that if I am too loud, I will disrupt the phenomenon.

"The hermitess of Astellum Plain."

"Is she Luvesti?"

He urges Zenith onward again. "She's lived out here her whole life. Prefers to keep the company of solas instead of people."

I can't say I blame her.

A narrow path laid with shimmering stones reaches from the front door. Dozens of rounded bushes cloaked in butter-yellow flowers crowd a lovely, cultivated garden within the wild tangles of prairie grasses.

"I'd like to meet her," I say.

"Really?" Holden turns around as best as he can, pegging me with a concerned look before facing forward again. "Didn't you hear me say she's a hermit? Believe me, it's for a reason."

"I know what it's like to be on the outside," I say, pressing closer to his back.

"Well, my father brought me there as a child and it traumatized me. And . . ."

"And what?"

"Nothing was ever the same after that."

When Holden doesn't continue, my chest constricts. I let out a slow, impatient breath, wishing I could pull his hidden thoughts out of his head and examine them one by one. But am I any less evasive? How easy it is to forget that others bear their own loads that are just as heavy as mine. Maybe heavier.

As we move past the cottage, one of the bushes straightens, and I reflexively grab Holden's sides.

"*Ow*," he wheezes.

"Sorry." I relax my grip and crane my neck to confirm what I witnessed. Zenith is moving at a steady clip, but I manage to catch a glimpse of a pale, wrinkled face and two black eyes fixed on me from under layers of linen the color of moss and feather grass.

"No, don't let go," Holden says. "I'm going to get Zenith into a gallop so we can have the best view before the sun comes up."

The exhilarating race pushes all other thoughts from my mind. I turn my face to the east and wait for the sun's impending inferno to set the whole sky ablaze. Moments before its fire spills over the horizon, Holden pulls on Zenith's reins and jumps down from his back.

"Come on, Amyrah." He offers me a hand, shaking it when I hesitate.

Curious, I slip my leg over Zenith's back, and Holden yanks me out of the saddle. I take a few unsteady steps to regain my balance.

"What is it?" I ask, blinking at the sunrise.

"No, not that way." He comes behind me, grabs my shoulders and points me to the northeast. Leaning in, he whispers in my ear, "There."

What I had thought was a ridge is really a smooth, towering stone wall in the distance, circling the base of a mountain. Except, it isn't a mountain at all.

"The shining city of Luvesta," Holden declares with no small amount of pride as the sun's rays shoot across the plain, casting the city in celestial glory. It catches the light and parries it back to us, a small star of its own.

I turn my face away from its blinding cast.

Holden stands beside me, and I watch his face as it shimmers with awe, delight, and longing.

"That, Amyrah, is home."

I dearly hope he's right.

37
SEYLA

SIX DAYS HAVE COME AND GONE since I parted with Téron, and for the most part I have succeeded in not thinking about him.

But it also feels like drowning.

Ordin and I have been kept occupied with the intake protocol for úramech returning to the Agmen from any posting outside of Tarriv. We have undergone several rounds of questioning and reports to our superiors, armor and weapon inspections, multiple visits to the Agmen healers to ensure that we are in good health, and intensive conditioning. There have been no other recent arrivals, so it has just been me and the cantankerous old fool I used to love to hate. We have hardly spoken because, until recently, it has never been our custom to acknowledge each other if we weren't required to. The silence feels incredibly awkward now, and I'm struggling to understand why.

Perhaps Ordin has changed.

Perhaps I have changed too.

I step into the stronghold courtyard, ready to take advantage of a small break in the intensive schedule. The busyness of it all used to be what I needed to keep me sane. Full days and a bone-weary body meant little time to think, followed by heavy, dreamless sleeps. I thrived on the challenge, the purpose. Now, I have grown weary of the hectic rhythm of my life in Tarriv, and it is no longer enough to staunch the memories and the weakness.

A cry reaches my ears. I snap to attention and run to the source, hand on my khukuri hilt. A group of off-duty úramech crowd around something I'm both anxious and terrified to see. I shoulder between them, my breaths quickening.

Two stoic soldiers half-drag a man between them. He is filthy, and the rusty stains of old blood surround slashes in his tattered tunic. Acid rises in my throat.

"Oh, come now." A smooth voice rises over the commotion. "You can't have all the fun with our foreign pet, Dekar." I rake my eyes over the onlookers and find Yanim's smug visage.

"The Imperii is not yet satisfied that we have extracted all we need to know from him," the taller of the two soldiers says briskly over his shoulder. He chuckles. "But I can put in a good word so that you can have the scraps."

I glance back at the beaten man, gripping my khukuri impossibly tight. He lifts his face and when he looks in my direction, my soul cracks in two.

Téron.

Pulse deafening in my ears, I plant myself in front of Yanim and draw my blade. "He has been claimed."

Every instinct within me screams against my actions, but I don't care. I *don't*.

The smile fades from Yanim's lips. "Is that so?"

My breaths come in quick bursts. "It is so."

He grits his teeth and lets out a slow exhale that ends in an ugly snicker. "How desperate you must be. It's too bad no man has found you worthy enough to bind. That amount of spirit shouldn't be wasted."

Dekar and the other soldier continue to haul Téron away, and it requires all my resolve not to break eye contact with Yanim and watch them go.

"Perhaps no man is worthy of me," I breathe, my voice barely controlled.

Yanim regards me coolly, hatred rampaging behind his handsome eyes. His body jerks and he swings his arm, backhanding me across the face.

I sprawl to the ground, khukuri flying, an explosion of stars consuming my vision. My ears fill with the sound of hideous laughter. I dig my fingers into the earth and try to call on my training to keep my emotions in line, but I cannot make myself think. When the ground stops pitching around me, I get to my feet, retrieve my khukuri, and crack its hilt into Yanim's perfect teeth.

38
WEHNA

MY HEADACHES HAVE RETURNED, and the dizziness along with them, as if the turbulent Haneth Sea has been bottled within my skull. It rages against its prison, thrusting my fractured mind about without mercy. Pain and nausea are the only constants in my life anymore.

And anger.

I suppose any of those things is better than the fear that used to define my days.

The knife slips on the skin of the onion and lodges itself in the fleshy tip of my forefinger. I stagger back and press a thumb to the throbbing wound. The knife clatters to the wood plank floor.

"*Heshïn*."

"Wehna, do not use such a filthy word." My mother gasps from across the room, where she is pressing fresh enatuberries through a cheesecloth-lined sieve. The blood-red juice drips from beneath and into an earthenware bowl. Her eyes land on my hands, widening when she sees the real blood trickling in a steady stream down my wrist.

"Mada, she's hurt," Arvo whispers, his hand freezing on its way to pop a berry into his mouth.

I make myself stay where I am as my mother hastens over, though I want to run and hide and scream. Her brows pinch and I wait for the next reprimand about my carelessness.

My mother's fingers are gentle as they assess the damage, but it is still enough to earn a pained hiss through my clenched jaw. "It looks like your fingernail saved you from something worse," she says before fetching a strip of white cloth and a little glass bottle. The scent of rosemary drifts through the air as she applies the balm to the cut and wraps the wound.

"Be more careful next time."

My chest deflates. There it is, that little reminder that I am not measuring up, that she is surprised I have survived in her absence.

I sit on the edge of a bed while Mother resumes her task with Arvo and wait for my emotions to form into something I can identify.

The thoughts that haunt me are as murky as the shadows that shift outside our door.

I am glad they are back, I tell myself as I watch my mother bottle the juice and wipe down the table. Arvo licks his fingers, and she tousles his hair as she passes him. *I'm glad. I am. Why wouldn't I be?*

This narrative cycles through my mind, my lungs growing heavy and my heart thumping quicker every time it repeats. I don't understand how I could have been so wrong about what happened to them, or how to come back from what I thought was my reality.

"Wehna, the washing needs to be done." Mother's eyes pass over my features, as if she can read my thoughts. I wouldn't be surprised if she can. She's always been able to root out the hidden motivation to every action I've ever made. Will she ever grow as weary of it as I am?

I blink at her as she holds out a basket piled high with rags, linens, and the bright purple cheesecloth.

"But, Mada—"

Her lips spread into a forced smile that comes across as more reproachful than consoling. "We all need to contribute, sweetie."

Tears prick my eyes and pain pricks my finger. I bite my lip and stand, holding up my wounded hand. "Even with this?"

A rush of white flashes over my mother's face. "Oh, Wehna, I'm so sorry. Of course not—"

I grab the basket from her hands and turn toward the door. "It's fine. I understand. You need to control something, don't you?" I spit over my shoulder as I rush out of the cottage, letting my words strike her where I can't see them do it.

The laundry falls at my feet somewhere between the chicken coop and the cottage, and I grip my face in my hands, muting a strangled scream against them. I spent weeks feeling like a stray, an unsolicited burden on Tress and Bryn. Now I miss their busy household, where my every breath is not measured and I don't second guess each action I make.

Being confined inside the cottage with my own family feels worse than either the headaches or the nausea, and I know that fact makes me a horrible person. But must I act as if we are now whole and the last months didn't happen? I'm not strong enough for that. If strength means I must clothe myself in a lie, I don't want it.

I draw in a shaky breath and drop my hands. The wren-sola titters from above, calling out my location. I throw it a pained look and move to escape from its glow. I cannot afford to be found right now.

Quickly, I walk across the clearing, away from my mother and brother, wishing the shadows would grow a backbone and swallow me for real.

How can Mada expect us to pick up the tatters of who we once were when everything has changed? She may pretend this is home, but our home ceased existing a long time ago. We have become the needy ones she used to dote on, and Arvo has no use for me now that he has our parents back. Even making and selling jewelry as an occupation is no longer something I can pour myself into. I would never be allowed to go to Utsanek's market square, the only logical place to sell it.

I don't have a purpose anymore, do I?

The sola glares in my eyes, sending a spike of pain through them, and its inexhaustible heat presses into my skin. I quicken my steps to get away from it. The bird is at once welcome and the most hateful thing in creation, mirroring the hypocrisy in my own mind. I can see how Elyōn led me and my brother and kept us safe through all our trials, yet at the same time, I feel so thoroughly abandoned by him.

"Going for a stroll?"

Father emerges from the goat shed, brushing his hands on the front of his tunic. I close my eyes for a beat and turn toward him, not bothering to put on a smile. It wouldn't be real, anyway.

"You shouldn't be out here alone," he says.

Scolding, again. His concerns for me may be legitimate, but all I can do is let out a dry, disbelieving laugh. "No, you're right. I shouldn't be alone. I shouldn't have *ever* been alone. I think we're beyond that now, though."

My anger, eager to discover a new outlet, turns on my pada. He still treats me as if I am the same demure girl who used to help around the home, cooking meals to take to the needy, watching my brother, and selling trinkets at the market.

His expression flickers, as if weathering a physical blow. "Wehna—"

My eyes widen in warning and my breaths congeal in my chest, building to a volatile pressure. "Don't do that. Don't tell me all the ways I need to try harder." Heat crawls up my cheeks, and I turn toward the narrow path that leads to Utsanek.

I break into a stumbling run when I hear him follow.

"*Wehna*."

Desperation takes hold, forcing all sense from my mind. All I know is I cannot let him catch up with me. Holding my hands out, I escape down the darkening path, my heartbeat deafening in my ears.

"Wehna, come back."

A root grabs at my foot, and I pitch forward, my left knee, palms, and elbows taking the force of my fall. A strangled wail bursts from my throat.

My father's footfalls come to a halt, and his labored breaths fill the gaps between my sobs. He stands over me, his feet weakly illuminated by a cluster of bolétis along the path. I don't dare look up at him.

He whistles out a long exhale as he crouches at my side. "You've hurt yourself." His hands find my forearms, fingers trailing to my wrists and turning them to expose my bleeding palms.

"I-I'm fine," I whisper, attempting to pull my hands back, but his firm grip presses my bracelets into my skin, holding me fast. I drag my reluctant eyes up to meet his, expecting to find the criticism that has so often defined his features from the moment of his return.

But his brows are not pinched with anger or judgment, and glimmering trails shine on his cheeks.

"I'm sorry, my girl."

"Sorry for what?"

His head dips, his shoulders angling forward. "For doing this to you. For making you hurt."

With trembling hands, he rips a strip of fabric from his own tunic, then another, and wraps them one at a time around my throbbing palms. He has always been adept at fixing anything he touches, nothing ever staying broken for long in our home.

But wounds are different, requiring time and space to breathe.

He binds mine with tenderness.

"I have been harsh, expecting the impossible of you since we returned. It's not because I don't love you, Wehna. It's because I don't know how to live in a world where it's my fault you are broken, and . . ."

The fabric eludes his control, and he surprises himself with a sob before silencing it with a clack of his teeth.

"And I am the one thing you can't fix," I finish.

I pull away and get onto my knees, ignoring the pain, and lay my hands on both sides of his face. "I will be fine, Pada. It's not that bad."

His eyes stay fixed on the ground between us. "No, it *is* bad. All of it. And you're right: you shouldn't have been alone at all. How can I forgive myself for thinking anyone in this world needed me more than you and Arvo?" His words break apart between unabashed sobs. "How do I come back from that? W-what can I do to m-make it right?"

You need to be strong, Wehna.

It's an odd time to think of the words that my conscience so often screams in accusation. Now, they come as a gentle reminder of the kind of strength that possesses the power to bring life from destruction.

"You don't have to. I-I forgive you."

His eyes dart up to meet mine, and I allow them to see past the prickly exterior I've kept between us.

"Just love me the way I am *now*. Wounds and all."

His lips fall open, like he wants to correct me, but then he presses them together, stopping the outpouring of words.

"Can you do that, Pada? Please?"

He sucks in a slow breath. Fresh tears run down his cheeks and dampen his copper beard as he whispers, "Yes, I can do that," and pulls me close, blessing my forehead with a warm kiss and a slow exhale.

My heart squeezes with the closest thing to affection that I've felt in months.

After a while, he struggles to his feet and helps me up. I wince at the pain in my leg and test it out. Nothing is broken or sprained, perhaps only bruised from the fall. I think of my mother, how she lurches about the house on unsteady footing, and I am ashamed for not considering what she might be battling to complete the mundane tasks that never cease needing to be done.

Everyone bears wounds, but only we can understand the extent of our pain.

"So where were you off to in such a hurry?" my father asks, turning to face the blackened path.

I bite my lip, unsure if I should tell him that my heart desired to find the one place I found a small measure of comfort while he and Mother were lost to me. A sigh escapes me. If anything is going to strengthen this strange relationship we are navigating, it's honesty.

"I wanted to visit Tress and Bryn," I say. "He's not well, you know. A kaligorven attacked him when he—" I stop. The knowledge that Arvo and I have been in real danger in my parents' absence can't help matters.

But Pada doesn't seem to notice how I trail off. He stares ahead, his face made visible by the bolétis glow. "Bryn. My friend," he murmurs, running a hand over his face. "Yes, I would like to see him too." He goes to the side of the path and bends low, and I watch him, uncomprehending, until he straightens, clutching a handful of the bioluminescent mushrooms to his chest. "It wouldn't do to get lost on the way to Utsanek, would it?"

Awkwardly, we walk together. The silent hike through the trees is terrifying, although it shouldn't be, considering I was literally chased by one of the Shrouded beasts the last time. The fact that I now know what lurks in the black, that I am intimately acquainted with what could devour me if we should come upon it, makes this path dreadful.

Or perhaps letting go of my rage has made room for fear to resume its hold on my heart.

When I hear something moving through the low bushes to my left, I cross to my father's side of the path and grab his arm with one hand, wrangling the little mushrooms with the other.

"Easy, Wehna. Elyōn sees us, even in the dark."

I let out a lurching breath as Utsanek's sola glow comes into view through the spiraling swathes of ténesomni. "He sees, yes, but is that the same as caring?"

A small laugh shakes from him. "He is nothing but care." I feel his eyes on me and I can't bear to meet them. "Or so I remind myself, especially when I don't understand him."

We dump the bioluminescent mushrooms outside the gates and enter Utsanek. I try to keep my head down, to appear inconspicuous as we enter the streets. I hope my father won't be recognized, since he has been gone for so long, but the same can't be said for me. I have not forgotten that Myrzeth threatened punishment the last time I was in the city.

An aroma of rich meat and spices makes my mouth water as we pass a street corner food stand. "I'm glad Vo isn't with us," I say, thinking about the time I lost him because of a meat pie.

Pada looks at me questioningly, but I decide it's best to keep the story to myself. Arvo's safe now, isn't he? My parents don't need to know about what got him there.

Pain pulses through my temples, my vision blurring, and I hold my breath and wait for it to pass.

"I would rather have you all with me," my father says. The sola bone glare shifts across his face as we pass under the lights. His expression is hard like stone, but I can see the hairline cracks where sadness seeps through. "No matter the danger."

"Why would you want to put us at risk like that?" I ask, running my hands up and down my arms, as if I can wear away the bitterness grafted into me like a second skin.

The streets stretch before us, untold evils lurking around every corner.

"Before our family was torn apart, your mother and I thought nothing about the dangers of what we were doing, as long as we could shelter you and Arvo from the consequences."

"But we were never safe, Pada."

Father's red hair glows like fire in the light. He combs his fingers through it, his mouth taut at the corner. "No. We thought we could separate our family life from the calling the Highest put on our hearts, but we were wrong."

We continue in awkward silence. How can I respond to that? It would be wrong to condemn him again, and I'm not the one who can absolve his guilt. I force my thoughts to fixate instead on our surroundings.

A palpable uneasiness roams the city. The busiest streets are well-lit, almost pleasant by Vale standards, and yet for all the illumination, there is no laughter, no giddy excitement that brighter days have come. A spark of hope flashes in my soul—hope that the valefolk aren't being taken in by Myrzeth's empty promises of prosperity after all.

"What in Atsun?"

My father stops, staring at what used to be the secret entrance to Ellithïm. It's now a passageway like any other.

"They had to get rid of all the bolétis." I slip my hand through the crook of his elbow. "The kaligorven were bound to discover it, and Bryn didn't want to take the chance of bringing their wrath down on the fidrélas."

Moisture reflects in my father's eyes briefly before he blinks it away. "What a shame to see it robbed of its beauty. This place was supposed to be a stronghold for the weary."

I apply gentle pressure to his arm. "It still is."

I am met with a shriek at the Perens' front door.

"Wehna! You're back."

"We're just visiting." Struggling to fathom her undeniable joy, I extricate myself from Elodie's embrace. Her smile falters and I feel horrible. "But I am glad to see you," I blurt in a rush to fix it.

She brightens, grabbing my hand and squeezing. "Come see Pa. He's doing so much better, and he asks about you all the time." She starts to pull me into the house, but her face blanches when she notices my father waiting behind me.

"H-hello," he stutters, raising his eyebrows and offering a small smile. It eases my heart to see him feeling so awkward, like a boy sent on an errand for his father. "I'm Arlyn Qaith."

Recognition dawns and Elodie shoots me a glance, at a loss for words.

"Meet my father," I say.

Her unintelligible exclamations draw her sisters from the kitchen, who scamper in bearing several disgruntled kittens. Amid the squeals and exuberant greetings, we are each handed a feline and dragged to the same room where I spent so many days after my head injury.

"Pa, Ma, you'll never guess who is here," Elodie says, out of breath.

I look furtively to the bed, relieved to find Bryn sitting up and looking much better than when I was last here.

"By the Highest!" Tress straightens in front of the fire, the iron tongs clattering to the hearth as she runs across the room to embrace my father. His expression is a strange mixture of joy and shame.

Tress pulls away and smooths the tears away from her cheeks. "If I didn't believe in miracles before . . ." She purses her lips as she struggles for words. "How can it be that Elyōn is so good?"

My father makes several unsuccessful attempts at a reply, then carefully sets the kitten on the foot of Bryn's bed like the furball is made of glass.

Tress shifts so she can see through the doorway. "And where is your wife? I can't tell you how I have missed my friend. I want to make her hug me back for once."

My father tries to respond, but she laughs and presses a hand to her forehead before he finds success. "Why didn't I consider the possibility that you were fine? Of all the doubting fools. You aren't leaving this house until we have had a full account of what happened, Arlyn."

Bryn laughs weakly. "My dear wife, give our friend a chance to speak."

"Rael is well," my father finally manages to answer. "She is with Arvo back at the Cantar cottage."

I tune out the rest of my father's explanation—I've heard it before—and let my eyes lose focus on the mewling white fluff in my hands.

"I'm glad you're here." Elodie nudges me with her hip and retrieves the kitten from my apathetic grasp. "I would have been worried sick if

Orlagh hadn't assured us that you and Arvo made it to safety."

I bite my lip. "Sorry. I should have found a way to send word or . . . or something."

"You had other things on your mind," she says dismissively.

It's true and there's nothing to add. I have been consumed by those 'other things' for what feels like months, years. Always anxious for my parents' safety when they would head into the most light-devoid parts of Utsanek for some humanitarian effort, then for Arvo when I was all he had. Always fearing that we would starve to death or be hunted down by the kaligorven. That I would fail at all my parents expected of me.

Always terrified of the shadows themselves.

"How does it feel?"

I gape at her, trying to quit feeling sorry for myself long enough to work out what she's asking. Her expression is so expectant, so innocent. So *wrong*. "*Hmm*?"

"How does it feel to have them back?"

"Oh." I trap the lie between my teeth. "It's great." Averting my eyes, I cinch my arms around my waist and try to ignore the way my head pounds.

Elodie watches our parents as they speak in low tones. I have lost track of their conversation and I don't even care.

"After what my pa went through, I might understand," she says softly. "The thought of losing him is almost too much for me to bear." She gulps and blinks. "Speaking of which . . ." She raises the crying feline and plants a kiss on its head. "Lissi insisted I take Bear back after you left."

I reach out and give the cat a halfhearted scratch between the ears. "I thought you didn't care for him anymore."

Elodie sinks her weight into a hip and gives me the most incredulous look, as if to say *what girl in her right mind could resist a kitten*?

I laugh lightly, and it feels good. "Obviously not, then."

Bryn breaks into a deep cough, and Elodie drops the kitten to rush to his side, offering him a glass of water before Tress takes a single step toward him.

"Thank you, my strong, beautiful girl." He takes a long drink, then cups his daughter's cheek with one hand while pressing his other palm flat against his abdomen.

A worried frown creases Tress's mouth and eyes.

"You need to be careful," my father says, mirroring her concern.

A wheezy laugh huffs out of Bryn. "I have spent all my life being careful, Arlyn, but now is the time to be a man of action." He turns his pale face toward my father. "What do you say?"

Say to what? A chill races through me. *What is my father being asked to give now?*

He is silent for a long, heavy moment before his shoulders lower and he nods resignedly. "Yes, Bryn. You're right. And I will stand with you."

Elodie's sharp fingernails bite into my forearm, and I turn to her, my eyes wide. "What are they talking about?"

"Myrzeth is calling a citywide meeting in a week. I heard my parents talking about it earlier."

"Well, that's not so unusual, is it?"

Her face darts to her mother, then back to me. I stuff down my own dread. "I guess not," she says. "But, Wehna, I'm still afraid."

"Why?"

She catches her bottom lip between her teeth and takes a quick breath. "My pa and ma are planning on attending."

I look up to find my father's eyes trained on mine.

It would seem he will be going too.

39
AMYRAH

SCATTERED FRACTALS OF LIGHT DANCE over my skin in every color. I approach the crystal walls of Luvesta like a fleck of dirt, like a drab particle drifting toward a diamond. A palpable hum emanates from the wall's spires, permeating the marrow of my bones, but it's off-key, out of beat, and my heart remains cold, closed, and silent.

Shouldn't it know the song?

Holden approaches the immense front gates, leading Zenith with one hand and trying without success to brush away the accumulated dirt from the journey with the other. He's like a boy of twelve returning for supper after a long day of getting up to no good.

"Let me," I say, pushing aside my own apprehensions and stepping toward the horse.

Holden gapes at the reins in his hand, then chuckles and gives them to me. "I guess I'm a bit nervous about returning. It's been years, and I look nothing like who I was when I left."

"Will that matter? You're Luvesti, aren't you? They'll be thrilled to let you in." I finger the blackened half-crown braid, hating how it reminds me of what happened in Ketsé. I wish I could trade it for my missing necklace. They wouldn't doubt me if they saw its argentilum pendant glowing.

Abandoning his attempts to straighten his appearance, Holden lets his gaze find me. "They'll be glad to see you too, Amyrah."

"Will they?" I force a weak smile. "That will be a new feeling."

Holden pivots, takes two large steps, and grips my shoulders. His eyes are wide, insistent. "Yes. I'll make sure of it."

My pulse thumps a deafening racket in my ears. Until now, Holden has been so carefree and confident. I have put complete trust in him, but in this moment, he is wild, almost as if he is desperate to hang his apprehensions anywhere other than on his own shoulders.

"How can you be so sure?" I whisper, unable to trust my voice at any other volume.

A shadow of misgiving ripples over his stern expression. "If they accept me, they'll accept you. Believe it."

He waits until I acknowledge him with a fluttering blink and dip of my chin before dropping his hold and turning toward the gates again.

Tugging Zenith closer, I slide a hand up his neck and lead him to follow Holden up the wide pathway.

Elyōn, I hope he is right.

My fingers grow hot against the horse's neck, and I yank them away, frowning. The sensation dissipates as I rub them together. I look at Zenith, and he lets out a bored, snorting exhale.

I turn my attention to Holden, who is standing before the gates and spreading his arms wide as if he would embrace an old friend. There is no one hidden in the shadows, no watchman posted above. How different the city of Luvesta is from Ketsé, where the walls were alive, and one could not pass five steps without the sensation of being watched. Standing outside of Luvesta is cold, unfeeling. Like there could never be a hope of entering if you found yourself on the wrong side of these walls.

"Holden, how will they know we are here?"

He doesn't need to answer. With a mighty, cracking shudder, the gates break apart, opening outward foot by foot.

A rush of warm wind pushes my hair behind my shoulders, and I hold Zenith's reins tighter as he stamps his feet and whinnies.

Luminescence shoots through the gap like a brilliant arrow.

Looking over his shoulder, Holden smirks at me. "They don't have to know. The gates always open to the Luvesti." He turns forward again and presents himself to be swallowed by the light.

"How clever," I mutter. A metal that glows when the Luvesti are near, and now gates that will allow only them to enter.

No wonder the rest of Atsun can't stand us.

Pulling Zenith close by his bridle, I follow.

I am met by a crescent of soldiers in shimmering white armor, angling their swords at my throat.

The horse is snatched from my grasp by a woman with hair as bright as the sun, like liquid fire rippling over her breastplate.

Her eyes take me in from foot to ink-stained braid. I am filthy before her pristine presence. She tilts her head in challenge. "And who gave you, child of darkness, the right to lead one of our horses?"

I look around in vain for Holden.

"Fix your gaze to me, girl, for I am the one who will decide your fate." The woman hands the horse to another man and stands in front of me. Around her, the armed guards lower their blades.

I stare at her in witless silence.

"She came with me. I am responsible."

My heart's tempo slows a tick as Holden steps into the circle.

The woman's eyes widen, but she refuses to look his way. Her murky irises remind me of the holes the men carve in Loch Skythe's ice to fish in Vestri. "The young man is Luvesti, I see, otherwise the gate would not have permitted you entry. That fact is what's keeping you *both* alive." Her hands twitch toward her own blade hanging at her side. "But speaking for this girl does little in her favor."

"Yara."

I don't dare look away from the woman, but I can see Holden motioning to her in my periphery.

Focus faltering, she finally regards him. Her mouth drops open. "It can't be," she utters in a hoarse whisper, as if she has seen a ghost.

But her show of weakness is momentary, and she straightens, snapping her wrist across her chest. "Hail, Holden, returning Prince of Luvesta."

Everyone but me and Holden repeats the phrase, fists whacking armor with dull thuds and voices crying out in unison as their eyes fix onto the man whom I thought I was beginning to know.

Their *prince.*

I turn to him now, and when he refuses to return my bewildered gaze, my confidence in him shatters.

"We had no word of your coming," Yara says, ignorant of my imploding heart, and nods to a boy standing off to the side. The silent command is met with swift obedience as he races away.

"I didn't have the means to announce myself beforehand, did I?" Holden replies tersely. I wonder what kind of reception he had hoped for if this is not it. He jerks his chin at the retreating boy. "I assume you sent him to notify my father. You needn't have done that since that's the first place I intend to go."

Yara's brows raise. "I would advise caution, my prince. The king is not well."

"What?" Holden's face blanches, his eyes growing large. "Is he alright? Why did no one send for me?" He steps forward, gaze fixed to the top of a street that winds ever up and up between rigid walls of stone, where the crowning structure of Luvesta perches like a white wolf on a mountain.

Yara lays a hand on his shoulder. "Just as you had no means of giving us warning, we have had no means of informing you. And, yes, he will be notified so we can be sure he is well enough to receive you." Her voice lowers, tinged with the barest note of compassion. "The king does nothing in haste these days. You need to prepare yourself for entering his presence."

Holden's breaths leave in forceful lurches, and I struggle to hear his pained question. "Is he really that bad, Yara?"

The woman's expression is impassable but not stern. She watches him for a few measured breaths. "Yes."

A moan leaves Holden's lips. "I should have returned seasons ago."

"Take time to prepare yourself, and someone will send for you when he is ready," Yara says.

I approach him, hesitating before resting a hand on his arm. He doesn't recoil from my touch. "Holden, I—I'm sorry."

Low gasps echo around me, and I glance up, confused. Yara glares at the casual interaction. I jerk my hand away and look at Holden. His jaw tenses, Luvesta's diamond glow trickling over his face as he turns to me. When his eyes meet mine, there is a brokenness in them.

"Disease is the way of life, Amyrah." His voice is tinged with defeat, and he shoves himself between the guards.

I stand there, alone in the middle of a crowd, struggling to stuff down hurt.

"That leaves you to deal with." All the tenderness with which Yara treated Holden has left her raspy voice.

I blink twice and swallow, meeting her gaze. Her hair may be luxurious, and her armor polished to a blinding gloss, but the ever-glowing city walls reveal so much more. Like the lines rimming a mouth held too long in a grimace and the jagged scars across her knuckles cast in stark relief from the directional light. Pity clinks unexpectedly in my chest. I suppose anyone who has lived her whole life in a place where every flaw is dispassionately laid bare could end up like her.

Whether Yara throws me out, locks me up, or makes a public spectacle of me, I can no longer be sure that Holden will be my advocate. I must face this on my own, just as I am.

It's oddly liberating.

Maybe the burden of my heritage will no longer weigh on me. This could be the moment all the pretense and mystery are removed, and I can simply be Amyrah, an average girl who gained the gift of Elyōn by fluke.

Yara once again assesses my road-weary appearance, her lip curling. "You cannot stand before the king in this state." She waves a hand to one of the younger guards—a girl with a burnished bronze plait and a smattering of freckles that eclipses my own. "Oriole, escort her to the house of cleansing."

With another command, the guards of Luvesta's gates disperse, and I am left to Oriole's care.

She considers me for a moment, her mouth slack, then recovers and slides her blade into her sheathe. "Sorry. Forgot I was holding that." Her fair cheeks turn bright pink. "I've never met anyone from . . . from *out there*." She wilts, as if ashamed of her rudeness.

My chest aches. How strange it is to go from a kingdom of darkness to a kingdom of light, yet to find an ignorance shared by both.

"It's fine." I grip the strap of my satchel. "I've felt the same about everyone I've met outside of the Vale."

Clearing her throat, Oriole points up the silver-paved street. "This way."

We ascend the main roadway, where everything gleams unapologetically white except for the doors. They are crafted from a rich wood with veins of copper slivering them from top to bottom. When I drag a hand across their grain, I find it warm to the touch. This whole light-exuding city feels oddly cold, except for the doors.

My escort pauses, glancing at me with a curious expression.

"What kind of wood is this?" I ask, letting my hand fall and catching up with her.

A sad curve clings to Oriole's mouth as she turns toward the roadway again. "*Luvem Artus*. Wood from the Trees of Light. They grew all over Atsun, they say, in the ancient days." Her steps slow, a wistful expression possessing her features. "They were Elyōn's gift to the world, spun into being at the same time as the firelights, which were beautiful but distant, unable to be touched. The Highest gave his people the trees out of compassion for their darkness-bent souls, knowing they would crave light among them. Wherever they grew, people gathered underneath their branches. The Trees were the seeds of the great cities of Atsun.

"But the stories also say that the wildlands were volatile, that a festering evil shifted beyond the light's reach. The people grew fearful and restless, heeding the whispers and ignoring Elyōn's promises. Rather than tending the trees, they cut them down, thinking that they could spread out the light, carry it wherever they desired, or fashion items they could set on their mantles and tuck in a pocket to ward away daemons. But the trees' brightness was not meant to be used in that way and it did not last."

Oriole's narrative has enraptured me, distracting from the ache of my muscles. Her shy persona has completely disappeared, replaced with an obvious love and passion for the lore of her kin.

"Instead of returning to Elyōn in remorse for their rash actions," she continues, her expression pained, "the people raged against the god who would give them such a fleeting, weak gift." Oriole falls silent for several steps and when she speaks again, there is a bite to her voice. "Anger burned in their hearts hotter than the Highest's light ever had, and it is said that was what Érechlys, an ill-burning firelight whom Elyōn had cast from the skies, needed to gain purchase in the depths of Atsun. She was the one who had been hissing in the shadows, and when the people began to listen to her, giving heed to doubt, her power grew."

I swallow. "That's . . ."

A blush blooms on Oriole's cheeks. "Not what you asked about." She hides her face in her hands. "Sorry again. I have always loved the old tales, but there are few Luvesti who want to hear them anymore. None, really, except for the old hermitess, and my parents don't approve of me visiting her." She tosses me an apologetic glance. "I took advantage of your listening ear."

I laugh lightly, a smile perching on my lips. "No, it's fine. I know so little of the history of Atsun, and your account means more than you know. Please, continue."

Oriole stares at me for a moment, as if she can't fathom my interest. Eventually, she resumes her narrative, and we keep walking. "Despite the people's rebellion, Elyōn had compassion for them. He sent out his messengers, who would bear the light to the farthest reaches of Atsun. In this way, his presence dwelled with the people, though it resulted in strife between them and the Shrouded beasts of Érechlys."

"He gave them the solas," I whisper. The image of their bones hanging over Utsanek's streets clouds my mind's eye, and I feel so, so sad. "But people have found a way to take advantage of them, too, haven't they?"

"What do you mean?" Oriole's brow crinkles.

I recall Holden's surprise when I told him how the valefolk hunt the solas to abuse their light. Caution blares in my chest. "W-well, people will always want to take anything good and keep it for themselves, won't they?"

"Yes, I suppose." She is silent for a few steps before turning to me. "I still haven't answered your original question, have I? You asked me about . . ."

That wary knot loosens in my stomach. "The wood."

Her gaze drifts to the beautiful doorways, a long breath escaping her lips. "There were a few who grieved how their kin ravaged the trees' glory, and the Highest was grieved for them. Though it pained his heart, he instructed the faithful to cut down the few Light Trees that remained so they could not be abused by the followers of Érechlys and commanded the light to a different use. When the wood was crafted into the framework of their city, its luminescence would pass into its walls. As long as it was never removed or altered, the city would have light that would endure." She looks at me, an ancient pride brimming in her eyes. "The wood remains, preserved exactly as it was in the ancient days, and Luvesta still shines."

Oriole lets me contemplate her story on my own, and I marvel at how the Highest can turn something born of destruction into good.

But the splendor of this fact soon fades as I weather more and more glares from the Luvesti, young and old alike. I am a blight in their branches, a snag in their garment. No one seems able to fathom how someone so repulsive could exist within these sacred walls.

The truth sinks in that, even here, in a place I'm supposed to belong, I don't, and all I can think is that Belwyn is right. There is more to kinship than blood and heritage.

Oriole casts me a sidelong glance, biting her lip. She is a sweet girl, not yet hardened in the way Yara is. I can't be bitter toward her. I wonder what her life has been like, kept within physical walls where all she knows is the brightness of day. Does she long for a reprieve from illumination's glare like I longed for a reprieve from the ténesomni?

I would ask her, but I have expended my energy for conversation, and I'm not sure I want to make room in my heart for yet another person whom I'll either push away or bring to harm.

Stopping, I lean on the wall to catch my breath.

My escort is maddeningly placid, as if we haven't just hiked up a mountain. "Imagine doing this a dozen times each day," she says with a grin.

"I can't even fathom it," I huff.

"Fortunately for you, this is as far as you need to go."

Without a farewell, the girl leaves me, and I am handed off to three different waves of servants who subject me to various levels of bathing. A young attendant takes my homespun dress with pursed lips, not bothering to hide her revulsion at handling such a weathered, soiled garment. I make a feeble request that it be kept for me, but by the way she raises her eyebrows, I have little confidence it will. The book and satchel she tosses onto a bureau with no regard.

I force myself to keep silent, to hold in my questions of why this is happening, why it is imperative that I lose three layers of skin before meeting the King of Luvesta. Most of all, I want to know where Holden is and if he will still be a friend when we meet again.

No amount of scrubbing can rid my hair of the black stain. "What on Elyōn's fair earth has the child done to herself?" a maid gripes to another, and I pinch my lips to hold in a laugh. I am less amused, though, when my damp locks are braided, wrapped, and pinned so tightly to the base of my skull that I get an immediate, throbbing headache.

A cream dress with flowing sleeves in fabric softer than any I've felt is presented to me, along with a jeweled belt that clings to my hips, angling down in a "V" across my abdomen. By the way the metal glows, I wonder if it is made of argentilum. Both items seem far too luxurious for me. They are finer than anything the Foremost's wife wears in the Vale and would be out of place even among the Ketsé's Nocilium. Even the servants here dress better than most of the denizens of the Vale and the forest city.

I reach to my throat, needing to feel the angles of the little star to ground myself, but cold sadness consumes me when I remember that it is lost. Without it, I feel like the Vale has been cauterized from me like a wound.

Can the scar of who I am be so easily erased?

The head attendant clicks her tongue, hands on her hips. "I suppose that will have to do." She throws a resigned look to her friend. "Hildi, you'd better pray His Majesty doesn't think we're offering him insult."

Embarrassment coats me from head to toe, and I want to melt into the cracks in the stone floor. After all this effort, I'm still unfit to—

"Do you know my father at all?"

The rude woman spins around, bumbling with a rushed apology and inclining her head to the prince.

Holden leans on the doorframe, his hard expression passing over the scene. I hold my breath, but his eyes settle on the two curtseying women.

"The last thing Amyrah could be is an insult."

Warmth paints my cheeks and I shoot him a grateful smile, which he returns with a dip of his chin. He seems back to his usual, carefree self. Perhaps his iciness toward me was just a result of finding out his father is ill.

As relieved as I am that he is here, I almost don't recognize him. His outfit, though still fine, seems subtle for a prince. He wears a gray tunic embroidered with beautiful designs in silver thread at the cuffs and collar, a pale leather jerkin with a belt like mine, though far more masculine, and a navy mantle flowing down from his shoulders. His feet are clad in black boots that reach up to his knees, with midnight-blue pants tucked into them.

He clears his throat and holds out his palms in a conciliatory gesture. "They got a hold of me too."

I fidget with my hands. There is no book in my pocket, no necklace to hold, no hair to card my fingers through. There is nothing to hide behind. Just . . . me.

Holden's mouth tips, then he jerks his chin toward the hallway. "Well? Are you ready to meet my father?"

40
AMYRAH

YARA WAITS FOR US IN THE MAIN STREET, her armor exchanged for a dress that is even more forbidding, perhaps because of the severe black belt and dirk sheathed at her waist. Her garment is woven of dusty-blue thread, inlaid with silver designs that jag across her abdomen. With a closer look, I see subtle plates of armor worked right into the fabric. The dress falls in strict lines from her shoulders and hips without a single wrinkle, hitting a hand breadth above her black-booted ankles. The outfit both hides and accentuates her curves, and her white-blond hair twists in one limp spiral over a shoulder.

"Prince Holden." She dips her chin, making no attempt to acknowledge me. "Your father awaits your presence."

Holden makes a point of extending his hand to me. "Come, Amyrah. You have nothing to fear."

My eyes flick to his face, and I wonder at his optimism.

When I take his hand, Yara's mouth quirks downward, her brows overshadowing her eyes. She says nothing and motions for us to follow.

Thank Elyōn, there are only two sets of stairs to climb between us and the palace. I'm filled with so much anxious energy that some extended physical exertion might have done me good, though. The walk still helps to quiet some of my clamoring thoughts, at least.

Holden seems confident, but there is a downward pull to his mouth, a slight curve to his shoulders that is all wrong. It must not have been easy coming home to the news that his father is ailing, to be made aware of all the days he has missed with him.

I can empathize. My own father was often plunged into terrible lows as he battled depression, and I never knew how I would find him. His sickness may not have been visible on the outside, but it was every bit as real.

My grief returns like a wallop to the throat. The light had hardly broken through for Pada before—

No. I can't do this now. Sadness does not belong here, in this kingdom of light. I banish it back to the forgotten places in my mind and try to steady my heart with deep breaths. I focus on what this day will bring, but that isn't much better, because I can't shake the feeling that I am back in the forest city, about to face the Nocilium.

If Belwyn were with me now, I'd beg him to come in with me.

The thought twists my stomach, casting doubt on every decision I have made since my gift was revealed.

It's not a gift, Amyrah. It's simply a quirk of your heritage, I counter, pressing my book close so I can feel its angular corners biting into my ribs. I insisted on going back for it, much to Yara and Hildi's annoyance, because if there is any place for it, it's here, in the halls of my mother's people. Of *my* people.

A faint flutter of hope wriggles free from my guarded heart. The ever-present, aggravating thing demands I give it space.

There's every chance this could end up like it did in Ketsé, or even worse, I tell it.

A stuttering exhale collapses my lungs. *But you can rely on Holden now*, Hope answers back.

I pull in a slow, deliberate breath. *Only if he doesn't remain silent and leave me to defend myself again*.

My fingertips seek to graft themselves into the leather of the book. It is both soft and unyielding, and I let it anchor me as we approach massive, gleaming wood doors. The guards open them for us, their eyes glued to Holden as we pass.

Palace Luvesta's halls escalate every noise so that the smallest click of Yara's boots on the polished floor is like the snap of brittle timber. It feels like I will be set ablaze, consumed in a moment. I apply pressure to Holden's hand and hope by that small gesture, he understands what his kinship means to me.

We come to the end of a curving passage, where two more Luvesti guards stand with strict posture on either side of an ornate cased opening carved with a myriad of creatures and starbursts.

Solas. I slow my steps, my mouth agape. I'm awed by the skill and beauty of the sculptor's hands.

"Amyrah, come." Holden tugs my hand.

Reluctantly, I follow him into a cavernous room with mullioned windows reaching at least fifty feet high along every wall, except for the one behind us. A gasp slips from my lips, amplified tenfold by the otherworldly acoustics. The throne room is fashioned in such a way that the entire course of the sun can be observed from dawn until dusk. We must be facing south, because to my right, the delicious hues of twilight drift across the sky in broad swathes, washing the room in a gentle pink hue. The ever-glowing walls of this city hide much of the sky, but up here it's as if I can see the whole of Atsun stretching out around me.

Holden might insist there is nothing like a Luvesti sunrise, but I do believe I love the sunsets most.

"My son."

My eyes snap to the center of the room, where an imposing throne of that dark, copper-lined wood sits like a gateway to the shadowlands. A figure rests on it, slouched to the side, white-gold robes flowing over the wood and down the steps like spilled starlight. He is almost too bright to look at, like the solas in the Vale.

Holden's hand goes limp in mine, and I let it slip away as he takes a tentative step. "Father."

The man on the throne moves to get up, the attendants on either side rushing to support him. His hair is fairer than Holden's, tinged with silver, and his face is hidden as he coughs into his sleeve. The brightness around him ripples in response.

Holden lengthens his strides and jumps up the steps to catch his father by the shoulders.

The king swallows him in an embrace, burying his face in his neck.

I do not belong here.

This is a holy moment, saturated with weeping and laughter, with dread and incandescent joy. My eyes prickle as I imagine what a reunion with my own father will feel like in the place where death no longer has dominion and all tears shed in fear, pain, and sorrow have been wiped away. That place where Elyōn dwells and calls the firelights by name.

Lock it away. Lock it away. Lock the pain away.

I turn to give them this moment of privacy.

"You have returned to us at long last," the king rasps, his voice muffled at first but becoming clear as he pulls back to peer at his son.

"I should never have stayed away so long," Holden answers, his voice thick with emotion.

"Nonsense. You were doing as I told—"

Another violent bout of coughing interrupts the king's words, and my eyes jump up. The tall man curls over his son's arms, suddenly small and childlike. His shoulders heave as Holden lowers him back to his seat and crouches, gripping his hands.

"Don't push yourself, Father. Perhaps this reunion should wait until you are feeling better."

"Nonsense. Joy should be felt no matter the state one finds himself in." The king places a hand on Holden's cheek, his expression dripping with delight. His gaze soon drifts past him, hitching on something that causes his face to pale.

On *me*.

I smile awkwardly, but it is a fragile thing that shatters as soon as the king speaks again.

"Wh-who have you brought with you, Holden?" His voice is a labored whisper, an Elberu wind carrying the first hint of Morpa's decay.

My face fills with heat, and I hug my arms around the beat-up volume.

Holden's face snaps to mine, his normally sharp eyes muddied. He gets off his knees and crosses the floor, extending his arm toward me.

"This is Amyrah, Father. I met her in Ketsé, and she is undoubtedly Luvesti. She has—"

But Holden does not get a chance to finish his sentence. Ignoring the protests of the attendants and Yara, the king rises from his throne and struggles down the steps, outstretching his arms and passing his son by. I swallow hard, unsure of what to do, what to say, other than to let the older man close the distance between us and grab my face in his warm, fleshy palms.

"It cannot be." His voice is a deep ocean of sadness and disbelief.

"Your Majesty," I say, the scent of medicinal herbs and cloves swirling through my senses.

Jeweled tears that mimic the gemstones in his crown cloud his eyes, slipping down his face's many creases. He stifles a sob, and as aged as he is, I can see a strong resemblance to his son.

But how could I have broken a king I have never met before? My eyes flick to Holden, who looks as astonished as I feel.

"No, no." The king shakes his shaggy head and blinks, his eyes clearing. They are not green like Holden's but a pale, striking blue. A familiar blue. "Do not call me by such a formal title." He smiles weakly. "My daughter would not have wanted that."

"Father, what are you talking about?" Holden's voice is tremulous.

A breathy laugh parts the king's lips. "I cannot mistake this face, those eyes, that smile." With a great amount of exertion, he stands tall, places an arm behind my shoulders, and throws out the other one as if to present me to an entire court of people, though it is only the attendants, Yara, Holden, and me in the room. "And beyond that, my heart confirms it. Holden, this is the child of Luvesta's lost daughter. My only granddaughter—"

I gasp, my knees buckling, and it is no small miracle when the king—my *grandfather*—holds me upright.

"—and your niece."

Silence that gives a whole new meaning to the word dampens his pronouncement like a heavy snowfall. Fingernails biting into my palms, I stare hard at Holden, looking for any indication he knew and kept this from me. His jaw is slack, and his hand is frozen in his hair mid-rake. It would have been easier to accept this if I had someone at which to aim my shock, my anger. I frown, and his mouth snaps shut. *Is that guilt?* I deny the thought. How could he have known and not said anything? He had been traveling through the Grovesha and living in Ketsé for years without a single family member to fellowship with. If he had known I was his niece, wouldn't he have said something to me when his Luvesti heritage was revealed? Over our days of journeying together?

It would have made traveling with him a whole lot less awkward. A small, surprising grin shifts over my lips.

But heat creeps up my neck when Yara chokes out a dry laugh. I wish the floor would turn to water beneath my feet and let me sink through it.

The king's grip tightens on my arms, a tremor running through his fingers. *I shouldn't make him exert himself like this.* I shift my feet and try to stand on my own.

"Your Majesty, forgive me, but that claim is rather far-fetched." Yara gestures impatiently at me. "What proof do we have that she is of the Luvesti?"

"I can attest to it, Yara," Holden says, chin jutting and eyes wide with exasperation.

Yara snorts. "Forgive me if I don't accept your word."

Holden makes a sound like a growl, and the king raises a palm to still him. He turns to Yara, a warning in his tone. "Commander, you are forgetting your place. It would go better for you if you bridled that flame of a tongue."

The web of anxiety around my ribcage loosens, and my mouth twitches at Yara's sour expression. *I don't think I'll mind being related to this man.*

Rubbing a palm over the lower half of his face, Holden gives Yara an annoyed look. "Can't you see how the argentilum belt she's wearing glows?"

"You *have* been gone a long time, haven't you, Prince Holden? We are in *Luvesta*. Everything glows."

Holden strides a pace with his arms folded, his sharp gaze locked on Yara. "Is there a reason you don't want this to be true?"

Yara crosses the floor and stands before me and the king, her shrewd eyes taking in and discarding every facet of my being. "The world has grown dangerous. I only wish to correctly divide friends from foe." Her right hand dashes across her torso to her sheathed weapon. In a quick motion, she grabs my left hand from its grip on the book, draws the dirk, and drags it across the meat of my palm.

I cry out and pull my hand back. Red blood blooms along the cut, pooling in my hand's folds and dripping down my arm. Staining the sleeve of the pristine dress.

The king's arms shake around me, but no words pass his lips.

"What in the blazes is wrong with you, Yara?" Holden shouts, running to me and pulling out a kerchief to wrap around my hand.

I watch his firm movements, shock numbing my senses and making me forget to breathe.

Yara takes a step backward and smirks at the king, holding her crimson blade at eye level. "Do you see, my king? She bleeds like the common world. She can never be more to you than an illegitimate descendant."

"Silence!"

My ears ring with my grandfather's deafening shout. He sags against me, all his strength sapped. As if snapped from a daze, Holden jumps forward to bear his weight. I help as best as I can to get him to his throne, although it isn't easy with a useless hand.

Yara stays where she is, wiping the blade with the hem of her sleeve before returning it to the sheathe.

"Thank you, my son," the king wheezes after a long bout of wet coughing. "I am fine. I am fine."

He sounds the furthest thing from it.

I slip to my knees on the raised dais, lifting my throbbing hand in front of my face and holding my mother's book tighter to my chest. Tears warp my vision.

Holden wheels on Yara, his voice still at that strident pitch. "What did that prove? If she had a Groveshan father, did you really think her blood would shine like ours?"

"It proves I am not worthy, Holden," I say, lowering the book to my thighs and blinking so I can make out the golden words etched into its burgundy cover. My heartbeat thunders in my ears. Holden's fingers press down lightly on my shoulder.

"What are you holding, dear child?"

I glance up to discover sorrow and confounding compassion on the king's face, and a faded spray of freckles across his nose and cheeks.

"If this would help to prove to you who I am, Majesty, please take it." I hold the book out, and the king extends his weathered hands to accept it. His eyes seek mine, curiosity piqued. "It was my mother's," I say, a catch in my voice. "Do you recognize it?"

He looks at the cover, his eyes shining with tears. "*Avis ténesomni, luvem*," he whispers, then swallows and lifts the cover as if afraid to frighten away a phantom memory. "E. C.," he says in a tone as ephemeral as an Elberu frost.

"Oh," I rush to explain. "It stands for 'Ellehra Cantar.'"

The king's eyes glisten. "So, she married, then." He laughs. "She never did like the way her name sounded with her maiden name, 'Ardaire.'"

Ellehra Ardaire. Daughter of the King of Luvesta. Eldest sibling to Holden and . . .

"Myrzeth." I didn't mean to utter my uncle's name, and I press my fingers against my lips. Yara's boots shift audibly on the marble behind me.

The king's eyes jerk up, surprise carving new lines across his craggy features. "Do you know of him?" There is an odd cadence to his words, like they are pronged things that tear through his chest.

I nod but do not risk explaining.

He looks away, as if he desires to hide his regrets from me. "Yes, Myrzeth was my second child. He and your mother were always at odds well before Holden came into the picture."

A quick glance at Holden reveals he's clinging to his father's words tighter than I am.

"Myrzeth had a bent to his mind that compelled him to search out every shadowy corner of both this city and our history. He was drawn to the *erychélus nathura*—the dark nature that all Luvesti are trained to deny from infancy. And it was in Ellehra's nature to seek and amplify the light, no matter how small it may have been. She always saw the hope for good in Myrzeth when others could only foresee evil."

The king stops to catch his breath, and I'm grateful for the reprieve. My heart feels wrung out, aching as though it will crack under the weight of this moment, when all I have been searching for since I left the Vale is being realized.

I wipe my eyes and look at Holden, whose head hangs low.

"When even she could no longer find a reason to argue for him, it was decided that he could no longer be counted among the Luvesti," the king says, smearing away the speckles of stale perspiration and fresh tears. "It was the belief of some that banishment from Luvesta would disrupt his connection with his abilities, or at the very least prevent him from tapping further into the *erychélus nathura*. Although he and Ellehra could not have been more opposed, she fought the decision." The king interrupts himself with a hoarse laugh. "Wonderfully, woefully stubborn girl."

I can't help but laugh, too, and it's an odd sound—sad and happy marbled together. "From what I've heard about her, I know that is true."

My grandfather's gaze shifts from me to Holden and back. "The last thing I should have done was agree to banish Myrzeth from Luvesta. It meant we not only lost a son, but your mother as well."

He bites his lip and returns his attention to the book. "She was both grieved by his rebellion and unwilling to leave him to his caprices. It didn't take her long to go after him, whether to look out for him or to make sure he didn't do more damage, I am unsure." He thumbs through the pages. "She must have taken this with her when she left. I thought it was lost forever."

"It nearly was. My pada tried to get rid of it when she died." I inhale and bite my lip. What if the king didn't know she passed?

He dips his chin, his joy washed away in a moment. "It's alright, my child. I know she is gone. The glow always dims in the city when one of our own is lost. And I felt it in my heart." He closes the book and stares at its cover wistfully. "Do you mind if we keep this here now? It is an heirloom of the Luvesti people. There is no ill-will borne to you for having it. You did not know, unlike my daughter, who certainly knew better."

Holden crouches beside me, and I realize how awkward, how earth-shattering this all must be for him. How old had he been when she left Luvesta? When she came to the Vale? When she died?

He rests a hand on his father's forearm. "Mother was right."

The king's feathery brows reach for his hairline. He looks hard at

Holden, waiting for him to explain, his expression caught somewhere between fear and hope.

"My brother is still alive."

He returns Holden's grip, clasping his son's forearm. "And—and is he—is he well?"

Holden's brows shadow his eyes. "He . . ." Hesitation consumes his words. "I haven't seen him, but there are reports . . . Well . . ." He turns to me, a silent plea evident in his raised eyebrow.

"He has taken over the Vale with the aid of . . ." I struggle to find a softer way to say it, but there isn't one. "Of the ténesomni and the kaligorven."

The king's eyes pinch closed, turmoil etching itself deep between his brows and in the soft creases around his mouth. "No," he exhales.

"Then, Majesty, I must urge for an extra measure of caution."

Yara's voice strikes my chest like a chisel on fragile stone. I had forgotten she was here. The fact that she has listened in on this conversation feels like a breach of privacy.

"If your own son who is full of superior Luvesti blood cannot rise above the draw of the *erychélus nathura*, why would we open the doors to someone"—she gestures flippantly at me—"who has been brought forth in the very darkness that seduced him?"

Cold spreads down my arms, like the cords of ténesomni are pulsing beneath my skin, waiting to be summoned. For a moment I see the sable strands staining me, but when I blink, they are gone.

She's right, I think. *I am one wrong action away from becoming him*.

A fit of hacking takes my grandfather, deeper and more violent than any that has gripped him yet. He coughs into his elbow, and when he pulls it away, speckles of luminescent blood stain the sleeve. Holden casts Yara an accusatory look and her olive-toned skin turns ashen.

"My father has had enough for today." He addresses the attendants on either side of the throne. "Would you help the king to his chambers?"

They move into action and as the king stands, Holden rests a hand against his cheek. "Rest now, Father. We can discuss this later; it will keep. You need to save your strength."

Acquiescing, the king presses his son's hand against his cheek and gives the order for the attendants to usher him out of the throne room.

Holden watches them leave with lips pressed together and eyes hooded.

"Well. I will leave you now. I assume you are capable of finding Amyrah a place to lodge." Yara doesn't bother to meet her prince's eyes or stay long enough to confirm if he heard her. Silence soon follows the sharp *clip* of her steps.

We stand there until the last tinges of purple slip beneath the horizon. The room does not grow dim with it, the luminescent walls of Luvesta preventing the soft cloak of night from settling over this never-ending day.

Holden shifts and lets out a long exhale, and I feel like it's alright for me to breathe again too.

I step forward hesitantly, trying to ease the mood with an unconvincing smile. "So, you're my uncle, then?"

Holden stretches his neck and regards me, his jaw tensing. Then, the lines around his eyes smooth and he chuckles, shaking his head. "Maybe Belwyn will stop acting so jealous of me now."

My face grows warm, but the embarrassment is a welcome change from every other emotion I've experienced in this room. I pluck a long, honey-colored hair from my dress. My eyes catch on my scarlet-stained sleeve cuff. "I hope so."

A half-formed grin dimples his cheek. "Whatever he assumed, the way I care for you has always felt different."

The anxious pressure releases its hold on my lungs. "Same for me."

He jerks his chin in an invitation to come over, wrapping an arm around me when I oblige. I rest my head on his shoulder and close my eyes.

"And now we know why," he says.

41
SEYLA

THE ACRID ODOR OF STRONG DRINK rises above the stench of human waste and garbage, dredging up specters from my childhood. Memories of dysfunction, hunger, and sleepless nights smack me like a physical blow. I breathe through my mouth, focusing instead on avoiding the murky puddles and slumped shapes that clog Tarriv's disjointed, ramshackle streets.

I ought to know the city of my youth better than the shape of my own thoughts, but tonight I am a stranger within it. Khukuri at my side, skills honed, clad in armor—yet off-balance. I can't discern whether it's because I am alone for the first time in a month, or because I have jeopardized everything I have strived to achieve.

I find a wall to lean against and pull out a paper, passing my eyes over the words again.

Seyla Bréinth is to be immediately stripped of rank and banned from the Tarrivan Agmen for the assault of a fellow úramech until such a time as a trial can be held to determine her fate.

Underneath the condemning sentence, General Entva's black seal is pressed into the paper.

Cursing, I crumple the sheet and toss it in a gutter.

You've been on your own most of your life, I remind myself. *This is nothing you aren't used to.*

But being alone has never been a choice I made willingly. It was a cruel reality to which I was forced to adapt or die.

Téron's broken body and gaunt face swims before my eyes, and I want to scream.

Was he worth risking everything for?

I push off the wall and continue through the streets, staying as out of sight as possible. My hands tremble.

A couple people shuffle by, observing me with confused expressions. Úramech are supposed to hold their heads high, yet I cower in the shadows.

I am unworthy of the armor I wear, yet what will I be without it?

Refusing to acknowledge their sidelong glances, I duck into the Hidden Hand Tavern, welcoming the consuming din of people who have lost all inhibitions. I hope to the ancestors I can disappear among them.

"Bréinth," a voice croaks.

I close my eyes, a nervous sweat emerging along my brow. *There is no way the news of your discipline has spread through Tarriv yet*, I remind myself. Attempting a neutral expression, I face the barkeep shouldering toward me through the mass of inebriated patrons.

"Haven't seen you in a spell. Ya got coin for me, darlin'?"

I select the version of myself whose heart isn't a pathetic, weak thing and meet his shrewd gaze. “That depends on whether you’ve kept my room for me, doesn’t it, Burgel?”

The burly man snorts. Reluctantly, I follow him as he circles around the counter to collect empty steins. “Not sure why I would have when it could belong to someone who’d bring in better business.”

Finding an empty stool, I lean against the other side of the bar, my braids sliding over my shoulders like snakes. “Because you know that arrangement would bring you more trouble than it’s worth.” I toss him a cinch bag, which he snatches from the air at the last moment. “And I pay better than any of them.”

How odd it is to act the part of someone I used to be.

Burgel loosens the cords and peers within. “Aye, that’s good. You’ll find everything as y’left it.”

“Well now, sweetheart,” a greasy voice wheezes. I grit my teeth and turn toward the man drooping over the stool on my left. His face glistens, and he takes a long draw from his stein, licks the remnants of his grog off his purplish lips, and leers at me. “This doesn’t seem the right place for all that getup.”

I breathe in a shard of breath as his hand slides across the leather plates on my shoulder, his filthy fingers finding the bare skin of my arm and hooking around the strap of my bracer. He has no way of knowing how much more dangerous today has made me.

“How ’bout you let me loosen that for you?”

Burgel throws him a narrowed glance as he slides a mug of steaming liquid—mulled cider by the smell of it—across the counter. The barkeep might require a sharp tongue to keep him in line, but he respects that I will not let a drop of alcohol pass my lips. I take the beverage, sipping with forced indifference as the drunken man ogles me.

Swallowing, I let the mug hit the counter with a loud thud. “Do you value your life?"

The man leans forward to flick one of my braids with his other hand. "Feisty, aren't you?" He lets out a chuckle. "I like that."

My muscles tense and I move my hand to the curved blade sheathed at my side.

But Burgel intervenes before I can teach the drunk a painful lesson and make a mess of his tavern. "Careful, mate. Wouldn't want you to lose that silver tongue of yers." He barks out a hoarse laugh. "The vixen's got teeth, of that I can assure you."

His hand drops away from my arm. I exhale, anchoring my eyes on the rows of bottles behind the counter, and let a brittle smile slant my lips. "Burgel's never had to experience my bite, but he knows what's good for him, unlike the average mongrel."

The man's sneer morphs into a scowl. A string of filthy words flies with his spittle, and he reaches to touch me again. I pivot, grab his hand by the thumb, wrench his arm around, and slam his knuckles into the counter. The man yelps, but I cut the sound short by shoving his face into the rough-hewn wood with an elbow to the back of his skull. Stringy brown hair spills over the counter like thin gruel.

The tavern falls silent, save for Burgel's rasping cackle, the man's groan, and the scraping of my chair on the dirt-caked floor.

"Thanks for the drink," I say, leaving the stunned crowd in my wake as I take the stairs near the back of the room three at a time.

Chest heaving, I slam the apartment door behind me and lean against it, pressing my fingers hard to my mouth. The familiar fragrance of spiced oils and dried herbs tries to greet me like an old friend, but it might as well be the stench of decay.

Heshïn, *Seyla. What has become of you?*

With shaking hands, I pull the straps that hold my armor fast, ripping off piece by piece of formed leather and hammered steel, letting them fall at my feet. Breathing does not come easier without the mocking uniform crowding my lungs. I peel off my sweat-drenched tunic and stumble across the dim room. Starving for air, for illumination to shake me from this debilitating panic, I grab the sheet hung over the window. The fabric catches and I tug it harder, a whimper slipping from my lips.

The rod cracks and the sheet rips down, sending a billow of dust to swirl in the glow of the full moon.

Sinking to the floor with my fists pressed over my eyes, the memories take me.

"Still your tears, Seyla. She will be fine. Your sister is strong."

My mother stood in front of me, gripping my upper arms until my fingers began to go numb. I craned my neck to see around her, which wasn't difficult with how skeletal she was, and watched as the man peered at Tetyan with hungry, hawk-like eyes. A sickening feeling pooled in my stomach.

"She'll make us proud."

My focus snapped to my mother's face. She was a beautiful woman, if her many suitors were any indication. Her olive complexion was perfect, her lips full. Glossy black hair hung in an obedient cascade all the way down to her knees, and thick, arched brows drew attention to her wide, copper eyes. Though she tried to mask it with the lie of optimism, guilt seemed to seep like oil from her pores.

"She'll make us arlum, you mean," I spat, hoping she could feel the heat from the ignati rumbling in my core. "To pay your debts."

A sigh hit my face, and my mother pinched her lips together. I had never seen her grow angry before, and I welcomed this new development. I wanted a fight.

But she surrendered too quickly, resting her cold hand on my cheek. "We're a family, aren't we, Seyla? We need to support each other, no matter the cause of our misfortune."

A jangling sound made me look back to Tetyan. *But she is sick*, I thought, helpless as the man circled my sister with his embroidered robes and fringe of tiny bells. She stood, obedient, back straight, hands clasped in front of her soft blue shift, chin tucked low to her chest.

"Yes, the High Seer will be pleased with you." The man's first spoken words sent a chill down my spine. He lifted her chin, and I could tell by the press of Tetyan's lips and the paleness of her cheeks that she was terrified.

"Don't make her do this." I found my mother's eyes again, pleading. "Let it be me."

A life in servitude to the fanum priests sounded like a worse fate than death, but for Tetyan, I would do anything.

"You are too old."

I struggled in my mother's grip, but her hands held tighter. "Seyla, don't ruin this for her. The temple servants are well-treated, the favored ones often receiving gifts of appreciation. Tetyan could do well for herself. Better than she could have hoped, really."

What do you know of Tetyan's hopes? I wanted to scream. I was the one who kept her warm at night when our house was unsafe. I was the one who hid her when strange men came by. I was the one who never let her feel the pangs of hunger, even if it meant starving myself to do it.

But what if my mother was right, and all the misery I had shielded her from didn't have to be her future?

Tetyan's eyes raised to find mine, and she nodded with more courage than I had ever shown in my life.

Succeeding in breaking away from Mother's brittle grasp, I launched myself at my sister and pulled her into an embrace that could crush her. The temple seer stepped back, alarmed, but he did not intervene.

"I won't leave you there, I promise," I whispered into her ear. Her bony frame trembled, but I couldn't tell if it was fear or a suppressed cough which shook her. "I'll find a way to pay the debts and bring you home to me."

Tetyan pulled away, resignation plain in her eyes. "Seyla, we have no home. Not anymore."

My face flinched. It was only half true. Our house still stood, but a burnt smell clung to our hair and clothes, a lingering gift from the fire that robbed us of the byre that had been our refuge. It was one of the nightly visitors who had dropped his lantern in the hay on his drunken stagger to fetch his horse. The same man to whom our mother owed insurmountable debts.

Mother had always promised she'd find a man that would bring us everything we could have wanted. Instead, she found one who robbed us of all we had.

Tetyan's simple statement was the inferno that transformed me, burning my soft, hopeful heart until what remained was hard, sharp, and misshapen.

"Home is where we're together," I said, tucking a strand of hair behind her ear.

Impatiently, the seer placed a large hand on Tetyan's shoulder. Intimidated by his size, his ownership, I backed away and stood beside my mother. At sixteen years old, I barely reached her chin. She was tall and graceful, where I was shorter and wiry. Even if I wasn't too old to take

Tetyan's place, they would never have taken me. I had seen many girls chosen for temple service and none of them looked like me.

"Well, Fehlan? Do we have an agreement?" The man stepped forward and held out his other hand, a small sack of arlum clinking against his many rings. Behind him, my sister's shoulders shook as she tried to withhold the cough that had been plaguing her for months.

Pasting on the smile reserved for those she was most eager to impress, my mother bowed her head and accepted the money.

"Yes."

The seer's heavy beard swallowed his grin.

Don't let her leave, Seyla. Don't let her walk away, my mind screamed.

But I let her go.

That night, I resolved to get her back. The general was always looking for new recruits to train; I had quick reflexes, sharp wits, and tenacity. It would cost everything I had and was to be considered for the Agmen's training program, but what did my soul matter when Tetyan was at stake?

Within a fortnight, I had secured a position and received the advance pay for my future service to the Imperii.

But within a fortnight, Tetyan was dead.

Consciousness returns to me suddenly, as if ice water has been poured over my head. The moon's rays no longer shine through the window, and my body aches from the unforgiving floor.

Gasping as my joints protest the movement, I push myself upright.

I cannot relive the mistakes of my past. I will *not.*

Clawing up from the floor, I open a drawer and find a tunic to replace the one crumpled in the corner of my room and yank it on. The úramech uniform still lies piled in front of the door. I can't bring myself to put it all back on but decide to grab the belt with the khukuri attached, cinching it around my waist.

The Hidden Hand is quiet now; it must be well into the night. The streets are empty as I jog down the familiar route to the stronghold. Wearing nothing but threadbare clothes and a single blade, I am invincible. I no longer feel like the self-sufficient thirty-nine-year-old soldier of the Southlands.

I am sixteen-year-old Seyla, racing to save a man I have, against all logic, come to love.

42
BELWYN

My mother paints with a steady hand that defies her physical frailty. She nudges a strand of hair away from her face, leaving a streak of white paint on her cheek. Grinning, I approach quietly and look over her shoulder at the array of inventive canvases before her: a weathered shingle, a book with water-damaged pages, and a flat glass flask. All the items are splotched with thick paint, each brush stroke cleverly hinting at impossible light that trickles like weightless water through brooding forest and mountains.

How can she have the patience to sit in one place for days at a time or the imagination to create scenes she has never witnessed?

A sudden splashing noise followed by Korvin's scolding and Shem's gleeful laughter makes my mouth tip into a shadow of a smile. Korvin managed to convince Mother to move everything downstairs so she can be a part of the rhythms of life. At this moment, I'm glad.

Shemai fishes the heavy pot out of the washbasin and hands it to Korvin to dry.

I massage my mother's shoulder gently and lean over her. "I like what you've been working on, Mada," I say, the term of endearment like a different language on my tongue. My father always insisted such titles were too informal for his boys, correcting us to use the much more respectable *mother* and *father* in their place. It no longer matters what people think of us, I realize—what he thinks of me. I finger the ends of the brushes that are soaking in a jar of distilled pine sap to loosen the thick paints from their bristles. "It reminds me of what I've seen outside of the Vale."

A shriek crackles through the air, and everyone's eyes snap to the room's small window. I hold my breath, listening for any indication of where the kaligorven are, if they are close. If we should shutter the windows and hide until they pass.

The only other sound is water dripping from the sudsy plate gripped between Shemai's white-knuckled fingers.

I exhale. "Just echoes. We're safe."

Mother reaches back and clasps my fingers with hers, their subtle tremble the only indication that anything interrupted us. "I have been walking these landscapes in my dreams ever since you left. It was too real to ignore, so vivid that I could picture you walking beside me. I had to —" Her words catch, and she lifts her hand from mine to press her bent knuckles to her lips for a breath. "I had to believe that darkness did not await you like it did Rhun."

A dull ache laces through my chest. I bend to wrap my arms across my mother's collarbones, hugging her tightly from behind. Our grief twists together, but it does not overwhelm me. It lends strength that shouldn't be there.

I should have hugged her like this ages ago, when she would stand at the window for days watching for a son who would never come home.

My brothers soon forget the awful sound and resume the washing up with their usual squabbling and good-natured banter. Their prattle settles around us like thistledown.

I exhale all the fear, all the regret in a long breath. Why did it take tragedy for our family to realize that the only thing worth having was right here all along? The load would have been so much lighter if we had carried it together.

Mother sniffs. "I knew you had to be alright."

My stomach twists. She reminds me of Amyrah, with her stubborn, childlike faith. The way we parted still hangs over me heavier than the ténesomni. Though it ripped me to shreds, I am beginning to understand why she did it.

She believed I could change things for the better, that I didn't need her at my side to do it.

I straighten and grab the sword from the rack behind the door, securing the belt around my gray-blue tunic.

Mother's eyes widen, apprehension displacing her faith. "Must you go out again?"

A sharp bob of my head serves as my answer.

"But the Shrouded—"

"Aren't going anywhere unless something changes." *Unless I change it.*

There's a burning in my bones, my forever-simmering anger drawn to it like a moth to ignati. For the first time, I believe it can be used for good. What if my rage isn't meant to be starved out but simply directed at the right target? I won't know if I don't try.

But my mother is too fractured to bear these harsh realities. With a quick kiss on her forehead and a vague explanation of when to expect me back, I grab a lantern and slip out the front door.

A gravelly voice emanates from the street. "Where do you think you are going?"

I grimace. Has my father been sitting out here the whole time? I slow my steps and consider whether to turn around. This man has done nothing, nothing at all since I returned, except stay out all night and slump in a defeated heap on the stoop for the better part of the days he's home. Does he deserve a say in what happens around him? To his family?

A breath shunts from his broad chest. "There was a time when my sons respected me," he grumbles, but his words are dull, lacking that fine-toothed bite that used to tear into my confidence as if it were made of lichen. Or maybe I'm the one who has become harder, more capable of withstanding his opposition.

I turn to face him.

His scowling eyes are the clearest I've seen since before I left Utsanek with Amyrah. Brow folded, jaw flexed, his gaze catches on the sword belted at my side. His sword.

"Can't do anything that will help anyone with that piece of refuse," he mutters, gaze returning to the dusty doorstep.

I allow myself a dry laugh. "Then why did you think it was worth giving to me?"

He leans against the doorframe. "You looked ready for a fight that day, but it seems it's done as much good at your side as it did collecting dust over our mantle."

As if a string runs up my spine, my back stiffens, yanked tight in one quick jerk. My pulse beats harder, and though I may tower over my father now, I feel so small.

Give it back to him. Shove all the disgust and insults back in his face.

Look at him. Doesn't he deserve it?

The anger within begs to be let loose.

Instead, I firm up my grip on it and look at him—really look.

A finger's width of silvering hair tops his usually shaved head. Shadows swim around eyes that are almost lost in the deep hollows of his eye sockets. A fresh black slash crosses through the faded Foremost tattoo around his bicep. His shoulders and arms have shed the bursting, vein-corded appearance, and he looks so weak.

He's lost everything too.

"I'm going to the market square, Father. I'm tired of waiting for another Sola Vinari horn, for a scream to bounce down the streets, for a monster to crawl past our door."

"You act like there's another option." His voice grows quiet in a way that's unknown to me. "There's nothing else for us, Belwyn. Just this." He gestures lamely at the shadows and his shoulders sag further.

I step closer and raise a shaking hand, hesitating a moment before laying it on his shoulder.

The touch is uncomfortable, like hair combed the wrong direction. I have never dared reach out to him like this before.

"No, Father, you're wrong." I lick my lips, allowing my courage the chance to build. "We've been lied to our whole lives. This is not where we are meant to be."

He narrows his eyes, a scoffing huff hissing through his teeth before he shakes his head and looks away.

My hand falls to my side. "You can sit here if you want, or you can come with me." I mean to be firm, to give him no reason to doubt my confidence, but my voice falters at the end. I sound like a boy pleading with his father to spend time with him.

I haven't the faintest idea why.

He rubs his head and stares at me blankly. Well-accustomed to him not thinking much of what I say, I swallow and begin walking toward Utsanek's center.

"Belwyn."

My eyebrows spring up when he stands and staggers beside me. In the lantern glow, I see what little color he has drain from his face. Swaying, he reaches for a wall to cling to while his head clears. His lips flatten together and he drags in a slow breath, nostrils flaring.

"I'm coming with you."

I stare, slack-jawed, until I notice how dry my mouth is.

It's what I suggested he should do, isn't it? So why does this terrify me more than him purposefully ignoring me?

Maybe he can change, is changing. Maybe there's hope for the weak, the broken, the corrupted things.

But when the ominous drumbeats race down the alleys of Utsanek to meet us, that timid burst of hope burns out.

43
WEHNA

"CURSE THE MORVUS WHO DECIDED that the Vale needed a fleet o' drums to announce every little thing." Orlagh bustles free from the throng that issues from Utsanek's North Gate, joining me, my father, Elodie, Tress, and Bryn at the outskirts of the gathering. The older woman brushes down the front of her skirts and swipes her wiry gray hair away from her flushed face, scowling toward the far end of the clearing. "Never in all my years have I seen such pomp."

"It's effective, though," Bryn says, his mouth tilting down as he takes in the scene.

"Effectively givin' my heart convulsions each and every time, yes." Orlagh sighs, her eyes scanning over each of us until they land on me. "Ah, there yeh are, Wehna. Take these home with yeh to yer ma and that sweet brother. Tell him my spiced buns haven't been the same without his help." She hands me a netted bag from which an aroma of fresh herbed bread emanates.

I raise my lantern to peer within and find a small paper parcel spotted with grease sitting atop two large loaves. "Thank you, Orlagh." The smile I offer her is poor payment. "Arvo will be pleased."

She winks at me. "Aye, well, remind the lad it's not all for him."

"Right. Yes. I'm sure my mother will take charge of them the moment I step through the door." *She always does.* I can't keep the bite from my tone, and my father gives me a strange look.

I press a thumb to the knife gash in my finger, calling up the heat of pain to punish myself, because I know what his look means. I hear it as if his voice is right inside my skull. *You are being unfair. Ensuring things are in order is the way she keeps her mind from going to the worst places. She loves you, but she's damaged too.*

I want to shout back, *Yes, yes, yes, yes. I know all those things,* but I hold it in because I want it to be easier for my father to love me. Mother said I could unravel now that I have both my parents back, but I doubt she was prepared for the tangled mess I'd become.

The commotion around us grows to be too much to ignore, and I blink, trying to take it all in. The Reckoning Grounds are rapidly filling with people, and they keep pouring in. Buffeted out of my unstable thoughts, I shift closer to Elodie. Worry coats her features, making her appear much younger than she is. Vulnerable.

She shouldn't be here.

"We need to get closer to the platform before it's impossible." My father looks at Bryn, uncertainty pushing one of his brows low. "Are you sure you feel ready for this?"

Bryn releases his wife's hand and stands taller. "Absolutely."

I see the fretful narrowing of Elodie's eyes and reach for her hand, squeezing it with as much assurance as I can manage. She's concerned for her father, who shouldn't be here in his condition. Knowing him, I'm certain he would not listen to the protests of his daughters or his wife.

"Let's not waste any time, then," my father says, turning to address me. "Will you stay with Elodie and Orlagh?"

"I beg yer pardon, young man," Orlagh says, incredulous. "I'll not be brushed aside while the menfolk take care of business, thank yeh kindly."

Elodie hides a smile behind her palm, and my father stares at the baker with apparent astoundment. "Alright. That's settled." He inclines his chin, motioning for Orlagh to proceed ahead of them.

"We'll be fine, my dearest." Tress bestows Elodie's cheek with a gentle pat before tucking herself under Bryn's arm. A stranger might think she's a timid woman who doesn't have the self-confidence to leave her husband's side, but I know the truth. She's actively supplying the strength he lacks, like she does for everyone around her.

"Do you want to get closer to the front?" I ask Elodie once we are alone at the edge of the gathering.

The younger girl shakes her head adamantly, fingering the end of her braid. "Pa didn't want me to come, but Ma insisted I should be informed of what's happening in the Vale if . . . if . . ."

She doesn't finish, and she doesn't have to.

If the worst happens to them.

Is it the nature of parents to put too much on their oldest children? I bite my tongue to keep from saying something that will hurt Elodie, that I'll regret.

Closing my eyes, I shove my own fears into an obscure corner of my mind, though the anxieties are never content to stay there. Sometimes they seep through the fault lines, and I can picture my parents lying, lifeless, on the side of the road as if their deaths really did happen. I believed that image for so long. How can I remove the stain of it from the fabric of who I am?

I take a slow breath and loop my arm through Elodie's elbow, pulling her farther up the side of the clearing, close to the trees. I'm not keen on being in this situation either, but here we are. What would be the point of it if I can't hear what's going on?

Myrzeth stands at the northernmost edge of the grounds, where sola bones are set atop poles around a large platform. His robes drift around him like strands of ténesomni, weaving him into an obsidian garment.

He watches over the sea of people, his sharp eyes focused, taking everything in. When his gaze slows, I can almost swear it has found me.

"It's not safe so close to the forest."

Startled, I look to see who spoke. A tall form eases out of the shadows, a lantern swinging at his side.

"It's Wehna, right?" he asks, one eyebrow popping up.

"Yes," I say hesitantly, a frown forming. He's familiar, but my exhausted brain struggles to comprehend why. A younger boy, similar in features to the other but with lighter hair, follows closely behind.

"Hello," the second boy murmurs when he sees my eyes on him.

"Korvin, what are you doing here?" the first young man chastises, spinning around.

Elodie sucks in a rapid breath, her fingers finding my forearm and squeezing hard. "Wehna, that's *him*," she whispers into my ear. "The boy I took you to find."

Confused, I look back at the pair of them.

"I saw you and Father leave and I . . ." Korvin tries to explain, his apologetic expression shifting into something more determined. "I want to be a part of what's happening in the Vale."

Korvin's brother frowns, his tone scolding. "But Mother—"

"She'll be fine, Bel. I left Shemai with her and she isn't going to go anywhere on her own." Korvin looks imploringly at his brother. "And I . . . I don't want you to leave us again."

My heart constricts at the honest statement, but I force myself not to dwell on it. Instead, I let the pieces come together in my mind. *Belwyn.* I've only met him once, but I feel stupid for not recognizing him. This is the young man Amyrah secretly adores, no matter what she's told me. And if he is here, then maybe . . .

I crane my neck to see past them, my chest thrumming with the hope of finding another familiar face close behind. "Is Amyrah with you?"

When silence answers me, I look at Belwyn. He winces and scratches his arm, seeming to struggle with words. A pendant in the shape of an eight-pointed star catches my eye, lashed to his wrist with leather cords. It's finely crafted, delicate. I recognize it.

Heart leaping to my throat, I gasp for breath. *Elyōn, no.*

"She left." Belwyn lowers his hand and frowns. "We parted ways in Ketsé." His eyes seek mine. "She was fine when I left her," he says, voice dropping low.

He doesn't offer any other details. I'm relieved to learn my friend is safe, but hearing the name of my home on the lips of a person who shouldn't know it exists causes a swell of emotion to overwhelm me. It's a wave swallowing a boat that's already sinking.

"Ketsé," I breathe, the word a drop of honey on my tongue.

I close my eyes and imagine its vertical gardens and walkways lined with glowing stones. I can hear its worship gatherings held in elaborate tree cathedrals open to the main streets, free from the fear of Shrouded beasts or the threat of being reported to a corrupt authority. *Ketsé*, my mind repeats. Cries. Mourns.

I flit my eyes up to Belwyn again. "What did you think of my home?"

Elodie's brows lift like she expects me to correct a slip of the tongue, but I release my hold on her arm and angle my face away from her.

"No, Elodie. I'm not from this awful place, and I could never think of it as my home," I say, the words coated in frost to keep her from questioning me.

Belwyn glances from me to Elodie, a puzzled bent to his brow. "Truthfully, I didn't find it all that different from here."

I straighten my spine, defensiveness rising. "Is that right?" A strangled laugh jumps from my lungs. "So, when you were there, you were scared every time you stepped outside? You had to rely on the bones of murdered Light Creatures to see your path? You needed to lie to make yourself believe you had a single scrap of goodness in this *heshïn* darkness?"

Elodie steps away from me as if I am some wild thing she doesn't recognize.

Belwyn shakes his head in a single, decisive motion. "No, but that's not the similarity I was talking about."

I press trembling fingers to my temple, rushing to cut his argument off at the knees. "How could you suggest Ketsé is anything like Utsanek? You must not be the person Amyrah thought if you can't see the blatant difference between shadow and light."

Belwyn blinks, a tendon standing out along his neck. I hug my arms around my chest, refusing to let myself feel remorseful for snapping at him. Bad things have been happening all around us, all the time, every day, and I'm tired, so tired, of trying to find the good in them.

"Where did Father go?" Korvin asks, a welcome break from this tense conversation.

I wish the throbbing pain in my head was so easy to push aside.

Turning to his brother, Belwyn jerks his chin. "He disappeared a few blocks from the grounds. I don't think he could stomach coming back here again."

Korvin's mouth twitches.

Belwyn shifts his attention to Elodie, addressing her with compassion that grates on me. "I'm sorry. This is probably a bit confusing." He motions with his chin for Korvin to step forward. "This is my brother. Can you two stay together and push a few rows into the crowd?" His troubled gaze passes over the towering trees. "I'd feel better if we weren't so exposed."

Elodie casts me an uneasy look, but I don't want to acknowledge it. I don't want to see her opinion of me displayed on her face, or to witness how the shattering of my faith might impact hers. Grasping the skirts of her dress, she turns back to Belwyn and responds with a shy nod.

His brother extends his hand to her like someone much older and more mature. "I'm Korvin." A dimple presses into one cheek the way a stitch pulls tight in a soft garment. "If you didn't already catch that."

Elodie stares at his hand as though it is the most terrifying thing. She seems to remember herself and accepts it with a small smile. "El-Elodie."

If I weren't so self-absorbed and bitter at everyone around me, I might find this moment sweet. Even if it is happening in the worst place in Atsun.

With a calm demeanor, Korvin leads Elodie away right as the drummers cease pounding.

The silence that replaces the racket is so complete, I'm afraid to breathe and shatter it. From deep within the woods at our back, something growls and breaks it for me.

"Like I said," Belwyn says roughly, locking a hand around my forearm and dragging me closer to the crowd, "it's not safe so close to the trees."

The shiver of fear racing down my spine is enough to keep me from protesting.

"Why did you send them ahead?" I ask, going along with Belwyn as he forces a path through the startled people. Barely contained panic thickens in the air, carried by whispers, harried conversations, and exclamations of alarm that spread from person to person.

"Because I wanted you to understand what's at risk here."

I plant my feet to prevent him from going farther, pegging him with a question when he looks back at me. "What's at risk?"

He sighs. "The darkness that's at the heart of Utsanek isn't only threatening the lives of the valefolk. It's threatening *everyone*." Belwyn's eyebrows go up at that last word and stay there, waiting for me to comprehend the fullness of that statement.

"I don't understand."

I don't want to understand.

He scans the crowd, leans in, and says in a low voice, "The Ketsé you know and love, the one filled with life and the memories you cling to? It's been overtaken by ténesomni."

I yank my arm from his grip. "No. You're wrong."

"Wehna, I've been there. And I think that what happens here, right now, will affect all Atsun."

My world is crumbling, splintering, disintegrating bit by bit. I blink and swallow a couple times. "Why?"

Belwyn straightens, tilts his chin. "Why what?"

The question I want to ask is, *Why didn't my parents tell me what's happening outside the Vale*? But it doesn't find my lips.

"Why have you been to Ketsé?" I say tersely, annoyed by how danger and darkness seem to sharpen him yet cripple me.

"It wasn't safe for Amyrah to stay in the Vale anymore, and she needed . . . she needed answers." He closes his mouth, clearly unwilling to say more.

But I don't need him to. I recall how the argentilum pendant shone when it got close to Amyrah's skin. The precious metal has always been rumored to glow in special circumstances, and no matter how I tried, I could never get that hateful star to do anything abnormal. The moment Amyrah got close, though, it twinkled like starlight.

"Because she's Luvesti," I say for him.

Belwyn grimaces, rubbing the back of his neck. "Yeah. That."

I've heard many horrid things said about the Luvesti, a lot of them from one of the friends I left in Ketsé. Most people spoke of the race of light-bearing people as if they were perfect, but wasn't that because the Luvesti never ventured close enough to the Shrouded lands to do much of anything at all, right or wrong? My friend Jaki had laughed at the lore as if it were the most ridiculous joke, and her attitude was contagious.

Now I know that the Luvesti are as human as the rest of us. How could I think badly of them after knowing Amyrah, however briefly?

But I also recall why Jaki hated them so much, and it homes in on my rotten thoughts like a vulture.

"So where is she? Isn't she supposed to be fixing this?" I motion to the shadows undulating around us. "Because that's all the Luvesti are good for." I try out Jaki's words, unsure if I like the taste or if I believe them.

Belwyn lets the lantern hang loose at his side. "She tried."

My hands shake. "Tried? Past tense? And, what? Gave up?" I don't understand my anger. She was—*is*—my friend. But what do I really know of Amyrah, that aloof girl with a hero complex and easy faith that puts mine to shame?

Belwyn stares at me for a while, clearly stunned by my volatile emotions. "It's not something she can control, Wehna."

I snort. "Something she can't be bothered to control, you mean."

"Welcome, my good valefolk," Myrzeth calls above the brain-rattling hum of voices, closing Belwyn's window to argue with me.

I turn my focus to the Foremost. Even from this far away, I can see his wide grin and the confidence radiating from his entire person in a way I can't fathom.

A question surfaces in my mind. If Amyrah is Luvesti, what does that make her uncle?

I shiver. He must be Luvesti too.

I hope he isn't as weak as her. I hate myself for thinking it.

"It's another beautiful day in the Vale, is it not?" Myrzeth smiles broadly, as if he expects a favorable reaction from the valefolk. When they repay him with silence, he does not seem perturbed. He spreads his arms at his sides and opens his palms, and the black above us ripples.

"*Caelaveth*," he shouts, and the ténesomni rolls back on itself, retreating from the immediate vicinity so that the grounds are encased in a bright dome. The blackness moves in frothing waves outside of it. Exclamations of approval slink around the clearing as the vast number of tightly clutched lanterns illuminate the space far better than before.

I slip a finger underneath my braided bracelet and spin it around my wrist. Myrzeth has power that I cannot begin to comprehend. If he wanted, he could reveal the sky and explain its existence to the valefolk. I can't think how that would serve his purposes, though.

"Do you believe me now?" he asks, and this time he is repaid with a hearty cheer.

"It's sick how easily they can be led," Belwyn whispers, leaning close.

I nod, though I understand their response more than I care to admit. Sometimes it is preferable to cling to momentary comfort instead of assessing the ugly truth.

"I've summoned you here today for a rather unique Blood Reckoning Ceremony," Myrzeth says, moving across the platform in long strides. "I understand that within the walls of Utsanek it can be difficult to grasp the importance of Sola Vinari and how hunting down a Light Creature can benefit our people. Our kaligorven protectors are more than a means of survival for us, however. They are our strength. For you to understand, you need to witness it for yourselves." Myrzeth turns, motioning behind him.

Chill bumps cover my arms, my neck.

Several men emerge from the wall of ténesomni, guiding a large cart forward. A heavy canvas drapes over a bulky shape on top of it, and the whole thing angles as the men push it up a ramp concealed behind the platform. Myrzeth hops to the ground to make space, gazing on it with smug anticipation. The men position the cart in the center of the stage, then retrieve blocks of wood from the corners of the platform and place them before and behind the wheels to keep them from rolling.

A strange sound exudes from within the covering, caught between a wail and a chilling melody. It is unlike anything I have ever heard, and dread grows to an unbearable level in my chest.

Has he really done this? Has he caged one of the Shrouded in some twisted attempt to convince the valefolk that these beasts are worthy of our worship? It is the most nonsensical plan I could imagine, and I am at a loss to comprehend how it could strengthen his position.

Another wail erupts, and from the corner of my eye I see Belwyn flinch. I turn to him fully, noticing his face's white pallor, and reach out to him. "Belwyn, are you—"

But the question hangs incomplete. In a moment, his face beams with a blinding light, and startled cries fill the air. I hold up a hand to shield my eyes, trying to make sense of how he can be *shining*, until I grasp that it isn't from him. He's reflecting what is happening at the platform. I turn around.

The canvas has been stripped away from the shape in the wagon, and what lies beneath isn't a kaligorva.

It's a sola.

I close my eyes. The presence of the burning creature does nothing to relieve my fears, like it did when the sola wren appeared to me in Ellithïm and outside Utsanek. It has left me feeling naked, exposed. The sharp responses and the bitterness I have nurtured within my heart condemn me, and the thin garment with which I had tried to cloak my failings has been yanked away.

Please, Elyōn! I scream inside my mind. *This light . . . It is too much. It will consume me.*

"My dear valefolk, do not be alarmed." Myrzeth's voice carries over the people's confusion. I latch on to it. "Lower your hands, open your eyes, and gaze upon the creature that wars with those to whom you have sworn loyalty."

Murmurs circle around the throng and my heartbeat pounds in my ears. "Belwyn," I whisper, keeping my eyes closed. "I don't want to look."

"It's alright," he says, and he sounds calm. Maybe not calm. Resigned. Sad.

The brilliance slices through me when I open my eyes, but I grit my teeth and will myself to look.

An enormous form crouches behind the bars of a crude cage with barely enough room to turn around. I squint. The shock of the light ebbs, and soon I can see it.

"What is it?" I ask.

The thing has hooves and a long face that resembles a ram's. Its horns are so large they curl back around themselves, catching between the bars of the cage. A wide, fan-like tail brushes the floor. The creature's muscular body glistens as if it has just stepped out of a pool of molten gold, and the twisting patterns across its skin reach into the air in shimmering wisps.

It's . . . beautiful.

"Some sort of hoofed mammal," Belwyn says, a strange tremble in his voice that doesn't match him. "Does it matter? It's going to die."

The simple statement sours my stomach and I take a slow breath to ease it. "Is he going to do it himself, in front of all the people?"

"I suspect that's the plan." Belwyn grimaces.

I buckle with a disbelieving laugh. Will the valefolk allow that?

Myrzeth signals to his men, and piece by piece, they dismantle the bars that surround the sola. It becomes clear the cage was not a means to contain it, but a way to give structure to the canvas covering. Once the bars have been removed, I can see thick ropes binding the Light Creature to the cart's base.

Ropes? The sola looks to be made of pure muscle. It could break them with one easy motion. And how do the bonds not burn away at its touch? Surely the sola is made of liquid starlight.

The creature is being offered like a lamb to the slaughter, and it shows no desire to be free.

Pathetic. Weak, a voice whispers in my mind.

I bite down. I need this battle to be won right here. I need light to challenge darkness, to come out the victor.

When a silhouette blocks out the glow for a moment, my struggling faith flickers. Two people climb onto the platform, one steady and strong, the other needing assistance.

My eyes widen.

I know, I know, *I know* there are at least two men in this crowd who won't let this happen, but can they be this reckless, this foolish? I should get closer, or run away, but I can't move, can't think other than to wish that when the light reveals the faces of the figures, they won't be the ones I am terrified to see.

"This bloodshed needs to end," one of the silhouettes bellows, and the familiarity of his voice stabs through my chest.

"He's going to get himself killed," Belwyn says under his breath, and I swallow a sob.

Pada. My mouth forms the word, but my voice can't find its way through my terror-gripped throat. *How can he do this to us? Stand against a power he can't dream of challenging, hang his life in the balance? Risk leaving us on our own again? How can he let Bryn stand by his side when it would take almost nothing to leave his five daughters fatherless?*

If this is what Elyōn requires of those who trust in him, then I don't want it.

Something grim and hard grips my insides and compels me forward. Ignoring Belwyn's warnings, I twist, I sidestep, I shove between bodies, my eyes glued to that platform while everyone else fades into the background.

Amused laughter spills from Myrzeth. I am close enough to the front of the clearing that I can see him better now, with his white face and white hair and the sable folds of ténesomni clinging to him. He holds a hand in front of his face and turns it over, inspecting his palm. A wry smile plays with his lips. "It needs to end, you say? And why should your opinion be of any significance?" Lowering his hand, he raises an eyebrow. "Who are you?"

The sola bones backlight my father as he turns to the crowd. "It should not matter who I am. The question is who *this* man is." He addresses the valefolk with a raised voice, sweeping his arms to indicate

Myrzeth. "You accept him because he claims to have knowledge beyond the Vale. You trust him because he frightens you with a show of power, but you do not know the truth."

The expression twisting Myrzeth's features is unreadable. He folds his arms and stares down my father, and my palms begin to sweat.

"And what is the truth?" the Foremost asks, his voice quiet. Dangerous.

"Men like you have kept the valefolk in ignorance about what lies beyond these borders and lied to us about the true nature of the kaligorven. They are the reason this void of light exists in the first place. Elyōn created Atsun as a place of brightness, but wickedness has perverted your understanding of the nature of that light. This darkness has not been persecuting the rest of the world like it does the Vale until very recently."

The valefolk grapple with what any of that could mean, their confusion evident. I can see the fear, the anger on their faces, and it's justified. My father has taken a sledgehammer to their delusions.

Jaw slackening, I struggle to fit the bold man before me together with the one who exists in my memories, the one who avoided confrontation as much as possible. My parents always chose to tend to the needs of the valefolk quietly from within our home, never taking their beliefs to the streets. Theirs was a humanitarian effort which was intended to show Elyōn's love to people with actions more often than words. They spoke of and loved the Highest openly within our doors, hoping that they would effect change without ruining people's conception of the world.

But in the dwelling place of darkness, nothing is more confrontational than light.

This not the father I remember.

A chorus of deep roars challenges his speech, echoing from all sides of the clearing. Screams move toward me like a wave, and the throng presses in close as if to escape some unseen horror, making a clear path for it to pass.

The Shrouded have arrived.

44
AMYRAH

ELYŌN IS NOT LIKE THE PEOPLE of the land, that he should deal falsely with them. There is nothing that can sway his mind. What he promises, he fulfills. What he wills, he makes good. Though he dwells in unapproachable splendor, he also plants light within the hearts of those who seek him. In compassion, he also shares that light with those who curse his name, that they might not be wholly consumed by the ravenous dark.

Fanning my fingers out against the old pages of my mother's book, I raise my eyes to take in the bright room, where the king wastes away with his son at his side. For several days, Luvesta has remained in an uneasy state, as if waiting for a Vestri blizzard to fall. But nothing has changed. The king lies in the same bed he retired to after revealing who he is to me and adding yet another layer to my life that seems both significant and meaningless at once. I came here to find out who I am and to get help controlling my Luvesti abilities, but all I've gained is another family member to lose. Even here, I can feel the shadows occupying my veins.

Shivering, I close the door on those thoughts and focus instead on the king—my *grandfather*. His breaths are labored, perspiration beading on his forehead. Holden sits on the other side, hiding his face in his hands. He hasn't said much these past few days, other than to send me to bed and ask his father what he can do to help whenever the king regains consciousness. The answer is always the same: *Stay with me.*

I barely know the man, can hardly accept that I am connected to this scene of anguish. The sadness circles around me like a wren with no place to land.

So, I read. I read of light I cannot see, love I cannot feel, and hope I do not recognize.

"Can you sing, my daughter?"

I blink several times and look at my grandfather, bewildered. Holden jumps to his feet, the stool clattering to the floor, and leans over him.

"Father, you should—"

The king raises a hand to still his son, bloodshot eyes not straying from my face. Holden straightens, slipping his hands into his pockets and frowning.

Remembering myself, I close my mouth and shake my head. "Not really."

Holden cocks an eyebrow at my response.

"I don't know many songs."

"That book is filled with songs, I believe." My grandfather shifts on his bed, trying to sit up. Holden hastens to assist him, steadying him by the shoulders and tucking a pillow behind his matted hair. "Though, the melodies have been lost to time. Or perhaps we have willfully forgotten them." He rests his head back, closing his eyes and patting Holden's hand. "Thank you, my son."

"I'll send to the kitchens for some broth," Holden says quietly, turning toward the hall. He sends me a pointed look before he disappears behind the door frame, as if to say *make sure he's alright.*

I watch him leave, my mind stuck on what the king told me. "I do know a song," I say, turning the book's pages until I come to the place where several are missing. "And it's from this book." I glance up and meet my grandfather's gaze. "Would you like me to sing it?"

He sucks in a quick breath, flattening his mouth into a thin expression I can't decipher. "Please," he says in a hoarse whisper.

My voice struggles to find the notes at first, and the sound disperses into the large room. The words quickly become like rich fare for my soul, strengthening my heart as the air swells with melody, with promise. I give myself over to the sola's song.

When it is over and the arched ceilings cease echoing the music back down on us like gentle rain, I return my attention to the king. His chin is raised as if he is imagining the heavens that hang above, and tears cut across his cheeks into the shadowy stubble lining his jaw. "You say this song is written in that book?"

When I nod, what little color he had leaves his features. He motions for me to bring the book to him, but I cannot move, cannot breathe. "I'm so sorry. The pages are missing." I nearly choke on the bitter words, remorse for having burned the Shaluth Cantu in a moment of desperation filling my chest.

He makes a noise not unlike a moan of pain. "And where—*how*—did you come to learn it?"

Stricken to see the emotion that drowns my grandfather, I close the book with shaking hands and kneel at his bedside. "I don't know. I first heard the melody from a sola in the Vale, and then I remembered the words, as if from a long-forgotten dream. I wondered if my mother had taught them to me."

He passes a hand over his face, smearing away his tears. "H-how can that be?" he whispers, but the question does not seem to be for me. Wetting his lips with his tongue, he fixes his gaze on me again. "I do not know if that is the case, but I remember that melody." Lowering his chin, he grips my hand in his. "My late wife, your grandmother, suffered much in her last days. It was like all she knew had been stripped away from her. Often, she did not recognize me or her own son. Delirium stole the last of her days from us, but always, always, she hummed a song. *That* song. She had a voice that could make even the hardest soul weep, and though reason abandoned her, her gift for music never did."

A sob lurches through his chest and I reach to steady him.

"No one could make sense of her words, and the lorekeepers came up empty after scouring Luvesta's records for some connection. I believed that it was the final surge of her beautiful mind before it blinked out, even though there was no proof that she was the one who wrote it."

"But they have lived in this book the whole time." I set it on the bed, withdrawing my hand. It is too precious of a thing for me to possess.

There is so much I don't understand. Will I always be caught like a leaf on a current, never able to forge a different course or make ripples of my own?

Silence lengthens between us, broken only by my grandfather's ragged breaths.

"It has a twin, you know," he finally says.

I blink away tears I didn't realize had formed. "A twin?"

"That is perhaps the wrong word for it." His dry lips pucker in thought. "But in every way this book is good and full of light, its counterpart is all that is evil and dark."

"Why would such a thing exist?" The question emerges from me, unbidden. "What purpose can something like that serve?"

The king gestures vaguely. "Knowledge of self, I suppose. To grasp the wickedness of which we are capable, don't we need to see it laid out without justification, without embellishment?" he asks, taking a moment to draw in several slow breaths. "It was never meant to be read, you understand, but kept close by as a grim reminder of the depths to which the Luvesti could plummet."

I nod, but I don't really understand. It sounds like a tempting thing for anyone who might be less than satisfied with the way of life the Luvesti have chosen.

Someone, I realize with a growing sense of dread, *like my uncle*.

My grandfather catches my hand in his. "Fear not, my dear. It is kept under lock and key, as it has been for generations."

"And what about my mother's book?" My eyes hitch on the tome lying benignly on the crumpled linens. "Was it just a symbol as well, kept within reach of our people's hands but far from their minds?"

His silvering hair flops as he dips his chin to his chest, a soft chuckle escaping him. "You inherited your mother's quick tongue, I see. Yes, you are correct. It was hidden in the archives—preserved, I suppose we would call it—but rarely was it ever drawn out and consulted. Just adored by a bright Luvesti girl who could never tire of the light. And, it would seem," he laughs, fondness evident in his expression, "taking books that did not belong to her."

He's quiet for a while, his gaze traveling somewhere beyond me, yet nowhere at all. "Ellehra would be lost for days amid the archive shelves." He releases my hand and trails his fingers over the book's worn cover. "This book disappeared the same time she and her brother left us."

"That must have been so hard." My thoughts drift to the years of growing up with my father. I have seen grief cripple a person; I cannot imagine the weight of not knowing whether someone you love is living or dead.

"Losing both her and Myrzeth at the same time was what stole my wife's mind in the end," the king says, as if his thoughts are one with mine.

Weeping takes him in a furious billow, and I am helpless to know how to comfort him, other than to circle my arms around his shoulders and try to weather the battering. The aching sorrow shifts into a bout of coughing that turns his lips blue and splatters his sleeve with gold.

"Amyrah, I think you should leave."

My heart sinks at the coldness in Holden's voice. I turn to find him standing in the doorway, a bowl in his hands and a pained expression shadowing his face. My hurt melts, softened with the balm of empathy.

When I met Holden, I would have never suspected that his life had been altered by tragedy. But he is so much like me, having borne the weight of living in a world that is *wrong*. He's a living reminder of loss to a father haunted by sorrow, just as I once was.

The king's voice, though still breathless, turns hard. "This is not her doing, my son. These are old wounds that cannot heal until the rot has been dug up and seared away."

Jaw clenching, Holden enters the room and sets the broth on a side table. "You look worse, Father," he says, producing a cloth from his pocket and using it to dab the sweat from the king's forehead.

"Nonsense. I feel better."

His weak smile fools no one.

The lines etched between Holden's eyebrows deepen, but he lets the argument drop. "The city is darker today," he says, changing the subject as he bends to set the stool right.

I move to the window, eyes roving over the rooftops and to the midday sky. The view faces south, and a chill runs through me when I see a black shadow rolling over the Astellum Plain.

Has it found us here too?

"It must be a shift in the weather?" the king says, as if it's a question and not a statement.

Holden gives a weary sigh. "No, it's as blue a day as I have seen. This is different, and no one here will understand because it's caused by the ténesomni."

"Impossible!" My grandfather is repaid with a horrible coughing fit for not moderating his outburst. Letting its ugly sound and Holden's gentle tones blur to the back of my mind, I stare at the irrefutable evidence before my eyes.

Taking a drink of water seems to settle my grandfather enough for him to finish his thought. "The black stain is confined to the Vale. The borders have not been breached in—"

"I know, Father. A hundred years. It's been growing stronger as of late, though, pressing its territory into the Grovesha, stone by stone."

My heart thumps faster and faster; my breaths come quick and shallow. I tear my eyes from the blackening horizon and look down at my hands braced on the windowsill, heart stuttering when I see fluid veins of ténesomni shifting across my skin like tiny tributaries. I turn my back to the window, searching for a way of escape that will not draw attention, but there is none.

Holden glances at me suspiciously, and I hide my arms behind my back. Did he see the proof of my tainted heart squirming across my flesh? Does he know what a dangerous, cornered thing I am?

He gives me a look that seems to say *it will be alright*, eyes not straying from my face.

I don't believe him.

"H-how can that be?" his father asks, and I feel like I will throw up.

Reluctantly, Holden breaks his attention from me and looks at his father. "I don't know, but only one thing has changed in the Vale of late, and that is Myrzeth."

The king's lip trembles, his face growing paler.

"I'm sorry, Father, but there is no other explanation. He hasn't only taken control of the Vale. He's given himself over to the *erychélus nathura*, making the ténesomni stronger because of it."

"No, not my boy." A moan forces from my grandfather's lips. He hides his face in his hands. "Was it me? Am I the one who did this to him? Is it because he was banished from this place that he surrendered himself so wholly to darkness?"

"No. Father, *no*." Holden falls to his knees at the bedside and pulls his father's hands away from his face. "Don't take the weight of his choices on your shoulders. He chose this path, not you."

"But if he had stayed, *perhaps—*" My grandfather's grief strangles him, and he struggles to gulp in a breath. "Perhaps he could have learned to live in the light."

Holden has no response to this, except to keep his eyes fixed on his father's face, compassion angling his eyebrows up in the middle.

"And now this evil has once again reached our doorstep because I failed him," the king whispers.

Digging my nails into my palms, I utter a half-formed prayer to Elyōn for control, for courage. I can't stand to see my grandfather shoulder blame when the real culprit stands in the same room.

"My king, Myrzeth is not the one who is responsible for freeing the ténesomni to roam."

"Amyrah, don't—"

"No, Holden," I bark at him, my teeth clacking against each other. "Let me speak. Let me admit what I am."

I walk forward, pushing up my sleeves and holding my arms to the side so that the shadows are visible. My grandfather's eyes fall on them, widening.

"Do you see?" I ask, my voice cracking. "Myrzeth is not the only one tainted by the *erychélus nathura*. It lives and thrives in *me* as well. I tried to hold the ténesomni back, to keep it from swallowing towns and cities whole, and all I accomplished was shattering its prison. I have undone our people's labors because I am weak, and when it mattered most, I called to the dark."

There is a commotion outside, echoing up the hallway. Quick footsteps follow panicked shouts. Holden twists to look out the bedchamber door, but my grandfather's eyes lock on mine. They don't hold the condemnation that a twisted part of me craves.

They glisten with compassion that will be my undoing.

"My child," the king whispers, acting as if he has not noticed the noise welling up within his castle, "the dark will always seem like it answers, but that is because it wants you to believe there is no greater power." He beckons me closer and takes one of my arms in his hands, his warm palm weighing on it, smothering the icy shadows.

"But I have cried out to Elyōn and he doesn't answer," I say. "I'm yearning to be free, not condemned to this battle between what I want to do and what I'm powerless to stop."

My grandfather's hand presses down firmer. "Shadow lies at the heart of all people, more visible in some than in others. It isn't the presence of that shadow that should frighten you. No, much more alarming than the darkness is the absence of a war against it."

I frown at him.

He presses on, insistent. "When people love darkness more than light, when they grow weary of fighting against the all-consuming shadow, it is then that they have become servants of Érechlys. But the one who sees the stain in herself and finds her soul in anguish because of it truly is—can only be—a daughter of Elyōn."

Tears streaming, I bite down on my lip to deny the sobs that threaten to rip through me, unsuccessfully. "Then why can't I master it?" I cry.

Holden looks back, his frown melting into amazement. "Amyrah," he says, crossing the room and standing before me. "*Look.*"

Confused, I follow his gaze to my arms. The bands of ténesomni have grown languid, shrinking into thread-like wisps before they disappear completely.

"Elyōn hears you," my grandfather says through tears of his own.

I sink to the bed and wrap my naked arms around my stomach, curling forward and letting the fear and wonder and relief crash like breakers over my head.

A gentle hand rests on my back.

"You are his, Amyrah. No matter how much damage the ténesomni has wrought through you, I have confidence Elyōn can still use this for good," my grandfather says.

"What damage has she done?"

We all turn toward the door, where the armored form of Yara stands, hand resting on the hilt of her sword.

She could not have shown up at a worse moment. I refuse to avert my eyes, even though the flames in hers threaten to burn me.

No one answers her question.

"Yara." Holden clears his throat, looking toward the window.

"What's happening out there?"

The side of her mouth twitches, but she makes sure I feel the weight of her glare before she answers, "It is the solas, my prince. The ones within the walls have grown restless, and we've received reports from the Astellum Plain. Others are emerging from the Sighing Woods as if they have been chased."

My grandfather's hand slips from my back. "Chased? By what?"

Yara grimaces. "The kaligorven."

45
WEHNA

I FEEL THE DRIP OF SWEAT under my arms; I can smell the stink of fear. Both make me sharp, freeing me from my paralyzing thoughts and grounding me in the physical world. I cut through the mass of people until I am below my father, right in front of the platform.

"Pada, we have to go," I plead, but either he doesn't hear, or he ignores me. Bryn seems equally unaware of my existence. I glance around, hoping to see Tress somewhere so she can help me talk sense into them, but I can't find her.

Only one person watches me. Only one sees.

Myrzeth inclines his face, assessing me with eyes like a new moon night. My conscience urges me to say something, to challenge him like I have done in the past, but my mouth is empty.

His gaze is cold, so cold, yet as I hold it and see his lips twitch downward for the briefest of moments, confusing, idiotic, alarming empathy awakens in my chest.

Myrzeth blinks, breaking the connection, and turns back to his people. "Peace. Let the kaligorven pass through. If you keep your wits, I assure you, no one is in danger here." Patiently, he waits for the commotion to settle.

"Well, Foremost? Are you going to tell us what he means?" someone speaks up.

Myrzeth tips his head in acknowledgment, his hair falling before his face. "Almost everything this man has said I would agree with." He pauses. "Yes, I do have knowledge of what lies beyond this place. Yes, I do hold a special power bestowed upon me by my Luvesti lineage. However, these men speak of those things as if they are shameful, and on that I disagree. Recall, if you will, that I was not the one who established this pattern of ignorance. Many a Foremost before me sought to scrub the knowledge of the lands of light from the Vale's existence. I am not to blame for your current situation."

Bryn grunts his disgust. "If that's the case and you truly are so noble, then why don't you enlighten them once and for all?"

Myrzeth chuckles as if he has been anticipating this, and the sound is both disconcerting and allaying. I would love to laugh at opposition like that.

"Are you sure that is what you want?" he asks, raising an eyebrow at the two men, but their grim expressions remain unchanged. "If you think they will benefit from the shattering of their world, then so be it.

"Friends, what you know of your world is a lie. These men are correct. You were once a people who were free to roam all Atsun, partaking in both darkness and light alike."

The valefolk look around at each other, speaking in a hush of low, confused murmurs.

"But do you know who did this to you?" His voice rises over them, tinged with anger. "It wasn't the Shrouded, like these men would have you believe. No, it was the worshippers of Elyōn."

The blight-cloaked beasts roar; the valefolk respond with shrieks.

My eyes dart to my father's crestfallen face. The Foremost is twisting the intentions of my father and Bryn to his advantage, and the terrifying thing is that he is right. The Luvesti have done this.

The revelation has a profound impact on the people. A woman's raised voice reaches me from the left, her tone accusatory.

"*You*. You have always promoted Elyōn, haven't you? I've seen you escorting people past my front door time and time again, speaking the name of the Highest as if he were a lover. Don't you dare deny it."

Someone is thrown to the ground at the front of the audience, and Bryn cries out. He looks as if he wants to leap off the platform, but my father holds him back.

The prostrate figure raises her arm above her head. "I'm fine," she wheezes. Orlagh steps from the crowd and kneels with difficulty to see after the woman, who I realize is Tress.

The people's anger rises to a dangerous level behind them.

"Peace," Myrzeth intones. "Do not persecute them for something they followed in ignorance."

This seems to calm their fervor.

Myrzeth grins, pleased. "Your strength has always been your open-mindedness, and that was what the light-lovers could not stand. They confined your ancestors to the Vale with all the ténesomni as if you were every bit as volatile as the kaligorven."

The expressions around me turn bitter with rage.

"We may come from that heritage, yes," my father says, "but is that who you will choose to be? Emissaries of shadow? Or will you distance yourself from that sordid history now and choose to forsake this wretched darkness?"

"It protects us," someone shouts, met with cheers of agreement.

My father's mouth gapes.

"Look at you," Myrzeth says, gesturing toward his people. "Look at what you have accomplished in a hundred years. Not only have you adapted to this harsh sentence, but you have also achieved a balance that seemed impossible. Can you not see the advantage you have, crafting this allegiance with the kaligorven? I have been abroad, and I can assure you that, although there are places where the ténesomni does not touch, they are lands of prejudice that would still seek to purge your people from the face of Atsun if they had the chance. They do not overtake us because they fear the might of the kaligorven.

"Would you go back on your agreement here? Now?" Myrzeth crosses the open space in front of the platform and stops an arm's reach away, eyes trained on me. "Would you break your bargain with your guardians?"

"Please, please do not be taken in by this man's clever lies," my father begs, his voice wavering.

Myrzeth ignores him. "Choose this day whom you will serve—the light or the shadow it cannot overcome—and the Shrouded will act accordingly."

Gasps fill the air, and I am startled by the reaction from valefolk who seemed so certain of their allegiance a moment ago. The throng ceases to jostle me, to squeeze me from both sides. I glance left and right to find that everyone has pulled away, and I am standing alone.

A look of insane glee dominates the Foremost's face.

The air temperature drops impossibly low and my breaths puff in frozen bursts. My heart staggers when I hear the dull thumps of slow footfalls. My father finally notices that I am standing in front of him, but his focus shifts to something behind me, terror melting away his remaining bravado.

Don't turn around, I plead with myself.

Oh, but I can't help it.

A monolith of living death reaches above, twice the height of a man. Barely contained within a twisted shape, it blurs the line between man and beast. It seethes and rumbles, its elongated, fang-studded muzzle splitting with a growl. Hot air hits my face. I choke on the stench of burning rot. When I lift my gaze to meet the kaligorva's, my stomach quakes. Its eyes are molten on the inside, ice on the outside. I can feel myself burning while the warmth from my flesh drains away.

If there is a moment to cry out to Elyōn, it's now, yet my thoughts are a thick, bitter haze. I close my eyes to shut the monster out, resigned to whatever will come.

A cold hand slips around mine, and I blink up into the face of Myrzeth. Without breaking eye contact, he draws me to the side and out of the path of the kaligorva.

I don't know why I don't fight him; I don't know why I can't speak.

Releasing my hand, he moves to the front of the cleared path before the beast. "Will you throw in your loyalty with the solas," he says, waving behind him at the pitiful Light Creature, which scrapes the ground with its golden hooves, "or the kaligorven?"

The throng hurriedly parts in several more places, issuing more alarmed gasps. A dozen kaligorven cut through the clearing on all sides, and a few others materialize from the blooming black behind the platform.

"Welcome, my friends," Myrzeth says warmly.

"They're all around us," someone shouts, and I want to laugh at how unnecessary that statement is.

"Indeed, they are." Myrzeth spins in a slow circle, arms outstretched. "As intimidating as this might seem, I assure you it is a mere fraction of their numbers, which are growing daily. Do you want them on your side, or would you rather take your chances against them?"

Complete silence consumes the listeners, and Myrzeth's voice softens in the stillness. "Darkness is patient. It waits everywhere, needing but the briefest flicker in the light to assert itself." He turns to look directly at me. "And it is always a single breath away."

I am frozen; I am entranced.

"Please, please, my people." My father's voice cuts through the spell of Myrzeth's words, and terror like I have never known hits me when I look at him. Bryn, quiet by his side, rests his hand on my father's shoulder. "This is nothing more than a counterfeit power. Stand against them while you are still able," Father says, voice cracking.

The plea is suspended above the clearing like a hand offered to a drowning soul. Will the valefolk reach up and take hold?

The kaligorven growl, and Myrzeth observes the scene with a barely discernible narrowing of the eyes.

"We choose the kaligorven." The young woman I've noticed shadowing Myrzeth before steps out of the crowd and raises her chin high. "We choose the side of strength."

No one contradicts her, and my mind screams one terrible thought: *My father is going to die.*

A sudden gale rushes up the channels the kaligorven have cut through the valefolk, sending my hair into my face and blinding me momentarily. When I push it away, I find the platform encircled by the obsidian beings, hunched on all fours, legs ready to spring. And Bryn and my father are right in the middle of them.

My feet move of their own accord.

I am not strong like my mother, bending everything into order around her to maintain a sense of control, a sense of self. I am impulsive, reckless even, driven by the fear that I am one step, one tiny, altering step, away from losing everything.

"Myrzeth." I gasp, breathless, stumbling on legs that can't bear my weight. I fall to my knees and grasp the hem of his tunic, searching his face. His eyes pierce my soul like a blade. "Please, spare my father," I whisper.

He regards me, face impassive. For a terrible moment, I wonder if I have misread the signals I've received from him in our few interactions, if he really is the tyrant I'm supposed to have no doubt he is. He turns back to the platform, raising his hands in the air.

A swirling vortex of ténesomni descends, dancing above the Foremost's hands. Blue appears beyond where the shadows have been siphoned from the sky. Flicking his fingers, he sends the black geyser careening toward the platform the moment before the kaligorven spring. It collides with my father's chest, throwing him over the beasts' horned heads and out of their path, then disperses back beyond Myrzeth's domed ceiling once more.

I scream, pressing a fist to my mouth to stifle the sound. My teeth draw blood from my knuckles. I asked for my father's life, but did I think of Bryn's?

As I lurch forward, Myrzeth's hands clasp around my forearms, preventing me from throwing myself in to fix my terrible, terrible mistake. A dizzying tempest of sola light and shadow consumes the platform, and all I can do is watch. Nothing about what I'm seeing makes sense. Horrific, ear-bursting shrieks erupt from the center of the writhing mass. The sounds are wicked, guttural; they cannot be from the sola. No, I know that it does not, will not, fight back. As the Shrouded tear it apart, it doesn't utter a sound.

Golden, blinding blood spills over the sides of the platform, and even the people who chose this cannot bear to look. Some cower, some cover their faces. Others turn and flee.

Myrzeth releases his hold on me. I fall to the side and vomit.

"By the blood of the Light Creature, you will be made into a mighty people," Myrzeth cries, his voice tinged with insanity, "and soon you will see the rest of Atsun kneel in submission." He laughs, long and loud, sending chills down my spine. "You may cower in fear now, but let it be temporary. What you have started can no longer be stopped. What you have chosen, you can no longer deny."

I drag myself through the river of the sola's lifeblood to where my father lies on the ground, pressing a hand to a wound above his left eye.

"Pada, please. We need to go now."

He blinks and groans as he sits up, eyes wide. "No. *No,*" he wheezes. "*Bryn.*"

"He's gone, Pada," I say, but it's more like a yelp. "He's gone and you will be, too, if we don't leave."

My father shakes his head, but I don't care what he thinks. Getting to my feet, I haul him by his upper arm into the crowd, no longer concerned about drawing attention. I'm not quick enough, though, to avoid catching a glimpse of Elodie's fair, terrified face as she breaks into the clear space and buckles to her knees.

I pull harder on my father's arm, expecting him to resist, but he falls in step behind me, like someone half asleep. When we escape the clearing and find the street that will take us to Amyrah's cottage, I still can't bear to slow my steps. I do not want to think about how my hasty appeal to the enemy has still left a gaping hole in the world.

I needed the light to defeat my darkness today.

But the darkness won.

46
BELWYN

CHAOS PRESSES IN, but it is no match for the feral thing that rages within my chest.

What am I doing?

My boots pound the packed earth and I crash my shoulders against the frothing mass of people, throwing them out of the way with ease. Behind me, the lifeblood of a sola drains between the clawed feet of the kaligorven, illuminating the valefolk's faces.

I'm running away like the *heshïn* coward I will always be. I'd ask myself why, but I know the answer. Nothing could be strong enough to counter Myrzeth's wickedness.

Maybe Amyrah was right to be afraid of what she could become.

"Belwyn, where are you going?"

I halt reluctantly. There are very few things that could convince me to stick around this bloodbath, but my brother's voice is one of them. I spin to face him. "Mind your own ignati, Korvin," I spit, grimacing when his eyes widen. "No one needs me here," I say with forced gentleness.

His lips grow taut. "That girl you sent me with—Elodie. I think her father may be hurt."

That gets my attention, and I approach him. His fair head appears like it's rimmed with gold in the glow of the sola's blood. He glances back toward the horrific scene. I don't blame him for being concerned, but she's a stranger. She can't mean anything to him yet, can she?

Then again, it only took one moment with Amyrah for her to become my whole world.

I grab his forearm to get him to look back at me. "That's more of a reason for us to leave. *Both* of us," I say, hoping he will abandon this misplaced bravery and heed me. "We aren't safe. I can't . . . I can't keep you safe here."

He only frowns.

Unwilling to entertain any argument from him, I put a firm hand behind his shoulder to encourage him along, but he shrinks away from my touch.

"This isn't about Rhun. And it isn't about me, either. I can't leave her. It would be wrong," he says, the last word cracking.

I straighten and stare at him. Did I know his voice was beginning to change? I swallow and move closer, lowering my tone. "Do you see what's going on back there?"

The Shrouded's cackles and screeches fill the air. Korvin winces but says nothing.

"*That* is not something we can hope to defeat. *That* is an evil that wants to consume the entire world. And *that* is not our responsibility."

Korvin shakes his head adamantly.

Ignoring him, I pull his arm and turn back toward the city.

But his quiet voice roots my heels to the ground. "The most important place to stand against evil is at home."

It's like burning coals have been poured over my head.

"You taught me that," he says.

His arm falls from my grip and my lungs deflate. I rub a hand over my face, refusing to look at my brother. "There comes a point when you have to accept that some evils can't be defeated," I mumble, hating myself for saying such a thing. For believing it.

"I think that's only true when the people that were supposed to do it have given up."

Jaw clenching, I turn back to ask my brother what made him so wise, but he's already disappeared into the crowd.

Fine. Let him learn his lessons firsthand, like I did. I try to push him out of my mind and stalk toward the city. Each step becomes more difficult to take, and when I get to Utsanek's North Gate and find my father slumped against it, the driving tempest of fear and anger dissipates.

"Quite the show the Foremost is putting on," my father says, bobbing his chin toward the ruckus.

I swallow, throat tight.

"A better man than me would put a stop to this." My father's words fade into a distracted lull, and he seems to shrink in stature right before me. He blinks. As if in denial of his own show of weakness, he scowls and turns his gaze on me. "But there are no better men to be found in all of Atsun."

My anger flares, quick and hot. "What do you want of me, Father?" I step into his personal space, letting him see how we now stand eye-to-eye. "Why must you always cut me down?"

He regards me with equal contempt. "If you had ever shown one scrap of manhood, it wouldn't be so easy."

I bark out an incredulous laugh. The single thread of respect I held for him snaps, and my lungs burn with my hatred. "Do you expect me to take that from someone like you?" My temper is explosive and I can feel it transforming my face.

Father takes a faltering step backward, and there is something new in his expression, something I have never seen before. Fear.

It shakes me to my core.

Trembling, I hold my breath and fight the intoxicating desire to unleash years of retribution for his abuse.

You would be the same as him, were it not for the grace of Elyōn.

The thought that whispers through my mind employs my voice, yet it is not mine at all.

My rage dies. I raise my eyes again, looking to the far end of the Reckoning Grounds where the platform swims in terrible light.

There is a much more deserving target for my anger.

I put my hand to the hilt of the sword that once belonged to my father. "I will be a better man," I whisper, my words filled with confidence in someone beyond me. Someone much, much better.

Stooping forward, I lose myself once again within the folds of the denizens of the Vale.

"Myrzeth."

My voice belongs to a stranger. Deep, assured, commanding. The voice of a man.

The Foremost loiters in the middle of the sola-blood-soaked

platform, his book held open in front of him. Ill words fall from his lips. I suppress a shudder when I see the kaligorven waiting behind the platform, their mouths dripping with glowing, blood-stained saliva. My heart falters. They seem larger than before, as if consuming the life of a sola has fed into their physical presence.

Is that how Myrzeth extended the ténesomni's reach? By feeding his hungry dogs?

Sobbing rises over the whispers of the valefolk and Myrzeth's mutterings, and I glance to the side. Korvin kneels before a mounded tangle of cloth, flesh, and blood, the young girl who was with Wehna wrapped in his arms. Another woman stands by, racked with violent sobs and hiding her face in an elderly woman's shoulder. The older woman is Orlagh, I realize, but I do not recognize the other. I suck in a sharp breath and avert my gaze, my insides twisting with remorse for dismissing Korvin's concerns.

Myrzeth's mouth twitches, but he doesn't look up. I draw my sword slowly from its sheath, earning gasps from the people closest to me.

"You have chosen a foolish moment to challenge me, Belwyn Kovah," he says calmly, eyes not straying from his book.

My grip constricts around the sword's pommel. "Foremost, I invoke the rights of Privotus Vimorteth."

That is enough to clear his face of that smug smile. His eyes raise to mine, narrowing as he slowly closes the book.

"Interesting," he says, coming to the edge of the platform and hopping down. He crosses the ground until he's an arm's length away. "And what makes you think I will abide by this archaic practice?"

The sobbing of Elodie and the woman I assume to be her mother quiets. My courage falters the slightest amount, but I stand firm and motion over my shoulder with my chin. "Because although you may have succeeded in swaying these people with your cheap tricks, there is one thing they will always gravitate to time and time again."

Myrzeth's face grows stormy. "Oh really? And what is that?"

"Tradition."

Myrzeth laughs, sharp and abrupt, and pushes around me. He lifts a hand to the silent valefolk. "And what do you say to that?"

Please, Elyōn. May they be what I hope they are, I think, turning and glancing from face to face. To their eternal credit, not a single person protests my challenge.

"We would have tradition observed," an older man at the front of the crowd says firmly, and a chorus of agreement rises from multiple others.

"Well, then." Myrzeth faces me and tucks his book under an arm. "If you indeed are prepared to manage all of *this*," he says, gesturing to the valefolk, to the half circle of rumbling kaligorven behind the platform, "then what is preventing us from proceeding with the battle for Foremost this very moment?"

I was prepared for this, and for the first time in my life I am grateful for the years of tutelage my father subjected me and my brothers to as sons of the Foremost. "The custom of the ritual states that I have seven days to prepare myself." Hoping no one can see how my hands shake, I sheathe my sword, taking my time and rolling my shoulders back nonchalantly. When my eyes find Myrzeth's face again, it gives me enormous satisfaction to see his calm façade has faltered. "If we are going to observe the rules of the challenge ceremony, then we are going to observe *all* of them."

When I nod at Myrzeth and face the crowd, they have already cleared a path for me to pass through. Most of the people's faces are wary, uncertain, but a few shine with pride, and it may be the first time I have ever seen that feeling directed toward me.

"K-Korvin," I say, my voice cracking with emotion.

My brother whispers something to Elodie and gets to his feet, crossing the open ground to stand at my side.

"We're going home."

No one—not Myrzeth, not the kaligorven—attempts to stop us from leaving the Reckoning Grounds, and my mind cries to Elyōn with an endless flow of wonder and praise.

I don't know what flows through my veins, but at this moment, I'm confident it isn't ténesomni.

47
AMYRAH

"HOLDEN, *STOP*." I make a grab for his wrist and sink all my weight into it.

He spins around, his forehead crinkled and eyes opened wide. "What? What, Amyrah? What is it you want?" The palace's glossy walls amplify his exasperated voice, and the fierce *clip* of Yara's boots fades as she proceeds down the hallway ahead of us.

Surprised by his unhinged response, I draw away from him.

"My father is dying, Luvesta might soon be under attack, and the brother I was sent to bring home is terrorizing the whole of Atsun." He grabs handfuls of his hair, making it stand tall at the roots. "What could be more important than any of that?"

"Nothing." I bite my lip, tears pricking the corners of my eyes. "Nothing is more important."

He lets out a long exhale, grimacing. "I'm sorry. I'm so sorry you're caught up in all of this." He attempts a laugh, but it's shaky. "What a fantastic family reunion we've had," he says, tugging me into an embrace.

I wait until the drum of his heart matches my own, until I am confident I have gained control of my emotions, before pulling away.

"It's fine," I mutter, then laugh dismissively. "I'm used to it by now."

"No, it's not fine. You deserve more than this dysfunction. You're as much a part of all this as any of us, and it's unfair of me to treat your concerns as nothing." He attempts a thin smile. "Please. What did you want to tell me?"

"The other book your father—" I blush, then quickly amend, "—*Grandfather* mentioned . . ."

"Yes?"

"I need to see it for myself."

Holden tilts his head. "Why would you need to do that?"

"I have this feeling . . ." I shake my head. "I don't want to say anything until I know for sure, but can you take me there?"

"My prince, you are needed at the gate. Now."

Both of us turn to find Yara standing several feet away, her stony brow etched with more ridges than normal. She flashes me a scathing glance. My skin crawls. There is something *off* about her, but I don't know what it is. Perhaps she is fiercely loyal to the throne and believes she's serving it by being so ruthless.

I can't blame her for being distrustful of me when I can't trust myself.

Holden looks between her and me, taking silent note of the tension between us. "I understand, Yara, but it would be worth our while to listen to Amyrah."

Yara makes a skeptical noise in the back of her throat, but Holden lifts a hand.

"I'm certain we have a bit of time before the kaligorven manage to scale Luvesta's walls," he says dryly. "Escort us to the vault."

She glowers at me, the muscles along her jaw flexing. Her reply tears reluctantly from her flat lips. "Yes, sire."

Jerking her chin to indicate we should follow, Yara leads us through a series of side halls and several flights of stairs. Down every passageway, the white walls glow with uncanny luminescence, broken only by the wooden doors with their copper veins.

We come to a narrow hall with two guards stationed at the far end, clutching long halberds with deadly ax heads. The door to the vault is different from all the others. Bands of a shining silver metal curve across the gleaming wood, fortifying them. They appear impenetrable.

"Give us entry," Yara commands the guards, who stare at her blankly.

"Commander, we are under orders to not open these doors for anyone but—"

"Anyone but the king?" Holden asks loudly, stepping from behind Yara. "Would his son be a suitable substitute?"

The guards' faces blanch. "Our apologies, your Highness. We did not see you."

"Well, get a move on," Holden says, raising his eyebrows.

Hurriedly, they obey, fumbling with the bulky locking mechanism.

The doors' hinges protest with loud screeches, belying how long it's been since this room was opened. I was expecting it to be well-lit like the rest of this city, but there is an unnatural cloaking of shadows within, and the air smells of dust and disuse. Holden and I enter with caution. The space is cavernous and empty, except for a single pedestal in its center with a silken shroud draped over it.

Yara waits outside, making low conversation with the soldiers. I follow Holden to the pedestal and look at the distinctive rectangular shape outlined underneath the delicate fabric.

"Here it is: the book of darkness."

I sip in a shallow breath, relieved that my fears seem to be unfounded. "Not a very imaginative title, is it?"

Holden's mouth tips. "I believe the words inscribed on the cover are *prae daiet, ténesomni*. 'After the day comes the darkness.'" He reaches for the covering, slipping it off with a quick motion.

Dust blooms and we both cough.

Waving my hand to clear the air, I catch my breath and stare at the cover, confusion mounting. "Wha—what is this?"

Holden grabs the tome and holds it up, and my heart sinks. *Felenti's Book of Frightfables* is printed across the cover in bold letters.

"Guards, what is the meaning of this?" Holden says as he flips through the pages of what indeed appears to be a children's book.

They do not answer.

I was right. With a growing sense of dread, I reach to take hold of Holden's arm. "Your brother must have—"

He brushes past me into the hallway. I chase his steps, running into his back when he stops abruptly.

Both guards lie on the floor at his feet in pools of their own glowing blood.

"I had hoped to keep this from you," a voice says from behind us.

We wheel around. Yara leans against the doorframe, a gold-dripping dagger balanced between her fingertips.

Holden's back straightens, his teeth bared in what can only be described as a snarl. "How long have you been serving him?"

"*Him*? Whoever do you mean?" Yara raises an eyebrow and looks at Holden, feigning confusion. "Oh, you mean Myrzeth. Well, it's not really *him* that I serve, is it? It's Érechlys, but I would think that's rather obvious by this point."

"And how long ago did you steal the book for my brother?"

She makes a show of thinking, tracing the flat of her blade. My eyes are drawn to her fingers, which are wrapped in the ténesomni's snaking black cords. "*Hmm*. That must have been several years ago by now, when your mother died, you left, and your father was too distracted by his grief to care what happened within his kingdom."

An impassioned curse slips off Holden's tongue. He takes a step toward her.

"Oh, no, no, no," Yara warns, dropping her dagger and grabbing the halberd that was resting against the wall behind her. She angles the ax head toward the wooden doors, clutching the shaft with both hands and widening her stance. "If you're not careful, you will be responsible for breaking the agreement Elyōn made with the Luvesti in the days of old. What was it? '*If the wood of the Trees of Light should be altered or removed from Luvesta, its light will be withdrawn*.'"

Holden's shoulders drop a fraction.

An oily grin spreads across Yara's lips. "Submit your life to me or witness the strength of your precious city fall."

When Holden doesn't respond quickly enough, Yara takes an incredible swing with the halberd, embedding the ax head into the wooden doors.

The illuminating walls flicker.

"Stop—*stop*!" Holden's voice is raw, breaking, and he raises a hand to Yara. "If I do as you say, you must promise to spare my people, to spare Amyrah and my father."

Yara's forehead folds in thought. "That depends on how well they behave, doesn't it? But you are certainly capable of making it go better for them if you do."

Holden hesitates, and Yara yanks the weapon from the wood and goes in for another swing.

"*No*!" The scream erupts from my lungs as I thrust my palms outward. A living river of luminescence jumps from my hands and crashes into Yara, throwing her against the door with a horrible *snap* and aiding the halberd's path, sinking its sharpened edge deeper into the doors than should have been possible.

The lights of Luvesta go out.

Cries of a city thrown into confusion tumble down the passageways, and the shadows echo with Holden's heavy breaths. "Amyrah," he wheezes. "What have you done?"

I grope around for Holden's hand, hoping he can't feel how mine shakes. "You are *not* giving up your life for the sake of a tyrant. I'm not letting you."

"But I could have spared the Luvesti."

"I don't care what Yara promised. No matter the evil, no matter how strong it is, we can't give in to it, Holden. We just . . . we *can't*." I try to drag him down the hall, but he frees his hand and returns to the vault's doors, crouching next to Yara, searching for a pulse.

I can't bear to look at her.

He returns to me with a grim expression. "But, Amyrah, now Luvesta's light is—is *gone*."

"I don't think she ever intended to let it endure," I say, struggling for breath. "A hatred like that can't abide it. Trust me, I've seen it with the kaligorven. Dark cannot dwell with light." I offer him my hand again, and he takes it.

We move down the halls, leaving that horrible scene behind, and as the distance from it grows, so does the light around me. It's *my* light, I realize. The light that has been overshadowed for so long by my fear.

Even with Holden's grip growing firmer, I can still feel my hand trembling. He doesn't fight me, though, and runs by my side through the Palace Luvesta. We stop when we come to the grand entrance hall.

"Wait. Where are you going?" Holden pulls his hand from mine and spins me around by my shoulders. I jerk out of his reach.

"I shouldn't have come here, Holden. It changed nothing. What did I learn about myself except that I am too self-absorbed to stand by the ones I love?"

The sun's rays spill in through the high windows in the hall, but they have an unnatural, dirty quality, as if filtered through a sky choked with smoke. Holden's eyes appear like the color of dried moss.

"You learned more about your mother, didn't you?" he asks, one eyebrow raising. "And we both learned what we are to each other. As surprising as it might be, we're family." He stoops lower and looks straight into my face. "That's not nothing, is it?"

I look at the toes of my shoes sticking out from my old rust-colored dress, which, by some miracle, the maids returned to me after it was laundered, and puff out a breath. "No, it's not, but I'm nowhere closer to learning how to manage the Luvesti side of me."

He lifts my chin with a finger. "Aren't you?"

I frown.

"Back there with Yara, what did you default to using—the light, or the darkness?"

My mouth gapes. Instinct had driven me, and it wasn't the shadows that came of it. I look at him, wide-eyed.

Holden grins. "Exactly."

Shouts carry in from outside the doors, and my sense of urgency reawakens. "I can't stay here, though. If I killed Yara—"

"Don't you dare claim that guilt. She needed to be stopped."

"*If* I did," I say, eyes squeezing closed for a breath, "then it's going to be more difficult for you to explain why I should stay, especially since it was my blow which ensured the lights would go out. No matter how you defend me, I'm going to draw suspicion until the truth of Yara's betrayal is acknowledged, and that is not what you or your father need right now."

Holden's eyes narrow like he wants to contradict me, but I know he can see the truth in my words. He paces a few steps, then gives his head a vicious shake and faces me again. "But what if you're needed here, Amyrah? I could use you against the ténesomni, if indeed it's going to try to consume us too."

I smooth my palms down the front of my dress, the soft fibers under my skin bringing a small measure of calm. "There's a whole city full of Luvesti here, Holden. I'm sure you will be able to inspire them to fight it, just as you inspired me. But out there, in a land swimming with ténesomni?" I attempt a weak smile, which makes Holden's frown deepen. "That's something I *do* understand."

If Myrzeth's shadows have reached us all the way here, I shudder to think what it's like there. *Is Belwyn alright*? I squash down the possibility that he's the only reason I want to go back. I broke his heart. How do I know he'll want me?

I hug my arms across my ribs as his words come to mind. *Maybe you didn't mean to wake me up, but you did anyway. You showed me what I was missing. There's a reason you were supposed to be that for the Vale.*

No, I can't only think of him. I must think of the valefolk—*equally my people*—whom I left because I couldn't fathom facing their darkness again.

Holden rests a hand on my arm. "I don't know why you're the epicenter in all of this, but you are not the only one to struggle with who you are," he says, his voice lowering.

My eyes flick to his, and I catch a glimpse of the turmoil he has kept so expertly bottled away.

I shake my head. "I don't belong with people who have never tasted ténesomni. I need to stop being afraid of all the ways I can fail and go where I am most needed."

And where there's no longer any light to steal.

"Amyrah, *no.* My brother, he—" A sound like a growl escapes Holden, and he fists a hand and thumps it against the stone wall. "What makes him dangerous isn't his power; it's that he doesn't care for anyone but himself. Not even a mother who adored him." His head droops. "Can you imagine watching someone you love sink further and further away while being helpless to stop it?"

"Yes," I say, although it is hardly more than a breath. "I can." Holden glances at me, surprise raising his brows. My admission hangs between us, catching the threads of our shared sufferings and weaving them together.

"I'm so sorry, Amyrah. I didn't realize."

My nod is too quick. "It's alright. I don't find it easy to talk about what happened with my father when we lost Mother." I suck in a breath, knowing I can't give grief a chance to muddle everything up right now. "Don't you see? This is *why* I need to go back. Myrzeth needs to be stopped."

He passes a hand over his cheeks, like he's wiping away tears. "The thing is, I would go with you in a heartbeat if it meant I could save him. Not because he deserves it or anything, but because it would ease my father's mind." His expression hardens. "But Myrzeth is beyond redeeming."

I would have said the same of my father, with his many ups and downs. And yet the light found him when I least expected it. "Don't give up hope, Holden. I-I've seen Elyōn do some impossible things."

Holden regards me for a few breaths, then exhales slowly.

"You're right," he says, straightening. "I shouldn't let the ténesomni possess my mind as well as my city." He raises his eyes to the buildings that run ever up and up to the top of the mountain. "What's happening here has been brewing for a long time. And if someone as strong as Yara was swayed by Myrzeth, there's no telling how many others there may be."

I snatch my blackened lock of hair and run its soft ends between my fingers. Perhaps Jaki has met Myrzeth as well. Could my uncle's reach really be so broad?

Holden chuckles humorlessly. "Your arrival caused quite a stir, didn't it? It's no wonder Yara was so eager to have you thrown out."

Though everything is horrible, I force a fragile smile that shatters when I contemplate what lies ahead.

"Will you come with me?" I ask, and it's a stupid, impossible, selfish request.

"How can I?" Holden rubs both hands behind his neck. "My father isn't well, and Luvesta is going to need someone who is a bit more accustomed to navigating the shadows around here." He gazes down the once-bright halls. "They are already in a panic as it is. No, I need to sort through who has been tainted, like Yara, rally the Guard to meet the ténesomni, and defend Luvesta."

It's the right response, but I can't help the feeling of disappointment it dredges up. *Stop depending so much on other people to help you deal with your trials,* I tell myself.

Growing up motherless, I still always had Orlagh. When my father died and it was no longer safe to stay in the Vale, I had Belwyn. And when I became one part the warrior Atsun needs and one part the thing that's consuming it, there was Holden, promising me protection and a place I could find answers.

No, it's time I figure out who Elyōn meant me to be without falling back on someone else when things get difficult.

It's time I go home.

I turn away from Holden, pushing one of the palace doors open and starting to leave. "I'm sorry. That was unfair of me to ask that of you."

He stops the door. "And that means what, exactly? That you need to punish yourself by setting off on foot, with no provisions, nothing?"

I slide my hands up and down the dull, wooden door. It's cold. "I've already asked too much. And . . ." I look out through the gap and see the billows of ténesomni in the distance. "I don't think there's any time to waste."

I should have known Holden wouldn't let me run off without making sure I'd been cared for. Leaving the palace kitchens, I swing the heavy satchel over my shoulder and whisper a quick prayer of thanks to Elyōn for providing what I will need for the long journey back to Utsanek.

It's a much different experience going from the palace to the Southern Gate. The roads are all downhill and I don't feel like my lungs are filled with shards of hot glass. My presence drew attention the first time I came through with Oriole, but now there are much more pressing things on people's minds than a single stranger. The smooth walls and cobbled paths are ordinary and dull, devoid of their illumination. I witness a few people simply standing and staring at them with tear-streaked faces. Even though the Luvesti must still possess the ability to cast their own light, this loss has been a devastating blow, like going from the luxurious warmth of a bonfire to a single, flickering wick. I try to tell myself that this was Yara's goal, not mine. That I'm not the one at fault for robbing yet another city of luminescence.

Holden waits for me at the stables within the city gate. I gape when I see which horse he's selected for me to ride. "No, Holden. You can't give me Zenith."

"I absolutely can and I will." He passes a hand over the stallion's gray neck, his smile a little sad. "He's been a good companion for me, but this is my place for now. There are a dozen other horses I can ride, but only Zenith knows you." Holden checks the saddle strings fastened around the bundle of my cloak and bedroll.

"Well, then, thank you." I walk toward the horse, uneasy. "But if something happens to him—"

"I'm more concerned about something happening to you. Zenith is sure-footed and intuitive. He's used to the ténesomni, and he'll bear you to safety if you should lose your way." Blinking, Holden stares hard at me. "No, I'm not going to let you change my mind."

I chew my lip. "But will he let me ride him without you?"

Holden's expression softens. "I think so. He's intelligent, and he'll be able to compensate for your limited experience as a rider."

"More like no experience at all." My stomach swirls thinking about controlling such a large animal. On our long journey together, Holden gave me a few brief lessons on horsemanship, but there was never an occasion for me to command the horse without him present.

"You're familiar with the basics, and Zenith will take care of the rest."

I purse my lips, trying not to think about how my ineptitude with something as simple as riding a horse does not bode well for facing an entire forest that could be filled with enraged kaligorven, but I manage to mumble my gratitude.

Holden flashes me a grin. "You're welcome, niece."

"*Don't* call me that." I swat his arm and begin to mount Zenith.

Holden steps forward like he wants to help me up, but he seems to think better of it and stays back.

It's strange how much my confidence grows by this simple acknowledgment of my competence. I hike up my dress and swing my leg over the saddle.

Holden hands me the reins. "One last thing."

I turn, trying to ignore the pang I feel at the thought of riding away from the only family I have left in the world. "What is it?"

Looking down, Holden rummages through a sling bag at his side and unearths a fabric-wrapped parcel. He offers it to me. "I know my father wanted to keep this here, but you will have a greater need of it. If you're going after Myrzeth's book, it makes sense to have its opposite."

I unwrap it. Golden words swirl across burgundy leather, blurring together as tears gather in my eyes. "After darkness, light," I whisper.

Holden nods, a fondness on his face. "My sister would want you to have that." He takes hold of Zenith's bridle and runs a hand up and down the bridge of the horse's long nose.

Sorrow clutches at my throat. I wish this world was different, that I didn't have to choose between my heritage and my heart. I wish it wasn't so difficult to discern between true light and all that would consume it. I wish I could sit at my grandfather's bedside and ask all the things I have wanted to know about my mother before it's too late.

But there is no time.

With an order from Holden to the guards, the enormous doors of the South Gate swing outward. Holden lets his hand fall from Zenith's bridle and stands watch as I exit Luvesta.

"May the Highest hold you," he says, pressing a fist to his heart.

Painfully, I drag my eyes away from him and inhale, echoing his prayer as my eyes take in the wall of shadow looming above the vast Astellum Plain.

48

SEYLA

BLACK DOESN'T BEGIN TO DESCRIBE this night, but the expanding reach of ténesomni is the last of my concerns. If Dekar's statements can be trusted, then Téron does not have long in Tarriv. Or perhaps even this life.

I don't waste time trying to convince the úramech stationed by the stronghold gate to let me in. News of my dismissal has undoubtedly traveled through the ranks, and although I have a knack for talking my way out of tricky situations—especially with a blade in hand—I am not confident the tactic will work any longer. But that does not dampen my determination. A wild, unhinged confidence fills me in a way I have never experienced before. Twenty-three years working toward a goal, and now I am throwing it away.

I have never felt so free.

Crouching behind a crumbling stone barricade, I bring down my heart rate with three intentional breaths. I can't afford to make any hasty mistakes. I observe the movements of the guards, then sprint to the wall when there is a small break in the patrol. It is to my advantage that the palisade was built to keep the soldiers and prisoners in rather than people out. I jump and grab the beams that run perpendicular to the wall's vertical poles, hoisting myself up noiselessly. Repeating the motion, I climb to the top and straddle the wall between the sharpened spikes.

Only two shapes are visible in the courtyard, one checking in with the guards on the other side of the gate, and the other leaning against the main building. The latter looks to be occupied with lighting a long, curving pipe. Judging by the position of the moon, this is the last shift before dawn—a perfect time to take advantage of the weariness before the change of the guards. With another quick glance to ensure the way is clear, I drop to the ground. The tails of my long braids jerk, flicking me in the face.

The prisoner cells are housed within the main Agmen barracks. I see no one stationed by the main entrance, but that tells me nothing. What lies beyond is completely out of my sight, and I'm going to have to take my chances.

I steal along the walls of the barracks, pushing open one of the doors wide enough to slip through. The hall is dimly lit within, and I distinguish no movement in the shadows. To the left of the main hall, the general's quarters sit closed and quiet, and beyond that lie the cell blocks. I slip past as quickly as I can, hoping no one chose to work through the night. I won't stick around long enough to find out.

The only unknown I care about is which úramech has been left to monitor the cells, and if I can think fast enough to get past him or her. Holding my breath, I grip my khukuri's hilt, drawing it part way out of the sheath, and round the corner into the narrow cell block passage.

A rounded silhouette paces away from me toward the end of the row, and my heart lurches to my throat.

Must I harm a fellow úramech to attain my goal? Would Téron understand my actions? No, he would only see a hardened daughter of the Southlands.

Before I can decide why that even matters to me, the guard spins around, keys clanging against his hip. His large mouth falls open, eyebrows raising the heavy folds of his forehead.

"Seyla?"

Relief washes over me, and I slide my blade back into its sheath. "Ordin," I pant, erasing the distance between us. "Thank the ancestors. I need your help."

"What in Elyōn's name are you doing here?" he whispers, eyes darting past me.

The cells are mostly empty and from what I can tell, none of them house Téron. I bite back a frustrated growl. "Where is he?"

Ordin's tone drops low. "Foolish woman, forget that man. He's as good as—"

I shoot out a hand and grip Ordin's upper arm, digging my fingers in. His eyes find mine, growing large like crow's eggs. "If you ever cared about my mother, Ordin, then *help me*."

He looks stricken. I have yet to ask him how he knew my mother, or what she meant to him, but I know enough to hope that whatever the relationship was, it still holds power—or better yet, guilt—over him. Ordin holds my gaze for several heartbeats before letting out a heavy exhale. "Aye." He inclines his head. "I can do that."

Turning, he leads me to the very last cell, tucked away to the right. It appears to be empty, but then my eyes fall on a heap of rags pressed into the corner. My chest tightens.

"I can't give you long. Shift is due to change soon," Ordin says, fumbling for the correct key.

"That's fine," I try to say, but it is only a whisper. "I'll take what I can get."

He unlocks the door, swinging it open. Its hinges shriek into the early morning stillness. Cringing, Ordin holds out his lantern for me to take and jerks his chin toward the cell. "Well, get in. Say your goodbyes."

A lump forms in my throat. It's true, then. The Imperii has had his way with Téron, found his information to be wanting, and has sentenced him to execution to rid Tarriv of the waste of resources. Legs weak, I cross the rough stone floor and kneel at his side.

For a moment, I simply stare at his face. Dirt and blood are worked into every line, and the hollows of his cheeks are pronounced. And yet, there is a serenity about him in this moment that I regret disturbing. With shaking fingers, I brush a limp tangle of hair away from his forehead. He reacts to my touch, groaning softly and stirring.

"*Shh*," I hush, slipping my hand beneath his head. "We must stay as quiet as possible."

Téron blinks at me, confusedly, struggling to sit. I help him upright.

"What—what are you doing—here?" he manages to wheeze through fits and starts. He rests back on the stone wall and closes his eyes.

I ball my hands to keep from fussing over him. "You represent a considerable investment. I needed to make sure it was not for nothing."

Téron laughs dryly, opening his eyes and letting them find mine. His lips pull into a grimace. "You should leave, Seyla. I'll only drag you down with me."

"That is for me to decide. You ought to know that I don't take kindly to anyone dictating my fate." I take one of his hands. It's as cold as ice. "And I came to ask you a question."

Téron's brows raise uncertainly, but he waits for me to continue.

"When I first brought you back to my tent, and you were delirious with fever, you said 'forgive me.' I didn't catch most of what came out of your mouth, but that was clear. What did you mean? For what do you need forgiveness?"

He presses his lips into a line, his brows quirking downward in the middle. "Why would you ask me that?"

"I need to know—" The rest of that sentence refuses to find its path to my lips, though it clouds my thoughts.

What kind of man you are.

Téron licks his cracked, bleeding lips, a tremor traveling across his shoulders. He swallows a gasp, wincing as he gives a mere hint of a nod, as if resigned to reliving something he would rather forget.

"I-I didn't allow my daughter to enter my pain for years, and I refused to share the burden of hers. When I finally woke up to the error of my ways, it was too late. She lost her mother before she had a chance to know her, and I . . ." He takes a shaky breath to compose himself. "And now she has no one." His eyes mist over. "I left her alone again, and I have no way of knowing if I did enough to save her."

I hold his hand tighter, bringing his battered fingers to my lips. "But you tried. That's what's important. You didn't abandon her or pretend you hadn't done anything wrong."

"No, but what good did it do in the end?"

A smile possesses my mouth. *Yes*, I think. *He is exactly who I need him to be*. "To have someone who loves you well enough to bear their own failings without excuse, pretense, or justification?" My voice catches and I take a moment to steady it. "Believe me, Téron, it is the rarest, most powerful force for good in the world."

From outside the cell block comes the jingling of keys and an angry voice. I hurry to my feet and glance down the passage. I see Ordin's large silhouette approaching, followed by another. The hairs on my neck stand on end. Spinning, I return to Téron's side.

"You have to trust me," I hiss, not daring to take another look to assess how much time we have. I draw my khukuri and find one of my thinner braids, tracing it back to its roots behind my ear. With a careful motion, I cut it off.

"Do you trust me?" I ask again, this time searching his eyes.

Téron gives a slow blink. "What?"

"I said, *do you trust me*? Please, you must."

His eyes narrow, but he dips his chin. "Wholeheartedly."

I motion at him, palm facing the ceiling. "Give me your hand."

Not breaking eye contact, he holds it out. With a quick movement, I slide my blade across my own palm, then his. He hisses but does not withdraw his hand. I press our wounds together. Holding the loose ends so it can't unravel, I wrap the braid twice, three times around our pressed palms. "Repeat after me: A life unbound I now forsake for these bonds which would weave my soul with another."

Téron's lower jaw falls, his face paling in the lantern glow. "Seyla, no."

The noise down the hall increases. I grip his hand tighter in mine and lean in close. "Yes. It's the only way. Please." I lift a shaking hand and rest it against his cheek. "Say it."

Some intense, inner turmoil crosses his features, and I know what I am requiring of him costs more than anything he's ever been asked to give before. But he relents, his chest deflating, and I lead him in the words that will forever alter the course of our lives.

"By this vow which none shall break, I take you, as you take me."

When he repeats the final words in a husky whisper, my tears fall unexpectedly between us, splashing onto our bound hands like rain, carrying our blood away in a reddened stream. I am afraid to look at him, to see his resentment for forcing him into such a reckless action.

But he runs a finger slowly down my wrist, and I swallow a gasp.

"Seyla Bréinth, you are on disciplinary leave, are you not?" General Entva's booming voice sends splinters down my spine, chasing away the heat that had gripped me.

"Yes," I answer, my voice shaky, refusing to turn around. Worry claims Téron's eyes, and he reaches with his unbound hand to thumb one of my tears from my cheek.

Trust me, I mouth. Plead.

He nods.

"Then what is the meaning of coming here tonight? You are banned from the stronghold. No new information has been gleaned from this man. The Imperii has declared him to be a useless cast off from the Vale. Since he is not of the Southlands, there is no reason to keep him here, draining our resources. He will be executed come sunup."

I hold Téron's hand tighter and angle away from him, revealing the bloody hands wrapped in my own braid. Slowly, determinedly, I lift my eyes to meet General Entva's.

The Tarrivan general is not the kind of man anyone would expect to hold such a high position. He isn't tall, nor is he broad-shouldered. Still, there is something in how he carries himself, in the shrewdness of his gaze that strikes fear into the hearts of all who stand before him. He is the type of man no one in their right mind would consider crossing.

I hold our bound hands higher, our mingled blood dripping between our fingers. "This man is my bonded. According to our custom, he is a member of the Southlands now, is he not?"

The general's eyes narrow, but his face does not reveal his surprise.

Ordin's makes up for it.

"What have you gone and done now, you stupid—"

General Entva holds up a finger. His graying brows loom over his eyes, and he looks around me to question Téron. "Is this true? Have you taken the vow?"

My heart thumps painfully in my chest. Téron could deny the ceremony's validity right now, and that would be it. He could take the fall and there would be no way I could rescue him.

I hold my breath. If he denies it, I will kill him.

"Yes," he says, his voice weak. "I have."

I breathe again.

"That puts this in a different light, doesn't it?" General Entva paces across the entrance to the cell, forehead knit with thought. "It can hardly be considered an improvement to your current situation, though, can it?"

"Perhaps not," I say on Téron's behalf, taking a moment to swallow and gain control of my shaky voice. "But he now has ties to the Southlands, and as such, he deserves the right to a proper trial like any other citizen."

The general regards me silently for a while, then exhales. "Seyla Bréinth, you were once one of our most promising female recruits. I had heard the rumors that you had grown soft as of late, but I didn't believe it until I saw it with my own eyes. And now you would throw it all away for the sake of a stranger?"

Perhaps if I had been the recipient of this speech a season ago, it would have hit me with more force. Tarriv's Agmen has been my life for over two decades. I poured everything I had into it, but what was it all for? To patrol a beach? To put men twice my size in their place? The latter is gratifying, yes, but as far as life goals go, rather pointless. At first, I joined to free Tetyan from a life of unspeakable servitude, but when she died, all I had left was myself.

What good is a life alone? Who would care if I live or die?

My gaze falls on Téron. "He is no longer a stranger to me."

The general scrutinizes me, then turns to Ordin. "Lock them both in. If she wants to throw in her lot with this refuse, so be it. We will deal with this mess in the morning."

Not bothering to acknowledge me again, General Entva leaves the cell blocks.

Téron grips my hand tighter, calling for my attention. "Has anyone ever told you how infuriating you are?" he asks.

I laugh dryly. "Only every day. Isn't that right, Ordin?"

My former partner makes no reply as he backs out of the cell and swings the door inward. It clangs shut, and he inserts the key.

"Ordin," I say, waiting for him to acknowledge me. He doesn't. "Why did you tell the general that I was here?"

The man is quiet for a while as he secures the lock, then he raises his eyes to meet mine. "I promised Fehlan I would watch out for you. You've given enough of yourself for this outsider." Ordin looks at me, pleading. "I thought it was time you let him go, Seyla."

Shaking my head, I turn back to Téron. "No, I am done letting people go."

Ordin breathes out heavily. "Yes, I see that now. What good it will do anyone, I have no idea. At least I've done what I can to make you see sense," he mutters as he leaves.

Quiet fills the cell, and I busy myself with unwinding the braid from around our hands. I tear two strips of linen from the edge of my tunic and bind the wounds. His first, then mine. I avoid looking at his eyes, which I can feel are trained on my face. My hands shake as the full implications of what we have done settle on my mind. I am bound to a man the Imperii has indicated he wants dead.

But at least he is no longer alone.

"So what now?" Téron asks, taking his hand from me and tracing the makeshift bandage with a finger.

I undo the clasp of my belt, surprised when I realize that they left me my khukuri. Maybe General Entva is hoping I'll regret my decision and take out Téron for him. Or perhaps he thinks the shame of my new circumstance will be enough for me to wish to end my own life. Bending, I lay it along the outer cell wall. "We await a proper trial. The Southlands may be brutal, but they are also fiercely loyal. That dedication is what has made us strong as a people living under the shadow of the Vale. I know you may not have confidence in our version of justice, but I hold hope that it still exists, even here." I settle next to him and lean my head against the wall. "We will have to take it one moment, one new morning at a time."

"Thank you," he says quietly after a while. "I have never had someone stand by me like you have done."

"Do not thank me." I allow myself a mirthless laugh. "As much as I hate to admit it, Ordin was right. It would have been better for you if we had left you to the wiles of Loch Skythe."

"Perhaps." Téron raises a wry eyebrow at me. "That might also have been easier for you, but one thing I wish I would have learned much sooner is that dwelling on what might have been will only leave a person entrenched in the past, unable to move forward. Nothing good can come of that. I wasted thirteen years with my daughter that way, and I don't intend to repeat that mistake."

I think of Tetyan's resigned face as the seer handed my mother a bag of arlum. I recall all the days where I broke my body to earn my place in the Agmen, though my sister was long gone and my mother might as well have been dead. Climbing ranks may have felt like a way to move forward from all the failures and disappointments in my life, but Téron is right. I have been allowing myself to be entrapped exactly where I was for twenty-three years.

It is time to start moving forward.

I take his hand again. "With this action, we have forged something new. And tomorrow, when the sun rises, we can face the day *together*."

Nothing else is said between us as the early morning slips away and the sounds of life begin to fill the stronghold, but whatever promising new dawn I was anticipating doesn't arrive.

Because the sun never comes up.

PART THREE

believe

You.
You I have chosen,
Not because of who you are
But because of who I am.
I sent the blood to course through your veins;
I formed every facet of your being;
I know who you will become.
But it is your heart that I have called,
Your heart that I love.
Do you hear me, child?
Do you trust that I knew my mind
When I sunk the flame of my mark
Deep within your being?
Your heritage declares your outer inclusion,
But my love declares your soul.
If you hear my voice, then come.
Come, come.
I will give you true light.

49
WEHNA

I SHOULD TELL THEM WHAT I'VE DONE.

"Wehna, you're hurting me."

The comb slips from my hands, falling to the floor with a dull *thud*. I hold my trembling fingers in front of my face, stretching them out, then curling them in.

"I'm sorry, Arvo."

My brother places his hands protectively over his scalp and frowns up at me. "I want Mada to do it," he says, and it shouldn't cut me like it does. It's a simple task, detangling his hair. It's been my responsibility since our parents disappeared from our lives, but now they are back.

"Fine. No problem. Have it your way." I wave my hands and storm to my bed on the other side of the room, dropping myself onto the mattress. "You always do."

My mother's brows slash downward, and I brace myself for the reprimand. Technically I did nothing wrong, but sometimes it's like she can read my heart's attitude like a book.

Like she can probably read my guilt right now.

The cottage door creaks open, letting in a rush of night air and sparing me from further scrutiny.

"Arlyn." My mother turns to him, breathless with surprise. "You're back so soon."

Father enters the cottage without a word, dragging a chair close to the fire and falling into it. He covers his eyes with tight fists.

Mother retrieves the comb from under Arvo's swinging feet and sets it on the table. "Do you think we can take care of your hair tomorrow?"

My brother's eyes jump between me, my mother, and my father. "Yep, but I changed my mind. I want you to do it, Wehna."

I shut my eyes, feeling the walls shiver around my heart. If he didn't love me so much, it would hurt less to hurt him. But any semblance of penitence seems like too much for my fragile mental state. Afraid of muddling up everything worse than it already is, I pretend I don't hear, slip beneath the woolen coverlet, and turn to face the wall.

The cottage snaps with tension.

I hear my mother's soft footsteps crossing the wooden planks, the scrape of a chair across the floor. The creak of the wood as she sits. "Was it as you feared?"

A long pause chokes the room. "Yes." My father's answer is muffled, like his lips don't want to let it exist in this world. "Bryn is dead."

They can never know what I've done.

I shed silent tears until I fall asleep.

50
AMYRAH

BURNING ARTERIES CRACKLE AND FLASH within the thundercloud ahead. I urge Zenith on, grasping his mane with the reins to keep from being thrown from the saddle. An uncomfortable pressure of urgency to get to the Vale swells within me, molding my fears into a solid, driving force, but the Astellum Plain is bigger than I remember, and the unnatural tempest will only increase in strength the longer I take to reach it.

Why did I assume I could pass through its midst unscathed?

The closer I come, the smaller I feel. It's less of a storm and more the physical embodiment of my fears: Elyōn's light and Érechlys's shadow locked in a terrible battle.

Zenith, heedless of my apprehension, does not slow as foamy sweat coats his neck. Alarmed, I pull on the reins and command him to check his pace. He resists me, even at the brink of exhaustion, but I manage to bring him to a trot. My heart rate comes down with the rhythmic pounding of his hooves.

Reluctantly, I return my focus to the phenomenon.

A line of solas stretches across the plain to the west and the east, forming a golden wall between Luvesta and the ténesomni. It is almost too difficult to make out any sure detail, but I can see smaller bursts of brightness in between the larger ones. Land creatures of all shapes and sizes roam the ground, slowing the black cloud's advance, while winged solas flit, curbing the higher shadows. For the moment, their efforts appear to be working.

Yara was wrong, or maybe she intentionally spun the truth to plant seeds of fear. Now that I'm out here, I know the solas weren't fleeing the woods at all; they were coming to shield Elyōn's light-favored people like a wild, wonderful army of stars.

I wonder if the Luvestans will come and stand with them or if their faith is too shaken by their loss.

"A-Amyrah?"

The sound of my name almost makes me fall off my horse. I rein Zenith to a halt and glance around.

"What are you doing out here?" Oriole stands amid the wildflowers, staring at me with her wide, gray eyes. Her freckles are dark against her pale face. Behind her, the hermitess's cottage hunches in the middle of the open field like a forgotten haystack.

"I'm going back to the Vale. What are *you* doing here?" I slide from Zenith's tall back, pass the reins over his ears, and lead him closer to Oriole.

She closes her gaping mouth, looking at the ground sheepishly. "When Luvesta went dark, it felt like my faith in Elyōn was snuffed out with it. I went to the only place I felt safe."

I raise an eyebrow.

"She's not crazy, like they say she is," Oriole seeks my face again. "She's lived away from the brightness of Luvesta for so long, I knew she wouldn't be as rattled as the rest of the city."

You don't have time for this, I tell myself, my eyes straying back to the gloom-strewn south.

"Is that her?" An abrasive voice spills from the shack's open door, and a small shape appears shortly after.

"Who, Hermitess?" Oriole asks, stepping aside and turning to face the shrunken woman.

"None of those ridiculous titles for me, Finch. You ought to know my name by now."

Oriole leans in close to me and whispers, "She seems to forget that she's never told me what it is."

A scowl crosses the woman's thin lips, but she turns her attention to me. "Aye. Here you are at last. Finally found your way back to me like you promised?"

"I didn't—"

But the hermitess crooks a beckoning finger and disappears inside her dwelling.

"I find it's best not to put her off," Oriole says, the corner of her lips twitching. She snatches Zenith's reins from my hands. "Go on. I'll take care of him."

Sighing, I relent and follow.

A confused aroma of spices, perspiration, and damp thatch overwhelms me when I step inside. I blink, letting my eyes adjust to the odd, shifting glow. Shelves line the circular walls of the room, stacked with so many bottles and books that the wood sags in the middle. I bite back a shriek when little sola creatures with big ears and long tails scurry to the hermitess and dive into the folds of her shabby garments. *Mice!*

"Now, let me see it," the woman croaks, holding out knobby hands.

I frown, not understanding. She huffs out an exhale. "I don't like wasting words, little bird. Hand over that book."

Perplexed as to how she can know about it, I unearth my mother's book from my bag.

The hermitess yanks it out of my hands and flips through it, her eyes scanning the pages hungrily. The book falls open to the section with conspicuous jagged edges crowding the crack.

"What in the sola's shine have you done here, child?"

I open my mouth and squeak out a couple noncommittal syllables.

She slams the tome shut, bopping it on my forehead. "Do tell me you have something inside that skull."

My cheeks warm, but before I can come to my defense, she's turned her back and begun muttering to herself, waving her arms about. A haze of snow-white hair drifts around her head like a cloud caught in a lazy Elberu breeze. Hefting up a stack of old papers and books, she spins and thrusts it into my chest. "Don't root yourself there like an old stump. Help a body out."

I glance out the door, wondering if I should get out now or indulge this person who, I hate to agree with Holden, seems absolutely insane.

"Could'a sworn I made that willowy thing scribble me a copy."

"Are you looking for what was on those pages?" I venture from behind the stack of items that I now struggle to see over. A sparkling sola ladybug creeps across one of the spines. "Because I know it by heart."

"Ah, there be brains." The hermitess bustles around me and motions to an empty section of shelves. "Be a doe and set that there."

When I'm free of my burden, she thrusts her chin toward a lumpy, bed-sized pillow on the floor. "Seat yourself."

Awkwardly, I obey, trying not to care about the other unidentifiable sola critters that scurry away when I do.

Pulling out a three-legged stool, the hermitess perches on it, looking like a fluffed-up grouse that's lived through Vestri a few too many times. She peers at me down her sharp nose with wide, shadowed eyes.

"Are you going to wait until the sun drops into the Vestri Sea? Sing!"

My breathing quickens and my palms begin to sweat. I cast a longing glance out the front door, wishing to the skies that I had kept riding. From this angle, I can see Zenith pawing the ground and Oriole staring toward the south. Twilight has settled on the plain, bathing everything in a warm hue. The blinding line of the solas curves into view, holding back a sea of obsidian night.

That sight is all I need to coax the Shaluth Cantu's sweet promise to find my lips.

"My eyes have seen a glimmering beam
Piercing through doomed bracken's core
And although it has made my heart to hope,
I fear I shall see it no more.

Thus grows the ever dark'ning gloom
From the glen to the ne'er ending moor.
And although Light has filled me with wealth unknown
I fear it has left ye poor."

"That'll be enough," the hermitess says, a sharpness to her words. She holds up a flat palm. I bite my lip, feeling foolish for getting so lost in the melody. The woman climbs down from her stool and shuffles again through her stacks of books and parchment.

"And?"

"And *what*?"

"You sang it. Tell me, what does it mean?"

"Well, it's . . ." My neck grows hot when she turns from the shelves and stares, feathery eyebrows all but consumed by the creases in her forehead. A shimmering mouse peaks at me from a fold of her shawl. "It's about a sola coming into the Vale and—"

"Wrong."

"Ex-excuse me?"

"Why?" Her features scrunch to the middle of her face. "What did you do?"

"No, *you*—" I grit my teeth and take a calming breath. "*You* said I was wrong about the song."

"Well, you were, weren't you?"

"But *how* was I wrong?" My exasperation increases when she clicks her tongue. "How can that song be about anything other than a sola coming into the Vale's darkness?"

"I'll tell you how. It was written by a girl who had never been to the Vale before."

I frown, thinking of my conversation with the king. "My grandmother, you mean?"

The hermitess shakes her head with exaggerated patience. "No, not *her*. Your mother."

It feels like the walls are pressing in around me. I struggle to remember to breathe.

"She must have taught the song to her mother in her dying days. The girl didn't think it was much, but I knew the moment I heard it that it deserved to be added to that book she carried around. Wrote it in myself. Quite the little song wren, wasn't she? And you're not much different, I see."

I have to concentrate to keep my mouth from sagging. "But how could she have known what was going to happen in the Vale?"

"That's the problem with you Luvesti. Navel-gazing to the point of willful ignorance, the lot of you." She dismisses my stricken look with a wave. "That song is about so much more than what it appears. Darkness isn't an affliction reserved for those physically lost in it." Her eyes dip to my arms as if she can see the ténesomni I'm sure is lurking below my skin. "You ought to know that better than most."

Suddenly, I feel so, so tired. I swallow hard and get up from the cushion, shaking. I'm not sure how Oriole could ever find solace in this woman's company.

"This was a waste of time," I say, freezing when I find a battered book wrapped in leather cords held out before my nose. "What's that?"

"Left it with me, the dear lamb, when she took herself into Atsun's heart. Couldn't stop her, so I sent a whole fleet of solas to keep an eye on her until her father put an end to that."

The woman shakes the book until I take it. I unwind the cords, my heart unspooling as the pages are freed. I don't have to ask who 'she' is, because I can read the name written in precise handwriting inside the front cover.

Ellebra Ardaire.

The older woman grunts. "Impetuous, bright girl. Saw beyond the pride of her people and did what no one else had the heart to do."

"To do what?" My fingers cling tightly to the book. I recall Myrzeth's glee when he sought to offer me to the kaligorven. He employed Yara to steal the book of darkness and spread seeds of distrust throughout the Grovesha. My mother couldn't be more different from him. A dry laugh tumbles out. "To chase after a wicked sibling who never deserved the love his family gave him?"

The hermitess gives me a hard look as if to question if that's truly what I believe. I drop my gaze.

"She chose to follow someone into a blackness everyone preferred to ignore, although she knew there was precious little hope," she amends for me.

A tingle passes through my body. *And am I making the same mistake as her*? I hold my breath and gently turn the pages, which are filled with the same handwriting as inside the cover. "What's all this?"

"Wouldn't know, would I, girl? Not about to go reading someone's private journal."

My breath catches. All this time searching for information about my mother, and now I hold more than I could have ever hoped in my hands.

"And you want me to—"

"Keep it, obviously." She crosses her wiry arms and gives her head a disbelieving shake. "Perhaps 'brains' was too generous a word."

My cheeks flush and I turn to the door, slipping the book into my satchel. "I should leave. It was a mistake to stop here."

"No, girl. The mistake was running away."

My blood grows hot. I wheel around to face her. "What do you know about me?" An incredulous laugh pops out. "And *what* am I running away from?"

"From who you are."

All my fight fizzles out with her matter-of-fact reply. "I know who I am. I'm a reminder of pain; a weak vessel; a waste of a gift. And I'm no one special."

"Aye, that could all be true to some degree, depending on who you talk to, but you're also a child of Elyōn. That's beyond negotiation."

Tears sting my eyes and my throat constricts. "What use is that if I can't defeat the wickedness that dwells inside me?"

The old woman lurches forward, grabbing my face between her hands. "Foolish girl. No one can. That's why we leave it to the Highest. What you can do is go where he leads and trust that despite the mess you are, he *can* and *will* work his splendor."

I gulp, and her expression softens. She threads her arm through mine and tugs me outside. I am too stunned to resist.

"The light in you is not *of* you," she says, leading me through her front garden of low bushes and wildflowers. "Quit insulting Elyōn by claiming it as yours and let him do with it what he will. He'll burn that darkness out of you, one shade at a time."

I almost laugh. "And that's it? I'm supposed to accept that I'm this helpless thing and just *wait* on him?"

A rush of wind rolls over the plain, and in an instant the air fills with hundreds upon hundreds of butterflies. They burst with luminescence like they did when Holden and I passed through the first time on horseback. Some land on my arms and in my hair, while the rest flutter around me in a dizzying haze. The shadows crumble before these fragile beacons.

"Elyōn delights in choosing the most unlikely creatures imaginable; there's no human sense or reason that can justify it," the woman says in a reverent whisper. "And if nothing else gets through to you, then these silly, frivolous insects might."

Tears choke me as hope brushes my heart with its golden wingbeats.

I don't know if I'll always win against the shadows inside me, or if I'll survive the journey south, but I might be able to trust in the one who has put his mark on my soul, who chooses such insignificant creatures as these to prove his promise.

"Keep on flying, starling," the hermitess says, approaching Oriole and Zenith and reaching to tweak the cheek of the former. "Fly headlong into the thickest night and don't give two bolétis about the shadows. You might be surprised what Elyōn will enable you to do."

As I follow her to Holden's horse, the flock of sola butterflies settles back into the low foliage. Their glimmer dims, but the hope does not fade from my heart. I rest my hand on Zenith's neck, close my eyes, and whisper a bumbling prayer of gratitude.

Beside me, Oriole gasps, and when my hand heats up and I open my eyes, I do too.

Streams of illumination jump from my fingers, hitting Zenith with sparks and crackles. A shimmering wave passes over his muscular body, like fire engulfing old paper. Within the span of a few breaths, he has been transformed into something brighter than the burning stars above.

And from his burnished back unfolds a resplendent pair of feathered wings.

51
BELWYN

"Hold the sword like you mean it. And straighten that old woman of a spine."

I bite back a retort and comply with my father's demands. He hasn't been this animated in a while, which must be a good sign even if it means bearing some routine humiliation.

"Keep your eyes on me at all times, but also be aware of what's around you." He circles in the tight quarters of the derelict alley behind our house, holding a long stick in his fist. The shadows are thick, but a single lantern set on a windowsill illuminates him well enough. With a lunge, he jabs his stick hard into my ribs. I double over.

"I said, pay attention," he says, his lips curling in an amused sneer.

"I am," I grind out between gasps, retaking a defensive stance.

"Really?" My father draws back, his face plastered with mock surprise. "My mistake." His eyes travel past me, and he gives a slight nod.

Before I have time to interpret what that signal means, pain explodes across my temple and hot blood pours down my face. I press a hand to the unexplained wound, spinning to identify my attacker.

Shemai lowers his slingshot with an impish smile, which dissolves when his gaze clashes with mine.

"Sorry, Bel. I didn't mean to hurt you like that."

"What are you using in that thing? Glass?" I spit.

Shem cowers.

I hold my hand in front of my face. In the diminutive light, the blood looks like Mother's black paint. I hiss out a curse.

"No apologies, Shemai. You're doing your part to prepare him." Father cracks his stick across my hand holding the sword, dropping it from my grip. I abandon all deference and lunge at him.

He sidesteps my enraged advance. Too late, I see the foot held out across my path. My legs are kicked out from beneath me and I sprawl, earning a face full of dirt.

My father's amused laughter hits me like a blow to the gut.

"Get up. Retrieve your weapon."

Embarrassment warms my cheeks, my neck. Breathless, I stoop and take the sword. With a lazy swing, my father bats it from my hands.

"I said retrieve your weapon."

Jaw clenched so hard it could crack, I snatch my sword up again and position myself so Father and Shem are both within my field of vision.

"See that, Shemai? He's learning," Father says.

My patience reaches its tipping point. "Myrzeth's not going to come at me with weapons. He bested you when he challenged you for your position, didn't he? How can you think I will learn anything worth knowing from you?"

I fling the sword onto the ground and pace away, letting out a frustrated shout. When I hear footfalls, my back tenses, anticipating retaliation from my father. But it doesn't come.

"Oh dear. What's all this about?"

It's my mother's voice, and I spin around.

"Men's business, Ketur. Nothing you can be of use with," Father says with a heavy exhale and a dismissive wave.

I glare at him, wondering why he always has to be such a boar, then hurry to Mother. She's carrying a basket with both hands, and it looks like it might be enough to topple her.

"What happened to your head?" she asks, eyes thinning with worry.

"A lesson in awareness." I lift the cloth in the basket to reveal a jar of Korvin's specialty soup and a dozen biscuits smeared with a small amount of enatuberry preserves. My stomach growls with hunger, but she slaps my hand away when I reach for one.

"These are not for you."

I stare at her, bewildered, until Korvin emerges from behind bearing a scraggly bundle of wildflowers in one hand and a lantern in the other.

"Mother and I are going to visit the Perens," he explains, his eyes slipping away from mine when I raise an eyebrow.

"Who?"

"Remember, Belwyn? Elodie. We met her at the Reckoning Grounds on the day that . . ." He chews his lip and clears his throat, obviously still troubled by those events. "She has four sisters, you know. It's been three days since they lost their father. I want to know how she—how *they*—are. And I thought . . . I thought they could use some encouragement."

Korvin's bashful compassion softens my edge. "You know where to find them?"

Smiling wanly at Korvin, Mother covers the biscuits again. "Elodie told Korvin where she lived when they first met. We're going to take a stroll and see if we can find it."

I begin to protest her going out, but she won't hear it. "I'll be fine, Belwyn. I'm feeling better than I have in days. The walk will do me good."

Her eyes linger on my face for a breath, and she gives a sudden sniff, blinking to stymie tears as if she is afraid that once she starts crying, she won't be able to stop. "I want you to know how proud I am of you," she says in a tight voice, first patting my cheek, then squeezing Korvin's shoulder. "You both give me the courage to keep going."

A painful lump lodges in my throat.

Mother straightens and turns toward my father, who skulks at the edge of the alley. "Dravek?" she says softly.

He grunts his acknowledgment, turning slightly as she approaches him with slow steps. Reaching out white fingers, she hesitates before brushing them along his jaw. "Come home to me."

Those words are not meant for my ears, but hearing them splits something wide open inside my chest. It's a longing for pain and dysfunction to end; for our family to be mended. For good to gain the upper hand over wickedness.

My father stands statue still, his flaring nostrils the only evidence that he heard her. In a moment, his hardness melts away, and he leans into her touch, raising a hand to hold her fingers there for a breath longer.

Mother lowers her hand back to the basket, spotting Shem crouched in a doorway. "Why don't you come along?"

He stands, slipping the slingshot into one of his trouser pockets, and runs to catch up with Korvin.

"Sorry for the cut, Bel," he mutters out of the side of his mouth as he passes me.

I watch them all fade into the ténesomni.

"Well? Ready to continue?"

A weariness clings to my limbs. Crossing to where the sword gleams from the ground, I grab it, extending my arm and considering the mirror-like blade. My sad reflection is enough to deflate me.

"You realize I'm not going to become the best warrior overnight, don't you?"

A grunt is his reply.

Grimacing, I cinch my grip tighter on the sword and turn around. When I find him slumped against a wall, head in his hands, however, I lower my arms and approach him.

"Why, Belwyn?"

My steps falter.

"Why did you invoke Privotus Vimorteth?" he asks, dropping his hands. A brokenness dominates his face. "Did you think you needed to prove yourself to me?"

I want to answer, but the words stick in my lungs like a fly in a spider's web.

"Because you don't . . . I never meant . . ." He slams a fist against the stone. "I wanted you to be more than I ever was. My father was hard on me, and I chose to believe it made me strong. I know no other way. But now you, your brother . . ." He clenches his jaw, and when he speaks again, his voice has an undeniable tremble. "I can't stand the thought of another pointless death. I-I can't lose you too."

Stunned, I lean against the wall beside him. "I'm not doing it to prove anything," I say softly. "I know it might upset you to hear it, but I've been freed from that burden. All I care about is doing the right thing, whether it's easy or not."

Father stares morosely at the ground.

"I know there's little chance I'll beat Myrzeth. Trying to do so might even cost me my life, but if there is a hope that this could wake people up to stand against his evil, then I need to take it."

I drag in a quick breath, realizing I know exactly who taught me that. I close my eyes and allow my heart to plead for Amyrah's safety, wherever she is.

"You were right." My father's raw voice breaks the silence.

I angle my head, unsure if I heard him properly. "Right about what?"

"You are stronger than I thought." He raises bleary eyes to mine. "I'm sorry I ever said otherwise." He claps his thick hand behind my neck and awkwardly drags me closer.

I find it hard to breathe as he holds me there for the span of five slow breaths.

His eyes are clouded with moisture when he releases me, but a familiar hardness soon possesses them. "If anyone can send that daemon back to Ikktar, it's you."

52
AMYRAH

THERE IS NO FREEDOM LIKE sitting astride a glorious winged sola and soaring beneath the heavens. When the feeling of Zenith's hooves pounding the ground was exchanged for the incredible lurching power of his wings, blinding fear threatened to drag me back to the earth. But the hermitess told me to fly. Resolved to heed her, I fought the impulse to direct the horse back to the land.

Now, the terror has vanished.

I wish Holden could see Zenith transformed into a breathtaking Light Creature. The horse has been infused with more than light: delicious heat radiates from his body, and intelligence shines in his jeweled eyes. If Holden thought he was special before, what would he think of him now?

Although my touch sparked the change, I know better than to think the transformative power originated in me. It, like my ability, like all good things, was a gift of grace.

The wind whips my hair into impossible tangles as the hidden leagues pass below. I cannot express the delight of feeling the sun's rays warming my skin as it rises during the day, and at night I feel as though I could pluck the stars like ripe enatuberries.

From this height, I can see the extent of the ténesomni's roiling blanket suffocating Atsun. Farther to the southeast, it grows ever darker. Although I have no map to follow and every conceivable landmark has been blotted from view, all I need is to look for the blackest of black shadows to find my way home. The Askonnet Mountains should also be visible at some point in the journey, piercing the kaligorven's shroud and guiding me in.

Whenever I sense that Zenith is growing weary, we glide back to the earth, circling a few times to be sure of what kind of landscape we're dropping into. Each time we pass through the shadows, a reflexive shiver races up my spine. Zenith's illuminating warmth soon chases away the chill, though. Thankfully, we haven't encountered any kaligorven back in their domain, and our rest has been undisturbed. I sleep with Zenith's large wings sheltering me from all the world.

I feel the seventh morning dawn, even though it cannot be seen, and Zenith and I ascend above the layer of ténesomni to find an ominous red sunrise awaiting us. A gnawing urgency blooms in my soul.

I've kept careful watch of the shadows, and they are thicker than ever. *How could it ever get blacker than this*? The Vale must be close. I worry that I have become disoriented, that we have traveled days in the wrong direction. The sobering thought dredges up the familiar fears of my incompetence.

Was I a fool to take this journey alone?

My weary eyes scan the horizon, seeking any change in the endless sable sea. Despair wells within my chest, as tangible as the shadows below. The sun reaches its zenith.

Until *there*. Edging out of the undulating ténesomni, the angular peaks of a mountain range come into view. Relief silences my oppressive thoughts.

I lean forward and hug Zenith's neck. "Well done, friend."

He whinnies and shakes his silken gold mane.

"We'll be there by nightfall."

53
WEHNA

When I was Arvo's age, Mada had me help tend her beautiful hanging gardens. Life was uncomplicated and I was naïve. I didn't grasp the significance of caring for something so fragile, of protecting an unassuming seedling until it had struggled through the hardships and grown to maturity. I delighted in the tiniest bud, in the rocksquash that went from soft green to deepest ocher, never appreciating how miraculous the transformation was.

Pada would harvest the ripe fruits and vegetables in Elberu while we prepared the jars and pots to preserve some of them, clearing cellar shelves to store the rest. I hated the dank, windowless room, but when I was with him, there was never a reason to fear the dark.

Sometimes, though, the gourds would rot even when the circumstances were ideal and every precaution had been taken. The soggy flesh would make me feel sick when I helped Pada clean up the mess. I would ask him why some of the vegetables were fine while others turned to fuzzy mush.

Only Elyōn knows, he'd answer.

I wander down sparse, green rows now, lifting broad leaves and holding up a lantern to search for the ripe fruit that should hang beneath. Utsanek's flat fields north of Loch Skythe are nothing compared to Ketsé's vertical gardens, but this picked-over, deer-ravaged section reserved for the Vale's destitute holds a beauty of its own.

A distant drumming fills the air and my stomach churns. I grit my teeth and ignore it.

"I got a good one," Arvo declares, seemingly unaffected by the foreboding sound.

A lantern bobs over to him as my father goes to inspect the find. Patting Arvo on the back, he slips the diminutive squash into his bag.

We used to have everything we could ever want, and now my family has been reduced to scrounging through people's scraps.

Angry tears threaten, but I swallow down the urge to cry. How can I lose my composure now when my parents and brother seem to be handling everything we've been through without a problem?

I'm beginning to think that I am a fruit that was destined to rot while all others around me flourish.

The night bell rings, and I turn to face Utsanek. My mother's crouched silhouette straightens as she stretches out her back.

"We'll stay out a bit longer," she says, turning to catch my eye. "The valefolk should be occupied for a while yet. There's no need for us to get in the way."

She cuts across the rows to hug my father's side. He wraps his arms around her and bows his head.

Turning my back to them and breathing through waves of guilt, I crouch and lift another leaf. I jump back when I discover a blackened, hollowed-out husk of a rocksquash crawling with maggots underneath.

54
BELWYN

SIX BEATS OF THE DRUMS, six beats of silence.

I take slow breaths as the bell tolls to signify the passing of another day.

My palms are wet, and I drag them across my tunic to wipe away the nervous perspiration. Amyrah's necklace catches between the fabric and my skin, reminding me of its existence. Not caring how odd it will look, I raise my wrist to my mouth and press the little star to my lips.

The pendant is abnormally warm to the touch.

A frown wrinkles my forehead, but my confusion doesn't have the opportunity to take root.

"Has your week of preparations served you well?"

I drop my arm and stare across the clearing to where Myrzeth's eyes scour me, livid.

"It's been what I needed," I say, far too calmly.

I start toward him but pause when I hear my father's voice.

"Son, here."

He steps into the cleared space, holding out my bow and quiver.

I raise an eyebrow. "Father, no. I can't use that with all the valefolk around. I don't want to hurt anyone else."

The lines around my father's mouth deepen. "Take it, Belwyn. Don't be the fool who puts his hope in a single weapon." He says no more, but I can almost hear the rest of his thought.

As I did when Myrzeth challenged me.

Nodding, I take the items, fitting the quiver to my back. I can't imagine a situation where this will be useful, even though archery is something I've always been more partial to, but he may be right. It would be foolish to have no other option.

My gaze moves past him to the stoic form of my mother standing with my brothers at her side. Korvin is as tall as her now, and Shem clings to her midsection. My confidence cracks, seeing them here. How can I put them through this scenario again?

My hands threaten to shake until I tighten them.

"If something should happen to me—"

"Are you being a coward *now*?" my father asks in his usual, gruff manner. I wince. He tips his chin down and makes a great effort to moderate his tone. "I don't mean that. I-I don't. What I should have said was that I am not going to entertain any thought of your failure until I see your lifeless body hit the dirt."

I gape at him, then choke back a bubble of odd laughter.

Father claps me on the back. "You've done Rhun proud, son."

Suddenly sober, I dare to ask, "And what about you?"

His eyes narrow and his lips stretch thin. The tension is unbearable.

"Yes, I am proud too," he finally mumbles.

The admission would be no less painful if it were ripped from his own flesh, but his mouth angles in a subtle grin.

"*Please.*"

Cold laughter sounds from behind us. No part of me desires to turn around and face Myrzeth again, but I do.

"I've never been one for family reunions," he says, flicking something off the page of the book held out before him. "Can we not get this ridiculous challenge out of the way, *hmm*?"

"Certainly. When you're done reading your bedtime story."

Stifled laughter swirls around the Reckoning Grounds, and Myrzeth's leer slides from his lips. He snaps the book shut, then holds it out to the side and gives it an impatient shake. Ketra runs forward to take it from him. I'm reminded of this exact scene at the last Privotus Vimorteth, but instead of planting a passionate kiss on Myrzeth's lips, Ketra cranes her neck and finds me instead.

I'm almost certain she's been crying. I frown, and she quickly looks away and accepts the book before slipping into the crowd.

"Approach the center of the clearing," Myrzeth instructs.

With one last glance at my father, I obey.

"Now, tradition states that the ceremony will be concluded when either one of us forfeits, but my men assure me that this has never been a rule set in stone. Seeing how tenuous these times are, might I suggest a more *permanent* conclusion?"

I shut my eyes for a breath when I hear my mother gasp. My racing thoughts do all they can to incapacitate me. "So you would either kill me or—"

"Or make sure you have blood on your hands, yes." I can hear the wicked grin in Myrzeth's voice.

"Belwyn, *no*," Korvin whispers hoarsely.

If this is what it will take to defend the people I love, so be it. Opening my eyes, I wet my lips and draw my sword. "I accept."

"Excellent. Let the challenge commence."

He flicks his fingers toward me, and I am swallowed in darkness.

"That's cheating!" I hear Shem squeal. "You can see but he ca—" His protest cuts short, like someone has clapped a hand over his mouth.

Myrzeth replies with a cold laugh. I orient myself toward the sound and hold out my blade and try to wave away the shadow.

No good. I experiment with running a few steps to the right and left. The ténesomni seems to follow me wherever I go. A crunching tread draws close, and I swing out my sword, hitting only air. I shiver, realizing that I could have hurt a bystander without knowing it.

"Shem, Korvin," I call, shirring up my grip on the sword. "Show me where my boundaries are."

Within moments, an alarmed shout rings out across the way, then another and another. A grin claims my face. Shem must be shooting stones over the clearing with his slingshot, targeting people at the edge of the crowd. I position myself in the middle of the noise where I know I won't hurt anyone and concentrate on listening for the one sound that matters.

Myrzeth's careful footsteps echo from the right, between me and Utsanek's Northern Gate. I throw myself into a run toward the sound and swing the sword in a wide arc, hoping that if I can't see him, then he can't see me either.

My sword connects with something soft, and the ténesomni clears around me with a hiss. I look around wildly, my eyes finally latching onto Myrzeth. He stands a few paces to my left, holding up his forearm and assessing a long gash across it.

"Clever," he says, raising his eyebrows as if impressed. He shakes out his arm and strolls to the left. I mirror his movements to the right.

Myrzeth's eyes lock on mine. He raises an open hand to the sky, drawing down the living shadows until they rage above his palm.

But this is a tactic I have seen him use before, and when he flings his arm down and forward, I am prepared for it. I lunge to my left, tucking and rolling out of the path of the obsidian battering ram.

Screams erupt from the valefolk standing closest to where I was, and my blood runs cold. I may have avoided the blow, but Myrzeth still made me feel it.

Determination renewed, I grope around on the ground for my sword, but it's nowhere. I risk looking away from the Foremost, and discouragement rears its ever-present head when I spot the blade laying on the other side of my opponent.

A wide, toothy smile slices across Myrzeth's face. "What horrible luck." He reaches to the sky again and repeats the maneuver. There is no time to prepare for it. Reflexively, I hold a forearm in front of my face, bracing for the blow.

A deafening, shattering sound fills the air with the impact, but the ténesomni breaks against me like a thin sheet of ice. I lower my arm, staring at it in wonder. The argentilum star pendant glows brightly, as if resting against Amyrah's skin, but I don't have the time to admire it or to question why it's responded like this.

Myrzeth's eyes cling to the necklace wrapped around my arm. "Interesting. Where, oh where did you manage to find that little gem?"

I stand, dusting off my hands. "From the girl you tried to offer to the kaligorven."

A puzzled look crosses Myrzeth's brow.

"You might remember her, considering she was your own niece."

I can hear the people muttering their surprise, their disgust, and a warmth of satisfaction rushes through my veins.

Yes, hate him. See through his manipulation to the horror he is.

The forced amusement evaporates from Myrzeth's face. "It seems I've underestimated what kind of tricks you've had time to prepare. I wonder, though, how many more can you have?"

Dread constricts my chest. *What do I have left to fight him with*? Helpless, I glance around. My father stares at me with a level of impatience bordering on explosive. His lips move. I can't hear his words, but it's still as if he is shouting them at me.

You morvus!

I reach behind my shoulder. By some mercy, the bow has remained on my back, along with the quiver. I sling the former off and whip an arrow out, draw the string to my jaw, and aim at Myrzeth's chest.

He backs away at first but appears to call my bluff. We both know there is no way I'm going to fire an arrow in any direction that will put anyone in danger but him. With quick steps, Myrzeth advances on me.

I force myself to keep the arrow tip from sagging, hoping to the skies that my arms don't give out on me as I back away. This show of defense is all I have left. My last hope is that I can lead him to where no one else can be hurt on my account.

Chuckling, the Foremost drawls, "Where do you think you are going? I thought we agreed that there would be no forfeiting this fight. If you run now, I swear I will hunt you down and kill you for your cowardice."

"You think this is a forfeit?" I ask, glancing quickly behind to make sure the way is clear. "You seem to have become better acquainted with Vale customs over the last several days. Tell me: Are there any rules that dictate *where* the Privotus Vimorteth must be held?"

Myrzeth slows, doubt flickering his gaze. He looks to the edge of the crowd, where his black-clad followers are gathered. One of them—my gut wobbles when I see that it's Flip—raises his hands apologetically, palms to the sky. Myrzeth glares at him, then me. "You are stalling for time."

I don't waste the moment, backing toward the city gate and keeping him in my sight, as my father instructed. "No answer? Well, it seems Dravek was a better Foremost than you. He made sure all his sons were well-versed in Utsanek's traditions." I glance to where my father stands. Even from this distance, I can see how pale he has grown. His eyes, however, are steady, and they lock onto mine. "Would you mind informing our new leader who gets to decide the venue for the challenge ceremony?" I ask, loud enough for all to hear.

He hesitates before stepping forward. "In the event that the rights of Privotus Vimorteth are invoked, the challenger may choose a new location for the battle if he or she should find it unsuitable to a fair fight." His voice was uncertain at first, but now it has grown to its former, confident timbre. Like the leader he used to be. "This prevents the current Foremost from abusing his authority in the Vale to weight a challenge in his favor."

The Foremost's eyes snap to mine, like he would end my life here and now, but I have already backed all the way to the city gate.

"In case you haven't figured it out, I reject this location," I shout, then turn tail and run.

Of course, Myrzeth was right: Bringing up the customs of Privotus Vimorteth and taking to Utsanek's streets was a desperate bid for more time. The fact is, I have no idea how to defeat him or how to get out of this with my life. All I know is that getting Myrzeth away from where he can feed off an audience has to work in my favor.

I dart down the side streets while keeping as direct of a path through the city as I can.

Where to go?

The question screams through my mind on an endless circuit. Should I face him in the market square? No, there are too many blind spots, and the area is much too closed in.

The last option is to take the fight to the produce fields that lie between the loch and the city. It's nearing the end of Zomré and the fields will soon be ready for harvest, but what other option do I have?

Horrible shrieks echo down the passage behind me, growing ever closer.

Myrzeth must have signaled the kaligorven to pursue me.

Shades.

I really have no chance, do I?

Banishing the thought, I lower my head and beg Elyōn for the stamina to make it out of Utsanek.

55
AMYRAH

I PAUSE TO GIVE ZENITH A MOMENT to rest his wings on one of the mountain peaks in the late afternoon. The temperature is freezing and the air is thin, but I need him to be as fresh as possible because I fear what we'll find when we reach the Vale.

By the time I decide to take the plunge beneath the ténesomni, the sun has dipped below the horizon. We circle over a dip in the shadows that must be where the valley lies. I try to judge its approximate location, but it's impossible to know for sure.

Zenith tugs against my hold on the reins, anxious.

It's a feeling I share. "Alright, boy," I soothe, leaning forward. "Let's do this."

He responds to the subtle shift in my body weight, angling for the descent, and I marvel yet again at his intelligence.

This time when I slip through the shadows, it's like they aren't only brushing my skin on the outside; they pulse from within, demanding to be let free.

"Burn the darkness out of me, one shade at a time," I whisper to the Highest.

Zenith's light reveals the forest that has witnessed so many wonderful and terrible moments of my life. Although I've never seen it from this vantage, and I am nothing like the girl who left, I still feel like I'm coming home.

A chorus of hideous roars emanates from the trees, scaring birds into the thickened air. I hold on tighter to Zenith, a shiver running down my spine. The kaligorven must know we are here.

Smoothing tears away with a palm, I focus on what lies beneath.

We have come through the barrier a bit farther from the city than I hoped, but ahead, the trees open into a semicircle, with dull dots of light beyond.

"It's the Reckoning Grounds," I say to Zenith, as if he can understand me. "That's the perfect place to land."

We glide close to the forest, Zenith's hooves skimming the leafy tops, and I attempt to prepare myself for what we will find within Utsanek's gates. Who should I seek out first? Belwyn? Orlagh? My uncle?

I don't think I'm ready for—

My thoughts abandon me when the clearing opens beneath us like a mouth. The Reckoning Grounds are crawling with a steady stream of people moving through Utsanek's gates as if a ceremony has just concluded.

I bite my lip. What kind of evil have they witnessed? If I hadn't delayed this afternoon, could I have intervened?

The valefolk shriek and point and shield their eyes, some of them ducking for cover. Concerned by the upset Zenith's appearance has caused, I tug him upward. I have no idea what has transpired here since I left, and I can't take the risk of exposing him to their violence. After all, they seemed to have no qualms letting my uncle offer me to the kaligorven.

And those *are the people you want to save*? He *is the person you returned to confront?*

I almost laugh. As far as foolhardy plans go, this one isn't promising, but I can't deny the peace it has settled in my soul.

Fixing my eyes ahead, I direct Zenith over Utsanek's gate. The winged horse casts disorienting beams down every twisting passageway. I rack my brain to think of a suitable place to land him, but there is nowhere within the city.

Reaching down to pat Zenith's neck, I whisper, "We'll go to the fields north of Loch Skythe. You'll get the break you deserve there."

56

BELWYN

When I make it to the fields, my lungs feel like they have been submerged in boiling water. The metallic taste of blood lingers on my tongue, and no matter how many ragged breaths I take, I can't get enough air.

I struggle as far as I can into the fields before folding onto my knees in the fragrant earth, hoping the kaligorven are not as close behind me as I fear.

What now?

My gasps morph into unhinged laughter. I sit back on my heels and raise my face to the sky, closing my eyes. I'm out of ideas. There isn't anything funny about this situation, yet I laugh.

It feels so much better than fear.

"Belwyn?"

My madness evaporates in an instant. I squint against the shine of a lantern as it draws close.

"Wehna." Scrambling to my feet, I throw out an arm in a fervent gesture. "Get out of here. *Run.*"

She blinks at me, confused and much less alarmed than she should be. Understanding quickly sets in when a vicious roar rends the air.

Wehna scrambles to the side of the field, yanking a small boy after her.

I fix my eyes to the north side of the fields, where blackness congeals like blood in a wound. A hole appears at its center as if a giant worm has bored through clay, and a gargantuan kaligorva emerges, prowling on all fours with a triumphant Myrzeth sitting on its back.

Blood rushes to my head, and I hear nothing beyond my spastic pulse and the rasp of my breaths.

I reach for my bow.

"There's no escape for you now, I'm afraid," Myrzeth says, his voice carrying unnaturally well. He makes a motion with a hand, clearing a dome around us. The glow from Wehna's dropped lantern fills the area like normal light should. Several more Shrouded shapes materialize from the wall of ténesomni, flanking the Foremost.

One of my hands cinches around the bow, and the other grasps for an arrow. "If you expect to keep the people's respect, then you will finish this challenge in your own strength, not with these abominations."

The kaligorven hiss and growl.

Myrzeth tilts his chin and slips off the kaligorva's back. He approaches me with slow steps, crushing the flourishing crop underneath his boots.

"If you insist, then I will leave them out of it. However, I must warn you. It might appear that I have control over them, but they are wild beasts that feed off fear and hatred. If they should be provoked to attack because of your careless choice of words or my untimely demise—" His shoulders shake with a humorless chuckle, causing the shadows to ripple overhead. "—I think nothing will be able to stop them."

An expression of unfettered rage eclipses Myrzeth's easy-going mask, and he throws his hands in the air, drawing down every particle of ténesomni to come to his aid.

I draw the bowstring to my jaw. It cuts into my fingers.

"Wehna, look at the stars," a tiny voice squeaks to my right. "They are *dream* bright."

My eyes flick up. Myrzeth's lust for darkness has exposed the sky in its fullness, and my heart stutters. The stars might be shining clearer than ever before, but there is one coming closer, outshining them all.

When Myrzeth breaks his concentration to gape at it, I let my arrow fly.

57
AMYRAH

THE CITY FALLS AWAY BEHIND US, time suspending when a fair-haired man comes into view beneath a swirling tempest of shadow. A figure faces him, bow drawn.

My heart lurches, recognizing its own.

The tension in his arm releases and a horrifying roar fills the sky. The wall of ténesomni behind my uncle releases like a foul wave, splitting into lupine shapes with horns and claws and Ikktar-red eyes.

Terror fills my empty spaces.

Grabbing Zenith's mane, I lean as far forward as I can, sending him crashing to the earth in a blaze of furious fire. He obeys and cuts a burning streak between Belwyn and the incensed kaligorven. Zenith comes to a running stop, rearing to his hind legs and throwing me from the saddle.

The wind is knocked out of me, and I gasp and wretch as a line of white flames jumps across the verdant rows, cutting off Myrzeth's kaligorven horde. Smoke fills my nostrils. Those are *real* flames. The solas can literally set the world ablaze.

Another roar, this time human, breaks through my stupor, and I scramble to my feet.

Myrzeth shouts again as he snaps something off near his shoulder. An arrow. *Belwyn's* arrow. It has missed my uncle's heart.

Relief fills me briefly, but I do not understand it. I do not accept it. Why should I care about whether Myrzeth lives or dies?

Holden would care. My grandfather would care. And my mother cared. Perhaps Elyōn would show compassion to even the most wicked person for the sake of those he loves.

That mercy is too good, too pure for Myrzeth to fathom. He gathers the darkness above him like a mountain and advances on Belwyn.

And I run to stand in the gap between them.

58
WEHNA

I watch Myrzeth summon all his power into a thundercloud. I watch a shining figure run between him and Belwyn. I watch a single spark challenge a tidal wave of fury.

She holds out her hands. White ignati leaps from her palms, spreading a shield between her and Myrzeth. It's a small circle at first, but with a fumbling prayer from Amyrah's lips, it grows outward and upward, pressing against the shadows until Myrzeth loses his grip on them. With a deafening rush of wind and an even brighter flash of incomprehensible light, the ténesomni flees the Vale's skies completely.

Myrzeth tries to draw down the shadows again, but there's nothing to grab. Just the firelights playfully winking at the earth. He lets out an enraged bellow, pacing along the border of Amyrah's light like a caged wildcat. "*What are you doing here*?"

"Wehna, Arvo, get back," someone whispers abrasively. I turn. My mother and father stare at me from a distance with huge eyes, hunched forward with their hands outstretched, motioning for us to come to them. I release Arvo, but I need to witness what happens with my own eyes. I face forward again, spurning their protests.

Amyrah lowers her shield until it blinks out, her chest heaving. "I'm giving you a chance."

"W-what?" Belwyn asks incredulously, but she ignores him.

The fire from the winged sola creature flares up behind Myrzeth, backlighting him so he looks like some specter from Ikktar before it gutters out. Rancid smoke curls through the air.

The Foremost cackles. "I have not come this far because of the charity of others. I certainly don't need it from you."

Amyrah raises her chin. "Look behind you, Uncle."

Myrzeth raises an eyebrow before doing what she says. When he turns and sees, he seems to shrink.

Beyond the charred line in the field, not a single kaligorven remains, and neither does the sola horse. The line of terrible beasts has been replaced with a growing crowd of valefolk.

Whipping around to face his niece again, Myrzeth forces out a sharp laugh. "Do you think this temporary reprieve will win them to your side, or that the shadows of Érechlys can be defeated by one untested Luvesti?" He moves a few steps to his right, then turns and paces back. He stops short when he sees me.

"She isn't alone," Belwyn says, moving to stand beside Amyrah.

Cries of agreement ring out from the valefolk.

I drag my eyes away from Myrzeth's as he continues edging toward me. A weight settles on my chest when I watch Belwyn take Amyrah's hand.

She looks surprised, but a small smile finds her lips. She faces

Myrzeth again. "The light will always do good for those who call on it. Can you say the same of your darkness?"

I stare at my former friend, whose honest statement has pierced my soul with ruthless accuracy. My vision blurs at the edges, and I wonder how we can have such extreme opposite life experiences. Because I have spent the last months crying, screaming, begging for the light to break me from this place of shadow, but it abandoned me. And waiting for it has bled me dry.

"No, Arvo!"

From the corner of my eye, I see a small shape pop up between the rows of rocksquash, and Myrzeth darts toward it. There is a scuffle and a blood-chilling scream. Too late, I understand why he had been edging toward me.

My brother, who must not have returned to my parents as I assumed he would, struggles in Myrzeth's grasp, and my chest convulses when I see the glint of a blade clutched in a bloody hand beneath his chin.

"I would think carefully about any further action you intend to take against me," he says, tugging Arvo toward Loch Skythe's beach.

"You *heshïn* daemon!" Father makes a move forward but falters, falling deathly pale when blood blooms along the edge of Myrzeth's blade.

Amyrah's voice cracks. "W-we won't hurt you. Just let the boy go."

Myrzeth cackles and continues dragging my brother with him. "Forgive me if I don't take you at your word," he says, now walking backward. His feet find the stony shore. The five of us—Belwyn, Amyrah, and what's left of my family—follow at a careful distance, reeled in by this unthinkable scene.

With a strange Atsunic command, the black loch begins to bubble and churn. An enormous, serpentine shape emerges from the water in four oily humps. My stomach flips. Is Myrzeth going to feed my brother to some waterborne kaligorven?

But the terrifying beast isn't here for a meal. With precise waves, it draws out a wooden shape from beyond an outcropping of rock and circles it, shifting it closer to Myrzeth and Arvo. Pressing the knife closer to my brother's throat, Myrzeth backs into the troubled waters and reaches for the boat with his other hand.

"You will let me leave this place, and this boy will ensure that I will not be followed."

My mother wails, and I run to get away from the sound of her fears manifesting before mine have had the chance to paralyze me.

"Myrzeth, *wait*," I beg.

He regards me, his mouth arcing downward.

I stumble, my heart thudding far quicker than it should from such a short sprint. "If—" My mouth has gone dry, and I swallow. "If all you need is surety that you will make it to safety—"

Amyrah gasps. "Wehna, no."

"—th-then take me in his place."

My mother sobs, and an unbearable silence follows. Why would Myrzeth consider such a ridiculous thing? Why would *I* think it could work? But I can't help it. I fight for my brother because that's what I do, what I will *always* do.

Even if no one will fight for me.

Myrzeth lowers the blade.

Arvo scrambles out of his grip and sprints to my mother's outstretched arms. She weeps against his curly head, and I wait for her and Father to beg for mercy on my behalf. Mother's terrified eyes find mine, but she is frozen, and no sound passes her lips. Father is on his knees assessing the gash in Arvo's neck, taking no notice of me.

The light doesn't want me.

I turn to Myrzeth. He extends his hand.

But the darkness does.

"Wehna!" Arvo yells.

Ignoring my brother's outcry, I go with Myrzeth as my mother's shrieks and my father's curses chase me into the boat.

"Please," I whisper. "Please, Elyōn. Don't forget me."

59
AMYRAH

PLUMES OF SHADOW SWALLOW the little vessel, taking both my estranged uncle and a sweet friend from my life.

I'm too weary to know how to feel.

Valefolk begin to fill the ravaged fields, their hushed murmurs growing in volume. I draw in a breath and hold it there until the urge to scream, to cry, to shout in victory goes away.

"Amyrah." Belwyn breathes out my name like an exhale, and it breaks apart against my weary heart.

My gaze drops to the fingers inserted between mine. I follow the line of his arm until I am looking at his sweat-and-dirt-streaked face.

He's embracing me before I have a chance to utter a word of apology, arms strong around my back, hands sliding up my neck, fingers firm against my scalp. He draws my mouth to his. The kiss is hesitant, like he's not sure how it will be received. I press in closer, claiming it fully.

When we're both breathless, I pull away, biting my lip to hide its trembling. Belwyn touches his forehead to mine, then angles back so his hazel eyes can drink in my every detail. Warmth creeps up my spine where his palms forge a path.

"What's happened to you while we've been apart?" he asks, attempting to comb his fingers through my hair. They snag in the wind-tousled tangles and I wince. He chuckles and instead runs his hands up and down my forearms.

I let my eyes travel above him to the foreign sight of burning stars hanging above the Vale. "I don't know where to begin." I drop my gaze back to his eyes.

He gives a small, understanding nod, his lips pulling into a lopsided smile. "Me neither," he says. His expression grows serious. "But the ténesomni. You've learned to control it?"

Breath catching, I shake my head. "No, not really, but I'm not going to live in fear of it. Elyōn will expose it when the time is right and teach me to overcome it."

A slight frown presses his brows low, and I wonder if I have upset him. Perhaps talking of the Highest makes him uncomfortable. Perhaps he still does not trust him.

But the look passes, and he nods. "I don't claim to know him as well as you do, but, yes, I think you're right."

Something strange flares around him, like a brief pulse of light. When I blink, it's gone, and he pulls me in again, holding me with such tenderness that the excitement, the fear, and the overwhelm all decide to come out at once. I sink to the ground, and he sinks with me. He keeps his arms tight through the sobs and the tears and the snot, like this is not my grief alone, but one we share together. My breaths soon slow, and I inhale the scent of *him*.

I am whole in his embrace.

Brushing my hair away from my face, Belwyn gives me a mischievous smile, then turns and fiddles with something around his wrist. I gasp when he holds up my necklace between us. "Amyrah—"

"I *knew* you had taken it."

"—be my second half?"

I forget about breathing, then gulp in air when the world starts to spin around me. A laugh presses through my lungs and dissipates in the space between us. Doubt flickers across his features. I want to smooth it away, as I want to smooth away all the hurt I have caused him, all the days we've spent apart. I slide my hand up his neck and lose my fingers in his hair. It's longer, wavier than when I last saw him.

"I think I already am."

He doesn't get the chance to tie the necklace around my neck before I'm the one kissing him.

Sunlight streams through the window in mote-swirled rays. My fingers cut through them, savoring the warmth.

"It's strange, isn't it?" Belwyn whispers into my hair, tugging me closer. "Not having to battle shadows anymore."

I give in to him and pull my bare feet up onto the dusty couch, tucking my head into the alcove beneath Belwyn's chin. "But it's right." I listen to his heartbeat. "Even if it does still feel like a dream."

"Do you think the darkness will come back?" Belwyn traces the underside of my wrist with his knuckles.

I shiver and attempt to keep my thoughts in line. “I don’t know. It seemed like it only retreated, not like it was defeated for good.”

Belwyn is quiet for a while. “But at least we know one thing.”

Shifting, I angle so I can see his face. “What’s that?”

One side of his mouth pulls higher. “You made your song come true.”

An intense awareness of my unworthiness bears down on my chest. I let the Shaluth Cantu circle around my mind.

All the darkness will fade away . . . And all of the Vale will be free.

I chew the inside of my cheek. “Did you know my mother wrote that song before coming to the Vale?”

Belwyn’s eyes widen.

I glance down at our hands, threading my fingers with his. “I’m not sure what inspired it, other than her heart’s desire that a terrible wrong would be made right.” A small smile finds my lips. “A very odd woman I met in Luvesta told me that song isn’t about the Vale at all, but about a broader darkness coming to its end.”

Silence envelops us, and Belwyn squeezes my hand. “Either way, something beautiful came from it, didn’t it? And I think we can look forward to something beautiful coming from it again.”

My cheeks flush as I consider this. Maybe that’s the nature of all pure promises. They offer a temporary joy when we see them come to pass in the present but also foreshadow a bigger fulfillment that isn’t for us to know.

A clatter sounds from across the room, where Orlagh crouches before her shed-sized oven, pushing a long-handled ember scraper across the flat stone inside its mouth. She hacks out a cough and straightens when a cloud of ash mushrooms into the air.

“I don’t know what kind of beasties last made use of my beloved Bertha, but if I ever find out, there’ll be words.” She huffs, brandishing the flat-edged implement like a pitchfork.

I hide a laugh behind my palm. How did I never know her oven has a name? Belwyn, too, shakes with silent mirth.

Orlagh leans against her table and wipes her damp forehead with a kitchen towel. “But I shouldn’t be complainin’. Just bein’ back in this place is more’n I could’ve hoped for.”

Myrzeth’s sudden disappearance and the breaking of the ténesomni cast illumination not only on our streets, but in many of the valefolk’s hearts. It has only been a few days in the light, and already people have begun the painful, yet healing, task of making amends with their neighbors. The fact that Orlagh has been able to move back into her old home is evidence of that.

But there are some families here who can never heal.

“It’s more than I could have hoped for too.” I get up and cross the small room to slip my arms around her. “Thank you for offering to let me live with you. After everything that has happened to Wehna’s family, I couldn’t think of making them leave the cottage now.”

And I can’t go back there after losing both Wehna and my father. I let the bite of sadness have its moment in my soul, hugging Orlagh tighter before letting her go.

She reaches back to pat my cheek. “You’re a kind bairn, but don’t give up hope of returning. I have been beseeching the Highest for many happy memories there yet.” She winks at Belwyn and sprinkles grated cheese over the pale ball plopped on the floured work surface. Her powerful hands plunge into the dough, swiftly kneading it together.

Puzzled, I pull out a chair and sit next to her. Belwyn moves to a seat on the other side of the table.

“Orlagh, it’s too painful to think about going back,” I say. “I don’t want to be where I’ll see my father in every corner.”

Her hands still and the color drains from her flushed cheeks. "Oh, oh child. How could I have forgotten?" She brushes her silver hair away from her face and turns to me, her eyes glassy.

I wince. "Sorry. I-I didn't mean to sound like I thought you were insensitive."

"Nay." She gives her head a decided shake. "That's not what I meant. I forgot to tell yeh what happened."

Dread presses on my stomach. "What do you mean?"

Her lip trembles and she struggles to form the words. "Amyrah, when tha' wicked man intended to offer yeh to the kaligorven, and your father thwarted the whole thing . . ."

My heart hammers in my throat.

Orlagh's legs buckle and she sags to a stool, staring out the window. "I brought several of my sweet older lasses back to see about caring for his body."

I swallow a sob.

Blinking, Orlagh faces me. Tears course freely down her face. "Dear Amyrah. He was alive."

"W-what do you mean?"

Belwyn reaches across the table and traps my hands under his, but I am numb to his touch.

"There was a sola creature with him, and it was like its illumination was sustainin' him despite his injuries."

The room spins around me and I feel like I will faint. "Where is he?"

She worries her lip, but the color has returned to her face. "We were afraid the kaligorven would return and finish him. Between the three of us and the help of a few strangers, we managed to move him around the city to the shores of Loch Skythe. Tha' bewildering fox creature followed us the whole way there. We saw no other option other than t'put him in a skiff and push him out into the loch with a prayer tha' Elyōn would guide him to safety."

My dizzying thoughts dip under a sudden weight, and I press trembling fingers to my lips, fighting to breathe. Belwyn gets up and rounds the table to wrap his arms around my quaking shoulders.

I am safe within them. I am home.

"How can—how can we know if he is a-alive or not?" I manage to push out between gasps.

Orlagh dusts off her hands, comes close, and slips them under my chin. "Sweet child," she whispers, the warmth of her fingers pressing into my bones. "Have faith."

And I realize that, against all reason, I do.

EPILOGUE

Commander Verrek paces the southern shore of Loch Skythe, holding a ruddy lantern out into the swirling mists. The shadows had deepened quickly that afternoon, and when the Shrouded beasts began emerging from the waters, leaving his men alone and prowling through bushes and low hills of the moors, he knew it was the day he had been watching and waiting for. The day he had been promised would come.

Look for me when the light has been exchanged completely for darkness, he'd been told.

But nothing could have prepared Verrek for how suffocating the ténesomni would be when it came in its fullness.

Like a parasite, doubt now feasts on his disturbing thoughts. Verrek straightens his back, calling to mind his years of discipline. This is not a time to show weakness.

The air is oppressive and still—suffocating. Then, there is a subtle shift in the black clouds ahead and the water begins to lap at the shore in front of the commander's boots.

"*Stand ready, úramech*," he shouts to the soldiers waiting in strict rows behind him. He has conditioned them well: they didn't speak a word in protest when he'd issued orders that stood in such stark contrast to what they had been accustomed to. Though he can't see them, he hears them draw their swords in unison.

A shape emerges from the shadows as the disturbance in the waters grows. At the helm of a small boat, a ghostly man stands, holding no lantern. Needing none. He parts the crushing ténesomni with a lazy twist of his hand.

The boat crunches against the sand in the shallows, and the man splashes into the water, taking a moment to steady the vessel while a young woman clambers out after him.

Verrek draws his own sword and raises it up in a salute.

"The Southlands welcome you, Lord Myrzeth."

The regiment echoes his greeting with an uproarious shout.

APPENDICES

BURN THE DARKNESS
OUT OF ME

ONE SHADE
AT A TIME

GLOSSARY

NAME PRONUNCIATIONS

Amyrah *(uh-MEYE-ruh)*

Anit *(uh-NEET)*

Arvo *(AR-voh)*

Askonnet *(ASS-kon-neht)*

Astellum *(ASS-tel-loom)*

Atsun *(AT-soon)*

Belwyn *(BELL-win)*

Dravek *(DRAY-vehk)*

Ellehra *(el-LAY-ruh)*

Fehlan *(FAY-lin)*

Izra *(EYES-ruh)*

Jaki *(JA-kee)*

Ketra *(KEH-truh)*

Ketsé *(KEHT-say)*

Ketur *(keh-TOOR)*

Korvin *(KOHR-vin)*

Luvesta *(loo-VESS-tuh)*

Myrzeth *(MEER-zehth)*

Nocilium *(naw-SILL-ee-yum)*

Orlagh *(OR-luh)*

Qortehr *(kor-TAIR)*

Rael *(ray-EL)*

Rhun *(ROON)*

Seyla *(SAY-luh)*

Shemai *(SHEM-eye)*

Tarriv *(TAIR-iv)*

Téron *(TAIR-uhn)*

Tetyan *(TEHT-yun)*
Utsanek *(oot-SAN-ehk)*
Veridree *(VAIR-ih-dree)*
Wehna *(WEH-nuh)*
Yara *(YAR-uh)*

ATSUNIC TRANSLATIONS

Agmen *(AYG-min)* : the Southland army
argentilum *(ar-JENT-ih-loom)* : a type of precious metal that absorbs and releases light and heat
arlum *(AR-loom)* : a form of currency used in the Vale
bolétis *(boh-LAY-tees)* : bioluminescent mushrooms
caelaveth *(chay-LAH-veth)* : become as one
caeruméni *(CHAY-roo-MAY-nee)* : a worship service
elïatova atéro *(EL-ee-uh-toh-vuh uh-TAIR-oh)* : take it into oneself
Ellithïm *(EL-ih-theem)* : paradise
Elyōn *(EL-ee-ohn)* : the Highest; deity of Atsun
erychélus nathura *(AIR-ih-kay-loos nuh-THOO-ruh)* : the dark nature the Luvesti strive to deny
fanum *(FAHN-oom)* : shrine
Grovesha *(groh-VEH-shuh)* : the Outerlands; beyond the Vale
heshïn *(Heh-SHEEN)* : a crass expression of frustration
ignati *(eeg-NAH-tee)* : fire
Ikktar *(ĪHK-tar)* : the doomed afterlife
Imperii *(im-PEER-ee)* : the leader of the Southlands
istilatum ideralis *(EES-till-a-toom EE-dair-all-iss)* : burning star
kaligorva *(kal-ih-GOHR-vuh)* : a lone Shrouded beast of darkness
kaligorven *(kal-ih-GOHR-vehn)* : the Shrouded beasts of darkness

ATSUNIC TRANSLATIONS
(continued)

maevotér *(MAY-voh-tayr)* : private tutor
morvus *(MOHR-vuhs)* : idiot; fool; moron
praecéro *(pray-CHAIR-oh)* : split; break apart
Privotus Vimorteth *(pree-VOH-toos vih-MOHR-teth)* : the right to challenge the Foremost to ritualistic combat for his or her position
Shaluth Cantu *(shuh-LOOTH can-TOO)* : salvation song
sola *(SOH-lah)* : a Light Creature
Sola Vinari *(SOH-lah vihn-AR-ee)* : the ancient custom of hunting the Light Creatures
sola brossa *(SOH-lah BROH-suh)* : the light-imbued bones of a Light Creature
sola kuvror *(SOH-lah KOOV-rohr)* : the incandescent blood of a Light Creature
ténesomni *(TAY-neh-SOM-nee)* : living darkness
úramech *(OO-ruh-mekh)* : a soldier of the Southlands

ATSUNIC PHRASES

avis ténesomni luvem *(uh-VEES TAY-neh-SOM-nee LOO-vem)* : "After darkness, light"
habith ténesomni eth noér lurum *(huh-BEETH TAY-neh-SOM-nee ehth noh-AIR LOO-ruhm)* : "Dwelling in darkness is our good"
Elyōn érit agértu *(EL-ee-ohn ay-REET uh-JAIR-too)* : "the Highest will act"
Noéth ignat u ténesomni ïth kuvrï ut luvem *(NOH-aith ig-NAHT oo TAY-neh-SOM-nee eeth KOO-vree LOO-vem)* : "We burn the shadows and bleed the light"
prae daiet, ténesomni *(PRAY DAY-eht TAY-neh-SOM-nee)* : "After the day comes the darkness"

DAYS OF THE WEEK

Sunday	Satus *(SAH-toos)*
Monday	Soporiat *(so-POH-ree-aht)*
Tuesday	Vindéré *(vihn-DAY-ray)*
Wednesday	Tavilun *(TAH-vih-loon)*
Thursday	Jotesta *(joh-TESS-tuh)*
Friday	Bézeqor *(BAY-zeh-kohr)*
Saturday	Xitus *(ZEE-toos)*

SEASONS OF THE YEAR

Ice	Vestri *(VESS-tree)*
Thaw	Niatev *(NEYE-uh-tehv)*
Sowing	Tiosh *(TEE-ohsh)*
Life	Zomré *(ZOM-ray)*
Harvest	Elberu *(ELL-ber-oo)*
Decay	Morpa *(MOHR-puh)*

SABINE'S BISCUITS & GRAVY

Ingredients

For the Biscuits

2 cups flour
4 teaspoons baking powder
1/4 teaspoon baking soda
3/4 teaspoon salt
2 tablespoons butter
2 tablespoons shortening
1 cup buttermilk, chilled

For the Gravy

24 ounces pork sausage patties
1/3 to 1/2 cup all-purpose flour, or as needed
4 cups milk, or as needed
Kosher salt & freshly ground black pepper

Directions

1. Preheat oven to 450 degrees.
2. In a large bowl, combine flour, baking powder, baking soda, and salt. Using your fingertips, quickly rub butter and shortening into dry ingredients until mixture looks like crumbs. Make a well in the center and pour in the chilled buttermilk. Stir just until the dough comes together. The dough will be very sticky.
3. Turn dough onto floured surface, dust top with flour and gently fold dough over on itself 5 or 6 times. Press into a 1-inch thick round. Cut out biscuits with a 2-inch cutter, being sure to push straight down through the dough. Place biscuits on baking sheet so that they just touch. Reform scrap dough, working it as little as possible and continue cutting.
4. Bake until biscuits are tall and light gold on top, 15 to 20 minutes.
5. While biscuits are in the oven, make gravy. Brown the sausage patties on both sides over medium heat until cooked through. Transfer sausage to a platter and set aside.
6. Whisk 1/3 cup flour into the rendered grease in the skillet. Whisk in the milk until smooth. Bring to a simmer over medium heat and cook until slightly thickened.
7. Chop the reserved sausage and stir it into the gravy. Season generously with salt and pepper.
8. Serve warm over fresh-from-the-oven biscuits.

SHALUTH CANTU

ACKNOWLEDGMENTS

I was not prepared for how different this journey would feel from that of my first book. Not only were my own expectations overwhelming, but I developed a fear of disappointing my readers, whose good opinion I was alarmed to learn I craved. As reviews for *Where Darkness Dwells* rolled in, complete with contradictory critiques, the pressure I felt to "get this one right" was unhealthy, as was my focus on approval.

Perhaps it's just my inexperience, perhaps it is what all authors inevitably go through, but I struggled in a way that felt almost *physical* to write this book. Weeks of not being able to get more than a few words on the page at a time made me believe I was an imposter. Despite assurances that all authors experience this, nothing made it less dreadful in the moment. There were days when I told myself I would never have a second book to offer my readers, that I had wasted my time and should admit defeat. That this series would be unfinished. Many, many tears were shed into my bathwater.

But God is faithful, even when we feel like we are one straw from breaking—especially then. He showed His kindness through friends who wouldn't let me give up (my dearly beloved Sisterhood) and brought me ludicrous joy and fellowship (the actual definition of the Flash Fiction Magic crew), through a husband who stoically weathered my verbal-processing gales, and through kids who granted me space, found my earplugs, and occasionally baked me cookies. He reminded me of my identity in Christ—of *who* I'm writing for—through the word of God, my pastor's faithful preaching, and my mom.

Despite all the trials, this beast of a book emerged. My struggles had woven themselves into my prose. My characters' battles with despair, doubt, and trusting God reflected my own. I wept with them as they lost sight of the light and rejoiced when the dawn burned through. All the things I had feared would be in this book—the imperfections, the oddities, the contradictions—were what made it believable, made it come alive. If my first book was my heart, then this one was most definitely my blood. Writing it wasn't an escape; it was the very real working out of my faith. And yes, there was plenty of fear and trembling involved.

Now I'm here, flabbergasted to be at the finish line. Just thinking of everyone who helped along the way makes me tear up. Rachel, Emily, and Kate: you read this story in its earliest form, and I can't begin to tell you how unworthy I feel of your friendship. My lovely beta readers gave me their unhinged reactions (as requested) and helped me patch the plot's holes. My amazing editor, Elle Fort, challenged my story in entirely new ways and made it stronger than I could have ever hoped. As for proofreading, Anne J. Hill's keen eye was exactly what this final version needed.

And now it's finished. It's in your hands, on your shelves, and engraved on my heart. My dearest hope is that God will do what God does best and use this weak thing exactly as He intended all along.

Soli Deo gloria.

After darkness, LIGHT.

ABOUT THE AUTHOR

Andrea Renae grew up on the Canadian prairies alongside her cat companion, thrilling in stories of all kinds. As an only child, she was usually lost to daydreams or finding new things to create with her hands. As an adult, writing became a way to process life's countless beauties and hardships while solidifying her hope in the Author of it all. A lover of all things beautiful and rich in meaning, she believes in the power of a good story to bring hope and truth in the most unexpected ways.

When her fingers aren't typing away, she can often be found teaching her children, playing piano, experimenting with different artistic mediums, or practicing for her inevitable fame on the GBBO. Her favorite activity, however, will always be spending time with her family, her friends, and her goofy goldendoodle, Charlie.

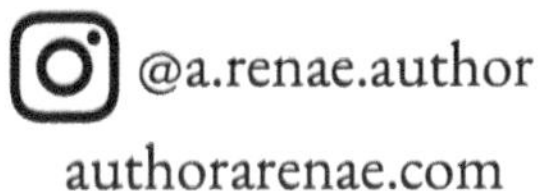

authorarenae.com

www.ingramcontent.com/pod-product-compliance
Lightning Source LLC
Chambersburg PA
CBHW020343310726
48979CB00015B/2492/J

* 9 7 8 1 7 3 8 8 6 4 7 5 1 *